P9-CET-552

Conner Bailey's SHORT STORY PORTFOLIO

with

cat the Rat

TABLE OF CONTENTS

THE LAND OF STORIES

AN AUTHOR'S ODYSSEY

THE LAND OF STORIES

AN AUTHOR'S ODYSSEY

CHRIS COLFER

ILLUSTRATED BY BRANDON DORMAN

LITTLE, BROWN AND COMPANY

New York Boston

This book is a work of fiction. Names, characters, places, and incidents are the product of the author's imagination or are used fictitiously. Any resemblance to actual events, locales, or persons, living or dead, is coincidental.

Copyright © 2016 by Christopher Colfer
Jacket and interior art copyright © 2016 by Brandon Dorman
Endpaper illustrations copyright © 2016 by Christopher Colfer

All rights reserved. In accordance with the U.S. Copyright Act of 1976, the scanning, uploading, and electronic sharing of any part of this book without the permission of the publisher is unlawful piracy and theft of the author's intellectual property. If you would like to use material from the book (other than for review purposes), prior written permission must be obtained by contacting the publisher at permissions@hbgusa.com. Thank you for your support of the author's rights.

Little, Brown and Company

Hachette Book Group
1290 Avenue of the Americas, New York, NY 10104
Visit us at lb-kids.com

Little, Brown and Company is a division of Hachette Book Group, Inc.
The Little, Brown name and logo are trademarks of Hachette Book Group, Inc.

The publisher is not responsible for websites (or their content)
that are not owned by the publisher.

First Edition: July 2016
First International Edition: July 2016

Barnes & Noble Edition ISBN: 978-0-316-31778-8

10 9 8 7 6 5 4 3 2 1

RRD-C

Printed in the United States of America

To Will,
for playing hours of How Do You Spell?, What's
Funnier?, Would a Ten-Year-Old Understand It?,
and other interactive games while I write.
Thanks for being my secret weapon.

"A WRITER IS A WORLD TRAPPED IN A PERSON."

—VICTOR HUGO

THE FAVORITE STUDENT

Willow Crest Unified School District spared no expense celebrating the retirement of a beloved principal. The community banquet hall was decorated so elegantly, there wasn't a trace of Senior Bingo from the night before. The tables were dressed with lacy tablecloths, floral centerpieces, and battery-operated candles. Each place setting had golden plates and more silverware than the guests knew what to do with.

Teachers, counselors, janitors, lunch ladies, and former students showed up in droves to say good-bye and wish the principal well. The retirement party was one of the classiest gatherings any of them had ever been to. However, as the guest of honor looked around at all the long faces, the occasion seemed more like a funeral than a celebration.

The newly appointed district superintendent tapped his champagne glass with a spoon and the hall became quiet.

"May I have your attention please?" he said into a microphone. "Good evening, everyone, I'm Dr. Brian Mitchell. As you know, we're here to celebrate one of the finest educators Willow Crest Unified School District has ever had the privilege of employing, Mrs. Evelyn Peters."

Her name was followed by a warm round of applause. A bright spotlight hit Mrs. Peters, who was seated at the front of the room beside Dr. Mitchell. She smiled and waved at the guests, but secretly she wished she had never agreed to the gathering. Special attention and compliments from her colleagues always made her uncomfortable, and tonight it was just getting started.

"I've been asked to say a few words about Mrs. Peters, which is very intimidating," Dr. Mitchell said. "It doesn't matter what I say, because rather than taking any praise to heart, I know she'll only be listening to my speech for grammatical errors."

The guests laughed and Mrs. Peters hid a giggle behind her napkin. Anyone who knew her knew it was true.

"It's easy to say someone is good at their job, but I know for a fact that Evelyn Peters is an *incredible* educator," Dr. Mitchell said. "Nearly three decades ago, long before she became a principal, I was in her first sixth-grade class at Willow Crest Elementary School. Prior to meeting her, my childhood had been very difficult. By the time I turned ten, both my parents were in prison and I was bouncing in and out of foster care. When I stepped into Mrs. Peters's classroom I could barely read. Thanks to her, by the end of the year, I was reading Dickens and Melville."

Many of the guests clapped, making Mrs. Peters blush. Most of them had lived or witnessed similar stories.

"We did not get along at first," Dr. Mitchell said. "She pushed me harder than anyone ever had. She gave me extra homework and made me stay after school and read aloud to her. At one point, I was so tired of the special treatment, I threatened to graffiti her house if it didn't stop. The next day she handed me a can of spray paint and a card with her address and said, 'Whatever you write, just make sure it's spelled correctly.'"

The hall erupted with laughter. The guests looked to Mrs. Peters to confirm the story and she nodded coyly.

"Mrs. Peters taught me much more than just how to read," Dr. Mitchell said, and his voice began to break. "She taught me the importance of compassion and patience. She was the only teacher I felt cared about *me* as much as my grades. She got me excited to learn and inspired me to become an educator. We're very sad to see her go, but had she applied for superintendent instead of retiring, we all know I would *never* have been hired."

Mrs. Peters wiped her glasses to distract the guests from

the tears forming in her eyes. Had it not been for this reception, she might never have acknowledged to herself all the differences she had made in so many lives.

"Now, please join me in a toast," Dr. Mitchell said, and raised his glass. "To Evelyn Peters, thank you for inspiring and teaching us all. Willow Crest Unified School District won't be the same without you."

Everyone in the hall raised their glasses to toast Mrs. Peters. When they finished, Mrs. Peters took the microphone and raised her glass back at them.

"Now, please allow me to say a few words," she said. "My late husband was also a teacher, and he gave me the best advice one educator could give to another. So, I would like to pass it along to you in case this is my last chance."

Everyone in the hall sat on the edge of their seats, especially the teachers.

"As teachers, we must not guide our students to become the people *we wish them to be*, but elevate them to become the people *they were meant to be*. Remember, the encouragement we give our students may be the only encouragement they ever receive, so don't use it sparingly. After twenty-five years of teaching grammar school and my brief administration experience, I can assure you my husband was absolutely right. And since that is the best lesson I can teach you, I'll say for the last time, *class dismissed*."

The conclusion of her speech was met with a standing ovation. After a few moments of applause Mrs. Peters urged the guests to sit, but it only made them cheer louder for her.

The lights were dimmed and a screen was lowered. Dr. Mitchell and Mrs. Peters took their seats and watched as group photos of Mrs. Peters's classes were projected, starting with her very first sixth-grade class from almost thirty years before. As the slide show commenced, the former students laughed at their eleven- and twelve-year-old selves and the ridiculous hairstyles and clothes they had sported in earlier decades. Especially noted was how little Mrs. Peters had changed over the years. In every picture the educator's hair, glasses, and floral dresses were exactly the same. It was as if Mrs. Peters were frozen in time while the world changed around her.

The slide show made Mrs. Peters more emotional than anything else that night. It was like watching a family album flash before her eyes. She remembered the name of each face she saw. Most of the students she still knew personally or she knew what they had gone on to become, but there were a few she had lost contact with completely. It was a painful feeling to have been so close to a child at one point, then later to feel as if they had disappeared into thin air.

Mrs. Peters's students were the closest thing to children she had ever had. She hoped they were all happy and healthy, wherever they were. If she was no longer a staple of compassion and guidance in their lives, she hoped they had found someone who was.

"Evelyn?" Dr. Mitchell whispered.

Mrs. Peters still found it strange for a former student to address her by her first name—even if he *was* the superintendent.

"Yes, Dr. Mitchell?" she whispered back.

"Did you ever have a favorite student?" he asked with a grin. "I know we're not *supposed* to have favorites, but is there one child who stands out to you? Besides me, of course."

Mrs. Peters had never thought about such a thing. She had taught over five hundred students in her career and remembered each for different reasons, but selecting a *favorite* had never been a priority.

"I definitely *enjoyed* some more than others, but I could never choose a favorite," she said. "That would require judgment, and I always thought judging a child is like judging an unfinished piece of art. Every child enters a classroom with his or her own set of obstacles to face, whether behavioral or academic. It's a teacher's job to identify those issues and help students overcome them, but never to belittle a student for them."

Dr. Mitchell had never thought of it that way. Even in adulthood, he was still learning a thing or two from Mrs. Peters.

"I may be a superintendent, but I'll always be your student," he said.

"Oh, Dr. Mitchell." Mrs. Peters laughed. "No one ever stops being a student in the classroom of life."

Even though she'd thought not answering was the best answer, Mrs. Peters quickly realized she was mistaken. A picture appeared on the screen of her final sixth-grade class, three years earlier. She scanned the faces of her former students and stopped at a pair of twelve-year-old twins named Alex and Conner Bailey.

Alex's hair was neatly tucked behind a pink headband, and she held a stack of books close to her heart. A large grin filled her face because school was her favorite place in the world. Her brother, on the other hand, was puffy eyed and his mouth hung open. He appeared to have just woken up from a nap and to have had no clue the photo was being taken.

Mrs. Peters laughed because they looked exactly as she remembered them, and the picture reminded her of how much she missed them.

Both of the Bailey twins had unexpectedly transferred schools before Mrs. Peters had a chance to say good-bye. Alex went to live with her grandmother in Vermont halfway through the seventh grade, and then Conner joined her the following year. Even though their mother still lived in town, Mrs. Peters had been assured they were better off with their grandmother.

As far as Mrs. Peters knew, Alex moved away to attend a school for advanced learners. But it was still a mystery as to why Conner had gone to join her.

The year before he moved, Conner had run off during a school trip in Europe with another student, Bree Campbell. The stunt seemed entirely out of character for both students, who had clean records up to that point. Had Conner stayed in Mrs. Peters's school, he would have been punished appropriately, as Bree had been, but Mrs. Peters never thought it warranted a transfer to another school district.

The entire situation was very suspicious and personally upsetting for Mrs. Peters. Conner had just discovered a natural talent for writing and was excelling in school for the first time. Wherever he was now, Mrs. Peters hoped Conner had found someone else to encourage him. To her, there was nothing worse in the world than a student's wasted potential.

The slide show ended and dessert was served in the banquet hall. After a dozen more complimentary speeches from former colleagues and students, the evening finally came to an end.

Mrs. Peters loaded her car with a stack of farewell cards and an armful of bouquets. She was looking forward to a quiet night at home so she could decompress from the long and emotional evening. On her way home, she unintentionally drove past Willow Crest Elementary School. Mrs. Peters slammed on her brakes and parked her car. The school reminded her of one more good-bye she had to make before officially retiring.

Mrs. Peters dug through her large purse to find the key to her old sixth-grade classroom. Luckily the locks hadn't been changed, and she entered room 6B without any trouble. But instead of feeling a wave of nostalgia like she expected, she hardly recognized the dark room.

The current teacher decorated very differently than Mrs. Peters had. The desks were arranged in groups instead of rows. The walls that used to hold shelves of dictionaries and encyclopedias were now lined with computers and tablets. The posters of world-renowned authors and scientists had been replaced with posters of celebrities holding their favorite books—books Mrs. Peters wasn't convinced they had read.

Mrs. Peters felt like an actor stepping onto someone else's stage. She couldn't believe how much a classroom could change in such little time. It was as if she had never taught there at all. The only similarity was the teacher's desk, which was kept in the exact place Mrs. Peters had kept her desk for twenty-five years. The retiree sat in the chair behind it and looked around the classroom bittersweetly.

She hoped the decor wasn't an indication of anything other than the new teacher's taste. She hoped the same morals and values she had taught were still being shared in her absence. She hoped the new technology was enhancing those lessons, and not replacing them with lesser ideology. Most of all, Mrs. Peters hoped the new teacher *cared* about teaching as much as she did.

Before getting depressed about it, Mrs. Peters reminded herself she would have felt worse if there *hadn't* been any change. After all, it was thanks to teachers like her that the current generation was progressing so effortlessly into the future.

And just like all the teachers who had come before her, it was time for Mrs. Peters to pass the torch to her successors. She hadn't expected letting go would be so difficult.

"Good-bye, classroom," Mrs. Peters said. "I'll miss the lessons we taught together, but even more, I'll miss the lessons we learned."

Just as she stood from the desk to leave, a sudden gust of wind circled the classroom. Papers blew off the walls and a vortex formed in the center of the room. A bright flash illuminated the dark classroom like a bolt of lightning and Mrs. Peters dived under the desk for safety.

Peeking out from underneath the desk, Mrs. Peters could see two pairs of feet appear out of thin air. One wore tennis shoes and the other a pair of sparkling slippers.

"Well, this looks a lot different from when we were sixth-graders," said the familiar voice of a young man. "*Aw man*, how come they get computers and we didn't? I would have stayed awake more if we had those."

"Sign of the times," said another familiar voice, that of a young woman. "I'm sure it won't be long before they stop building schools altogether. Every kid will be plugged into a device and taught at home. Can you imagine anything worse?"

"Let's focus on one crisis at a time," the young man said. "You look around the computer desks and I'll look through the file cabinet. My stories have got to be in here somewhere."

The feet split up into different corners of the room. Mrs. Peters knew she had heard those voices many times before, but she couldn't picture the faces they belonged to.

"If they weren't in her old office, what makes you think they'll be in here?" the young woman asked.

"It's the only place we haven't looked," he said. "Teachers are sentimental—maybe she put them in a time capsule or something? I just want to look everywhere before we break into her house."

Mrs. Peters couldn't take the suspense any longer. She slowly got to her feet and peered over the desk. As soon as she identified the newcomers she let out a loud gasp, causing them both to jump.

"Mr. Bailey! Miss Bailey!" she said. The twins had grown so much since the last time Mrs. Peters had seen them, especially Alex. Mrs. Peters couldn't help gawking at the long, beautiful gown she wore. It was the color of the sky and sparkled as she moved, like something out of a fairy tale.

Alex and Conner Bailey were just as stunned to see their former teacher as she was to see them.

"Um...hi, Mrs. Peters!" Alex said with a nervous laugh. "Long time no see!"

"Mrs. Peters?" Conner asked. "What are you doing here so late?"

Mrs. Peters crossed her arms and glared at them over her glasses.

"I was about to ask you the same question," she said. "How did you get inside without a key? Where did all that light and wind come from? Are you in the middle of some sort of prank?"

The twins stared at each other for a moment in silence, but neither knew what to tell her. Without any other ideas, Conner began prancing around the room waving his arms through the air like seaweed.

"Mrs. Peters, this is a dreeeeam!" he sang. "You ate some bad sushi and now you're having a nightmare about your former students! Leave the classroom before we manifest into large school supplies!"

Mrs. Peters scowled at his terrible attempt to fool her, and he quickly dropped his arms to his sides.

"I have a perfectly good grasp over my consciousness, Mr. Bailey," she said. "Now, will one of you explain how you *appeared* in this classroom or do I need to call the police?"

Explaining the situation to someone in the Otherworld should have been an easy task by now, but as the twins stood across from their former teacher in their former classroom, they felt like they were twelve years old again. Mrs. Peters was impossible to lie to, but she would never believe the truth.

"We would, but it's a really long story," Alex said.

"I have a master's degree in English—I *love* long stories," Mrs. Peters said.

The retiree's stern expression suddenly faded from her face. She looked back and forth between the twins, almost in disbelief. It was as if she had figured out the truth all on her own and was having difficulty accepting it.

"Wait a second," Mrs. Peters said. "Does this have anything to do with *the fairy-tale world*?"

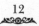

The twins' jaws dropped in perfect unison. This was the last thing they expected to come out of her mouth. It was like they were in a film that had suddenly skipped a scene.

"Um... *correct*," Conner said. "Well, *that* was easy."

Alex gave Conner a dirty look—certain there was some information he had forgotten to share with her.

"Conner, you told Mrs. Peters about the fairy-tale world?" Alex asked.

"Of course not!" Conner said. "It was probably Mom! She had to explain our transfers somehow!"

When the twins looked back at Mrs. Peters, she was making a face they had never seen her make before. Her eyes were large and glistening and she covered a huge smile with both hands. The retiree looked like an excited little girl.

"Oh my word," Mrs. Peters said. "After all these years, I finally know it was real.... I can't tell you how much time I've spent wondering if it was just a dream or a hallucination, but you've appeared just like *she* did... and in a dress just like *hers*...."

The twins couldn't have been more confused.

"*What* was real?" Conner asked.

"*Who* are you talking about?" Alex pressed.

"When I was a very little girl, I was sick in the hospital with pneumonia," she said. "Late one night, while the nurses were busy with the other patients, a kind woman wearing a dress just like yours appeared in my room. She brushed my hair and read me stories through the night to make me feel better. I figured she must have been some sort of angel. When she left, I begged her to tell me who she was. The woman told me she was a Fairy Godmother and lived in the fairy-tale world."

The twins couldn't believe their ears. They had known Mrs. Peters for years but never knew she had any knowledge of the fairy-tale world.

"Whoa, *small worlds*," Conner said.

"That woman was our grandmother," Alex said. "She and other fairies used to travel to this world and read fairy tales to children in need. Grandma said the stories always gave children hope."

Mrs. Peters had a seat on the desk and held a hand over her heart.

"Well, she was right," she said. "Once I was healthy, I devoured fairy tales for the rest of my childhood. I even became a teacher so I could share the same stories with others."

"No way!" Conner said. "That's why you made us do those reports on fairy tales when we were your students! This is *meta*!"

"Conner, I hate when you use that word," Alex said.

"I agree with Mr. Bailey—*this is meta*!" Mrs. Peters laughed. "Words can't describe how grateful I am to finally know the truth. All this time, you weren't living in another state; you were living with your grandmother in the fairy-tale dimension! That explains your abrupt transfers, why your mother was so vague about the details—and I'm assuming it has something to do with Mr. Bailey's abandonment of the school's European trip."

"Guilty," Conner said sheepishly. "I'm not a delinquent after all!"

"And your grandmother, is she still around?" Mrs. Peters asked.

She seemed so happy, the twins didn't want to break the news to her.

"Actually, Grandma passed away a little more than a year ago," Alex said.

"Yeah, just after she *slayed a dragon!*" Conner bragged. "But that's another long story that will only lead to longer stories—trust me, our future biographer is going to have his hands full—and right now we don't have time to explain! We're actually here for something really important."

"Oh?" Mrs. Peters said.

"Remember when you saved my short stories in a portfolio—for when I started applying to colleges? Do you know where those are?" he asked.

"You don't have your own copies?" Mrs. Peters asked.

"No, they were handwritten," Conner said. "It was painful enough writing the originals—my hand couldn't take making copies."

"Mr. Bailey, if you're going to be a writer, you need to learn to secure your work—"

"Yeah, I'm learning that the hard way," Conner said. "Look, something terrible has happened in the fairy-tale world, and we need my short stories to save it."

"I'm sure you have a million questions, but like Conner said, we're really crunched for time," Alex added. "If you know where they are, *please* point us in the right direction. A lot of people are depending on us."

From the tone of their voices and the urgency in their eyes, Mrs. Peters could tell they were very serious, so she didn't question them further.

"You're in luck," she said. "I have them with me."

Mrs. Peters retrieved her purse from under the desk and pulled a large binder out of it. She flipped through the binder, and the twins saw it was filled with hundreds of student essays, math tests, book reports, history exams, and artwork.

"Today was my last day before retirement," Mrs. Peters said. "I cleaned out my desk and I found *this*. It's a collection I've kept over the years of the student work that made me the most proud to be an educator. Whenever I had a particularly rough day, I would take a look through this and be inspired all over again."

When she reached the end of the binder, Mrs. Peters unclipped it and handed Conner a stack of papers with messy handwriting.

"Here are your short stories, Mr. Bailey," she said.

The twins sighed with relief. After a long search, they had finally found them! Conner tried taking them out of Mrs. Peters's hand, but she tightened her grip.

"I'll only give you these if you make me a promise," she said.

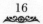

"He'll do whatever you want!" Alex said desperately.

Conner nodded. "Yeah, what she said!"

Mrs. Peters looked straight into his eyes. "When this troubling chapter of your lives comes to an end, promise me you'll go back to school and continue writing," she said.

Conner was expecting something much worse than that. "Okay, I promise," he said.

"Good," she said. "The world needs writers like you to inspire them, Mr. Bailey. Don't take your talent for granted, and don't let it go to waste."

Mrs. Peters released her grip on the papers, and Conner's short stories were finally in his possession. Alex was thankful it had been an easy exchange—she had been prepared to hex Mrs. Peters with a paralyzing spell if she needed to.

"I'm happy I made your binder," Conner said.

"I never thought I'd say this, Mr. Bailey, but you are the closest thing to a favorite student I'll ever have," she confessed.

"Me?" Conner said. "But...but...*why?*"

"Yeah, *why?*" Alex said before she could stop herself.

"With all due respect, Miss Bailey, when I'm old and my memory fades I won't remember the students who got the best grades or had the best attendance," Mrs. Peters said. "I'll remember the ones who progressed the most, and your brother has come a long way from taking naps in my class."

"I don't think I progressed any more than anyone else did," Conner said with a shrug.

"That's because no one has the privilege of looking at

themselves through someone else's eyes," Mrs. Peters said. "I watched you struggle after your father died—but you didn't let yourself struggle for long. Rather than wallowing in grief, you developed a strong sense of humor. Soon I was constantly condemning your clown antics in class. The following year, when I became principal, I had a feeling there was a remarkable imagination behind that wit. I had your teacher send me samples of your creative writing and my suspicion was right. You chose to *grow* from tragedy—and it takes a very strong person to do that."

Alex smiled proudly at her brother. Conner's whole face turned bright red—he was as good at taking compliments as Mrs. Peters was.

"Aw shucks," he said. "I guess I'm more sophisticated than I thought."

"You'd be surprised," Mrs. Peters said. "I learned a lot about you from your writing, possibly more than you intended to share. Perhaps as you look through your stories again, you'll learn a thing or two about yourself."

This made Conner a little nervous—how much of himself had he exposed? When he wrote, Conner only worried about telling a good story; he never thought about the fingerprints he left between the lines. He suddenly felt like he was in the shower and had forgotten to lock the bathroom door.

"Thank you, Mrs. Peters," Conner said. "For what it's worth, you've always been my favorite, too. I never would have liked writing if it weren't for you."

Mrs. Peters was so happy she had stumbled upon the Bailey twins tonight. Knowing she helped shape the twins into the wonderful and responsible young adults they'd become was the greatest retirement gift she could have received. She put the binder back into her purse and then glanced up at the clock. It was disheartening to see that the new teacher had obnoxiously decorated the clock to look like the sun.

"I can't believe it's past midnight," Mrs. Peters said. "I'm absolutely exhausted. If you'll both excuse me, I think I'll head—"

With another gust of wind and a flash of light, the Bailey twins disappeared into thin air. It made Mrs. Peters laugh because their quick exit confirmed something she believed with her whole heart.

"*Students,*" she said. "They come and go so quickly."

CHAPTER ONE

THE MASKED EMPIRE

The air was filled with so much smoke, you could barely see the sky. Every time it was cleared by a strong wind, it was quickly replenished from another pillaged town or forest fire. During the day, the sun looked like a weak lantern shining through a brown sheet. At night, seeing a star had become as rare as spotting a shooting star.

The fairy-tale world had faced many troubling times in recent years, but never anything like this. It was the first time in history that *happily ever after* seemed impossible to regain.

Over the course of one night, the Wicked Witch of the West's Winkie army attacked the Charming Kingdom and the Troblin Territory. Her flying monkeys were sent to terrorize the Elf Empire and the Corner Kingdom. The Queen of Hearts marched her card soldiers through the Center Kingdom and then wreaked havoc on the Eastern Kingdom. Captain Hook's band of pirates poisoned the waters of Mermaid Bay, sending the mermaids fleeing deeper into the ocean. Captain Hook's flying ship, the *Jolly Roger*, attacked the Fairy Kingdom, leaving the palace in pieces. Then the captain took the Northern Kingdom by storm.

The soldiers and villagers of every kingdom, who had once banded together to fight off the Grande Armée, were no match for these invaders. Their homes and towns were pillaged and burned to the ground. Their farms and stables were raided, and their livestock and horses were stolen.

All the fairies were presumed dead or in hiding. The kings and queens had lost their thrones, and their homes lay in ruins. The forests were slowly burned one at a time, giving the animals and refugees fewer and fewer places to hide.

The kingdoms and territories of yesterday ceased to exist. All the land in the fairy-tale world had been combined into one large empire ruled by the infamous Masked Man and his newly assembled Literary Army.

The elf, troll, goblin, and human civilians from all over the fairy-tale world were rounded up and marched into the

Northern Kingdom. They were pushed into Swan Lake, just beside the severely damaged Northern Palace. The lake had been dried out by the Literary Army, making it a deep, muddy crater, perfect to hold the civilians prisoner. By the time the lake was filled, the sun had started its descent in the western sky. The Literary soldiers pointed their captives' attention to a large balcony of the palace.

Doors opened and the Masked Man appeared. His entire head was covered in a mask made of rubies and jewels with only two slits for his eyes. His raggedy clothes had been upgraded to a well-tailored suit. He wore a long black cape with a collar that towered sinisterly over his head.

The Masked Man finally looked like the menacing ruler he had always wanted to become.

His entrance was met with a thunderous rumble of booing and hissing, which only escalated when the Queen of Hearts, the Wicked Witch of the West, and Captain Hook joined him on the balcony. The Masked Man held his hands out in front of him, embracing the noise as if it were applause.

"Now, now, now," he said. "Is that how you address your new *emperor*?"

The title was not received well by his imprisoned audience. Many of the civilians had stashed food in their clothing before being forced from their homes, and rather than saving it, they threw it angrily at the Masked Man. The self-appointed emperor was pelted with tomatoes, plums, and heads of lettuce.

The civilians roared with laughter. Even the Wicked Witch of the West cackled at the embarrassing scene. But the Masked Man wouldn't let his first moments as emperor become a mockery.

"SILENCE OR I'LL KILL YOU ALL!" the Masked Man yelled.

The food throwing stopped, and a tense hush fell over the dried-up lake. He had already destroyed their villages and homes; there was no telling how far he'd go to gain respect. A winged monkey brought the Masked Man a rag, and he wiped the food off his clothing.

"From this day forward you will no longer be the *people* of your pathetic kingdoms, but the *property* of this empire," he announced. "Disrespect me again, and I will not show you the same mercy as your weak kings and fragile queens. Anyone who dares to cross me will not only lose their own lives, but will first watch as I take their families' lives as well!"

Children throughout the lake began to cry, and their parents held them tightly. It seemed the darkest days were still ahead.

"I've brought you all here to witness the birth of a new era," the Masked Man preached. "But before we achieve a new future, the ways of the past must be destroyed—and the *leaders* of the past are no exception!"

The Masked Man gestured to a large wooden platform below the balcony, on the lawn between the palace and the dried lake. A very tall man in a long black cloak climbed to the top of the platform and placed a large wooden block in the center.

A dozen flying monkeys pulled a wagon out from behind the palace. It carried all the former kings and queens of the fairy-tale world: Cinderella, King Chance, Sleeping Beauty, King Chase, Snow White, King Chandler, Troll-bella, Empress Elvina, Rapunzel, Sir William, and even the young princesses Hope and Ash. All the royals had their hands tied together and were blindfolded and gagged with strips of white cloth.

The tall man on the platform withdrew a large silver axe from inside his cloak. The civilians began screaming and shouting in horror once they realized the purpose of it—*the Masked Man was going to have the royal families executed!*

Although they couldn't see, the kings and queens knew what was happening by the sound of the terrified crowd. They fought against their restraints, but they didn't budge. The civilians desperately tried to climb out of the dried lake to save their rulers, but they were kicked back into the mud. The card soldiers stood around the lake's perimeter and locked arms, forming a wall to block them.

The Masked Man laughed wildly at all the terror he was causing. Winkie soldiers pulled the royals out of the wagon and pushed them up the steps to the platform, then stood guard around it. The cloaked executioner sharpened his axe as he awaited his cue to begin.

"Start with the men, then the women, then the *children*,"

the Masked Man ordered. *"Your Majesty,* if you would please do the honors..."

The Queen of Hearts stepped to the edge of the balcony. With enlarged eyes and a devious grin, she looked down at the distressed royals like they were a delicious snack.

"OOOOFFFF WITH THEIR HEEEEEAAAAADS!" she roared.

The lake erupted in protest. The women cried desperate pleas for the execution to stop; the men yelled profanities at the Masked Man for being so cruel. The frightened royal families huddled together in a corner of the platform and trembled.

The executioner selected King Chance to be his first kill. He grabbed him by the arm and dragged him to the block. Cinderella and Hope screamed through their gags when they realized he was no longer standing beside them.

The executioner forced Chance into a kneeling position and placed his head on the wooden block. He held the axe above the king's neck and practiced swinging. With each swing, the civilians gasped, fearing it was the fatal blow. Finally, the executioner raised his axe higher into the air than he had raised it before. The pleas and screams from the helpless bystanders multiplied; the royals knew it was only a matter of seconds before the king lost his head.

The executioner brought the axe down—but as he did, he spun his body so it sliced the platform floor instead of the king's neck. Suddenly, the floor caved in, causing the executioner and all the royals to fall through the platform and disappear from sight. It was so unexpected, the panicked crowd went silent—this couldn't have been part of the plan.

"WHAT JUST HAPPENED?" the Masked Man screamed from the balcony. "GET THEM OUT OF THERE!"

Just as the Winkie soldiers went to inspect the platform, *three large horses burst out from inside it*! Porridge, Buckle, and Oats had been under the platform the entire time. They were pulling a carriage with the executioner and all the royals safely aboard. *The platform had been a large trapdoor!*

"NOOOO!" the Masked Man screamed, and leaned over the balcony as far as he could to get a better look.

To his horror, he saw Goldilocks on Porridge and Jack on Buckle! The couple steered the horses and the carriage into the forest beyond the palace, knocking over dozens of Winkie soldiers as they went. *The execution had turned into a rescue mission right before the Masked Man's eyes!*

Goldilocks glanced back at the rescued royals. "Is everyone all right?"

The royals moaned through their gags. Still blindfolded, they had no clue what was going on. The executioner threw off his cloak—*it had been the Tin Woodman all along*!

"Don't fret, Your Majesties!" he said. "This is a rescue!"

The Tin Woodman sliced off the royals' restraints with his axe.

"We're not out of it yet!" Jack said. "Everyone stay low! This is going to be a bumpy ride!"

Meanwhile, the elf, troll, goblin, and human civilians embraced one another and cheered as their leaders got away. The Masked Man was so furious, he was practically breathing fire. The visible skin around his eyes turned so red, it matched the rubies in his mask.

"AFTER THEM! ALL OF YOU!" he ordered the Literary Army. "DON'T LET THEM ESCAPE!"

The rescue party was chased through the forest by droves of Winkies and card soldiers on horseback. The fleet of flying monkeys followed them from the smoky sky. As the royals removed their blindfolds and looked around, an escape didn't seem likely—there was no way their carriage stood a chance against the approaching Literary soldiers. Luckily, Jack and Goldilocks had friends with a few tricks up their sleeves.

The Winkies and card soldiers were gaining speed and moving closer to the carriage. Goldilocks nodded to Jack and he whistled. Suddenly, Sir Grant and Sir Lampton appeared with dozens of their men on horseback. They formed a protective circle around the carriage of royals and knocked the approaching Literary soldiers to the ground.

"Sir Lampton, is that you?" Cinderella said.

"Hello, Your Majesty," he said. "I wish the circumstances were different, but I'm very pleased to see you're alive!"

Sir Grant and Sir Lampton's men weren't alone—they shared their horses with the Lost Boys from Neverland. When they were close enough, Tootles, Nibs, Curly, and the Lost twins jumped off their horses and landed in the carriage with the royals. The Lost Boys pulled slingshots out of their pockets and launched rocks at the Winkies and card soldiers, hitting them in the face and knocking them off their horses.

"This is fun!" Tootles said.

"Let's make it a game!" Curly said.

"Ten points for the big square ones, and five for the gold guys," Nibs decided.

"Deal!" the Lost twins said.

The Lost Boys giggled so hard watching the Winkies and cards fall off their horses that tears streamed down their rosy faces. They hadn't had this much fun since they left Neverland.

Thanks to the Lost Boys and Sir Grant and Sir Lampton's men, the number of Literary soldiers trailing the carriage had significantly lowered. But there were still plenty of Winkies and cards left to be concerned about. Luckily, the rescue party was close to the next phase of their plan.

As they raced farther into the forest, Goldilocks spotted an arrow sticking into the side of a tree—*it was a sign*!

"Jack, I see the arrow!" she said. "We're almost to the Merry Men!"

Porridge, Buckle, and Oats were getting tired and starting to slow down, so Jack was relieved to hear it. He whistled toward the treetops as loudly as he could.

"WAS THAT THE WHISTLE WE'VE BEEN WAITING FOR, OR DO MY EARS DECEIVE ME?" shouted a boisterous voice from the trees.

Jack rolled his eyes and whistled again.

"THERE IT IS AGAIN! OUR TIME HAS COME, MERRY MEN! ATTACK!"

Robin Hood and his Merry Men swung down from the treetops on ropes like monkeys on vines. Little John, Alan-a-Dale, and Will Scarlet slammed into the Winkies and cards. They knocked them to the ground and stole their horses. Robin Hood flipped through the air, landing in the carriage with the royals. He took off his hat and bowed to the queens.

"HAVE NO FEAR, LADIES, FOR THE TRUE HERO HAS ARRIVED!" he said. He winked at them flirtatiously and kissed Rapunzel's hand, which Sir William didn't appreciate.

"Gosh, I really hate that guy," Jack whispered to Goldilocks.

Robin Hood reached for the bow and quiver of arrows fastened to the back of his vest and joined the Lost Boys in shooting Winkies and cards off their horses. After hitting a few, the Prince of Thieves grew cocky and started showing off for the queens, striking ridiculous poses as he fired.

"DON'T BE INTIMIDATED, LOST BOYS," he said, and rubbed Tootles's head. "BATTLE IS MEANT FOR MEN."

Tootles snapped his slingshot against Robin Hood's buttocks, causing him to squeal like an injured swine.

"Tootles, save it for the enemy!" Goldilocks reprimanded.

"Sorry, it slipped!" Tootles said.

By now, the Winkies and card soldiers had all been knocked to the ground or had retreated to the Northern Palace. However, the chase wasn't over yet. Piercing screeches echoed through the forest as the flying monkeys descended upon the rescue party.

Jack whistled again. *"Peter, it's your turn!"* he yelled.

Like a rocket, Peter Pan flew out from underneath the carriage where he had been hiding. It happened so fast, he startled the royal families. The Boy Who Never Grew Up handed two bags of firecrackers to Little John and Alan-a-Dale, and matches to Will Scarlet. The Merry Men tossed the firecrackers to Will Scarlet, and once he lit them, Peter quickly scooped them up. The boy flew above the treetops and threw the firecrackers at the approaching flying monkeys.

Each explosion shocked and discombobulated the flying monkeys, and they fluttered to the ground. Peter and the Merry Men continued their firecracker relay until all the flying monkeys had dropped from the sky.

"Take THAT, you overgrown bats!" Peter chuckled.

Trollbella watched Peter Pan in astonishment. Her heart was beating so fast, if it had wings, she could have joined him in flight.

"It's like I was beheaded and went to heaven!" she said. "He's just like Butterboy—but he *floats* and *sparkles*! *I didn't know a boy so wonderful could exist!* Stop it, Trollbella! Pull yourself together! You promised yourself you wouldn't love again until the world was in better condition!"

Still, the Troblin Queen tried to catch the trails of fairy dust Peter left as he flew beside the carriage.

Finally free from the Masked Man's Literary Army, the royals and their rescuers could all breathe a little easier. Goldilocks and Jack took the reins of their horses and steered them into a sharp left, leading the party straight into the Dwarf Forests.

"Where are we going?" Snow White asked.

"Someplace the Masked Man and his army will never find us," Goldilocks said.

"Now, everyone keep as quiet as possible," Jack instructed. "The less noise we make, the better."

The royals obeyed his instructions. The rescue party spent the rest of the day traveling deeper and deeper into the Dwarf Forests. The kings and queens glanced around nervously at the thick forest, as most of them had never been to these parts before. They kept waiting for something frightening to appear, but the forest that infamously housed the most dangerous creatures and criminals in the fairy-tale world seemed rather empty.

They reached a hilly part of the woods just before nightfall. Goldilocks stopped the procession in front of a large boulder sticking into the hillside. She covered her mouth and made a peculiar shape with her hands.

"*Coo-KOO, coo-KOO!*" she called.

The birdcall echoed through the forest. The party waited anxiously in silence. A moment later, a faint birdcall came from somewhere beyond the boulder.

"Coo-coo-KA, coo-coo-KA."

The boulder was slowly rolled away by two monstrous black bears, revealing a hidden tunnel in the hillside. The sight of the bears frightened the royals and they held one another closely.

"Don't be scared, they're with us," Goldilocks whispered. *"If anyone has reservations about bears, it's me."*

The carriage moved into the tunnel, and the men on horseback followed. Once the entire rescue party was inside, the bears rolled the boulder back so the entrance was hidden again. The rescue party traveled down the tunnel for several hundred feet and then entered a cavernous mine.

The ground was covered in cart tracks that stretched into more tunnels going deeper into the hillside. Thousands of fireflies covered the stalactites above, illuminating the dark cave like earthy chandeliers. Dozens of sheets and quilts were draped over stalagmites to make several tents.

The royal families were very surprised to see they were among hundreds of other refugees. Families of humans, elves, trolls, and goblins were dispersed throughout the mine. There were also several groups of animals: foxes, wolves, badgers, bears, and birds of every kind. Even *the animals* were taking shelter during this terrible time—which explained why the forest was so empty.

There were a few familiar faces among the hideaways as well. Hagetta and Friar Tuck were cooking a meal together in a large cauldron. The Traveling Tradesman, the old geezer who sold Jack the magic beans that grew the infamous beanstalk, sat against a stalagmite as he counted a collection of chicken feet he kept in a small sack.

Queen Red Riding Hood was in the back of the mine, quietly sitting alone. Her granny and the Little Old Woman from the Shoe Inn sat nearest to her, knitting quilts to make more tents. Slightly, the Lost Boy who had turned into a baby thanks to a youth potion, was taking a nap in a bassinet beside the older women. Blubo, a young flying monkey, was curled up in the bassinet beside him. Thanks to Granny's bad eyesight, she thought he was an extremely furry infant.

Being the pets of high-maintenance women, Clawdius and Lester had become fast friends when they were brought to the mine. The animals also napped together, taking turns using the other as a pillow.

Rook Robins and his father sat in a group with others from their village. Since he had nearly gotten the royals killed a year earlier, seeing them filled Rook with unbearable guilt. He excused himself from his group and took a walk through the tunnels to be alone.

The rescue party's entrance caused quite a commotion. Everyone was so happy to see the royal families were alive that the mine vibrated with emotional cheers. The refugees surrounded the carriage and welcomed their leaders to the only sanctuary left in the fairy-tale world.

"Thank the heavens you're all right!" Hagetta said.

"All our prayers have been answered!" Friar Tuck said.

Jack climbed down from Buckle and then carefully helped Goldilocks off Porridge, an act that became increasingly difficult as Goldilocks's pregnant belly grew every day. It was only a matter of time before they welcomed their child into the world; they only wished a better world awaited it.

Robin Hood and the Merry Men eagerly helped the queens down from the carriage, kissing their hands as they did so, which greatly annoyed their husbands.

"Where are we?" Sleeping Beauty asked.

"We're in an abandoned dwarf mine in the West Hills of the Dwarf Forests," Goldilocks said. "It's not the extravagance you're used to, but we'll be safe here. Very few people know it exists and it's miles from the parts of the woods being burned down."

"We were taking shelter in a small cave in the Northern Mountains, but as you can see, our numbers have grown," Jack said.

"Where are all these people and creatures from?" King Chase asked.

"All over the kingdoms," Goldilocks said. "They're the few who managed to escape the Masked Man's army. Just like you, they've lost everything they had."

The royals were very sympathetic to the people around them, but clearly had hesitations about sharing the mine with the creatures from the forest.

"I assure you, everyone and everything in this mine is safe," Sir Lampton said. "We're all united by the same enemy and must stay so if we want to reclaim our world."

The royal families looked among themselves and nodded.

"You won't find any objection from us," Empress Elvina said on the royals' behalf. "We need to put aside our differences from the past, otherwise there'll be no hope for the future."

Since the elves had a long history of being ostracized by the other kingdoms, the empress's words spoke volumes. They had already lost so much; *unity* was something they couldn't afford to lose next.

"Where are all the fairies?" Rapunzel asked.

"In hiding, hopefully," Goldilocks said.

"Is it true the Fairy Council was turned to stone?" Trollbella asked.

"We don't know," Jack said with a long sigh. "Shortly after the kingdoms were attacked, Alex and Conner went to the Fairy Kingdom to find the council and get help, but they never came back."

Everyone in the mine looked to the ground with worried eyes and a heavy heart. This was the most distressing news of all. Without the Fairy Council or the Bailey twins, how would they ever defeat the Masked Man and his Literary Army? The future looked even bleaker than it had before.

"Alex was right," Cinderella said. "The Fairy Council

should have listened to her. Had they gone after the Masked Man like she requested, none of this would have happened."

"What about Charlie or that monster who took him?" King Chandler asked. "Has anyone tracked down their whereabouts?"

All the refugees turned to Red, but the queen remained silent. She didn't have the strength to relive it.

"Red and the Lost Boys found him at Morina's cottage," Goldilocks said. "The witch has imprisoned him inside a magic mirror. They also found the missing children from the Corner and Charming Kingdoms—they're under some sort of spell that's draining their youth."

With everything else that had happened, the royals had almost forgotten about the missing children.

"Can't we plan a rescue for them, too?" Rapunzel asked.

"The children have been cursed with very dark magic," Hagetta explained. "Moving them from their beds may take their life force away completely."

"But what about Charlie?" King Chandler asked. "How do we get him out of the mirror?"

"We *can't*," Red said weakly. "Once you're imprisoned in a magic mirror, it's nearly impossible to be freed. It takes powerful magic to put someone inside a mirror, but even more powerful magic to take someone out."

"She's right," said Snow White. "My stepmother spent her whole life trying to free the man from her mirror. She was as determined and capable as anyone, and even she needed *the Wishing Spell* to do it."

The Charming brothers didn't want to believe it, but there was no escaping the truth. There wasn't a silver lining in sight—for *any* of their worries.

"They're no longer missing if we know their location," Cinderella said. "We must find comfort where we can, otherwise we'll worry ourselves to death. God willing, the children and Charlie will be among many things we salvage in the months ahead."

"Yes, but how do we begin salvaging anything?" Sir William asked. "Have we ever faced a threat with such disadvantages?"

It seemed every question was only followed with more terrible news, so everyone in the mine went silent. No one wanted to accept defeat, but the little hope surviving in their hearts was dying fast. If something didn't happen soon, the fairy-tale world as they knew it would be gone forever.

The tense silence was broken by the Traveling Tradesman, who had been biting his tongue up to this moment.

"*Ah-hum.*" He coughed.

All the refugees in the mine rolled their eyes at the old geezer. Clearly, he was very unpopular among the survivors. When no one gave him the floor, the old man tried to get their attention again.

"*Ah-HUM!*" He coughed even louder.

Hagetta was the only one with enough patience to acknowledge him. "Yes, what is it, old man?" she asked.

"May I offer a suggestion?" the Traveling Tradesman asked.

His question was immediately followed by a chorus of loud sighs. Every time the Tradesman opened his mouth he only filled their heads with nonsense. But, to be fair to the old man, Jack raised his hands and silenced the exasperated crowd.

"Unless someone else has a suggestion to share, there's no point in discrediting his," he said.

Red grunted dramatically. "Everyone cover your ears," she said. "I've heard *crazy* is contagious in small quarters."

Despite the rudeness he received from his peers, the Traveling Tradesman went to the center of the mine so everyone could see him, and he offered them his suggestion.

"Perhaps we're all looking at the situation from the wrong perspective," he said. "In times as troubling as these, let's not torture ourselves further with questions we don't have the answers to—*let's ask the rocks!*"

He proposed the idea as if everyone else was supposed to know what he was talking about.

"ASK THE *ROCKS*?" Robin Hood said. "MERRY MEN, I BELIEVE THE STRANGE OLD MAN IS OFF HIS *ROCK*-ER!"

Robin Hood laughed wildly at his own joke, but no one joined him. The Tradesman was frustrated that he had to explain himself.

"Not just *any rocks!*" he said. "In my possession, I

happen to have *precious premonition stones* that are directly connected to *the will of the fates*!"

The wacky old man reached for his stones, but they were missing from his belt. He spun around in circles, looking all over the ground for where he might have dropped them.

"Where on earth are my precious stones?" he demanded. "Has anyone seen them? They were in a skunk-skin sack."

All five of the Lost Boys turned bright red.

"Oops," Tootles said. "We might have used those during the rescue."

"You did WHAT?" the Tradesman yelled. *"Those rocks are thousands of years old! They're meant for predicting the future, not slingshots!"*

"Sorry, we didn't mean to!" Tootles said.

"They didn't look like special rocks to us," Curly said.

"You really shouldn't leave your stones lying around," Nibs said.

"Yeah! There are kids in here!" the Lost twins said.

The Tradesman sat on the ground and wrapped his arms around his head. "Now what am I supposed to use to predict the will of the fates?" he asked.

The Lost Boys checked their pockets.

"Would *marbles* work?" Tootles asked.

The Traveling Tradesman let out a deep, apprehensive sigh. "Very well—hand them over."

Tootles poured a small bag of colorful marbles into the Tradesman's shaky hands. He closed his eyes, rubbed the marbles together, and whispered strange gibberish to them. Finally, he threw them on the ground in front of him and carefully watched them bounce and roll into one another.

"Interesting," he said. "*Very* interesting."

The Tradesman hemmed and hawed as if the marbles were speaking a language only he understood. It was much more of an ordeal than the refugees were expecting. Curiosity got the best of them and they formed a circle around him.

"What are the marbles saying?" Jack asked.

"Don't be ridiculous—*marbles don't speak*! They simply move as the fates command," the Tradesman said. "You see this gray one? Dull, dreary, and stuck in the dirt—*that represents us*! See the blue one and the pink one, moving together in perfect unison away from the gray—*those must represent the twins*! Fear not, the Baileys are alive!"

A few of the refugees cheered—but quickly stopped when they remembered the information was coming from an old geezer talking to marbles.

"But where are they?" Jack asked.

"They're far away from us by now, most likely in the Otherworld—*but wait*!"

All the refugees leaned in a little closer. Crazy or not, this was still the most entertaining thing they had seen in weeks.

"See how the blue and the pink rolled toward the silver, yellow, purple, and red? *Now watch*—the pink and blue are rolling back to the gray with the silver, yellow, purple, and red! *Look, all the marbles have knocked the gray out of the dirt! It's a MIRACLE!*"

The Tradesman leaped to his feet and threw his hands into the air in celebration. The refugees were on pins and needles waiting for the message to be interpreted. Even if the news was not as great as it appeared, the Tradesman's enthusiasm was infectious—they hoped this wasn't the *crazy* that Red was talking about.

"What does it all mean?" Jack asked.

"It means the twins will have to travel to places far, far away, but will return with help and save our world!" the Tradesman said. "But this will happen if, and *only* if…"

"*Yes?*"

"*Worlds collide,*" the Tradesman said with large, energetic eyes.

No one had a clue what the old man was talking about, but they were all so desperate for something positive, they took it as a good sign. Red, on the other hand, was not as enthusiastic.

"All I see is an old man who's lost his marbles," she said.

The other refugees slowly came to their senses, too. Just because this was the closest thing to good news they had received didn't make it credible.

"I agree with the old man," Goldilocks announced. "It doesn't matter what the marbles say or don't say—the Bailey twins have never let us down before. Just because we haven't heard from them yet doesn't mean we should give up on them. We have to have faith they'll return with help."

"But what do we do in the meantime?" Red asked.

"Wait," Goldilocks said. "It's all we can do."

CHAPTER TWO

GROUNDED

Alex and Conner left their sixth-grade classroom and found a neighborhood park where they could rest and form the next phase of their plan. It was an hour or so before sunrise, and the night sky was lightening with every passing minute. Everything was so quiet and peaceful, it was difficult to imagine how chaotic life was back in the fairy-tale world and what awful things their friends might be enduring.

The closer it came to sunrise, the more people drove past the park on their early work commutes. Naturally,

Alex had seen this many times before, but every car she saw gave her a small thrill. It had been a long time since she'd been back to the Otherworld, and it wasn't until this moment that she realized how much she missed it.

"It's nice to see how little things have changed here," Alex said. "The fairy-tale world changes so much, I've never had a moment to catch my breath."

Conner was only half listening. He flipped through the pages of his short stories and separated them into four stacks on the ground.

"Great, they're all here!" he said. " 'Starboardia,' 'Galaxy Queen,' 'The Ziblings,' and 'The Adventures of Blimp Boy'! Those are the stories with characters that can help us! We'll use the potion to travel inside the stories, find the heroes, and then take them back to the fairy-tale world to help us fight our uncle's army."

Alex had only agreed to her brother's plan because their options were so limited. The closer they got to actually going through with it, the more doubtful she became. It was one thing to travel into the books of classic literature, but an entirely different endeavor to go into short stories written by her brother.

"Your stories sound more elaborate than I was expecting," Alex said. "I thought you wrote about our experiences in the fairy-tale world and just changed all the names."

"That's how it started," Conner said. "But after I got the hang of it, I might have exaggerated things a bit and taken some liberties. All good writers do—I think."

"Liberties?" Alex asked fearfully. "Conner, what exactly are we getting ourselves into?"

Conner waved it off like it wasn't a big deal.

"Relax, there's nothing more dangerous than what we've already been through," he said. "'Starboardia' is a pirate adventure, 'Galaxy Queen' is about space exploration, 'The Ziblings' are a group of superheroes, and 'The Adventures of Blimp Boy' follows a young archaeologist. It'll be a piece of cake."

The summaries didn't comfort his sister at all. The twins were lucky they had survived their adventures over the years. If his stories were based on those experiences, Alex wasn't eager to relive any of them—especially if they had been exaggerated by her brother's warped imagination.

"Are you sure this is going to work?" Alex said. "I don't mean to sound like a snob, but maybe we should stick to *published* stories."

"Stop worrying," Conner said. "There are no evil enchantresses, no dragons, no French soldiers, and no literary armies. All my characters are based on people we know and love. They have the same bravery, intelligence, and compassion as our friends—they'll *want* to help us. We'll be in and out before the antagonists even show up."

"What are we going to do with your characters after we bring them out?" Alex asked. "Where are we going to keep them?"

Conner had been so worried about *finding* his stories,

he hadn't thought about what they'd do after they found them.

"Good point," he said. "We need a place they can stay while we recruit the characters from the other stories. We also need someone to keep an eye on them so they don't wander off—someone we trust completely, who won't totally freak out about what we're doing."

The twins thought about the perfect place and the perfect person for the job, but the candidates were few and far between. It had to be someone in the Otherworld who already knew about the fairy-tale world, someone who had seen magic before and wouldn't be alarmed by it. The person had to be responsible enough to supervise several fictional characters and have enough space to host them. Alex and Conner came to the same conclusion at the exact same time. They looked at each other and knew they were thinking the same thing—there was only one person qualified for the task.

"Mom!" the twins said in unison.

The resolution was immediately followed by an avalanche of guilt.

"I can't remember the last time I talked to Mom," Alex said.

"Neither can I," Conner said. "She's probably worried sick."

"We've been so busy trying to save the fairy-tale world, we never had a chance to call home and check in," Alex said.

"We're good people, but *terrible* children," Conner said.

"Regardless of whether she wants to help us or not, we need to visit her so she knows we're alive," Alex said. "Let's just hope she cooperates."

The twins were in complete agreement. Conner gathered his stories, and they headed out of the park. Alex followed her brother but was confused by the direction he was walking in.

"Where are you going?" she asked him.

"Home," he said.

"But home is *that* way."

"No, home *used* to be that way," Conner said. "Mom and I moved in with Bob after they got married, remember?"

Alex's guilt was doubled by another avalanche—she was so out of the loop, she didn't even know where her own family lived anymore. Whenever she thought about her mom and stepdad in the Otherworld, she always imagined them living in the rental house they had moved into when her and Conner's dad passed away. Perhaps the Otherworld had changed more than she thought.

"I'm the worst daughter in the world," she said. "This isn't going to be a fun visit, is it?"

"Nope," Conner said. "Mom's gonna be pretty upset when she sees us, and I won't blame her."

They reached the edge of the park and Conner came to a stop.

"Aren't you forgetting something else?" he said.

"What?" Alex asked.

Conner looked his sister up and down, like it was obvious. "Alex, you're dressed like the Tooth Fairy," he said. "You can't go walking around the suburbs like that."

"Oh," she said. "You're right—one second."

With a quick spin, Alex transformed her sparkling dress and shoes into a T-shirt, jeans, and sneakers.

"I forgot how comfortable Otherworld clothes are," she said.

"You look like *you* again," Conner said. "Now come on, the quicker we do this, the better."

They walked through the neighborhood streets until they found Sycamore Drive. By now the sun had risen and Alex could see all the spacious homes on the street. She was delighted her mom and Bob lived in such a lovely neighborhood. Alex knew which house was theirs before Conner pointed it out because the flower beds were covered with their mom's favorite roses.

"Hopefully they'll be home," Conner said. "They're usually starting a day shift or ending a night shift around this time."

The twins walked up the curved path and knocked on the door. A few moments later, their stepdad answered. Bob was still in his pajamas and on his first cup of coffee. His eyes were puffy, like he had just woken up. The doctor did a double take when he saw Alex and Conner standing behind the door.

"Good morning, Bob," Alex said cheerfully. "Nice to see you again!"

Bob rubbed his eyes and scratched his head. He wasn't convinced he was awake yet.

"Um . . . *hi*," he said. "Well, this is a surprise."

"Is Mom home?" Conner said. "We have to talk to her."

"Yeah, she's upstairs getting ready for work. Boy, she'll be very glad to see you," he said. *"Charlotte, you have visitors!"* he called into the house.

The twins heard a window open above the porch. They looked up and saw Charlotte looking down at them from the second story, already dressed for work in her blue scrubs. Her face had many expressions at once—shock that she was looking at her children, relief that they were all right, joy that they had finally come home—but it settled on anger.

"Hi, Mom," the twins said apologetically.

"INSIDE. NOW," Charlotte said, and slammed the window.

Conner gulped. "We're off to a good start."

Before they knew it, Alex and Conner were seated on the living room sofa and their mother was furiously pacing in front of them. She was so upset, she couldn't form the words to scold them. Bob sat in an armchair beside the twins. He peered cautiously over his coffee, afraid for their safety.

"The new house is really nice," Alex said. "I really like how you decorated—"

"Quiet," Charlotte said. "Do either of you have any idea what you've put me through? I've been so worried, I haven't slept in months!"

"We're really sorry, Mom," Conner said. "We didn't mean to worry—"

"Less talking, more listening," she said. "Do you know what it's like to go to the grocery store and be asked 'How are your children doing?' and have absolutely no clue yourself? Do you know what it's like to tell a school district 'My children have transferred schools' with no proof of a transfer? Do you know what it's like to hear nothing from your children for weeks at a time except 'Sorry we didn't call you back, Mom, we had to fight a dragon,' or 'Got to go, Mom, an army is invading the castle'?"

Charlotte glared at her children as she waited for an answer, but the twins stayed silent. They didn't know if they were allowed to speak or if she was just pausing for dramatic effect.

"For your sake, I hope *your* future children show you more respect and courtesy than *mine* have shown me," Charlotte went on. "Because *not knowing* if your children are dead or alive in another dimension is the worst feeling you could ever have. It's worse than fighting enchantresses, it's worse than slaying dragons, and it's worse than battling armies, *I promise you!*"

Tears came to Charlotte's eyes and she looked away from the twins to wipe them with a tissue. The guilt the twins had felt before was nothing compared to the guilt they felt now. It tightened their stomachs and chests so much, they thought their bodies might implode.

"Mom, we weren't neglecting you on purpose," Alex

said. "We'd like to explain, if you give us a chance. Something really terrible has happened and we need your help—"

"I don't care what's happened!" Charlotte said. "There will always be another crisis in the fairy-tale world to tend to! Your family should come first! That's what your father and I raised you to believe, or so I thought."

"You did—and we do," Conner said. "But so many people's lives are in danger—"

"What about *your lives?*" Charlotte asked. "Since you were thirteen years old, you've been so busy saving other people, you've never taken care of yourselves. Do either of you even know what *today* is?"

Alex and Conner looked at each other, but neither knew what she was referring to. They quickly went through a mental list of possible holidays or special occasions that it could be, but both were blanking.

"Is it your and Bob's anniversary?" Conner asked.

Charlotte looked more heartbroken than ever. "No, today's your fifteenth birthday," she said.

The twins were shocked. How could they not have known it was their birthday? Suddenly, everything Charlotte said made perfect sense. They were so occupied with saving other people, they were missing out on their own lives.

Charlotte glanced at her watch and then grabbed her purse and car keys off the rack by the front door.

"I have to go to work," she said. "Both of you are *grounded.*"

Conner glanced at Alex. "Wait, can she still do that?" he asked.

"You bet I can!" Charlotte said. "I want both of you to go upstairs to your bedrooms and stay there until I get home."

"Do I even have a bedroom here?" Alex asked.

Charlotte was offended she had to ask. "Of course you do," she said. "When I get back, we're going to go out for a *nice family dinner* to celebrate your birthday."

"Mom, that sounds nice, but we're really pressed for time," Alex said.

"Alexandra Bailey, it's the least you can do for me," Charlotte said. "After we have a *nice family dinner* and discuss *normal family things*, we can talk about what you need help with—but only *after*. Conner, please show your sister to her bedroom."

Charlotte left for work, leaving her children in very uncomfortable silence. They were feeling so many things— guilt, shame, disappointment, anxiety—they didn't know which emotion to settle on.

Bob tried to break the tension, but even he didn't know what to feel.

"So . . ." Bob said. *"Happy birthday?"*

Chapter Three

THE FALLEN EMPEROR

The civilians were so thankful their kings and queens had escaped execution, they all stood a little taller in the dried-up lake. However, to avoid being the target of the emperor's building frustration, they kept as still and quiet as possible.

Inside the ruins of the Northern Palace, in a large chamber that Queen Snow White and King Chandler once ruled from, the Masked Man paced feverishly in front of his new throne. The large chair had been built from the pieces of all the other thrones of the kingdoms the Literary Army had conquered.

"I don't understand how your idiot soldiers didn't know the platform was rigged!" he yelled. "Why didn't they check it?"

The Wicked Witch of the West, the Queen of Hearts, and Captain Hook stood before the Masked Man. The new emperor had fallen into a daring routine of blaming the literary villains when something didn't go exactly as planned.

"*Our* soldiers?" the Wicked Witch of the West said. "You've been commanding our armies since we arrived! If you wanted them to inspect the platform before the execution, *you* should have ordered it!"

The literary villains had endured about as much as they could stand from the Masked Man. It was thanks to them he was emperor in the first place, but instead of fulfilling his end of their bargains, the Masked Man was bossing them around as if they were his servants. Power had clearly gone to his head, and *that* was far enough.

"I've heard enough about how *we* have failed *you*!" the Queen of Hearts barked. "It's time you coughed up what *you* promised *us*!"

"*You promised me Peter Pan!*" Captain Hook shouted.

"*And you promised me the silver slippers!*" the Wicked Witch of the West hollered.

"*And you promised me HEADS!*" the Queen of Hearts roared.

The Masked Man didn't have an ounce of empathy for the literary villains. Their frustration was nothing compared to the rage boiling inside of him.

"You will get what I promised once the royals have been recaptured and executed," the Masked Man said. "You agreed to make me an emperor, and I won't be a true emperor until all my adversaries have been destroyed!"

Footsteps echoed through the throne room. The Masked Man and the literary villains turned to see Mr. Smee sprinting toward them. The pirate was sweating, wheezing, and shaking—like he had been running from something terrible.

"Excuse me, Your Excellency?" Smee panted.

"This better be important," the Masked Man said.

"It's about the creature in the dungeon, sir," Smee said.

The creature responsible for turning the Fairy Council into stone was kept in the dungeon in the very same cell that once contained the Evil Queen. It was a monster of legendary power, so the Masked Man had ordered all of Captain Hook's pirates to patrol the dungeon and keep an eye on it.

"Yes, what about it?" the Masked Man asked.

Mr. Smee was trembling so much, his knees rattled together. No matter how he put it, he knew the emperor would be furious when he heard the news.

"It escaped!" Smee said. "Somehow it managed to take off its blindfold while it was in its cell! When the pirates went to feed it, they looked it in the eye and were turned into stone!"

Like steam from a teakettle, so much anger built up inside the Masked Man that a thunderous howl erupted from his mouth. He wrapped his hands around Smee's throat and strangled the pirate. The day had turned into an epic disaster, and unfortunately for him, it was about to get much worse.

A horn was blown outside to announce the return of the Literary soldiers who had been sent after the royal families. The Masked Man dropped Smee and bolted outside to the balcony. The Wicked Witch, the Queen of Hearts, and Captain Hook followed him.

From the balcony, the Masked Man could see the Winkies and card soldiers slowly emerging from the forest. They were all battered and bruised; many couldn't even walk without the help of another. They had come back with far fewer horses than they left with. The flying monkeys descended from the skies, but looked just as bad as the Winkies and cards, if not worse. They were so discombobulated that many missed the balcony and smacked into the walls of the palace.

Worst of all, there was no sign of the royal families anywhere. The Masked Man grabbed the closest winged monkey by its vest and shook him violently.

"WHERE ARE THE ROYAL FAMILIES?" he roared.

"They escaped!" the monkey screeched.

"HOW DID THEY GET AWAY? YOU OUTNUMBERED THEM TEN TO ONE!" the Masked Man screamed.

"They had a very strategic plan we weren't prepared for! They had backup waiting in the woods! Men on horses, men in the trees, *they even had a boy who flew!*"

The Masked Man felt like his heart had fallen out of his chest. If it weren't for his mask, they would have seen all the color drain from his face. He prayed he had misheard the winged monkey and that his ears were playing a cruel trick on his mind.

"Did you just say *'they even had a boy who flew'*?" he asked.

The winged monkey nodded. "Yes, sir," it said. "He wore clothes made out of leaves! He flew up from the trees and threw firecrackers at us!"

"PETER PAN!" Captain Hook growled. "You said he'd be trapped inside the book until we retrieved him!"

The Masked Man threw the winged monkey on the floor and clutched his chest. He felt like he was having a heart attack. Every time he thought the situation couldn't get worse, he was proved otherwise.

"No, this isn't possible!" the Masked Man said. "If Peter Pan managed to escape, that would mean my niece and nephew did, too!"

The Masked Man turned to the literary villains, and his fury quickly dissolved into fear. The Queen of Hearts and Captain Hook were more furious than he had ever seen them. With Peter Pan and the royal families out of his reach, the Masked Man wasn't capable of fulfilling his end of their agreements. They had followed him into the fairy-tale world and given him the use of their soldiers and cavalry for nothing.

"Listen, I can still give you what I promised," he said. "I just need more time!"

Captain Hook and the Queen of Hearts slowly moved toward him, backing him into the railing of the balcony.

"LIAR!" the Queen of Hearts roared. "No *royals*, no *HEADS!*"

"And you can't *give* me Peter Pan if you don't *have* Peter Pan!" Captain Hook said through a clenched jaw.

Afraid he was about to be knocked off the balcony, the Masked Man fell to his knees and groveled at the Wicked Witch's feet.

"I can still give you the silver slippers!" he pleaded. "Not all is lost!"

"I won't be fooled by any more of your lies!" the Wicked Witch of the West said. "Your reign ends today!"

The Wicked Witch of the West tapped the floor with her umbrella, and two of her flying monkeys grabbed the Masked Man by the arms. They flew him as high into the sky as they possibly could and dangled him above the forest. The civilians in the dried-up lake alerted one another to the sight, but no one knew what was happening.

"DON'T DO THIS!" the Masked Man cried. "YOU'RE MAKING A MISTAKE! MY NIECE AND NEPHEW WILL DESTROY YOU WITHOUT ME!"

"Our biggest mistake was trusting you!" the Wicked Witch of the West shrieked. She tapped her umbrella again and the flying monkeys dropped the Masked Man.

He plummeted toward the earth, screaming the entire way down, and landed somewhere deep in the forest.

"Look, the emperor has fallen!" The Wicked Witch of the West cackled.

It was obvious to the civilians that the literary villains had just staged a coup. Now that the Masked Man was gone, the civilians wanted to cheer, but the emperor's death didn't mean their troubles were over.

"If we aren't getting what we came for, then what should we do now?" Captain Hook asked. "Return to Neverland, Oz, and Wonderland?"

The literary villains thought it over, but now that they had seen the fairy-tale world with their own eyes, their own worlds weren't that appealing. With the Masked Man gone, they had unlimited power over the strange land, and power is easily addictive when placed in the wrong hands. It seemed the fairy-tale world had much more to offer them than their own worlds did.

"I rather like this world," Captain Hook said. "There are no Lost Boys, mermaids, or Indians to fight. And if Peter Pan is here, there's no reason to return to Neverland."

"There are no White Queens, Mad Hatters, or Cheshire Cats to pester us," the Queen of Hearts said. "Why return to Wonderland when I have plenty of heads to roll right here?"

"There are no wizards, Munchkins, or Good Witches to stand in our way," the Wicked Witch of the West said. "And I have more power here than the silver slippers could have given me in Oz!"

The literary villains shared a menacing smile.

"Let's stay in this world and rule the empire ourselves," the Wicked Witch said. "Perhaps if we work together, we'll achieve even *more* than what the Masked Man promised us."

The villains turned their gaze to the civilians in the dried-up lake.

From the way the three villains glared down from the balcony, the civilians knew the nightmare was far from over....

CHAPTER FOUR

A NICE FAMILY DINNER

The Storybook Grill was a popular place for dinner during the week. By seven o'clock each night, the diner was usually filled with families and teenagers ordering their weight in Goblin Fries and Midnight Milk Shakes. There were always loud and energetic crowds, and tonight was no exception.

However, the group in the booth at the very back did not match the liveliness of the other patrons, so they stuck out like a sore thumb.

Cindy, Lindy, Mindy, and Wendy—four teenage girls

recently reinstated as the Book Huggers—somberly sipped milk shakes and shared a basket of fries. The girls each had a copy of *The Adventures of Sherlock Holmes* by Sir Arthur Conan Doyle in front of them, but none of them seemed very interested in it.

"We should probably talk about the book if we're going to be a book club again," Cindy said.

The other girls nodded, but no one was eager to start. The quartet had recently taken a break from books to focus on other passions—well, *passion*—and started the Conspiracy Club. However, that club only made them more restless than they already were, and they had been advised to take up reading again.

"Did anyone have a favorite passage they'd like to share?" Cindy asked. "Or maybe a favorite character?"

All the Book Huggers were quiet, forcing Cindy to take charge.

"Lindy, let's start with you," she said.

Lindy was awkwardly hunched over her milk shake and staring off into space when Cindy called on her. Wherever her mind was, it wasn't on *Sherlock Holmes*.

"Um...I liked the *hound*?" Lindy said.

"*The Hound of the Baskervilles*?" Cindy asked.

Lindy looked uncomfortably from side to side. "Was there more than one?"

"Did you even read the book?" Cindy asked.

Lindy hunched lower than before and shamefully shook her head.

"Did *anyone* read the book this week?" Cindy asked.

The other Book Huggers slumped with embarrassment and shook their heads as well. Cindy let out a long and frustrated sigh.

"We can't revive our book club if we're not going to read books," she said. "But if I'm honest, I didn't read *The Adventures of Sherlock Holmes*, either."

"I started it," Mindy said. "It was just so hard focusing on a fictitious mystery when *the real-life mystery* has never been solved."

The Book Huggers nodded in agreement. No matter how hard they tried to inspire themselves with new interests, new hobbies, and new clubs, or by resurrecting old clubs, the only thing consistently on their minds for the past year was the disappearance of Alex and Conner Bailey.

"You'd think it'd get easier over time, but it doesn't," Lindy said.

"We only started asking questions about Alex because we were bored and had read all the books in the school library," Mindy said. "But every answer only gave us more questions, and the more questions we had, the more infatuated we became."

"I've read books and watched television shows about people with real-life obsessions, but I never thought I'd become one of them," Lindy said. "It's all I think about when I'm awake, and all I dream about when I'm asleep."

Wendy nodded—it was affecting her sleep, too.

"Bree Campbell knows something we don't," Cindy

said. "But until one of us gains telepathic powers—or waterboarding is legalized—I don't think we'll ever get it out of her."

"She's been absent from school for almost two whole weeks!" Mindy said. "I wouldn't be surprised if she's the next one to get '*transferred to Vermont*,' as they say."

Life had become exhausting to no end for the Book Huggers. They felt like mice stuck in a maze with no cheese.

"What are we going to do, girls?" Lindy asked the table. "I don't want this to affect the rest of our lives! I want to become a psychologist—not *need* a psychologist!"

"I'll never be a heart surgeon if I can't focus in medical school!" Mindy said.

"I'll never win my first presidential debate if I can't remember real issues!" Cindy said.

Wendy pointed to the ceiling and made an X with her fingers—implying she would never fulfill her dream of becoming an astronaut.

"It's gone too far, ladies," Cindy said. "This is just like *Nineteen Eighty-Four*, and there's no use fighting Big Brother anymore. We have to pull ourselves together while we still can. For the sake of our sanity and our destinies, we have to forget about the Bailey twins."

The Book Huggers raised their milk shakes and clinked them together. They were ready to turn over a new leaf. The undertaking wouldn't be easy, but it was necessary if they ever wanted to live normal lives again.

Unfortunately, the Book Huggers' noble venture was about to feel like the punch line of a great cosmic joke.

The front door of the Storybook Grill swung open, and the Bailey twins walked in with Charlotte and Bob. Wendy happened to glance up from her milk shake right at that second and was the first to notice Alex and Conner. For the first moments after seeing them, Wendy was certain she was hallucinating. They had *just* been talking about the Bailey twins—it was way too coincidental for them to be in the same diner at exactly the same time.

But the longer they stayed in her sight without disappearing, the more she realized they weren't a mirage—*the real-life Alex and Conner Bailey were right there!* Wendy was paralyzed with shock. The color drained from her face, and she couldn't feel her arms or legs.

"I think we should actually read *The Adventures of Sherlock Holmes*," Cindy said. "Next week, we'll come back to this diner and have a real discussion about it, just like we used to."

"I concur," Mindy said. "But can we do it a week from tomorrow? I'm getting my braces off a week from today."

"Congratulations!" Lindy said. "Will you have to wear a retainer?"

Wendy began humming to get the other Book Huggers' attention, but she was drowned out by the noise of the diner.

"Just for the first six weeks, then only at night after that," Mindy said.

"I was so relieved when I finally had mine taken off," Cindy said. "It felt like handcuffs had been removed from my mouth."

"My dentist said I don't need braces," Lindy said. "It's probably a good thing—I wouldn't have the patience for them."

Wendy couldn't believe they were talking about something so meaningless when something so extraordinary was right in front of them. She managed to regain feeling in one hand and lightly tapped Cindy on the shoulder with it.

"Wendy, are you okay?" Lindy said.

"You look like you're going to be sick," Mindy said.

"Was there something in your Midnight Milk Shake?" Cindy asked.

Desperate for them to see what she was seeing, Wendy used resources she hadn't used since the first grade—*spoken words*!

"Alex... Conner... over there!" Wendy peeped.

Her voice was high-pitched and squeaky like a baby bird's. The Book Huggers were so shocked to hear her make a noise, it took them a second to realize she had actually used *words out loud* and they had *meaning*. Once the message was interpreted, they jerked their heads in the direction of the door so fast that they pulled muscles in their necks. Once they all saw the Bailey twins with their own eyes, the Book Huggers went as still and pale as Mount Rushmore.

The twins were all eyes as they looked around at the diner's fusion of fairy-tale and 1950s decor. They knew

Cinderella's stepmother and stepsisters had opened a restaurant after moving to the Otherworld, but this was their first time seeing it.

Rosemary was in the middle of taking an order when she saw the Baileys out of the corner of her eye. The waitress abandoned the customers in mid-sentence to greet her old friends.

"Well, look what the cat dragged in!" Rosemary said, and hugged the twins.

"Hi, Rosemary," Conner said. "This place looks great!"

"Are Petunia and your mom around?" Alex asked.

"Mother has the night off and Petunia got another job, working for a veterinarian," Rosemary said. "Good riddance, if you ask me—she was a lousy waitress! I'll be sure to tell them you stopped by! Are you coming for dinner?"

"Yes," Charlotte said. "Table for four, please."

"Right this way," Rosemary said.

The stepsister grabbed four menus and sat them in a booth directly next to the Book Huggers. The girls quickly grabbed their copies of *The Adventures of Sherlock Holmes* and covered their faces with them, but Alex and Conner weren't paying attention. The twins were so amused by all the art and knickknacks throughout the diner, they didn't even notice their former classmates.

"How's Cinderella doing?" Rosemary asked the twins once they were settled in their booth.

"Well, actually—"

Alex was about to tell Rosemary the truth when her mother gave her a stern look. Anything that might get them off the topic of *nice family discussion* wasn't allowed at dinner tonight.

"*Just fine,*" Alex said. "Hope's growing like a weed."

"Wonderful. Please give them my best," Rosemary said. "I hope you enjoy the food. When you're ready to order, just wave me down—oh, we're out of the Beanstalk Salad tonight."

Rosemary went back to the customers while Alex and her family looked over the menu. It referenced so many people and places in the fairy-tale world, it was absolutely aggravating not to talk about the current crisis. The twins hoped their *nice family dinner* would end as soon as possible.

"So kids, what's new?" Charlotte asked. "How are your friends doing?"

She was so calm and casual, Alex and Conner knew she wasn't referring to the truth. They shared a curious look, and it suddenly dawned on them what their mother was doing. Their *nice family dinner* was a chance for Mom to pretend they were a perfectly normal family, living perfectly normal lives. The twins felt like they were in a play they didn't have the script for.

"*Good,*" Conner said. "Um . . . Goldilocks and Jack are expecting their first baby!"

"That's wonderful," Charlotte said. "Do they know if it's a boy or a girl?"

She knew as well as he did that the fairy-tale world didn't have ultrasounds, but he continued playing her game.

"Nope," Conner said. "I guess they're waiting to be surprised."

"Your father and I did the same thing when we had you," Charlotte said. "We weren't sure if we were having two boys or two girls, we just knew there would be two of you. Imagine our surprise when we had one of each—we didn't have to return any of the baby clothes."

Conner found this fascinating. "Really?" he said. "What would you have named us if we were two girls or two boys?"

"The firstborn was going to be an Alex no matter what," Charlotte said. "I've loved that name since I was a little girl—it was the name of my favorite doll. But if Conner had been a girl, his name would have been Sarah."

"What a coincidence! Before Margret passed away, we were planning on having a baby, and if it was a girl, we would have named her Sarah, too," Bob said. "Were Alex and Conner an easy delivery?"

Charlotte let out a long laugh as the memory came to her.

"Giving birth was easy compared to the days that followed," she said. "Their grandmother was so excited to have grandchildren, she visited us every day with someone new from the fairy-tale world. The first day she brought Mother Goose, who almost mistakenly switched Conner's bottle with her flask! Thank goodness I was an overly protective first-time mom and saw it happen! The second day we had the whole Fairy Council in the house. They were lovely, but kept magically upgrading our belongings into nicer things. By the time they left, we didn't even recognize our house!"

The twins had never heard this story before and laughed just as hard as Bob did. They could tell their mom enjoyed telling it as much as they enjoyed hearing it.

"Those were good times," Charlotte said with a bittersweet smile. "I miss them."

These were the moments of *nice family discussion* that Charlotte was so desperate for. The Baileys hadn't had them since the twins' father died. There was no talk of death or turmoil like in their usual conversations; they were just a family laughing and sharing stories with one another.

As much as Alex wanted to continue hearing stories about their parents, not addressing the issues at hand was eating her alive. Conner could feel the impatience boiling inside his sister. He knew it was only a matter of time before she ended their mother's game of pretend.

"Mom, I'm sorry you haven't had more moments to tell us stories like that," Alex said. "You're right, you and Dad raised us to put family first and we haven't for a long time."

"Thank you, Alex," Charlotte said. "That means a lot."

"But," Alex said, "I can't keep pretending everything is okay when we know it's not."

Conner covered his face with his hands. "Oh boy, here we go," he said.

"Alex, I asked you guys not to bring this up—"

"I'm sorry, but I have to," Alex said. "Right now, a lot of people need our help. I know Conner and I have given up a lot, and you've given up a lot by association, but we don't care what we'll have to sacrifice if it saves our friends and all the families like ours. We're *doing the right thing* because *that's* also the kind of son and daughter you and Dad raised. So please—*let us*."

Charlotte looked at her children differently than she had all day. She wasn't glaring at them with frustration or anger, but with pride. She reached across the table and held their hands with her own.

"I'm sorry," she said. "I guess I've been a little selfish. All I want is for you to have the same experiences every teenager gets to have before this time in your lives is gone, but I forget there's nothing *normal* about you. It doesn't matter what I want—you should be living the lives you were meant for. Forgive me, it was just so difficult losing your father; I hate feeling like I've lost you, too."

"I'm sorry we've made you feel like you lost us," Conner said.

"You're my children, but other people's heroes," Charlotte said. "Any mother would be lucky to be in my shoes, but that doesn't mean they're easy to wear. Sometimes at the end of the day, I just have to pretend you're both asleep in your beds."

Charlotte dabbed the corners of her eyes with her napkin. Alex and Conner couldn't blame their mom for wishing things were different—they did, too. The twins put so much time and effort into ending people's suffering, they didn't realize how much their own mother was hurting. But if their mom was willing, she was about to become more involved in their lives than she was prepared for.

"Now tell me what's going on in the fairy-tale world," Charlotte said. "And how in the world am I going to help you with it?"

Alex and Conner were relieved they could continue discussing their plan. Both opened their mouths to fill her in, but they were at a loss for words. After all, it was a complicated thing to explain. So much of it involved their uncle Lloyd, and they didn't want to overwhelm their mom with news of an evil brother-in-law.

"Long story short, a really terrible man has taken over the fairy-tale world," Conner said. "They call him the Masked Man."

"How'd he take over?" Charlotte asked.

"He stole a potion from Grandma that turns every written work into a portal to the world it describes," Alex said. "He traveled into *Alice's Adventures in Wonderland*, *The Wonderful Wizard of Oz*, and *Peter Pan*. Somehow he recruited the Queen of Hearts, the Wicked Witch of the West, Captain Hook, and all their minions and soldiers into a big Literary Army and attacked all the kingdoms."

"That sounds *terrifying*," Bob said. "Those villains used to give me nightmares when I was a kid."

"They're much worse in real life," Conner said. "Imagine how scary you *thought* they were, now double that image, cover it in butter, and leave it outside for a week— *that's* how frightening they really are!"

"Why can't the Fairy Council do something? Why does it always have to fall on your shoulders?" Charlotte asked.

"The Fairy Council has been turned to stone, and all the soldiers in all the kingdoms are no match for the Literary Army," Alex said. "If we don't find a way to stop them, no one will."

Charlotte hated that so much responsibility had fallen on her children's young shoulders.

"For the record, I am *not* okay with you two fighting these guys," Charlotte said. "But how are you going to stop them?"

Alex nudged Conner. "Tell her *your* plan," she said.

Conner didn't appreciate his sister's unenthusiastic introduction. "We're going to recruit our own army," he said. "We're going to use the same potion to travel into my short stories and bring back my characters."

Charlotte and Bob couldn't believe what they were hearing.

"Oh my gosh!" Charlotte said. "Is that really the only thing you can do?"

"Trust me, I wish I could file a report at the Pentagon," Conner said. "Sometimes you've got to fight fire with fire."

"I still don't see how I fit into all of this," Charlotte said.

The moment had finally come for the twins to tell her. It was such an absurd request, the twins were afraid to ask. If she refused, they weren't sure who could help them.

"We need you to look after Conner's characters as we bring them out of his stories," Alex said.

It was like someone pressed the Pause button on Charlotte and Bob. Without breathing or blinking, they just looked at the twins with open mouths and large eyes. They weren't taking it well.

Conner waved his hand in front of their faces. "Are you still with us?" he asked.

"Sorry," Bob said. "It's just—most parents of fifteen-year-olds only worry about getting asked for money to go to the movies, or driving permits."

Conner sat up excitedly. *"Oh-my-God-Alex-we're-old-enough-for-driving-permits!"* he said in one breath.

"One crisis at time, remember?" Alex said. "So, Mom and Bob, can you help us?"

Bob and Charlotte looked at each other and shrugged.

"If it'll save the fairy-tale world, I won't object," Bob said.

"What *kinds* of characters are going to be in my house?" Charlotte asked. "We just had the carpets cleaned."

"Oh, nothing crazy—*pirates, cyborgs, superheroes, mummies*—the usual fictional suspects," Conner said under his breath. "So, does that mean you guys are in?"

The twins held their breath. Charlotte was hesitant, but it might have been more concerning if she were completely fine with the idea.

"All right," she said. "It'll be an adventure."

The twins were so relieved, they sank a foot into their seats.

"Awesome!" Conner said.

"Fantastic!" Alex said.

Bob and Charlotte glanced down at the Storybook Grill

menus, but it was a very difficult conversation to follow with French fries and hamburgers. They both pushed the menus away.

"You know what, I think I've lost my appetite," Charlotte said. "Maybe we should go home and I'll cook something later."

"I agree," Bob said.

The twins weren't going to argue. They left the Storybook Grill with Bob and Charlotte and headed back home. All of them were completely unaware that their entire conversation had been heard by the patrons in the next booth.

The Book Huggers leaned so far out of their seats to watch them leave that Cindy and Mindy fell onto the floor. The night had consisted of the most important eavesdropping of their lives.

"Girls, did you hear everything I just heard?" Cindy said.

"I'm not sure," Lindy said. "My heart started beating so hard toward the end, I only heard every other word!"

"We've been right all along!" Mindy said. "They never went to Vermont—they were living in another dimension! Did any of us ever think of that?"

Wendy raised a hand—reminding the group it had been one of her suspicions from the very beginning.

"Forget Sherlock Holmes," Cindy said. "We've got our own mystery to follow."

CHAPTER FIVE

CRIES FROM THE CASTLE

Had someone told Bree Campbell two weeks ago that she would soon be flying above another continent on a World War II plane with three distant relatives, she would have laughed. Ironically, that's exactly where Bree was, and she wanted to cry. She had always considered herself a person of good judgment and respectability, but as she bounced around the Boeing B-17 Flying Fortress thirteen thousand feet in the air, somewhere between France and Germany, Bree suddenly felt like the lead character in a cautionary tale.

"Can you believe I haven't flown one of these since the sixties?" Cornelia called from the captain's seat. The old woman's hands clutched the controls, but from the way they jerked her back and forth, it looked like the plane was controlling her more than she was controlling it.

Bree, Wanda, and Frenda were strapped into their seats and holding on for dear life. They had been flying for nine hours straight, and thanks to Cornelia's questionable piloting skills, it had been the bumpiest flight of Bree's life. And from the way things were going, it might be her last.

"Aunt Cornelia, are you sure you don't need a hand up there?" Wanda asked.

"I'm fine, thank you, dear," Cornelia said. "It's just like riding a bike!"

"Yeah, *off a cliff*," Frenda said.

When Bree first met the Sisters Grimm and heard about their lives' work monitoring portals between the Otherworld and the fairy-tale world, she thought they were the most capable group of women she had ever known. However, she was learning the hard way that that capability did not include flying a plane.

"Cornelia, remind me again where you went to piloting school?" Bree asked.

"Well, *technically* I never went to school for it," Cornelia said. "My father was a pilot during the war—this was his plane. He taught me how to fly when I was about your age, Bree. He flew this baby to Germany many times. Thank goodness we're going under different circumstances."

"Your father fought in World War II?" Bree asked. "That must have been difficult with so much family in Germany."

"Most of our family left long before the war," Cornelia said. "Would you like a flying lesson, Bree?"

Bree wasn't convinced Cornelia knew how to fly, let alone give a flying lesson. She looked to Wanda and Frenda, and they motioned for her to go.

"You can't be any worse than her!" Frenda said.

"Learn everything she knows and save us!" Wanda said.

Bree was scared to unbuckle her seat belt, but she quickly unfastened it and dashed to the co-pilot seat beside Cornelia. There was an overwhelming number of buttons, switches, and levers before her.

"I don't think I can do this," Bree said.

"If you can operate that phone of yours so well, this will be a walk in the park," Cornelia said. "Besides, the co-pilot's job is the easiest."

"Wait a second," Bree said. "There should be *two* pilots flying this plane?"

"Traditionally," Cornelia said. "But it always takes two men to do what a woman can do on her own."

Bree would never have gotten on the plane if she'd thought it would lead to this. She was making the trip to save a friend, but who was going to save her?

As soon as she learned Emmerich had been kidnapped, Bree had a strong feeling it wasn't a normal Otherworld abduction. She had no evidence to support the suspicion, but she felt it with every fiber of her being and couldn't shake it no matter how hard she tried. Bree had pestered Frau Himmelsbach for more information about the incident, but Emmerich's mother grew tired of the questions and eventually ignored her calls. Bree had shared her hunch with the Sisters Grimm, and they agreed the circumstances were fishy.

"It is curious he was kidnapped so soon after being in the fairy-tale world," Cornelia said.

"If he was taken by someone from the fairy-tale world, we have tools that can prove it," Wanda told Bree.

"What kind of tools?" Bree asked.

"Cross-dimensional emission-tracking devices," Frenda said. "Whenever someone or something travels between worlds, the portal leaves a radiation-like scent on them. We have machines that can detect it."

"Awesome," Bree said. "All we need now is a way to get to Germany."

Cornelia had been cooped up in their Connecticut home for so long, she was looking for any excuse to get out of the house. She generously offered Bree a ride to Germany on their family plane. Bree was so desperate to find Emmerich, she didn't hesitate to take her up on the offer.

There was only one thing standing in her way: Bree had technically run away from home to find the Sisters Grimm. If she was now going to Europe, she needed a really good excuse so her parents wouldn't call the police. Luckily, Cornelia supplied that as well.

"Is this Little Eddy?" Cornelia had said to Bree's father over the phone. "It's your cousin Cornelia.... I know, it *has* been a very long time.... Darling, I'm calling to sincerely apologize to you and your wife. You see, Bree recently called me with questions about our family heritage. She was so interested, I invited her to come stay with me so I could tell her more.... Well, I *just* found out she never ran it by you.... My thoughts *exactly*—inexcusable! I'm sure you were both scared to death.... My intention was to send her home immediately, but I unfortunately had a bad fall this morning and injured my hip.... No, I'm not in any pain.... *Yes*, there is something you can do.... Would it be terrible if Bree stayed with me until the end of the week? I'm useless on my own.... Just until Wanda gets back into town, then we'll put her on the train home.... She's been such help.... You bet, absolutely no privileges whatsoever.... *Thank you so much, dear!*"

The next thing Bree knew, she and the Sisters Grimm were on their way to a small private airport. However, Bree, Wanda, and Frenda all thought Cornelia had hired a pilot to take them to Germany. They didn't realize Cornelia was planning to *fly the plane herself* until she switched on the propellers and launched them into takeoff.

Now, at just fifteen years old, Bree was sitting next to the old woman, being taught to fly the Boeing B-17 Flying Fortress. If Bree lived long enough to become an old woman herself, she wasn't sure her grandchildren would even believe the story she was currently living.

"Taking off is the easy part," Cornelia instructed. "You simply start the propellers with the blue dial, turn the red gear to Steering Mode to get the plane onto the runway, push down the green lever, and pull up on the controls."

Bree gulped. "Blue dial, red gear, green lever, controls," she repeated.

"Perfect," Cornelia said. "To fly, all you do is pull up on the green lever, turn the red gear to Flight Mode, adjust the altitude with the brown handle, and steer with the controls. Here, *give it a go!*"

Cornelia flipped a switch and the whole plane turned off. They entered a rapid descent toward the earth! Bree watched in panic as the numbers on the altitude monitor dropped hundreds of feet per second. Wanda and Frenda were screaming so loudly, she could barely focus.

"Green lever, red gear, brown handle, controls!" Bree said, mimicking everything Cornelia had just instructed.

The Boeing B-17 Flying Fortress stopped plunging toward the ground and glided smoothly through the clouds. In fact, it was flying much more easily with Bree at the controls.

"You're a natural flier!" Cornelia said. "It's in our DNA."

Bree thought there might be some truth to this. Since the magic in their family's blood came from Mother Goose, she wondered if a few of Mother Goose's flying genes had been transferred, too. There was actually a lot about Cornelia that reminded Bree of Mother Goose. They both

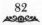

had the same twinkle in their eye when they put others in danger.

"How much longer until we're on the ground?" Wanda asked. "*Safely* on the ground!"

"We've already begun our descent," Cornelia said. "We'll land shortly after we pass over Füssen."

Bree recalled that the area didn't have many large cities. "Does Füssen have an airport?" she asked.

"We don't need an airport to land," Cornelia said. "To quote Coco Chanel, 'The world is your runway'!"

"Mother, she was talking about fashion!" Frenda yelled.

"Everyone stop worrying! This baby is built for combat," Cornelia said.

They didn't care what it was built for; landing a plane anywhere but at an airport sounded like a *crash landing* to them! Bree, Wanda, and Frenda tightened their seat belts until there was no slack left. Soon the small Bavarian city of Füssen came into view and Cornelia searched the ground for a smooth surface to land.

"That field should do," she said.

Cornelia jerked the controls and the Boeing B-17 Flying Fortress curved through the air, lowering toward a grassy field below. As the plane turned, Bree caught a glimpse of Neuschwanstein Castle peeking through the hills in the distance. It was as if she were seeing an old friend. The castle was just as majestic as it was the first time she saw it with Conner on Mary's Bridge.

"All right, time for your landing lesson," Cornelia said.

"You start by turning the red gear to Landing Mode, pull up on the green lever, turn the black knob to put down the wheels, and pull up on the controls so we're parallel to the ground."

"Red gear, green lever, black knob, controls—got it," Bree said.

"Splendid," Cornelia said. "Now land us."

Bree, Frenda, and Wanda were horrified. It was like Cornelia had a death wish or something!

"What? But I've never landed a plane before!" Bree said.

The plane was getting closer and closer to the ground—someone had to land it before it was too late! Cornelia looked over her glasses at Bree with total faith in her eyes.

"Sometimes, if we enter situations that scare us with both hands on the wheel, they don't seem as frightening," she said as calmly as ever. "Or in this case, *with both hands on the controls.*"

Bree couldn't believe Cornelia was making her do this. She could feel her heart beating in the back of her throat. One wrong move and they would all be dead!

Carefully and quickly, Bree turned the red gear to Landing Mode, pulled up on the green lever, turned the black knob to put the wheels down, and held up the controls to make the plane parallel to the ground.

"We're gonna crash!" Wanda yelled, and vigorously crossed her chest.

"Wanda, you're not Catholic!" Frenda said.

"I know, but we're gonna need all the help we can get!"

The wheels slammed into the grassy field and the plane landed like a rock skipping across a lake. It tore up large strips of earth, as if leaving a long message in Morse code. Finally, the plane decelerated and rolled into a shaky, sudden stop.

"Oh my God," Bree said in disbelief. "I just landed a plane!"

"Mother, how could you let a fifteen-year-old land a plane!" Frenda said.

Cornelia burst into a fit of giggles. "You're all so gullible," she said. "I had the autopilot on the entire time!"

The others didn't find this funny at all.

"You mean, all that was for nothing?" Bree asked with an angry scowl.

"No, no—you did quite well," Cornelia said. "Had the autopilot failed, we would have had a successful landing. My father did the same thing to me on my first flight. The best lessons are learned when it's *sink or swim*, and you're quite the swimmer!"

Once their hearts settled to a normal pace, Bree and the Sisters Grimm locked up the plane and headed for Emmerich's house. Bree thought leaving the plane unattended in a field was a strange thing to do, but Cornelia assured her that planes were very difficult to steal.

Bree led the women through the outskirts of Füssen and into the little village just below Neuschwanstein Castle called Hohenschwangau. Since Cornelia walked with a cane, Bree was worried the journey would be too much for her, but the old woman hobbled along, excited to be on another Sisters Grimm adventure. They walked past all the souvenir shops, restaurants, and inns dedicated to the castle, and found the Himmelsbachs' tiny home on the edge of town.

"There it is," Bree said, and pointed to the front steps. "That's where Conner and I met him."

The sight made Bree feel remarkably nostalgic. It seemed like just yesterday that she and Conner had told Emmerich they were secret agents so he'd take them into the castle after visiting hours. They hadn't been friends for long, but Bree and Emmerich had shared such an incredible once-in-a-lifetime adventure, she couldn't believe there was a time when the little German boy was a stranger. She just hoped they could bring him home, wherever he was.

"Here goes nothing," Bree said. "I hope Frau Himmelsbach is better at answering her door than she is her phone."

They walked up the front steps and rang the doorbell. They waited, but no one answered. Bree rang the doorbell again, holding it down longer. A moment later, Frau Himmelsbach answered the door.

"Kann ich Dir helfen?" she asked.

If Bree hadn't recognized her voice from the phone, she wouldn't have thought it was Emmerich's mother. The woman had brown hair and olive skin, very different from her son's pale skin and rosy complexion. She had puffy eyes and sunken cheeks, like she had been crying and not eating much. She wore a big black robe over a nightgown and probably hadn't changed clothes in days.

The woman wasn't what Bree was expecting, but she definitely looked like the mother of a missing child.

"Frau Himmelsbach, I'm sorry to disturb you," Bree said. "I'm Bree Campbell, your son's friend from the United States."

Emmerich's mother was not happy to see her, and especially not happy to see she had brought friends with her.

"What is wrong with you, child?" the Frau said. "I told you to stop calling me and now you've come to my home?"

"I'm sorry," Bree said. "I know you don't want to talk to me, but I couldn't stay away. These are my cousins, Cornelia, Frenda, and Wanda. We've traveled all this way because we want to help you find your son."

Frau Himmelsbach crossed her arms and shook her head. She wasn't easy to convince.

"You Americans and your egos," she said. "What can you do that the Bavarian police cannot?"

Bree looked to the Sisters Grimm, hoping one of them would have an answer.

"We're private investigators who specialize in child abduction," Cornelia said. "We've brought special equipment along with us that may point us in the direction of whoever took your child."

"The police searched every inch of my home," the Frau said. "They didn't find a single clue."

"With all due respect, ma'am," Wanda said, "the

Bavarian police can't find clues like we can. Please, may we come inside?"

The distressed mother looked back and forth among the women and tried to think of a reason not to let them, but she couldn't.

"Fine," she said. "I apologize, my house is a mess."

Frau Himmelsbach escorted Bree and the Sisters Grimm inside her home. The Frau offered them a seat in the sitting room and Cornelia and Bree happily accepted. From the sofa they could see into Emmerich's bedroom through an open door in the hall. The walls were covered in posters of superheroes. Bree remembered him saying he wanted to visit the United States because that's where all the superheroes lived. The memory made her miss him even more.

"May we have a look around?" Frenda asked.

"As you wish," the Frau said.

Frenda and Wanda went to work right away. They each removed a cross-dimensional emission-tracking device from their purse; the device looked like a long microphone connected to an old radio. They waved the microphone parts around the house and the radio parts beeped as they went.

They searched the sitting room and kitchen, but didn't find anything. The search continued in Emmerich's bedroom, and when they scanned the area by his window, the machines beeped like crazy. Wanda looked to Bree and Cornelia and with one nod she said a thousand words—*someone*

from the fairy-tale world had definitely been there. Bree's hunch was right.

"Was Emmerich taken through the window?" Frenda asked.

"Yes," Frau Himmelsbach said, surprised they knew. "The night it happened, Emmerich was sleeping in his bedroom while I was in here reading. I heard a noise, so I checked on him. His window was open and in the distance I saw someone in a black cloak running away with Emmerich over their shoulder."

She broke into tears recalling the terrifying sight and Cornelia offered her a handkerchief.

"I chased them, but they disappeared into the night," the Frau said. "I called the police and they came to the house every day for a week. They never found anything, not even a fingerprint. How did you know he was taken from the window?"

If they were going to tell the Frau the truth, Bree figured it was best to start at the beginning.

"Shortly before Emmerich was taken, he and I made a crazy discovery," Bree said. "We did this thing, like a *blood test*, and it proved he and I are actually *related*. Our blood matches DNA from the Brothers Grimm."

"The Brothers Grimm?" the Frau asked.

"Yes," Bree continued. "Which means Cornelia, Frenda, Wanda, and myself are either related to you or to Emmerich's father."

The Frau was very confused. "I wouldn't know either

way," she said. "Emmerich isn't my biological son—he was adopted."

"Adopted?" Bree said in shock. "He never mentioned that."

"That's because I never told him," Frau Himmelsbach said. "He was abandoned when he was a baby. I didn't want him living life thinking he was unwanted."

Everything Bree thought she knew suddenly changed. She quickly abandoned her plan to tell the Frau about the fairy-tale world—clearly she didn't have all the facts straight.

"Where was he found?" Bree asked.

"Neuschwanstein Castle," she said. "My father used to work nights there as a security guard. One night, as he was patrolling the halls, he heard crying. He followed the cries to the Singers' Hall and found Emmerich wrapped up in a blanket in the middle of the floor. Someone must have left him during a tour earlier in the day. It was very strange, because my father swore he had checked the room multiple times earlier that night and never saw the baby."

Bree and the Sisters Grimm were all thinking the same thing: Emmerich wasn't related to the Brothers Grimm after all—*he was from the fairy-tale world!* Someone must have crossed through the portal in the Singers' Hall and left him in the castle!

The Frau's eyes suddenly grew wide and she covered her mouth fearfully.

"Wait a moment," she said. "That reminds me of something I completely forgot! There was a note pinned to his blanket the night he was found. Let me see if I can find it."

Emmerich's mom went down the hall to her bedroom. They heard her searching madly through all her drawers and belongings. A few minutes later, she returned with a piece of parchment. Her hands were shaking, as if she were holding a ransom note. She handed it to Bree, and the Sisters Grimm gathered around her to read the note.

To whoever finds this child, please take him to a loving home that will offer protection. His father is a very dangerous man and the child is not safe with his mother. Should the father learn of his son's existence, the child will be in grave danger.

It appeared that Bree and the Sisters Grimm had helped the Frau uncover a suspect in her son's disappearance— *Emmerich's biological father*!

"It was so many years ago, I forgot the note existed," Frau Himmelsbach confessed. "Even then, I didn't take it seriously. I never thought they would find him."

"Should we take this to the police?" Wanda asked.

"No, we can't!" the Frau exclaimed. "You see, I never *legally* adopted Emmerich. I fell in love with him the minute my father brought him home. At the time, we were very poor. I was afraid he would be taken away if we called the police, so we kept it a secret. If they found out now, I would never see him again."

Bree had so many questions, she could barely see straight. She always loved a good mystery novel, but she never thought her life would turn into one.

"If you're related to him, do you have any idea who Emmerich's parents are?" Frau Himmelsbach asked. "Do you know where they might have taken him?"

"I'm afraid not," Bree said. "But I know someone who might."

CHAPTER SIX

A BEWITCHING OFFER

The Masked Man was awoken by a throbbing headache. He opened his eyes and discovered he was
somewhere in the forest, but he had no recollec-
tion of how he had gotten there. Even stranger, when he
looked around he noticed the ground was above his head
and the smoky sky was below his feet.

After further inspection, he realized he was upside
down. His cape was caught on a tree branch and he was
hanging several feet in the air. As he slowly returned to
full consciousness, the Masked Man remembered that

flying monkeys had dropped him there. He wasn't sure how long he had been hanging in the tree, but since he was still alive, he assumed his cape must have broken his fall.

He reached toward the branch piercing his cape to set himself free. The motion sent excruciating pain through his entire body and he screamed. The pain was so bad, he couldn't tell where it began or ended. Clearly, he had hit more than one branch on his way down. The Masked Man tugged on his cape and it ripped in half. He fell to the ground and landed on his back with a *thud*.

After a few minutes of lying on the ground, the Masked Man had a better idea of where the pain was coming from. His left arm was definitely broken, one of his right ribs was most likely cracked, and his right ankle was sprained at best. Half his mask had been ripped off by something he collided with during the fall, and bloody scratches covered one side of his face. Still, it was a miracle he had survived.

He moaned as he struggled to his feet. All the blood in his head rushed to the other parts of his body, making him woozy. He removed his damaged cape and ripped his suit jacket into strips to make a sling for his arm.

The physical pain was unbearable, but he was almost thankful for it—it was the only thing distracting him from his mental anguish.

The Masked Man was not a stranger to disappointment, but *losing an empire* was one colossal setback he never saw coming. After a lifetime of meticulous planning, he had finally achieved the power he had craved since childhood.

Only to then have it yanked away like a rug from underneath him.

After such a narrow escape from death, a different man would have abandoned his quest for supremacy, but the Masked Man's need for power was like a disease—and *fulfillment* was the only cure. Like a phoenix, he immediately began calculating his path out of the ashes. Somehow, some way, he would reclaim his power and destroy the literary villains who had taken it from him. But first, he needed to find a path out of the forest.

The Masked Man had no idea what part of the forest he had been dropped in, so he hobbled through the trees in search of an indication. After hours of limping aimlessly through the woods, he only found more and more trees the farther he went. Since the mythological creature had escaped captivity in the Northern Palace dungeon, the Masked Man was as cautious and quiet as possible just in case it was also wandering through the forest.

Eventually he stumbled upon a small clearing with three unusual boulders. They were tall and stuck out from the ground like trees themselves. The Masked Man had a seat against one of the boulders and tightened his makeshift sling. But his rest was short-lived.

A commotion traveled through the woods nearby. The sound became louder and louder as it moved closer and closer. It was a repetitive tremor, like the marching of several pairs of metal boots—*Winkie soldiers were approaching*! The Masked Man assumed the villains must have sent the soldiers to retrieve his body. He was too wounded to outrun them, so he dived into the bushes beside the boulders and was hidden from view.

A few moments later, two rows of a dozen Winkie soldiers entered the clearing, but they weren't alone. The soldiers were escorting the Wicked Witch of the West, the Queen of Hearts, and Captain Hook through the forest. The sight of the literary villains sent a rage through the Masked Man that was so powerful, his injuries were temporarily numbed. There wasn't a word in existence to describe the anger coursing through his veins.

The Wicked Witch of the West, the Queen of Hearts, and Captain Hook paced around the clearing like they were waiting for something to happen. They didn't appear to be looking for the Masked Man, so he wondered what on earth they were doing in the woods.

"Well?" Captain Hook growled. "Where is she?"

"Are we certain we're in the right place?" the Queen of Hearts asked.

The Wicked Witch of the West unrolled a scroll of parchment she held tightly in her hand.

"I'm positive," the Wicked Witch said. "Her instructions say, 'Take the path four miles into the Dwarf Forests and wait for me in the clearing of the three stone trees.' There hasn't been another clearing for miles. This must be it."

As the Masked Man knew all too well, *patience* was not

the villains' forte. The Wicked Witch, the Queen of Hearts, and Captain Hook became more restless by the second.

"Well, *whoever* she is, I don't like her," Captain Hook snarled. "She has some nerve to keep us waiting like this."

"I want to hear what she's offering," the Queen of Hearts said. "But if it isn't appealing, and we've come all this way for nothing, *I say we capture her and—*"

"Cut off her head?" the Wicked Witch asked mockingly. "There are *other ways* to execute someone, you know—most of which are more entertaining and far less messy."

"Like dropping the Masked Man to his death?" Captain Hook said with a nasty grin. "Watching him squirm and scream as he fell was rather fun, wasn't it? If only gravity affected *everyone*—my hook would be covered in Peter Pan's blood by now!"

The Queen of Hearts rolled her eyes. "I'm so sick of hearing that boy's name!" she hollered. "He's a child, Captain! *Let it go!* From the way you obsessively talk about him, I'd say he's taken much more from you than *just your hand!*"

Captain Hook intended to respond with a snippy comment, but the pirate went quiet. He leaned against one of the boulders and placed his hook on his hip, thinking about what the Queen of Hearts had just said.

From the bushes just beside Captain Hook, the Masked Man had a perfect view of a revolver dangling from the captain's belt. He was drawn to the weapon like a moth to a flame. If he got his hands on it, with three quick shots he could terminate the literary villains before the Winkie soldiers knew what was happening!

Carefully, when they were all looking in the opposite direction, the Masked Man reached his good hand toward the captain's waist and unfastened his holster.

It was a painful effort with his cracked rib and it took everything in him not to scream. Slowly, he removed the revolver from the holster with the captain none the wiser.

The Masked Man examined the gun—*it had three bullets*! He had exactly what he needed to shoot the villains! He cocked it and aimed the weapon back and forth at the three of them, indecisive about which one to kill first.

Captain Hook became agitated and started stomping around the clearing.

"I knew it was a trick!" he said in a huff. "We've been fooled! No one is meeting us in the woods today!"

The Queen of Hearts and the Wicked Witch nodded in agreement. But just as they were about to order the soldiers to take them back, they were interrupted by a voice from outside the clearing.

"Haven't you ever heard the phrase 'Good things come to those who wait'?"

The Masked Man lowered the revolver when he heard the voice. It sounded awfully familiar.

The villains and the Winkie soldiers heard footsteps next and quickly turned to see a hooded creature approaching them. The soldiers raised their staffs toward the

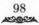

creature, but with a quick flick of its wrist, their weapons crumbled into dirt. The creature stepped into the clearing and lowered its hood—it was a beautiful woman with horns like a ram's that curved around the sides of her face.

"*Morina,*" the Masked Man whispered to himself. His desire to assassinate the villains was quickly replaced by curiosity. What did *she* want with them?

"Are you the witch they call Morina?" the Wicked Witch of the West asked.

"I am," Morina said. "And you must be the new leaders of this world. It's an honor to make your acquaintance. Defeating the kingdoms of humans and fairies is no easy task—you've achieved what the witches have only dreamed about for centuries."

The villains shared a proud look and stood a little taller.

"Since you're here, I'm assuming you received my letter?" Morina asked.

"It's not every day we receive an invitation delivered by a crow," the Queen of Hearts said. "Now tell us, what is the 'offer of a lifetime' that you wrote about?"

"It requires a lengthy explanation," Morina said. "Please, have a seat."

The witch waved her hand toward the three boulders and they transformed into large stone chairs for the villains to sit on. So far, the witch was very impressive.

"You see, the witches of this world have always had a long and unpleasant history with the people who ruled it," Morina explained. "Before you arrived there were rumors of an impending witch hunt. Those fears were all but confirmed when the Masked Man became emperor. We were certain that once he executed the royal families, it would only be a matter of time before he ordered our extermination. But luckily, that's all changed now that you've taken his place."

"If the Masked Man saw the witches as a threat, why should we view things any differently?" Captain Hook asked.

"Because the three of you are much wiser than your predecessors," Morina said. "Why become enemies when we have a glorious opportunity to become *allies*?"

The villains side-eyed one another. They weren't pleased with where the conversation was going.

"For your sake, I hope you're offering us more than *friendship*," the Queen of Hearts warned.

Morina smiled and her eyes grew wide. They could tell friendship was only the beginning of what she had to offer.

"Of course. I'll cut to the chase," she said. "Recently, I convinced the other witches that the only way we could escape the pending genocide was by leaving this world. We need a place to ourselves where we won't be controlled by fairies or ostracized by humans. So I formed a plan for the witches to invade and conquer another dimension, known as *the Otherworld*."

The villains were instantly intrigued. *"The Otherworld?"* they asked in unison.

"It's a world very similar to this one, but far greater,"

Morina explained. "It has hundreds of countries, thousands of cities, and billions of people. There are structures and machines you could only dream of, and more land and sea than we would ever need. The best part is that this world operates entirely without magic. With no fairies to limit us, we would be unstoppable!"

Her passionate description was hypnotizing. Still, the villains wondered if it was too good to be true.

"How can you prove it exists?" Captain Hook asked.

"Take a look for yourself," Morina said.

The witch's eyes suddenly lit up like the headlights of a car. Morina magically transferred images of the Otherworld into the villains' minds and their eyes glowed as brightly as hers. Visions of London, Paris, Tokyo, and New York City flashed before their eyes. They saw the Eiffel Tower, the Pyramids of Giza, the Great Wall of China, the Golden Gate Bridge, and the Taj Mahal.

The villains had never seen a world so grand and diverse before. The light faded from their eyes, but was replaced by the glow of desire.

"How do we get to the Otherworld?" the Wicked Witch asked.

"The late Fairy Godmother has portals hidden all over the kingdoms," Morina said. "But each one is difficult to open, and the journey takes a toll on anyone who's not a practitioner of white magic."

"Then how do the witches expect to cross over?" the Queen of Hearts asked.

"As luck would have it, the two worlds are scheduled to collide very soon," Morina said. "A *doorway* will open that will bridge the worlds like never before. Once it appears, we can charge into the Otherworld and take it by storm!"

The villains' suspicion grew as much as their interest.

"You seem to have it all figured out," Captain Hook said. "What exactly do the witches want from us?"

A devious smile grew on Morina's face. This was the part she was most excited to tell them.

"The witches don't want anything from you," she said.

"Then why do they want to become *allies*?" Captain Hook asked.

"You misheard me, Captain," Morina said. "The witches don't even know I'm here. I was speaking for *myself* when I proposed an alliance."

The villains shared a look, each more confused than the other. Morina waved a hand over the dirt and a fourth boulder shot up from the ground. She transformed it into a large stone throne, much taller than the villains' chairs, and she had a seat.

"I had every intention of *leading* the witches into the Otherworld," Morina explained. "Sadly, that leadership was stolen from me. Two witches with seniority, the Snow Queen and the Sea Witch, have taken the operation into their own clammy hands. But my frustration has taught me a valuable lesson: *Witches are not like wolves—we don't belong in packs.* Once we cross into the Otherworld, we'll

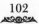

fight one another for dominance until there is only one of us left. So I've begun a new plan for *after* the witches conquer the Otherworld."

The villains shared a smile. Morina's plan was starting to make sense—and they liked where it was going.

"You're going to betray them!" the Wicked Witch said eagerly.

"Precisely," Morina said. "The Snow Queen and the Sea Witch plan to cast a spell on the late Fairy Godmother's granddaughter, a powerful young fairy named Alex. They believe if they curse her strongly enough, they'll be able to turn the girl into a weapon and use her to vanquish the Otherworld. I'm not convinced this will work. I believe there are more traditional ways of invading a new territory."

"You want our army!" the Queen of Hearts said.

Morina clapped her hands excitedly. "Exactly," she said. "I say we let the witches be our pawns. Let them invade the Otherworld and weaken its defenses. Once they've both exhausted all their resources, we'll charge into the Otherworld and steal it from them! We'll destroy Alex, the witches, and whatever is left standing in our way!"

It was the most thrilling and lucrative offer the villains had ever received. They were all fidgeting in their seats at the thought of the conquest. However, they still didn't know if Morina could be trusted.

"How do we know you won't just betray us in the end, too?" Captain Hook asked.

"We've already been deceived once by someone in this world—we won't let it happen again!" the Wicked Witch said.

"Unlike the Masked Man, I don't bite off more than I can chew," Morina said. "We'll divide the Otherworld evenly among us—we'll each have our own territory twice the size of this world. Surely that's more than enough land for each of us. Time is of the essence, so if you're interested, I need to know now. Do we have a deal, or not?"

The villains huddled together to discuss the situation privately, but Morina could tell they had already made up their minds. They were creatures of greed and couldn't refuse.

"We have a deal," Captain Hook said. "But if you disappoint us, we'll end you just like we ended the Masked Man!"

Morina laughed loudly. "You think you *killed* the Masked Man?" she asked.

"Of course we killed him," the Queen of Hearts said. "No man could have survived that fall!"

"Yes, but the Masked Man isn't a man—he's a *roach*," Morina said sharply. "Even if you cut off his head, he'd be back the very second a throne was left unattended. We haven't seen the last of him. But don't worry, I have something that will bring him to his knees should he try to sabotage our plan."

"And what is that?" the Wicked Witch asked.

The villains were curious, but not nearly as curious as

the Masked Man himself. He had very few possessions—
what had the witch stolen?

"Not *what*, but *who*," Morina said. "I've kidnapped his
son, a boy named Emmerich."

"The Masked Man has a child?" Captain Hook asked.

"Not one he knows about," Morina said. "But should he
ever cross us, the boy will stop him in his tracks."

The Masked Man was so shocked, he dropped the
revolver. He no longer felt any of his injuries or the anger
boiling inside him. He forgot all about losing his empire
and his desire to kill the villains. All he could feel was
adrenaline and his heartbeat. All he could think about was
the *son* he never knew he had.

"I should return to the witches before they get suspicious," Morina said.

The witch stood from her stone throne and with a snap
of her fingers, the boulders all returned to normal. The villains were buzzing with anticipation. If they could invade
the Otherworld today, they wouldn't hesitate.

"When will the invasion take place?" the Queen of
Hearts asked. "We want our soldiers to be prepared."

"It won't be long now," Morina said. "When the time is
right, we'll strike. I'll be in touch."

The witch covered her horns with her hood and disappeared into the trees. The villains ordered the Winkie
soldiers to escort them out of the woods and practically
skipped back to the Northern Palace.

The Masked Man was still so astonished, he stayed in the bushes long after the villains were gone. Having a son presented him with a world of new opportunities—opportunities he had never thought possible. If he played his cards right, the Masked Man could regain much more than just his empire—he could salvage *everything* that had been stolen from him. . . .

CHAPTER SEVEN

THE CAPTAIN AND HER CREW

I packed you both a turkey sandwich, chips, yogurt, a banana, two bottles of water, and a cookie," Charlotte said. "There's also a sweatshirt, a flashlight, a Swiss Army knife, a first-aid kit, matches, and a compass."

The twins' mother handed them each a backpack full of the items she'd packed. Alex and Conner appreciated the gesture, but traveling into a fictitious dimension was very different from going on a camping trip.

"Thanks, Mom," Alex said. "You didn't have to do that."

"Yeah, this isn't our first rodeo," Conner said, and looked through his backpack. *"Oh cool, chocolate chip! Thanks!"*

"It's just a few things—I'll feel better knowing you have them," Charlotte said. "So where's your first stop? Any idea how long you'll be gone for?"

Alex turned to Conner, just as curious as their mother. For the first time in their lives, she was leaving all the planning to her brother. She had offered to help a number of times, but Conner was determined to do everything himself. Not insisting was a gamble on Alex's part, but he seemed very confident he had everything taken care of.

"First up is my short story 'Starboardia,'" Conner said excitedly. "It's a pirate adventure set in the Caribbean Sea around the early 1700s. The story's about Captain Auburn Sally and her all-female crew as they search deserted islands for buried treasure."

Charlotte hid her concern behind a smile. "Sounds *progressive*," she said.

"Don't worry—we'll be fine," Conner said. "Auburn Sally is based on Goldilocks. We'll find her ship, tell her the situation, and bring her and her crew back to the house. It'll be easy."

"If you say so," Charlotte said, unconvinced.

"Go get 'em," Bob said, and patted him on the back.

Conner had organized his writing neatly in a binder with tabs separating the short stories. He opened the

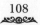

binder to the first page of "Starboardia" and set it on the living room floor.

"Are you sure there isn't anything we need before we go?" Alex asked one final time. "There's nothing you're overlooking or forgetting about?"

"Trust me. I've got everything under control," he said. "If there's one thing I know inside out, it's my short stories. I've actually been really looking forward to this. I bet my characters will be excited to meet me!"

Traveling into the short stories had been all Conner could think about since he'd first had the idea. Naturally, the circumstances to warrant the trip were terrible, but he still felt like the luckiest author in the world. Who else got to visit the worlds and meet the people that existed only in their imagination? Conner often fantasized about seeing a film or a play based on his writing one day, but *this* would be much better than that. It wouldn't be *someone else's* interpretation or adaptation of his words; everything would be purely as he'd envisioned it.

Conner removed Mother Goose's flask, which contained the Portal Potion, from his back pocket. He poured a couple of drops on the binder and then stored the flask safely in his backpack. The pages illuminated like a powerful spotlight, shining a bright beam of light toward the ceiling.

"Here we go!" Conner said. "Wish us luck!"

"Good luck!" Bob said. "We'll be here when you get back."

"Make good choices!" Charlotte said. "There's also some sunscreen in your bags if it's sunny out!"

Alex and Conner strapped on their backpacks, stepped into the beam of light, and disappeared from the house.

Just like it had when they traveled into *The Wonderful Wizard of Oz*, *Peter Pan*, and *Alice's Adventures in Wonderland*, the Portal Potion first took them into an endless space with nothing but words. Rather than printed text, words were *written* all around them, as if there were hundreds of invisible pencils moving through the air. Each word was in Conner's messy handwriting.

"Awesome!" Conner said. "It's like we've stepped inside my brain!"

"You've got to work on your penmanship," Alex noted.

The handwritten words stretched into shapes, then gained color and texture, and finally transformed into the objects they described. Conner watched in awe as the world of his first short story came to life around him. Alex was excited, too, until she saw the words *ocean waves* stretching below their feet.

"Hey, Conner?" she said. "Should we be worried about—"

Before she could finish her sentence, the twins fell into an ocean that formed under their feet. Strong waves crashed over them, pushing them farther and farther below the water. The water was difficult to swim against, but they kicked their way to the surface and spit out mouthfuls of

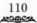

salty water. Conner saw his binder of short stories floating in the water nearby and retrieved it before the waves carried it away. If he lost the binder, the twins would lose their exit back into the Otherworld.

Alex angrily splashed water in her brother's face. *"Why didn't you say we needed a boat?"* she asked.

"Sorry!" Conner said. "I forgot the first thing I described was the ocean!"

By now the handwritten words had finished forming the world of "Starboardia" around them. They were bobbing up and down in the middle of the Caribbean Sea. The air was so misty, they could barely see each other, let alone any land or ships in the distance. Alex snapped her fingers and a small wooden rowboat appeared in front of them.

The twins climbed aboard and caught their breath. Conner put the binder in his backpack, where it would be safe. If anything happened to it, they would have no way back home.

"Well, *that* was a rough start," Alex said. "What's the *second* thing you described?"

"The *Dolly Llama*," Conner said.

"The Dolly Llama?"

"It's the name of Auburn Sally's ship," he said. "Don't judge me, I thought it was a funny name for a ship. We should see it any minute now."

A towering shadow appeared in the mist—something very large headed their way. The shadow grew larger and darker and details formed as it got closer. Finally, the twins saw that it was a pirate ship sailing straight toward their rowboat with no sign of slowing down. It was going to plow right into them!

"Abandon boat!" Conner yelled.

The twins dived into the water just as the ship smashed into their rowboat, crushing it to pieces. Once again, Alex and Conner were caught under the vicious waves. They swam to the surface and were sloshed around the choppy water as the pirate ship sailed right past them.

"Ahoy!" Conner yelled up at the ship. *"Twins overboard! Help us!"*

A few seconds later, a rope ladder was rolled off the ship, and it landed in the water next to the twins. They grabbed it, climbed up, pulled themselves over the ship's railing, and collapsed onto the lower deck. They were drenched and coughing up seawater.

Alex looked up and saw a large black flag flying above the ship with a llama skull on it.

"This must be the *Dolly Llama*," Alex said. She pointed out the flag to Conner, and a giant smile grew on his face. He leaped to his feet and helped his sister to hers. The flag was proof they were in his short story.

"We made it!" he exclaimed. "Alex, we're in 'Starboardia'!"

His excitement was cut short when they heard footsteps nearby. A dozen female pirates surrounded Alex and Conner, and they didn't look friendly. The pirates pointed their swords and rifles at the twins.

"Well, well, well," said a woman with an eye patch. "Look what we have here."

"What are you two scallywags doing in the middle of the sea?" asked a woman with enormous lips. "Too *young* to be in the navy, too *fair* to be pirates."

Conner almost stepped on a pirate behind him and jumped. Having no legs, the pirate walked on her hands and held a dagger with her teeth.

"My guess is they were *stowaways!*" the legless pirate said. "I'm surprised the sharks didn't find them first!"

Conner couldn't believe his characters were living and breathing before his eyes. The women were just as rough, dirty, and sunburned as he had imagined them. He grinned from ear to ear and jumped up and down.

"I'm so happy to see you guys!" he said.

The pirates tilted their heads at him like confused puppies. No one had ever been *happy* to see them before.

"Guys, it's *me!*" Conner said. "I'm Conner Bailey!"

The pirates raised their eyebrows and scratched their heads—should they know who he was?

"Who?" asked a pirate with a round, flat face.

"Oh, come on." Conner laughed. "I'm the *author!*"

"Author of *what*?" asked a pirate with bare feet.

"Of *this story*," he said. "I created this ocean, I created this ship, and I created all of you. Do you really not recognize me?"

Conner thought for sure it would have clicked by now, but the pirates still stared at him awkwardly, just as perplexed as before.

"He's been marooned for too long—the boy's gone mad," said a pirate with a peg leg, and the other pirates nodded in agreement.

Conner was getting frustrated. "I'm not crazy," he said. "Look, where is Auburn Sally? Let me talk to her. I'm sure she'll straighten this whole thing out. This is my own fault—I should have written you guys to be smarter."

The pirates stopped looking puzzled and began staring daggers at him. Alex covered her face and let out a sigh—this wasn't going to be as easy as her brother thought.

"*Oooooh, Captain,*" the pirate with the eye patch called. "There's someone down here who'd like to have a word with you!"

Suddenly, a woman did a backflip off the upper deck and landed directly in front of the twins. She wore a large black hat, a long brown coat, tall boots, and she had a sword and pistol attached to her thick belt. Alex knew this was Auburn Sally from the minute she laid eyes on her. If her acrobatics weren't enough to give it away, the captain looked exactly like Goldilocks. The only difference in their features was the captain's long locks of auburn hair.

"*Sally!*" Conner said like he was seeing an old friend—because, technically, he was. He stepped toward the captain to give her a hug, but Auburn Sally quickly drew her pistol and aimed it at his head.

"Am I supposed to know you, *boy*?" Auburn Sally asked.

Conner was shocked by the treatment he was receiving from his own characters. He had expected a warm and gracious welcome, but instead the heroine of his story was holding a gun to his head. Without him none of them would even exist! He wondered if this was what an underappreciated parent felt like.

He held his hands up and backed away from the pistol. "Okay, time out!" he said. "Everyone just calm down and let me explain! My name is Conner Bailey, and this is my sister, Alex. I know this is hard to believe, but I'm your *creator*! We are living in a short story I wrote for my eighth-grade English class!"

Auburn Sally looked at him with more perplexity than that of all her crew added together. "He's got yellow fever," she said. "Prepare the plank! We need to get him off the ship at once!"

"I'm not sick, either!" Conner said. "Fine! If you don't believe me, I'll prove it!"

He walked around the circle of women, pointing at each pirate.

"That's Winking Wendy, Fish-Lips Lucy, Somersault Sydney, Pancake-Face Patty, Stinky-Feet Phoebe, and that's Peg-Leg Peggy," he said.

"I prefer *Margret*," said the pirate with the peg leg.

"Fine, *Margret*," Conner said, and rolled his eyes. "In the back, that's High-Tide Tabitha, Catfish Kate, Too-Much-Rum Ronda, Big-Booty Bertha, Not-So-Jolly

Joan, and up in the crow's nest, that's Siren Sue. Your captain is Auburn Sally, this ship is called the *Dolly Llama*, and you're all searching the Caribbean for buried treasure!"

Conner crossed his arms confidently and waited for their apologies. The pirates were startled by how much he knew. They all looked at their captain, waiting to see how she would respond.

"There's only one explanation for how a young man we've never met before could possibly know so much," Auburn Sally said. *"He's a warlock!* Tie him and his sister up! We'll burn them at the stake on the next island we find!"

Before they knew it, the twins' backpacks were yanked off and they were pushed against the mainmast. The pirates wrapped ropes around their bodies, binding their torsos to the ship. Conner was so mad, he turned bright red.

"Let us go or you'll be sorry!" he yelled. *"Just wait until I get home! I'm going to write a sequel where you all get shipwrecked and have to eat your boots to survive!"*

The pirates laughed at his attempts to scare them. Winking Wendy pulled the ropes even tighter just to spite him.

"Keep it up, Wendy! We'll see who's laughing when I have a seagull peck out your other eye!" Conner warned. "Alex, can you believe this?"

"How did you expect them to react?" she asked. "What would you do if a guy showed up out of nowhere and told us we were characters in *his* story?"

"I would punch him in the face for making everything so damn difficult!" he said. "Alex, you've got to do

something! Zap them with a sleeping spell, turn them into sea horses—*anything!*"

"No!" Alex yelled. "I've been asking you for days if you needed any help planning, and you told me you had *everything under control!* Well, so far we almost drowned, we narrowly missed being crushed by a ship, and now we're being captured by *your* pirates! You and I have different definitions of *under control!*"

"Alex, don't be a child!" Conner said.

"Grow up, Conner!" she said. "This is *your* mess—*you* clean it up!"

"Fine, I will!" he yelled. "I don't need you or your stupid magic! I'll find a way out of this myself!"

Although Alex and Conner were tied up right next to each other, they each pretended the other wasn't there and pouted in silence.

A strong ocean breeze began clearing the mist and uncovered the sun. Soon the ship had a breathtaking view of the ocean surrounding it. There was nothing to see but the bright blue Caribbean Sea for miles around them.

Captain Auburn Sally returned to the upper deck and wrapped her hands around the large helm. She looked out at the open water and a radiant smile spread across her face. There was nothing keeping her back and no one to stop her; she was surrounded by an abundance of freedom and possibilities. Conner remembered writing about that expression—it was the expression he always wished the real Goldilocks could have more often.

"Once again, it's a beautiful day to be a pirate," Auburn Sally said to her crew. "Ladies, *lower the sales!*"

The twins looked up, expecting the sails above them to come down and fill with the ocean air. Instead, Siren Sue peeked out of the crow's nest with a treasure chest full of scarves, jewelry, hooks, and weapons. The other pirates gathered below her with hands full of gold coins.

"You heard the captain—time to lower the sales!" Siren Sue announced. "For a limited time, everything is half off! Scarves are two coins, earrings are four coins, necklaces are six coins, and the rifles are eight coins! Get your accessories while the sales are low!"

Siren Sue sold off the items to the pirates below until there was nothing left in her chest. The women ogled their new purchases and showed them off to one another. It absolutely baffled Alex, and when she glanced at Conner, he looked just as confused as she did.

"I don't understand what's happening," he said. "I never wrote *that.*"

"Did you mean to write *lower the sails?* Like the *normal sails* on a ship?" Alex asked.

"Oops," Conner said. "I must have spelled it wrong."

To his relief, once the *sales* were over, the pirates lowered the *sails*, too. They were made from cream-colored cloth, the exact color of Porridge's coat. They filled with the ocean breeze, and the *Dolly Llama* sailed into the horizon.

Auburn Sally turned the ship's wheel back and forth as she guided her vessel through the rough waters. She kept a watchful eye on the entire horizon around them. The longer the ship sailed, the more a familiar expression grew on her face—one that the twins had seen Goldilocks wear many times when they'd first met her. The captain seemed a little sad, like she was hoping something would appear in the distance, but it never came.

Conner recognized this face, too, and began to worry.

"Oh no," he said. "We're getting close to the part of the story when the navy shows up."

"How can you tell?" Alex asked.

"From the way Auburn Sally is looking out over the ocean longingly," he said. "The pirates are about to get company."

Like clockwork, Siren Sue climbed down from the crow's nest in a panic.

"Captain!" she shouted. "Look, in the east! A ship from the British Navy is approaching!"

Auburn Sally quickly unfolded a long telescope and scanned the eastern horizon. Alex and Conner squinted and could barely see a small speck moving in the distance. The captain smiled as she spotted the ship—this was what she had been hoping for.

"It looks like Admiral Jacobson has finally caught up with us," Auburn Sally announced to her crew.

"Any orders, Captain?" Winking Wendy asked.

"I'm tired of playing the admiral's game of cat and mouse," the captain said. *"Hoist the sails and prepare for battle!"*

The pirates all saluted her and went to work right away. They loaded the cannons on deck and sharpened their swords. The sails were rolled up and the ship slowed down, allowing the admiral's ship to gain on them. The small speck the twins saw in the distance quickly grew into an enormous ship twice the size of the *Dolly Llama*. Soon they could make out a British flag waving from the tallest mast and the ship's name painted along its side: the *Royal Tantrum*.

While the pirates scurried around the deck preparing for battle, the captain gazed at herself in a compact mirror. Auburn Sally applied lipstick and blush, she brushed her hair to give it extra volume, and she wiped off all the smudges on her clothes. The captain wasn't getting ready for *combat*; she was getting ready for a *date*!

"That's how she prepares for battle?" Alex asked her brother.

Conner nodded bashfully. "Just wait," he said. "In about five minutes it's all going to make perfect sense."

When the *Royal Tantrum* was getting close to the *Dolly Llama*, the pirates dropped the sails and sailed around the navy ship. The twins could see that the *Royal Tantrum*'s lower deck was full of British sailors running amok. They spotted Admiral Jacobson standing on the upper deck.

The admiral was posed regally, with one foot on the railing and a long sword in his hand. He was a very handsome man with broad shoulders and pitch-black hair in a neat ponytail. He wore a blue coat with several gold buttons and badges. The closer the pirate ship sailed around the navy ship, the more familiar he seemed.

"Conner, is it just me, or does the admiral look exactly like *Jack*?" Alex asked.

She glanced between the captain and the admiral. Just like her brother said, it all finally made sense.

"Oooooh," Alex said. "I get it now. Auburn Sally is based on Goldilocks, and the admiral is based on Jack. 'Starboardia' is a love story! That's so sweet!"

Conner grunted like his sister had just insinuated something very crude.

"Excuse me," he said defensively. " 'Starboardia' is a *pirate adventure*! It might have *elements* of love, but it is absolutely *not* a love story!"

Alex raised an eyebrow at him. *"Sure,"* she said mockingly.

By now, the *Dolly Llama* was sailing around the *Royal Tantrum* with gusto. The British sailors ran across the deck to watch the pirates circling them. Winking Wendy took the wheel and Auburn Sally went to the railing to see the admiral. She mimicked his pose on the railing of her own ship, and the two commanders locked eyes. If Alex hadn't known there was something between them before, she definitely knew it now.

"Good afternoon, Admiral," Auburn Sally said. "What brings you to this part of the Caribbean today?"

"You're a wanted woman, Auburn Sally," the admiral said.

"You mean, by more than just you?" the captain said playfully. "Honestly, Admiral, you're so persistent, I'm starting to think you have a little crush on me."

The pirates roared with laughter. Even the navy soldiers were amused and covered their mouths to hide their chuckles. The whole scene felt like it should have happened in a high school hallway instead of the Caribbean Sea.

"The entire British Navy is just *smitten* with you, Captain," the admiral said. "They've asked me to personally escort you back to land. Come willingly and I won't sink your ship."

"Admiral, may I remind you I am *literally* sailing circles around you," she said. "It's *your* ship I'm worried about. I'd hate to destroy it and embarrass you in front of all your men. By the way, *nice tights, gentlemen!*"

"So it's going to be the hard way, is it?" Admiral Jacobson said with a grin.

Auburn Sally laughed. "Oh, Admiral," she said, "haven't you learned by now I'm the kind of girl who likes—"

"PLAYING HARD TO GET!" Conner yelled, finishing her sentence.

The captain and her crew quickly turned to him, wondering how on earth he knew exactly what she had been planning to say.

"I told you this is my story," Conner reminded them. "I wrote the cheesy dialogue coming out of your mouths!

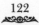

Would you quit the innuendos and just get to the battle already?"

Auburn Sally glared at him suspiciously for a moment, then turned to face the admiral again.

"I agree with the warlock," she said. *"Ladies, open fire!"*

As the *Dolly Llama* circled the *Royal Tantrum*, it was like the ships were joined together in a dangerous waltz and the pirates were taking the lead. They lit their cannons and fired them at the navy sailors, blasting large holes in the British ship. The admiral's sailors retaliated, but the pirate ship was much smaller and moving fast, making it a harder target.

The few times the pirates were hit, the entire ship rattled and swayed in the water. But the damage the navy was inflicting was nothing compared to the mark the pirates were leaving. The sailors looked to the admiral for guidance, but he seldom gave them orders. It was almost like he *wanted* to lose.

Cannonballs and chunks of wood flew through the air. Parts of the navy ship were set ablaze and the sky filled with smoke. Conner had written the entire battle, but writing it was nothing like living it. Even though he knew exactly what was going to happen, it was still terrifying to see it come to life.

"This is the most dangerous flirting I've ever seen!" Alex said.

"Don't worry, the pirates win!" Conner said, then

looked up at the captain. "Sally, would you hurry up and tell your pirates to aim for the navy's cannons already? I don't want to get splinters in my eyes!"

The thought had come into the captain's head just a moment before Conner suggested it. "How did you know I was—"

"JUST DO IT!" he yelled.

"Aim for their cannons, girls!" Auburn Sally ordered.

The pirates followed their captain's orders and aimed their cannons at the navy's. They blasted them off the ship, leaving the *Royal Tantrum* virtually defenseless. The pirates cheered and shook their swords at the sailors.

Winking Wendy jerked the wheel, and the *Dolly Llama* slammed into the *Royal Tantrum*, bringing the pirate ship alongside it.

"Now let's take their ship!" Auburn Sally ordered.

The pirates each grabbed a rope and swung aboard the navy ship. The battle continued with hand-to-hand combat on the decks of the *Royal Tantrum*. The sailors were barely trained for sailing and were no match for the pirates attacking them.

Winking Wendy flashed her empty eye socket at the sailors, scaring them and causing them to trip over themselves. Stinky-Feet Phoebe held her bare feet against their noses, and the fumes made the men temporarily lose consciousness. Having no legs made it easy for Somersault Sydney to tumble into the sailors and knock them down like bowling pins. Pancake-Face Patty seemed to enjoy head-butting the men, which explained the odd shape of her skull. Big-Booty Bertha simply turned her backside to any of the sailors charging toward her, and they bounced backward onto the deck.

Some of the pirates weren't as efficient fighters. Siren Sue sang high notes to hurt the sailors' ears. Fish-Lips Lucy irritated them with slobbery kisses. Too-Much-Rum Ronda drunkenly argued with the sailors about religion and politics. Not-So-Jolly Joan simply cried on their shoulders. These pirates offered perfect distractions for Peg-Leg Peggy (or "Margret") to sneak up behind the sailors and trip them with her wooden leg.

On the upper deck, Captain Auburn Sally and Admiral Jacobson walked around each other with their swords raised. They were so lost in each other's eyes that they almost forgot they had to fight to keep up appearances. When the two eventually started dueling, it resembled more of a passionate tango than an actual sword fight.

"This is the most nonviolent violence I've ever witnessed," Alex said.

"I kept it tame in case I had young readers," Conner said.

"That explains why the antagonists are so simple," she noted. "To be honest, I was really worried about what kind of villains your imagination would have come up with. I'm glad they're just men in tights."

"The navy sailors aren't the bad guys in this story," he said. "The bad guys are *way* scarier. They're based on people I've seen in nightmares. But we'll be long gone before they show up . . . *I hope.*"

Eventually, the sailors surrendered and the pirates rounded them up in the center of the *Royal Tantrum*'s lower deck. Auburn Sally pushed Admiral Jacobson off the upper deck, and his men caught him. The pirates raised their weapons in celebration—they had won the battle!

"You've lost, Admiral," Auburn Sally said. "The British Navy is going to be so disappointed."

"Sometimes a man fails in order to win," the admiral said with a smirk.

The navy sailors were stripped of their weapons, and their hands were tied behind their backs. The pirates placed a plank between ships and forced the sailors to cross it and board the *Dolly Llama*. Once everyone aboard the *Royal Tantrum* had been taken prisoner, the pirates blasted the navy ship with cannonballs until it sank.

"Put the prisoners in the cells belowdecks," Auburn Sally ordered, and glanced at the twins. "And I mean *all* the prisoners."

The pirates untied the twins and pushed them along with the sailors.

"Oh no," Conner said. "The bad guys are going to show up soon! I've got to convince Auburn Sally I'm the author of this story before they get here!"

"I'm willing to help you if it speeds things up," Alex said with a sigh.

"Well, I'm not willing to accept your help yet," he said. "I told you I can take care of this on my own!"

Conner managed to push past the pirates manhandling him and his sister. He dashed across the deck, but just before he was in reach of Auburn Sally, he was tripped by Somersault Sydney and tackled by Catfish Kate and High-Tide Tabitha.

"Captain, don't lock us up!" he pleaded from underneath the pirates. "I'm warning you! Something really bad is about to happen, but you can avoid it if you just listen to me!"

Auburn Sally laughed at his warning. "Take him away," she said, and turned her back on him.

The pirates forced Conner to his feet and dragged him away, but he wasn't ready to give up.

"I know what you stole from SMOKY-SAILS SAM!" Conner yelled.

The entire ship suddenly froze as if he'd shouted something obscene. Alex could tell that all the pirates and sailors knew who her brother was talking about. Just the mention of the name Smoky-Sails Sam sent a collective chill down their spines.

Auburn Sally turned back to Conner with large, fearful eyes. He continued his warning, desperate for her to listen to him.

"He knows what you stole from him, too—he knows about everything that happened on the island!" Conner said. "Smoky-Sails Sam is looking for you and your crew right now! He's going to see the smoke from this battle and be here before sunrise tomorrow!"

Conner knew that if anything would get through to her this would be it. The captain looked him up and down but didn't say a word.

"Your orders, Captain?" Catfish Kate asked.

Auburn Sally put on a brave face for her crew. "Throw this boy and his sister in the cells with the others," she said. "If he has tall tales to tell, he can share them with the other prisoners."

Auburn Sally turned around and faced the ocean. Conner struggled against the pirates, but it was no use. They were too strong to break free from—that's how he had written them. Conner and Alex were pushed down the steps to the cells belowdecks with the sailors.

"Well, that *totally* worked," Alex said. "Are you sure you don't want my help?"

"Give it a minute," Conner said. "She'll come around— she'll have to."

The captain looked down at the burning wreckage of the *Royal Tantrum*, and her eyes followed the trails of smoke ascending into the sky. Once all the sailors and the twins were belowdecks and there were no pirates around to bear witness, she pulled out a necklace she kept hidden in her shirt. Dangling from a golden chain was a bloodred ruby the size of a human heart.

While she refused to believe everything Conner had said, she couldn't deny that he possessed extraordinary knowledge of her ship and crew. If what he said about Smoky-Sails Sam was even remotely accurate, then the captain's greatest nightmare was about to come true.

CHAPTER EIGHT

THE WRATH OF
SMOKY-SAILS SAM

Things were calm belowdecks on the *Dolly Llama*.
Alex and Conner shared a small cell, while Admiral Jacobson and his men occupied four larger
ones. Everyone was silent, not from the embarrassment of
defeat, but from the sheer exhaustion of the battle. In all
fairness, the sailors didn't seem disappointed by their loss
and sat rather comfortably in the cells. Many were stretched
out and gently rocked to sleep by the sway of the ship.

"Don't worry, men," Admiral Jacobson said as he paced

around his cell. "We will find a way off this vessel and bring the pirates to justice! Those criminals may imprison us now, but soon we shall escape and make the British Navy proud!"

The sailors looked around the cells to see whom the Admiral was talking to, because none of them were too worried or eager to change the situation. After months of strenuous labor operating the *Royal Tantrum*, imprisonment was a nice change of pace for them.

"Save it, Admiral," Conner said. "The whole crew knows you've got the hots for Auburn Sally. No one is expecting to escape anytime soon."

The admiral was outraged by his insinuation. "How dare you suggest I *welcomed* the sinking of my ship or *allowed* pirates to capture my men!" he said. "I would never betray Britain with affection for a scoundrel like Captain Auburn Sally!"

Conner sighed and shook his head. "Raise your hand if you knew this was going to happen," he said. "Come on, don't be shy."

He raised his hand and Alex quickly followed. One by one, the sailors raised their hands, too, and the admiral was faced with a rude awakening. Despite his efforts to shield it, the heart on his sleeve was just as visible as the badges of honor on his coat.

"You mean, you've all known the entire time?" he asked.

The sailors nodded in unison with the twins.

"To be honest, Admiral," said the first mate, "I don't

think any of us knew you were trying to *hide it*. We don't hold it against you, though. The whole reason we joined the navy in the first place was to have an adventure, and there's never been a dull moment chasing these dames around the sea."

The admiral wanted to argue further, but the jig was clearly up. Instead of clearing his reputation, he just shrugged and had a seat on the floor.

"Well, I suppose that's a relief, then," Jacobson said.

The admiral lost all desire to form an escape plan. He put his feet up on the metal bars and enjoyed the quiet and calm of the cells with the rest of his crew. Conner, on the other hand, was growing more agitated by the second. His mission to locate and recruit his characters was going to be much more difficult now that he had refused his sister's help.

"So what happens next in this story?" Alex asked with a yawn.

"Auburn Sally is going to invite Admiral Jacobson to dinner in her chambers," Conner said. "They'll admit their affection for each other and then Jacobson will convince his sailors to join Auburn Sally's crew of pirates."

"Nice," Alex said. "And you still think 'Starboardia' isn't a love story?"

Conner grunted. "Okay, fine—*it's a love story*," he said. "You've identified your brother as a big sap. Are you happy now?"

Alex laughed. "I don't know why it's so hard for you to admit it," she said. "Plenty of men write romances."

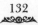

"I never meant to write a romance," Conner said. "I just thought Jack and Goldilocks had a really cool story. Everyone wants to be a hero, but Jack gave it up to be with the person he loved. He didn't care what people thought of him—Goldilocks was more important to him than his reputation. It takes courage to face a giant, but it takes a true hero to stand up to the world. I guess I wanted to celebrate that by putting it into my own story."

A smile grew on Alex's face as she listened to her brother. He kept his feelings hidden behind an emotional brick wall, but every so often she managed to knock a hole through it and peek inside.

"You're not a sap, but you're definitely a *hopeless romantic*," she said. "I think Mrs. Peters was right. You're going to learn a lot about yourself traveling through these stories."

Conner didn't want to agree with her, but he knew she was right. "Oh brother," he said. "Next thing you know, I'll be collecting porcelain dolls and listening to polka music."

The doors opened and Winking Wendy and Somersault Sydney walked in. They rattled the cell bars with their weapons to disturb their captives, but the tranquil sailors didn't even look up. The pirates unlocked the admiral's cell and pulled him out by the ponytail.

"*Ouch!*" Jacobson shouted. "What's the meaning of this?"

"The captain wants you to join her for dinner," Winking Wendy said.

The sailors hooted and whistled, making the admiral

blush. Winking Wendy flashed them her empty eye socket and they quickly quieted down. The pirates unlocked the door of the twins' cell next.

"What's going on?" Conner asked.

"Captain wants you two to join her as well," Somersault Sydney said.

Conner wasn't expecting this. Up to this moment, every beat of the story had followed his writing without a hitch. He hoped it meant his warning about Smoky-Sails Sam had caught the captain's attention.

The pirates escorted the twins and the admiral through the *Dolly Llama* to the upper deck. They opened a pair of double doors and pushed the twins and the admiral into the captain's quarters.

Auburn Sally's private chambers were the most elegant part of the ship. The walls were covered in red wallpaper and gold crown molding. A crystal chandelier hung over a long wooden table set for four. The captain looked like she was deep in thought when they arrived. She sat in the back of her chambers at a desk with several maps of the Caribbean spread across it. She was sitting with one foot up and spun a dagger on the desk like a dreidel. Her hat and coat were hung on a rack beside the desk, exposing her full head of long wavy hair.

"Your guests, Captain," Winking Wendy said as she presented the twins and the admiral.

"Thank you," Auburn Sally said. "You may leave us."

Winking Wendy and Somersault Sydney left the chambers, shutting the double doors behind them. Conner had written the next part of the story as a romantic dinner between the captain and the admiral, but obviously things had changed. As soon as they entered, Auburn Sally fixated on him with an inquisitive, unwavering stare.

"Since you seem to know *everything*, I imagine there's no point in pretending the admiral and I are adversaries," she said.

"Nope," Conner said. "You guys are in a complicated long-distance relationship."

"Just for the record," Alex chimed in, "I think it's *very* romantic."

Conner gave his sister a dirty look—she was *never* going to let it go. The admiral glanced between the twins and the captain, waiting for someone to fill him in.

"Will someone explain how this lad knows so much about us?" he asked.

"According to him, we're just characters in a story he's written," Auburn Sally said with amusement. "He believes everything in this world is just a figment of his imagination."

Conner didn't appreciate the disdainful tone in her voice. The admiral looked at him just like everyone else had after hearing the pronouncement.

"Have I done or said anything to *contradict* it?" Conner asked. "Because I'm pretty sure I've been right about *everything* so far."

Auburn Sally glared at him and a challenging look came to her face.

"I have something hidden underneath my shirt," the

captain said. "There are only four people alive who know it exists. Two are in this room, and one is the Queen of England. Guess correctly, and I *might* take you more seriously."

Conner knew exactly what she was referring to and didn't waste a minute to prove it. "You're wearing a necklace called the Heart of the Caribbean," he said. "It's the most prized piece of jewelry in the Western Hemisphere. It was given to Governor Connelly by Queen Anne as a token of her appreciation for governing the small island of Saint Ballena."

The intensity in Auburn Sally's face dissolved and her mouth fell open. She and the admiral were completely dumbfounded. The captain pulled on a gold chain around her neck and lifted a large ruby necklace out of her blouse. The ruby was brighter than the crown molding and the chandelier put together.

Conner pointed at the jewel. "*That's* what you stole from Smoky-Sails Sam," he said. "And you're wrong, by the way. There are *five* people alive who know it exists, seven including my sister and me. A pirate named Killy Billy saw you steal it. He's the one who told Smoky-Sails Sam you have it, and now Sam is on his way to take it back."

Alex was usually really good about filling in the blanks, but the lack of detail was getting frustrating.

"Would you mind sharing with the rest of the class who Smoky-Sails Sam is?" she asked.

Conner hesitated. He knew the story like the back of his hand; it just wasn't a pleasant one to share.

"Smoky-Sails Sam is the most feared pirate in the

Caribbean," he explained. "He's so powerful, the British Navy refuses to go anywhere near him. He has a fleet of five ships and hundreds of pirates. His ships burn rows of torches above their sails, leaving trails of smoke through the sky, so the whole Caribbean knows where they've been and where they're headed. They obliterate any ship they encounter, whether it's a threat or not."

Alex gulped. This was exactly the kind of villain she was afraid her brother would create.

"He sounds *charming*," Alex said. "How did he become so powerful?"

"Smoky-Sails Sam used to be a slave," Conner said. "He was captured from an African village by slave traders and brought to the Caribbean on a slave ship. However, on the way over, he broke the chains that bound him and led the other slaves in a mutiny. They killed the slave traders and took over the ship. Sam became the new captain, the liberated slaves became his crew, and he renamed the ship the *Vengeance*.

"Unfortunately, the power went to Sam's head. His crew wanted to go home, but Sam wanted to continue on and seek more revenge. He sailed the *Vengeance* to the small island of Saint Ballena and ordered his men to raid it. Governor Connelly sent word to the British Navy that they were under attack, but since the island was so small and valueless, the navy abandoned them. The governor and all the men on Saint Ballena were killed and their families were forced to work as servants.

"Since there was no government or authority on Saint Ballena, criminals from all over the Caribbean sailed there and joined Sam. Soon, he had enough men to form a fleet of pirate ships. They terrorized all the colonies nearby, growing stronger and stronger after every target they hit. The liberated slaves from the *Vengeance* wanted nothing to do with it, so they stole a ship from Sam's fleet and headed back to Africa. Sam was so outraged, he sailed after them and sank their ship. The smoky debris from the destruction is how Sam became known as Smoky-Sails Sam, and the whole Caribbean learned of his ruthlessness.

"As time went on, Smoky-Sails Sam had a daughter named Sumire. Governor Connelly's only child, a girl named Christine, was forced to work as her maid. The young women became very close and loved each other like sisters. Sumire helped Christine plan an escape from Saint Ballena. The Heart of the Caribbean was the only object of Governor Connelly's that Smoky-Sails Sam did not destroy, so Christine stole it back before she left. It didn't take long before Smoky-Sails Sam realized it was missing. To save her friend, Sumire took the blame. Rather than showing his only child any mercy, Smoky-Sails Sam made a gruesome example out of her. He cut her throat in front of his entire fleet, further proving his brutality, and no one ever stole from him again.

"Christine escaped from the island and sold the Heart of the Caribbean to a jewel merchant, but then stole it back the following day. The money she had acquired in the sale was enough to buy her own ship and hire a crew. She named the ship the *Dolly Llama*, and became known throughout the Caribbean as—"

"*Auburn Sally!*" Alex said, finishing her brother's sentence.

"Correct," Conner said. "When Jacobson became an admiral, his first assignment was to capture the sailing thief Auburn Sally. It was love at first sight, and they've been chasing each other around the Caribbean ever since. What the captain doesn't know is that Killy Billy told Smoky-Sails Sam that he saw her steal the Heart of the Caribbean. Sam's been following the *Dolly Llama* through the sea, too, and is getting closer by the minute. Since Sally's the only person who's stolen something from him and lived to see another day, he wants to make another gruesome example out of her."

"Conner, that backstory is so dark! Why would you write something so dreadful?" Alex asked.

"I told you, it was based on a nightmare I had," he said. "Besides, it's not like real pirates were any better."

Conner turned to Auburn Sally and Admiral Jacobson with desperation in his eyes. *"Now do you believe I created you?"* he asked.

The captain and the admiral were both astonished by Conner's familiarity with their lives. Whoever he was, wherever he came from, they could no longer deny there was something unique and eerie about him.

"I believe you put pen to paper about all of this, but I'm

still not convinced you *created* this world or the people in it," Auburn Sally said.

Conner had rolled his eyes so many times, his sockets were getting sore. "So you think I *plagiarized* it?" he asked.

"Explorers are quick to claim the places they find, but they don't *create* the land they raise flags on," Auburn Sally said. "Perhaps all writers are nothing more than subconscious explorers, sailing across a sea of other worlds, and you're just the first to discover ours."

Alex was intrigued by the captain's theory. She wondered if every fictional story she had ever read was more of an author's *discovery* than his or her *idea*. Perhaps *imagination* was a *subconscious map* to uncharted worlds of the cosmos. It certainly would explain why her grandmother's Portal Potion was so effective—it didn't *create* the world the text described, but simply provided a doorway into a world that had always been there.

Conner was getting a headache trying to understand it himself. "That sounds really deep and complex, but you're missing the point!" he said. "I'm trying to tell you that Smoky-Sails Sam's fleet is headed here right now! He's planning to kill all of you and take back the Heart of the Caribbean! But if you listen to us, we can help you avoid him!"

"How?" Admiral Jacobson asked.

"By helping my sister and me," Conner explained. "I'm about to make you an offer—it's going to be hard to grasp, so we might want to sit for this."

Auburn Sally, the admiral, and the twins took seats around the long table.

"Do you want me to explain this part?" Alex asked.

"I told you, I got this," Conner said, and cleared his throat. "You know that subconscious sea of other worlds you were just talking about? Well, for all intents and purposes, it exists! There's another world that's in big trouble—one I didn't write about. All our friends live there and a horrible army has invaded it. My sister and I are recruiting people from a bunch of different worlds to help us fight the army. If you come with us and help us defeat them, we'll bring you right back here."

Conner grinned like he was being more than generous. The captain and the admiral exchanged a puzzled look—something didn't add up.

"That's not an offer," Auburn Sally said. "An offer is an *exchange*. Taking us away from our problems, making us fight for you, then bringing us right back to our problems isn't an exchange—it's just more work for us."

"She's got a point," Alex said.

"Okay," Conner said, and quickly thought about something appealing to offer. "Well, if you help us, I'll tell you how you defeat Smoky-Sails Sam."

The captain and the admiral nodded as they considered it. Jacobson whispered something into Auburn Sally's ear, like an attorney speaking with his client.

"So you're telling us we *defeat* Smoky-Sails Sam?" the captain asked. "*Regardless* of whether we help you or not?"

"Duh!" Conner said with a snort. "That's the whole point of this story."

Alex slapped a hand against her forehead. Her brother was oblivious to what Auburn Sally was implying. She appointed herself as *his* attorney and pulled him aside to whisper in his ear.

"Conner, you basically just told them they don't need to help you," she whispered. *"You need to make them an offer they can't refuse."*

"Oh, dang it!" he said. *"I should never have written them to be so cunning. Thanks for the heads-up."*

The twins turned back to the captain and the admiral. Conner let out a low, slow, and menacing chuckle.

"Silly, silly Sally," he said. "What you don't know is that the road to victory is long and tedious. There are dozens of battles, hundreds of casualties, and thousands of miles awaiting you. It takes *years* to learn what I could tell you in a matter of seconds. If you help us, I will give you the *short-cut* to your triumph, and save you a ton of hassle. You'd be sparing your ship from a lot of damage and even saving the lives of a few of your crew."

Auburn Sally and Admiral Jacobson whispered between themselves again. They both knew they would have to face Smoky-Sails Sam eventually; there was no way of getting around it. If Conner could supply them with information on how to do it efficiently, they would have to consider his offer seriously.

They turned to the twins and presented a counteroffer.

"We'll help you if you help us defeat Smoky-Sails Sam *first*," Auburn Sally said.

Conner was about to rip his hair out. He silently vowed never to write another smart character into one of his stories ever again.

"Deal," he said through a clenched jaw.

Conner and Auburn Sally shook hands over the table. Alex wasn't convinced the captain and the admiral were being truthful and pulled her brother aside one final time.

"How do you know they're being honest?" she whispered.

"Because I wrote them to be just as trustworthy as they are calculating," he said. *"And I'll remind them about that shipwreck in the sequel!"*

"Let's discuss the details of our victory over dinner," Auburn Sally said. "I'm famished. Negotiating always gives me an appetite."

It had been hours since their last meal, so the twins were glad to hear it. The captain rang a bell and a few moments later, Fish-Lips Lucy entered the chambers pushing a cart with several covered serving trays. The quarters filled with a delectable aroma and the twins began salivating and their stomachs growled.

"Conner, what did you write for dinner?" Alex asked.

"Tomato soup, mashed potatoes, and rosary chicken," Conner said, and licked his lips.

"Rosary chicken?" she asked. "Did you mean *rotisserie chicken?*"

"Oh no," he said fearfully.

Fish-Lips Lucy uncovered the largest serving tray, and rather than a delicious roasted chicken, she revealed a live chicken wearing a Catholic rosary. The chicken panicked and fluttered amok around the chambers, squawking loudly and shedding feathers wherever she went.

Auburn Sally gave Fish-Lips Lucy a dirty look. "The chicken seems a little *undercooked*," she said.

"Sorry, Captain," Fish-Lips Lucy said. "I knew I was forgetting something."

Suddenly, Siren Sue burst into the chambers, causing everyone to jump and forget all about the chicken. Her eyes were large and she was out of breath, like she had come in a hurry.

"Forgive my intrusion, Captain!" Siren Sue huffed. "I saw smoke rising on the horizon behind the ship! I inspected it and saw a fleet of ships coming this way! Smoky-Sails Sam is following us!"

The captain, the admiral, and the twins stood up so fast, they knocked silverware and plates off the table. Auburn Sally darted to the large windows in the back of her chambers and looked through a telescope beside her desk.

"It's Smoky-Sails Sam, all right," the captain said, and then jerked her head toward Conner. "I thought you said we had until morning."

He racked his brain trying to figure out why they were so early. "It's because I rushed the battle!" he said. "There was smoke in the sky earlier than there should have been! You and the admiral were supposed to exchange a lot more witty banter before the first cannon fired! I accidentally gave Smoky-Sails Sam a head start!"

Auburn Sally put on her hat and coat and immediately went into damage-control mode. "Lucy and Sue, tell the women to drop the sails at once," she ordered. "I want every candle and lantern on this ship extinguished—we'll be harder to follow in darkness. Also, free the sailors from the cells. If they want to survive the night, they'll need to join our crew."

The pirates nodded and ran out of the chambers to inform the others. Auburn Sally hurried out on deck and the twins and Jacobson followed. She wrapped her hands around the *Dolly Llama*'s wheel and looked to Conner.

"Well?" she asked. "What do we need to do to defeat Smoky-Sails Sam?"

"It's not a *what*, it's a *where*," he said. "We need to head *west* immediately, sail through the Parakeet Islands, and pass the Isle of Skulls."

The captain didn't waste a moment asking questions. She spun the wheel so hard to her right, it almost broke off.

"Conner, where are you taking us?" Alex asked.

"Starboardia," he said.

CHAPTER NINE

SAILING CIRCLES AROUND THE BERMUDA TRIANGLE

The pirates scurried across the decks of the *Dolly Llama* like panicked ants. They blew out all the torches, lanterns, and candles until the ship sailed in total darkness. With the moon as their only source of light, they lowered the sails and took full advantage of the night breeze. The sailors were released from the cells belowdecks and put to work loading and positioning the cannons. All it took was the mention of Smoky-Sails Sam's name and the sailors didn't hesitate in joining the *Dolly Llama*'s crew.

Admiral Jacobson stood at the front of the ship with one leg on the bowsprit. He scanned the sea ahead to make sure there was nothing the ship might collide with in the darkness.

"It looks clear," he called up to the captain. "I'll let you know if that changes."

Auburn Sally kept a firm grip on her ship's wheel and a close eye on the approaching fleet of pirates behind them. With every minute, Smoky-Sails Sam was getting closer and closer to the *Dolly Llama*. The captain prayed Conner's shortcut would work and they could finally defeat Sam and his crew.

"You said to sail west to the Parakeet Islands, pass the Isle of Skulls, and then what do we do?" she asked.

"Then we'll sail to the right in a circle for an entire day," he said. "The legend states, if you travel *starboard* for a day in the Bermuda Triangle, it'll take you to Starboardia— hence the name."

"Yes, I know the *legend*," Auburn Sally said. "Every pirate has heard of the myth. Are you sure it's real?"

Conner was getting tired of repeating himself. "Yes, I'm positive," he said. "It's how you guys find it in the end of the story. I'm sure it'll work now, too."

"So, Starboardia is an actual location?" Alex asked.

"Why else would I name this story 'Starboardia'?" her brother said.

Alex shrugged. "I thought it was just a cute name based on pirate lingo," she said. "Is there also a Portworld or Portopia or Portland?"

Conner froze and thought about it for a moment. "No, but that would be a great name for a sequel!" he said. "Hmm... I should write that down."

"Let's stay focused on the original," Alex said. "Is Starboardia a country?"

"Starboardia is an ancient island," Auburn Sally said. "It's believed to be the only surviving land from the Lost City of Atlantis. It's nearly impossible to find because it floats around the Bermuda Triangle like a large ship, and never passes through the same part of the sea twice. They say the debris from all shipwrecks in the Caribbean eventually washes ashore on the island's coast."

"Nice backstory, Conner," Alex said. "How will Starboardia help us defeat Smoky-Sails Sam?"

"Hundreds of years ago, when the Europeans first settled in the Americas, an indigenous tribe was forced off their island by the white men who settled there," Auburn Sally said. "The tribe was outnumbered ten to one, so they had no choice but to vacate and hope they would find another island somewhere else in the Caribbean. They set sail and were caught in the middle of a horrible hurricane. When the storm finally cleared, they saw Starboardia in the distance. The tribe used all the wreckage on the island to build a magnificent fortress. The structure was carefully designed to help the tribe defeat an enemy that outnumbered them ten to one, should they ever be invaded again."

"Oh, I get it now," Alex said. "We're going to use the fortress! How fun!"

"Exactly," Conner said. "Including Sally's pirates and Jacobson's sailors, we have about fifty people on this ship. Smoky-Sails Sam has five ships and about a hundred pirates on each. The fortress should do the trick."

Suddenly, the twins and the captain were startled by loud eruptions coming from above. Everyone aboard the *Dolly Llama* looked up and saw red fireworks exploding in the sky. With each bright burst, the ocean and the ship were briefly illuminated by red light.

"Where are those coming from?" Conner asked.

They turned to the fleet of pirate ships in the distance and saw another set of fireworks being launched from their decks.

"Smoky-Sails Sam," Auburn Sally said as the fireworks exploded overhead. "They're using them to see us in the dark! Clever scum!"

Since all the light on board the *Dolly Llama* had been extinguished, the approaching fleet had lost track of them, and were headed in a slightly different direction. But now with the fireworks illuminating the ship, the fleet repositioned itself and was once again headed straight for the *Dolly Llama*.

"What do we do now?" Conner asked.

"Pray the wind is stronger with us than it is with them," the captain said. "Otherwise, we might not make it to Starboardia."

Conner paced the deck trying to think of a way to put distance between their ship and the fleet. At this point, Alex didn't care how much her brother opposed her help; she wasn't going to let his pride jeopardize their mission. When he was facing the other way, Alex covertly pointed at the sky. Almost instantaneously, thick clouds blew in and covered the stars. The atmosphere became too humid for the fireworks to go off.

Now that the fireworks were taken care of, the *Dolly Llama* needed a boost so the fleet wouldn't catch up. Alex took a deep breath and blew air toward the sails. A strong breeze came out of nowhere and pushed the ship a little faster, causing everyone on board to jolt.

"Captain, it's a miracle!" Siren Sue shouted from the crow's nest. "Clouds are blocking the fireworks and the wind is making us sail faster!"

The pirates and the sailors cheered in celebration. Auburn Sally stared at the sky in awe. Conner was surprised at how quickly the weather had changed in their favor—it was a little *too* convenient.

"Alex, cut it out!" Conner said. "I told you no magic!"

His sister shrugged innocently. "It wasn't me," she said. "Must be some kind of tropical storm."

"Nice try," Conner said. "But tropical storms don't blow clouds in one direction and ships in the other!"

Auburn Sally eyed the sky again and noticed the strange phenomenon he was referring to. "What's going on?" she asked. *"Your sister* is causing this?"

"Yeah," he said. "I forgot to mention she has magic powers—but don't encourage her! This is *my* story and *my* project. I can get us to Starboardia and help you defeat Smoky-Sails Sam on my own."

Conner stomped off the upper deck and joined Admiral Jacobson at the front of the ship. Auburn Sally's imagination had been broadened so much by the twins, *this* wasn't hard to grasp. She sauntered over to Alex and casually leaned on the railing.

"Men," she said with a sigh. "They always want to feel like they're in control."

"It's my own fault," Alex said. "He asked for my help earlier and I kind of embarrassed him about it. Now he thinks he has to prove himself to me."

"Rule number one on my ship: No woman is allowed to take orders from a man," Auburn Sally said.

"That's a philosophy I could get behind," Alex said.

"Then as your captain, I order you to leave Smoky-Sails Sam's fleet a few *presents* behind us," the captain said. "If you get my drift."

Alex and Auburn Sally shared a smile—Alex knew exactly what she meant. She turned toward the fleet in the distance and pointed at the water. Several clusters of sharp rocks stuck out of the ocean behind the ship.

"Attagirl," the captain said.

The obstructions and the wind helped the *Dolly Llama* gain distance from Smoky-Sails Sam's fleet. Soon the pirate ships had shrunk so much in the distance behind them, they could barely see the trails of smoke emitting from their sails.

The *Dolly Llama* sailed through the night, and by sunrise the Parakeet Islands appeared on the horizon ahead. Unfortunately, the rising sun gave the fleet of pirate ships a better view of the ocean, and the *Dolly Llama* was spotted again.

The ship entered a narrow channel between the Parakeet Islands, and the crew learned why Conner had named them so. The islands were covered with thousands and thousands of colorful birds. It was a beautiful sight, but the farther the ship sailed through the channel, the louder the birds' squawking became. As if they were competing for the pirates' attention, each bird tried to out sing the next. When the *Dolly Llama* reached the center of the channel, the sound became deafening. The whole ship covered their ears and moaned.

"PUT A SOCK IN IT!" Conner yelled at the birds.

"PUT A SOCK IN IT! PUT A SOCK IN IT!" the parakeets mimicked. "PUT A SOCK IN IT! PUT A SOCK IN IT!"

Alex couldn't stand the noise any longer. She snapped her fingers and birdseed rained on the islands. All the parakeets swooped down from the trees to feed and went silent. Conner shot his sister a look—but one of gratitude.

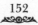

"Okay, I suppose *some* magic won't hurt," he said. "But nothing crazy—the *Dolly Llama*'s crew has to feel accomplished, too."

A twinkle came into Admiral Jacobson's eye as he watched the birds eat the seeds. "You know, the *red worm* is known to *cleanse* a parakeet's stomach," he said. "Perhaps we could leave a *nasty storm* behind for Sam's fleet?"

The twins made eye contact and mischievous smiles grew across their faces.

"Oh, Conner," Alex said, and clasped her hands together. "Please, please, please let me leave red worms behind!"

"Yeah—you've got to," he said. "It's just too good."

Alex jumped up and down giddily and snapped her fingers again. Small red worms rained down on the islands, too, and the parakeets happily dug in. The admiral and the twins laughed as they imagined the mess the birds would leave on the fleet later that day.

A few hours after exiting the channel, the *Dolly Llama* sailed past the Isle of Skulls. It was a creepy island with a permanent layer of fog hanging in the air. The shore had no beaches and was lined with dark eerie caves. The land was littered with large rocks that had been chiseled to look like large human skulls. Alex could have sworn the heads were following her as the ship passed them.

"Hey, Conner, watch this," Alex said. She cleared her throat and all the skulls started singing an obnoxious song by a boy band the twins knew from the radio.

"Oh baaaaby, please don't play this game,
My heart is so full of shame,
My love cannot be tamed,
I'm a moth and you're the flame,
And even though it's lame,
Remind me of your naaaaame!"

The twins were laughing so hard, their stomachs hurt. The rest of the ship screamed and pointed at the possessed skulls.

"It's the devil's music!" Winking Wendy shouted.

The pirates waved crucifixes at the island and shot the rocks with their rifles. Alex figured the joke had gone far enough. She cleared her throat again and the skulls returned to normal.

Once the Isle of Skulls was far behind the *Dolly Llama*, Conner excitedly ran from the front of the ship to Auburn Sally's side on the upper deck.

"All right, we've passed the Isle of Skulls!" he said. "Time to travel starboard."

"And if we sail in circles to the right all night, we'll find Starboardia?" Auburn Sally asked.

"More like Starboardia will find us," Conner said.

The captain stepped to the side of the wheel and presented it to him. "Would you like to do the honors, *Commander Bailey?*" she asked.

"Oh gosh," he said. "Sure!"

Conner had never even driven a car, so he wasn't going

to turn down the opportunity to steer a pirate ship. He put his hands on the wheel and could have sworn he felt the ship's heartbeat pulsing through it. It was an exhilarating sensation—with just the slightest movement, he had the power to change the ship's course and the crew's destiny. It reminded him of the feeling he had when he wrote, but it was ten times stronger. He was *living* and *breathing* the adventure he had only dreamed about.

Naturally, being chased by a fleet of dangerous pirates took some fun out of steering the ship, but it was thrilling nonetheless. Since they arrived, he had been angry, frustrated, anxious, and scared by different things, but the excitement of being in the world he created never left him. He wished every author got to feel what he was feeling right now.

As the sun started setting, it illuminated the ocean waves around the *Dolly Llama* like golden zebra stripes. Conner turned the wheel as far to the right as it would go and tied it down.

"Starboardia, here we come!" he said.

That night, all the pirates and sailors gathered in Auburn Sally's chambers so Conner could tell them what to expect the next day. It was strange to prepare them for a place he technically had never been before. He could only rely on the images in his head and hope they matched. The Rosary Chicken got cozy on Alex's lap and she stroked her feathers while she listened to her brother.

"Ladies, gentlemen, and chicken," Conner said. "Welcome

to Starboardia 101. I'm assuming by now, whether through eavesdropping or word of mouth, everyone knows why we're headed to Starboardia."

Not-So-Jolly Joan and Too-Much-Rum Ronda raised their hands.

"No one ever tells me anything," Not-So-Jolly Joan said, and burst into tears.

"I was told, but I don't remember," Too-Much-Rum Ronda said, and hiccupped so hard, she fell off her seat.

"No worries, I'll explain," Conner said. "We are out-numbered ten to one by Smoky-Sails Sam's fleet. There is a fortress on Starboardia that was designed for a group in our exact predicament. The fortress is filled with hundreds of booby traps; there are trapdoors, human slingshots, swing-ing blades, endless mazes, and much more. Once the for-tress is activated, the traps will go off every thirty seconds.

"Unless you want to be crushed, cut in half, or fall to your death—listen to this part very carefully. There are safe zones throughout the fortress painted in red. Five seconds before the traps are set off, you will hear a bell—when you hear the bell, find one of those safe zones immediately! I've come up with a motto to help those of us who have diffi-culty remembering directions. Repeat after me: *In Red, Ain't Dead.*"

"*In Red, Ain't Dead,*" the pirates and sailors repeated.

"Very good," Conner said. "Now, once we're on the island and find the fortress, we have to wait until all of Smoky-Sails Sam's men are inside before we can activate it. The fortress sort of works like a clock—a very heavy net of boulders pulls on gears located at the top, which turn and operate all the booby traps. The net is held up by twenty-one ropes and needs all twenty-one ropes to support it. Once one of these ropes is cut, another rope will snap under pressure every thirty seconds, causing the net of boulders to drop a little lower, which pulls on the gears, and activates the booby traps. Does this all make sense?"

The pirates and sailors stared at Conner like he was speaking another language. Even Alex was having a hard time following along.

"Those are just the logistics in case anyone was wondering," Conner said. "There's only one thing you have to remember—*which is*?"

"*In Red, Ain't Dead!*" the pirates and sailors said in unison. They were very proud of themselves and looked like dogs expecting treats.

"Great," Conner said. "Everybody break a leg tomorrow! Oh—no offense, Somersault Sydney!"

"None taken," the legless pirate said.

As the *Dolly Llama* sailed in large starboard loops around the Bermuda Triangle, the pirates, sailors, and the twins went to bed to rest up for the following day. In the sleeping quarters belowdecks, rows of white hammocks were stacked from floor to ceiling. It was chilly down there, so Alex and Conner were thankful their mother had packed sweatshirts for them.

The hammocks swung with the sway of the ship and

were very relaxing. Soon the pirates and the sailors fell asleep. Their snoring was so loud, the twins were worried the sides of the ship would burst open. Alex glanced down at the hammock below hers to see if Conner was still awake.

"Oh good, you're still up, too," she said.

"I don't think the dead could sleep through this," he said.

"Are you nervous about tomorrow?" she asked.

"A little bit," he said with a long sigh. "I just hope it all works out so the trip here hasn't been for nothing."

Alex could sense the doubt in his voice and she felt a little guilty. Had she been more supportive and encouraging in the beginning, he probably wouldn't be so cynical.

"Everything is going to be fine," Alex said. "You're a really great author, Conner. I keep forgetting to tell you how impressed I am by all of this. Every beat of your story is so well thought out and entertaining. The more it unfolds, the more intrigued I become. I can't wait for you to write your first book—there are millions of little Alexes and Conners around the world who are going to love it."

Conner was touched by his sister's words. It meant a lot coming from her, since he was convinced she had read every book in the world.

"Thanks, Alex," he said. "I would never have met Jack and Goldilocks if it weren't for you—so thanks for supplying all the inspiration."

"But think of everything you came up with all on your

own," she said. "You would have done just fine without me. I wish I had your imagination. What's your secret to making a story so good? Do you have any writing tricks or rituals?"

Conner had never thought about it before. He thought back to the very first time he wrote a story and recalled a tool that had helped him write ever since.

"Whenever I write, I imagine everything in Dad's voice," he said. "I try to describe everything with the same energy and enthusiasm he had when he read stories to us. Sometimes when I miss him the most, writing makes me feel like he's there with me. It's almost like he's telling me the story and I'm just writing it down."

The thought brought tears to their eyes. Alex knew exactly what he meant, because her dad's narrative was ingrained in her mind, too. Whenever they thought about John Bailey, they didn't think about the night they lost him, the funeral that followed, or the days they spent mourning him. They remembered the nights when he'd read them fairy tales by the fireplace in their old house, the animated gestures he'd make while acting out every scene, and the different voices he made for each character. Their father was a storyteller in every sense of the word, and Conner had inherited the same gift.

"Dad would be so proud of you, Conner," Alex said. "He would have loved everything about Starboardia."

"He'd be proud of you, too, Alex," Conner said.

"Other fifteen-year-olds would have given up on saving the fairy-tale world by now."

The twins laughed at the thought of another brother-and-sister duo going to the same extremes. Alex cast a spell so their roommates snored in silence, and the twins let the sway of the ship rock them to sleep, too.

Chapter Ten

STARBOARDIA

The following morning, the entire ship was awoken by a loud clanging coming from above deck.

"LAAAAAND HOOOO!" Siren Sue yelled, and rang the bell in the crow's nest.

The pirates, the sailors, and the twins quickly swung out of their hammocks and ran up the steps to the lower deck. They dashed to the bowsprit and joined Auburn Sally and Admiral Jacobson at the front of the ship. The sun had just started rising and slowly shed light on an island directly ahead. It had a beach littered with wooden debris and was covered in a thick forest of tropical trees. The crew could make out the tip of a large fortress towering over the trees in the center of the island.

"That's it!" Conner yelled. "That's Starboardia!"

There wasn't any time to rejoice because the discovery was immediately followed by the thunderous sounds of firing cannons.

"We've got company!" Siren Sue shouted, and pointed to the ocean behind the *Dolly Llama*.

Like a stampede, the twins, the pirates, and the sailors ran across the lower deck, climbed the steps to the upper deck, and crowded the railing at the back of the ship. The five large pirate ships of Smoky-Sails Sam's fleet were so close, they could smell the torches burning above the sails—and the ships were headed right for them.

The ship in the center was the largest and Alex knew it was the *Vengeance* without having to ask. It was the color of charcoal and flew enormous black sails. The *Vengeance*'s sides and bow were covered in metal spikes, making it resemble a large floating cactus. A flag with an image of broken shackles flew proudly at the top of the tallest mast.

All the decks of the five-ship fleet were swarming with pirates eager for a fight. The *Vengeance* fired its cannons at the *Dolly Llama* and cannonballs splashed in the water beside it. Each splash crept closer and closer to the ship.

"We've got to get to the island now!" Conner yelled.

Auburn Sally stood on a barrel and whistled to get her crew's attention. "Everyone gather as many weapons as you can carry and head to the boats," she ordered. "We'll lower ourselves to the water and row to the island."

"They're going to blow the ship apart!" Admiral Jacobson said. "We don't have time to lower the boats! We have to abandon ship now!"

Conner shared a fearful look with his sister and they read each other's mind—a little *more* magic couldn't hurt.

"Everyone follow the captain's orders," Alex said. "I'll keep the pirates busy until we get off the ship."

The crew nodded and split up at once. Alex stood on the railing and faced the oncoming fleet. She twirled her index fingers in the air and two cyclones rose out of the water between the *Dolly Llama* and the *Vengeance*. She pointed at the fleet and the cyclones whizzed toward the pirate ships like bulls released from a pen. The pirates abandoned their vessels and dived into the water. The cyclones crashed into two of the five ships and obliterated them completely.

While Alex stalled the fleet, the crew aboard the *Dolly Llama* unloaded four heavy chests filled with weapons. They stuffed their vests, pants, coats, and boots with as many rifles, swords, and daggers as possible. Conner ran belowdecks and retrieved the twins' backpacks. As he headed back up, he found the Rosary Chicken on the steps behind him.

"Bagawk?" the chicken asked, tilting her head.

"I'm sorry, but battle is no place for a chicken," Conner said. "You need to stay on the ship."

"Bagawk!" she squawked, horribly offended.

"I'm not *calling* you a chicken—you *are* a chicken!" he said. "This is ridiculous! I'm arguing with a typo!"

The Rosary Chicken puffed out her feathers and extended her wings. She had the heart of a turkey, the determination of a duck, and the bravery of a goose. Misspelled or not, she was ready for combat.

"Fine, but you have to stay in my bag," Conner said.

He tucked the Rosary Chicken into his backpack and left the zipper open enough so the chicken could peek her head out. Conner met his sister on the upper deck and handed Alex her backpack. They joined Auburn Sally and Admiral Jacobson in a boat and were lowered into the water. Once the entire crew was off the *Dolly Llama*, they rowed the boats to the shore of Starboardia.

Smoky-Sails Sam's men weren't too far behind. All five hundred pirates swam after the *Dolly Llama*'s crew. There was so much splashing, it looked like a school of hungry sharks was headed for the island.

"Everyone follow me," Conner told the crew. "The fortress is just through these trees!"

Alex, Auburn Sally, Admiral Jacobson, and the crew followed Conner as he raced through the tropical trees. The admiral's first mate gave Somersault Sydney a piggyback ride so she could keep up. Except for a few birds and a couple of large iguanas, the island was mostly deserted. They emerged into a clearing in the center of the island and found the legendary fortress of Starboardia.

"My God," Auburn Sally said.

"Conner." Alex gasped. "It's amazing!"

It was a breathtaking sight and everyone stopped in their tracks to take it in. The fortress was like a large Mayan pyramid constructed entirely out of broken pieces from hundreds of old ships. Everywhere they looked they spotted masts, bowsprits, sails, planks, bows, wheels, rudders, crow's nests, and flags all pieced together to form one massive structure.

It was twelve levels high and looked like a labyrinth of ladders, slides, rope bridges, swings, and tunnels. It was like a gigantic jungle gym, but it definitely wasn't for children. The structure was built on stilts over a shallow lake with sharp rocks that was home to dozens of alligators. The only way inside the pyramid was up a rickety staircase that led to the first level.

The *Dolly Llama*'s crew carefully climbed up the steps and entered the fortress. The inside was hollow and the bottom floor gave a perfect view of the eleven levels above it. Hanging in the very center of the pyramid like a chandelier was a heavy net filled with a dozen large boulders. It hung from a chain connected to a ceiling full of gears, and was secured by twenty-one ropes. Scattered all over the floor were the safe areas outlined in red that Conner had informed them about.

"Well," Alex said as she glanced around the fortress uneasily. "Is it like you were expecting?"

"That and more," Conner said breathlessly. "I feel like I planted a seed and all this grew."

The crew heard the trees rustling outside the pyramid. They walked to the edge of the first level and saw Smoky-Sails Sam's army of five hundred pirates emerge into the clearing. The men were so rugged and filthy, they made Auburn Sally's pirates look like contestants in a beauty pageant. They were soaking wet from their swim, and thanks to the red worms Alex had left on the Parakeet Islands, their raggedy clothes were stained with bird droppings. After a wild-goose chase around the Caribbean, the pirates were ready to take out their aggression on the *Dolly Llama*'s crew.

Most of the pirates were covered in tattoos and had missing limbs, teeth, eyeballs, and ears. Their appendages weren't replaced by traditional hooks and peg legs, but rather by daggers, razors blades, and metal spears.

Smoky-Sails Sam was in the last group of pirates to step into the clearing. He was seven feet tall with a long dreadlock beard. His coat, hat, belt, and boots were all made from black leather. A long sword proportionate to his height and a silver revolver hung from his belt. His appearance was just as intimidating as his reputation.

The pirate known as Killy Billy stood beside him. He had large bulging eyes and greasy hair. He was shirtless and his chest, arms, and back were covered with tattooed tally marks—each strike represented someone he had killed.

Just like the *Dolly Llama* crew had, Smoky-Sails Sam's men stared up at the structure in astonishment, as if they were facing a forgotten Wonder of the World.

"What do we have here," Smoky-Sails Sam said in a deep, raspy voice. "It looks like little Christine Connelly has discovered Starboardia."

"Look: up there!" Killy Billy said. He pointed to the crew on the first level of the fortress. "It's the *thief* and her hags! And they have Admiral Jacobson and his navy dogs with them!"

"Joined forces to finish me off, have you?" Smoky-Sails Sam chuckled. "It's going to take more than an ancient *tree house* to defeat my men."

The *Dolly Llama*'s crew gulped in fear. Auburn Sally put on a brave face and roared with laughter.

"Did you hear that?" the captain asked. "Smoky-Sails Sam thinks he has *men*! It's funny, because I don't see any *men* below us—I only see *swine*."

The pirates roared angrily at the women and men on the pyramid.

"Don't worry, boys," Smoky-Sails Sam said. "We'll put Captain Auburn Sally in her place! Just like everyone who steals from me, *she'll end up at the bottom of the Atlantic*! ATTACK!"

The pirates charged up the staircase and stormed into the fortress. The *Dolly Llama* crew spread out on all levels of the pyramid and Smoky-Sails Sam's men followed them. The clanking of swords echoed through the structure as Auburn Sally's women and Admiral Jacobson's men bravely took on Smoky-Sails Sam's crew.

Once all five hundred pirates were inside the structure,

Auburn Sally pointed her pistol at the ropes supporting the net of boulders and fired. The net descended several feet, pulling on the gears above, and the fortress came to life.

The pyramid worked more like a clock than Conner was anticipating. As the gears were pulled by the net, all twelve levels of the fortress rotated. The even levels turned clockwise, the odd levels turned counterclockwise, and the booby traps were triggered. The first chime went off and the *Dolly Llama* crew quickly found areas marked in red to stand on, crouch under, or hide behind.

Winking Wendy and the navy sailors were fighting Sam's pirates on the first level. They stepped into red circles drawn on the floor and watched as all the pirates around them fell through trapdoors and plunged into the lake below the fortress.

The alligators splashed around happily—the conflict above was going to supply the biggest meal they ever had.

The second level of the pyramid was covered in rope bridges. Sam's pirates chased Fish-Lips Lucy around one side and Pancake-Face Patty around the other, and the women met on a red platform between bridges. When the traps were set off, the bridges snapped like large slingshots and the pirates were launched off the pyramid.

Stinky-Feet Phoebe and Peg-Leg Peggy were dueling pirates in a long wooden tunnel between the third and fourth levels. Five seconds after the first chime went off, the women curled into a cubby outlined in red. A massive stone rolled through the tunnel, knocking Smoky-Sails Sam's men down like bowling pins. It rolled right past the women without leaving a scratch.

On the fifth level, Somersault Sydney and the admiral's first mate were battling eight of Sam's pirates each. They slid under a red platform just as stone blocks from the ceiling fell on top of their attackers. Somersault Sydney barely made it under the platform in time—she would have lost her legs if she hadn't already.

High-Tide Tabitha and Catfish Kate were fighting pirates back to back on a staircase between the sixth and seventh levels. They stayed on the only red step, and the rest of the staircase flattened into a slide. The pirates slid down the slide and into a shoot that dropped them into the lake below.

Big-Booty Bertha had taken a wrong turn on the eighth level and was surrounded by Smoky-Sails Sam's pirates. The floor was tiled and Big-Booty Bertha sighed with relief when she looked down and saw she was standing on the only red tile. Sharp spikes shot up from the floor and pierced through the pirates' feet. They grabbed their injured feet and hopped around in pain. Unfortunately, Big-Booty Bertha's backside was larger than the tile and one of her buttocks was scratched by a spike.

On the ninth level of the pyramid, Siren Sue was running from pirates shooting rifles at her. She dived behind a red door just as an avalanche of logs swept through the level. The pirates were knocked down and rolled off the pyramid with the logs.

Not-So-Jolly Joan and Too-Much-Rum Ronda wandered around the tenth level looking for someplace safe to hide. They weren't paying attention and fell right through a trapdoor and directly into a cage. It wasn't an ideal place to be, but the women figured they were safe enough. Too-Much-Rum Ronda and Not-So-Jolly Joan shared a bottle of rum while they watched their friends battle the pirates around them.

The floor of the eleventh level was covered with unstable floorboards that spun, teetered, or just broke as soon as they were stepped on. Auburn Sally and Admiral Jacobson fought Sam's pirates while keeping their balance on the stable floorboards painted red. To make matters worse, the eleventh level was also subjected to large swinging blades that the captain and the admiral had to avoid. The blades sliced into Sam's pirates and knocked them out of the pyramid.

From the twelfth and top level of the pyramid, Alex and Conner could see the *Dolly Llama* crew fighting the pirates on all the levels below. Conner heard something rattling at the bottom of his backpack and found that the Rosary Chicken had laid a bunch of eggs inside it—the excitement was too much for her.

"Not so brave now, are you?" Conner said.

The Rosary Chicken lowered her head in shame. The

twins threw the eggs at the pirates below, causing them to slip and slide off the structure. They caught the attention of Killy Billy, and the murderous pirate climbed up to the twelfth level, bringing a gang of pirates with him.

"Here, kiddy kiddies," the tattooed pirate called after them. "I've got enough room on my right arm for two more victims!"

"Go take a long walk off a short plank!" Conner yelled back.

Killy Billy and the pirates chased the twins around the top of the fortress. When they reached the south side, the floor crumbled under their feet. The twins spotted red monkey bars above and grabbed them to keep from falling. Unfortunately, Killy Billy and the pirates saw them, too, and hung from them as well. They swung toward the twins and tried to knock them off.

The Rosary Chicken fluttered out of Conner's backpack and began pecking at one of the pirates' fingers until they slipped from the bars. Then she moved on to the next pirate. Soon, Killy Billy was the only pirate left hanging. He kept one hand on the bars and reached for his rifle with the other. Alex gave him a nasty look and all the tally marks tattooed on his body magically turned into ticks. The pests dug into his skin and he screamed. He lost his grip on the bars and fell all the way through the fortress and landed in the lake below. The alligators dived after him, and Killy Billy never resurfaced.

Alex and Conner swung across the bars to solid floor. The Rosary Chicken crawled back into Conner's backpack and boastfully clucked up at him.

"Okay, you've redeemed yourself," Conner said. "Don't get a big head about it. No one likes a cocky chicken."

Every thirty seconds, another chime would ring, another rope would snap, and the *Dolly Llama* crew would find another red zone to shield themselves from the traps of the pyramid. Smoky-Sails Sam's pirates weren't so lucky. His men were dropping like flies around the fortress. Soon, they were reduced to half their original size, then to a quarter, and then the numbers between Smoky-Sails Sam's crew and the *Dolly Llama* crew were even. At this rate, it wouldn't be long before Sam's men were outnumbered.

Smoky-Sails Sam didn't care about his pirates as much as he cared about retribution. He pushed his way through the structure, carefully avoiding the traps, and headed for Auburn Sally.

When eleven of the twenty-one ropes had snapped and the pyramid was halfway through its course, all the traps ceased and the areas in red stopped being safe zones. Instead, the red platforms, cubbies, and tiles started transporting the *Dolly Llama* crew members to different levels throughout the fortress.

Winking Wendy was catapulted from the first level to the third by a spring hidden in the floor. Siren Sue was dropped into a slide on the ninth level that spat her out on the seventh. The platforms High-Tide Tabitha and Catfish

Kate stood on were connected and turned into a lift—High-Tide Tabitha descended into the level below, and her weight sent Catfish Kate into the level above.

Alex and Conner were standing on a red ledge when it suddenly collapsed and dumped them into a small cart. The cart rolled down a hidden track through the pyramid, and the twins felt like they were on a roller coaster. They tripped and pushed all the pirates as they zoomed past them and high-fived the *Dolly Llama* crew as they went.

On the eleventh level, Auburn Sally and Admiral Jacobson ran across a wooden bridge that suddenly dropped two levels down and swung through the air by chain ropes. Like a faulty elevator, every thirty seconds the bridge descended another two levels. The captain and the admiral would hop off the bridge, help their crew fight the remaining pirates, and then ride it down farther.

The element of surprise was exactly what the *Dolly Llama* crew needed to defeat the remaining pirates of Smoky-Sails Sam's fleet. The pirates lost all sense of the whereabouts of the men and women they were fighting, which left them confused and more vulnerable. By now there were fewer than fifty of Sam's pirates left in the fortress. Not wanting to end up in the lake or fall into a trap, the remaining pirates evacuated the fortress and fled into the trees.

The *Dolly Llama* had successfully reduced Smoky-Sails Sam's crew to nothing, but there wasn't cause for celebration yet. Smoky-Sails Sam himself was nowhere to be found.

When the captain and the admiral's bridge dropped to the fifth level, Smoky-Sails Sam appeared out of nowhere and leaped onto the bridge with his sword raised.

Auburn Sally and Admiral Jacobson fought the manic pirate as the bridge swung and spun violently through the air. All three had to keep one hand on the railing so they weren't flung off it.

The *Dolly Llama* crew watched in horror as the bridge descended through the center of the pyramid—but there was nothing anyone could do. The twins' cart reached the first level and slid across the floor. They narrowly missed being crushed as the bridge crashed to the floor beside them.

Smoky-Sails Sam's sword was bent in the crash, so he tossed it aside. The large pirate picked up Auburn Sally by her coat and threw her across the floor. Admiral Jacobson charged him with his sword raised above his head. Smoky-Sails Sam swiftly removed the rifle from his belt and shot the admiral directly in the chest.

"*No!*" Alex screamed.

"*Admiral!*" his first mate yelled.

Jacobson's eyes fluttered shut and he collapsed on the floor. Smoky-Sails Sam turned and aimed his rifle at Auburn Sally. Alex tried to think of something magical to save the captain, but she was so distraught, her mind went blank.

"Any last words, *Christine*?" Smoky-Sails Sam growled.

"Yes," Auburn Sally said. *"In Red, Ain't Dead."*

The final chime rang through the structure. Smoky-Sails Sam looked to the floor and saw he had thrown Auburn Sally directly into an area outlined in red. The last rope snapped, and just as Smoky-Sails Sam glanced upward, the heavy net of boulders fell directly on top of him. The Starboardia fortress had finished the job.

It was so quiet, the *Dolly Llama* crew could hear one another's heartbeats. All eyes were on the slain admiral. Everyone assumed the captain was in shock, because she just stared at Admiral Jacobson's body as if he would get up at any moment.

Tears rolled down Alex's cheeks and she buried her face in her brother's shoulder. "This is so sad," she said. "I can't look."

Conner rubbed his sister's back as he looked around at the devastated men and women throughout the structure. He scrunched his lips to hide a smile—he knew something they didn't.

Admiral Jacobson suddenly sat straight up with a loud gasp that startled everyone in the pyramid. He pulled on a gold chain around his neck and lifted the Heart of the Caribbean out from under his shirt. The bullet had been stopped by the large ruby.

"Ouch," the admiral said as he rubbed his chest. "That still really hurt!"

As far as anyone was concerned, it was a miracle! The

fortress vibrated from the crew's thankful cheers. When Alex saw her brother smiling, she hit him in the chest.

"You knew that was going to happen the whole time, didn't you?" she asked. "You knew the admiral was going to live, and you just stood there and let us think he had been killed! You were playing with our emotions for fun!"

His sister's angry accusation made him laugh so hard, he could barely breathe.

"I'm sorry, but I wanted to see your reaction to the end of the story," Conner confessed. "The fact that you were so invested in the characters and didn't see the surprise coming means I did something right, *right*?"

Alex was so mad at her brother, she turned her back and walked a few steps away from him to calm down. Auburn Sally got to her feet and helped the admiral to his.

"Aren't you glad I gave you my heart?" Auburn Sally asked.

"Both times it saved my life," Admiral Jacobson said.

The captain and the admiral shared a passionate kiss, and the *Dolly Llama* crew whistled and hollered at the lovebirds.

"We did it!" Auburn Sally declared. "We defeated Smoky-Sails Sam and his fleet! His reign of terror in the Caribbean is over!"

The men and women cheered even louder than before. They embraced one another and held up their weapons in victory. Not-So-Jolly Joan and Too-Much-Rum Ronda raised their bottle from inside the cage.

"And since Commander Bailey has so generously and bravely helped us with our enemy, we must return the favor," the admiral added.

The *Dolly Llama* crew went silent and their postures sank. They were hoping to go on a vacation after defeating the most feared pirate on the ocean.

"How do we get there?" Auburn Sally asked. "I hope it's not by sailing in circles to the *left*."

Conner pulled his binder of short stories out of his backpack and set it on the floor. He flipped it open to the glowing pages of "Starboardia," and the beam of light illuminated the fortress.

"It's much easier than that," he said. "We just step through the beam of light and we'll be there in no time."

The pirates and the sailors stared down at the glowing book nervously. Their captain and admiral nodded at them reassuringly, but even they were a little apprehensive. Conner tapped Alex on the shoulder.

"Are you ready to go home, or are you going to stay behind and pout a little longer?" he asked with a sly grin.

It took everything in Alex not to smile back, but after a moment she couldn't resist.

"Okay—I suppose you got me," she said. "You're right, I wouldn't have been so worked up if I didn't care about the characters so much. It's a testament to good writing, and you should be pleased with yourself. I completely forgot we were even in your story. For a few moments there, I truly believed with all my heart that we were living through... through..."

"What?" Conner asked.

"Well." Alex laughed. *"A pirate adventure."*

CHAPTER ELEVEN

CURSES

The Masked Man hobbled through the Dwarf Forests as quickly as his injuries would let him. Anyone traveling through the forests alone had the right to be worried, but with the mythological creature on the loose, the thick trees around him were especially intimidating. He held Captain Hook's revolver tightly in his hand and dashed behind a tree whenever he heard a noise nearby.

He followed a river deep into the forest until it split off into Dead Man's Creek. The Masked Man limped alongside the creek, and by nightfall he reached the site where the Witches' Brew used to stand on the banks of the creek. The tavern was nothing but a pile of ruins now, and a hundred or so witches were spread out around the creek.

The Masked Man hid behind a tree and searched the area for his son. Although he had never seen him before, the Masked Man figured he'd be easy to spot in the crowd of tattered women.

Just like the rest of the world, the witches had been chased out of their homes throughout the kingdoms by the Literary Army. They fled to the forest and formed a camp near their former headquarters, constructing huts from the wreckage of the tavern. The witches sat casually in groups around campfires and cauldrons. They chatted and flipped through spell books as if they were magazines.

Whenever a campfire started dying out, Charcoaline would hawk a flaming loogie into it and the fire would re-ignite. Tarantulene had spun a large web between trees and feasted on bats and owls that got caught in it. Serpentina's long tongue picked the bugs crawling through Arboris's bark skin, which pestered Arboris greatly. Rat Mary glared and hissed at a dozen cats that another witch had brought from home.

At the top of the pile of wreckage, two thrones had been erected. The infamous Sea Witch sat on a seat made of multi-colored coral while she supervised the camp of witches. She stroked her pet cuttlefish, which rested in a bowl of salt water on the arm of her chair. Beside the Sea Witch, the second throne was made entirely of ice that never melted, but the seat was empty.

Morina leaned against a tree at the edge of the camp, keeping her distance from the other witches. She scowled at the women around her with disdain. She couldn't wait to cross into the Otherworld and get rid of them. The horned witch watched the moon like it was a clock, counting down the hours till she would put her plan in motion.

The Masked Man had scanned the whole area for a child and finally spotted a little boy chained to the tree Morina leaned on. The boy looked around the camp of witches with large, terrified eyes like he had awoken to a nightmare. The Masked Man was expecting the child to resemble him, but Emmerich looked nothing like his father. His pale skin, rosy cheeks, and dark hair were all trademarks of his mother.

"He's the spitting image of Bo Peep," the Masked Man whispered to himself.

Unlike a normal father, the Masked Man didn't fill with pride or tenderness upon seeing his son for the first time, but only with the eagerness of a possible opportunity. All he needed was to get Emmerich away from the witches—he just didn't know how or when.

A sudden chill filled the forest air, and all the witches stopped what they were doing and looked toward the north. A wave of frost flowed down Dead Man's Creek and froze the water. They heard bells in the distance, and a moment later the legendary Snow Queen appeared on a white sleigh pulled down the creek by two monstrous polar bears.

Emmerich was so frightened by the bears, he closed his eyes and looked the other way. The sleigh stopped in the center of the camp. Arboris and Serpentina helped the blind Snow Queen down. She used a long icicle like a cane. She held up a white sack and exposed her jagged teeth in a wide smile.

"I've found it!" the Snow Queen announced proudly. "I've found the dust!"

All the witches were rather underwhelmed, but they didn't dare show it on their faces. Morina, on the other hand, couldn't have looked more unimpressed.

"Dust?" Morina asked. "You traveled all the way to the Northern Mountains to bring back *dust*?"

The Snow Queen growled and pointed her cane toward the sound of Morina's voice. "For someone so consumed with the future, you know nothing about the past," she said. "The contents of this bag will ensure our conquest of the Otherworld."

Morina grunted. "By all means, *enlighten* me," she said. "What's in the sack?"

The other witches throughout the camp were curious, too, so they gathered around the Snow Queen.

"Many years ago, before there were witches and before there were fairies, the world was inhabited by angels and demons," the Snow Queen said. "The demons created a magic mirror that transformed the reflection of something pleasant into something foul and grotesque. It made humans look like hideous monsters and landscapes appear as wastelands. The demons got so much pleasure out of torturing the world, they decided to fly the mirror to heaven and torment the angels with it.

"As the demons flew up to heaven, the evil living inside the mirror became so excited, it started to laugh. The closer to heaven they flew, the harder the mirror laughed, until it cracked and vibrated. Just as the demons reached the pearly gates, the mirror was so delighted, it burst into thousands and thousands of pieces that rained onto the earth like *dust*. Most people avoided the dust, but others weren't so lucky. The people that got the dust in their eyes never saw anything pleasurable again, but only the flawed and ugly qualities of everything. Others breathed in the dust and their hearts were filled with hate, anger, and jealousy.

"After centuries of sending blizzards through the kingdoms, I collected the remaining specks," the Snow Queen continued. "My snowflakes cleansed the air and rinsed the land, and brought the dust specks back to me in the North Mountains through evaporation."

The witches were mesmerized by the story, but Morina was still unenthused.

"And what do we need the dust *for*?" she asked.

The Sea Witch crawled down the pile of debris to join the other witches.

"The Snow Queen and I used the dust to curse Ezmia

the Enchantress," the Sea Witch hissed. "Long before she became the dreaded Enchantress, Ezmia was the late Fairy Godmother's apprentice. The favoritism made all the other fairies jealous, and poor Ezmia was often ostracized, heartbroken, and lonely. Many times she would travel deep into the woods away from the fairies and cry. Ezmia always found the same tree and wept into its roots as if it were a friend's shoulder. She cried so much, her tears watered the tree and it grew taller than any other tree in the forest.

"Once this became a routine for Ezmia, the Snow Queen and I covered the tree's roots with the dust of the magic mirror. One day while she was sobbing, she breathed in a piece of it. Immediately, her heartbreak, sorrow, and loneliness were heightened. Her desire to become the next Fairy Godmother and help people was replaced with the desire to seek revenge and inflict pain on those who had wronged her."

Shivers went up the witches' spines as they recalled the Enchantress's terrifying reign over the fairy-tale world.

"We gave Ezmia the steps to create a portal into the Otherworld," the Snow Queen said. "Once she mastered the seven deadly sins, and dominated the past, present, and future of this world, she would have manifested a portal. Our plan was to travel into the Otherworld, unleash the Enchantress, and take it by storm! Unfortunately, she was killed before the portal was complete."

"Well, lucky us," Morina said. "Thanks to *my prediction*, we know a doorway will be formed between worlds, saving us the hassle of building our own portal."

Charcoaline stepped forward and bowed to the Sea Witch and the Snow Queen before she spoke.

"Is your current plan to curse Alex Bailey with the dust and unleash *her* on the Otherworld?" she asked, and then quickly stepped back with the others.

"Correct," the Snow Queen said. "However, we already tried cursing Alex with the dust. It sent her down a destructive path, leading to the obliteration of the Witches' Brew and her departure from the Fairy Council, but it didn't last for long. Alex is the granddaughter of the Fairy Godmother and a child of both worlds—magic is very strong with her—so it's going to take more than one piece."

"How much *dussst* will it take?" Serpentina asked.

"A handful should be enough," the Sea Witch said.

Morina rolled her eyes. "Are you sure your dust hasn't expired?" she asked.

The Sea Witch was getting tired of Morina's disrespectful attitude. She snapped her claws and charged toward Morina, but the Snow Queen held up her cane to stop her.

"See for yourself," the Snow Queen said.

She opened the bag and the witches peered inside it. The dust from the magic mirror looked like silver sand. With her long, frostbitten fingernail, the Snow Queen removed one piece and blew it toward the polar bears. One of the bears breathed it in through its large nostrils, and its eyes turned bright red. For no reason whatsoever, the bear started uncontrollably beating the other bear.

A violent fight broke out between the polar bears, and the

witches quickly backed away from them. The Snow Queen and the Sea Witch cackled at the belligerent beasts. The Snow Queen whistled at the bears, and they sat straight up—resisting the urge to continue fighting.

"I'm still not convinced this will work," Morina said. "Even if Alex becomes as dangerous as the Enchantress and vanquishes the Otherworld for us, what's preventing her from unleashing her fury on us?"

All the other witches nodded—Morina had a valid point.

"Just like you, Morina," the Sea Witch hissed, "the dust has room to be improved. Together, with the magic of all the witches here, we'll cast a spell on the dust so that once it enters Alex's system, we'll be able to control every move she makes."

The Snow Queen pointed her cane at the ground and a large icy cauldron appeared. She poured the bag of dust into the cauldron.

"Ladies, please join us," the Sea Witch said.

The Sea Witch and the Snow Queen held their hands over the cauldron and the dust began to glow. One by one, the other witches throughout the camp raised their hands toward the cauldron as well. With each addition, the light shined brighter and brighter. Morina was the most skeptical and the last witch to join in. Once all the witches were united, a powerful spell was cast. The earsplitting sound of a thousand screams emitted from the dust and echoed through the forest.

"It is done," the Sea Witch said. "Now we must find the girl."

The Snow Queen removed the cloth covering her eyes, and her empty sockets lit up like trains in dark tunnels. She predicted where the young fairy was, and once the answer came to her, the lights faded and she re-wrapped the cloth over her eyes.

"She's already in the Otherworld," the Snow Queen said. "One of us must travel there and make sure she ingests the dust."

The witches looked around at one another, but there were no volunteers. Although Morina hated following any orders but her own, she knew she was the best candidate for the task. Besides, her plan to betray the witches wouldn't succeed unless their plan to conquer the Otherworld succeeded first. If she helped them with this, they'd never suspect a thing.

"I'll go," Morina said.

"You?" Rat Mary asked. "I'd trust a *fairy* before I'd trust the likes of you."

"Take a look around you, rodent," Morina said. "I'm the only witch who could possibly blend into a world of humans. Besides, I traveled there when I captured the Masked Man's son—I know the location of a portal and how to use it."

Morina made a good case, and the witches didn't argue any further. They turned to the Sea Witch and the Snow Queen and let the elders decide.

"Very well," the Snow Queen said.

"How long before the doorway opens between worlds?" the Sea Witch asked.

"In a fortnight," Morina said. "I will not have time to return, so I'll meet you on the other side of the doorway. It will open in the forest, in the clearing of the three boulders. It leads to a large city in the Otherworld. I'll travel there now, infect Alex with the dust, and be there when you arrive."

"Do not disappoint us," the Snow Queen said.

The Sea Witch scooped the dust out of the cauldron with her claws and poured it back into the white sack. A little begrudgingly, she handed the sack over to Morina.

"See you all on the other side," Morina said.

The witch covered her horns with her hood and journeyed into the forest away from Dead Man's Creek. She walked with so much determination, she strolled directly past the Masked Man without noticing him.

For the Masked Man's plan of revenge to work, he needed a way into the Otherworld as much as he needed his son. He glanced between Morina and Emmerich, and decided to follow the witch now and come back for the boy later. He trailed after Morina as quietly as possible.

The Sea Witch still had reservations about trusting Morina with the task.

"What if she betrays us?" the Sea Witch asked.

The Snow Queen's blue lips curved into a sinister smile, and a raspy laugh erupted from the back of her throat.

"Morina will *try* to betray us, but she will fail," she said. "Once Alex Bailey is under the dust's spell, nothing will stop her—*nothing*!"

Hearing this scared Emmerich more than anything else had since his kidnapping. He whispered to himself and prayed with all his might that Alex might hear him wherever she was.

"They're coming for you.... They're coming for you...."

CHAPTER TWELVE

MAKING A SPLASH ON SYCAMORE DRIVE

I t took the Book Huggers three days to find Conner's current address on Sycamore Drive. In their defense, the Bailey family had moved twice in the past four years and it was difficult tracking them down. After camping outside their previous house, the girls pestered the current residents until they finally gave them the forwarding address.

The four teenagers walked purposefully down Sycamore Drive looking for Bob and Charlotte's house. The

Book Huggers were on a mission to finally expose the Bailey twins once and for all. A bag with tape recorders and a Polaroid camera swung from Mindy's shoulder. Once they gathered enough evidence, their questionable reputation would be cleared and every school administrator, police officer, and representative in their community would owe them a massive apology.

It was a thrilling and nerve-racking endeavor, and their hearts were pounding as they walked down the street. Wendy got a little carried away and dashed from street lamp to street lamp and mailbox to mailbox like a secret agent.

"Wendy, knock it off!" Mindy ordered. "You're going to draw attention to yourself. Everyone act *natural!*"

Their anxiety was so high, the Book Huggers forgot what *natural* looked like. Cindy walked taller than usual and waved at all the neighbors like she was in a parade. Lindy swung her arms and swiveled her head like a cartoon character. Wendy skipped aggressively and broke a sweat.

"Too natural!" Mindy said. "Lindy, I told you to bring your dog! We would have blended in more if we were walking a basset hound."

"But Angela Lansbury has arthritis in her paws," Lindy said. "She has to be dragged around on a skateboard! That would have drawn even more attention!"

"Okay, fine, if we can't move clandestinely, then let's move quickly," she said. "The sooner we get out of the view of the public, the better."

By *the public*, Mindy was referring to an old man

watering his lawn, a pair of kids playing basketball, and an overweight cat napping on a porch. None of the neighbors were paying attention to the Book Huggers, let alone suspicious of them.

"There it is!" Cindy said, and pointed to one of the homes. "That's Conner's house!"

The Book Huggers bumped into one another as if Cindy were pointing out a poisonous snake.

"Remember," Mindy said, "if anyone catches us, we're here for a school project."

Not so *clandestinely*, they tiptoed up the house's driveway and crawled on their hands and knees through the flower bed. They regretted wearing shorts and short sleeves, because the roses' thorns scratched up their arms and legs—but there was no going back now. They slowly sat up and peered through the window.

Inside, the Book Huggers saw Charlotte Gordon vacuuming the living room. The house was spotless, but she was vigorously cleaning anyway, as if the home were covered in invisible dirt only she could see. It had been two and a half days since Charlotte's children traveled into her son's short story, and since she hadn't heard a word from them, cleaning was therapeutic for her overwhelming sense of helplessness.

Conner's binder of short stories was still in the center of the floor in the exact spot he had left it. Charlotte was afraid she might break something if she moved it, so she carefully cleaned around it.

"Honey, why don't you have a seat?" Bob said from the couch.

"Not now, I'm distracting myself from my thoughts," Charlotte said over the vacuum.

Bob got up and pulled the plug, but it didn't stop his wife. She wiped all the surfaces, fluffed all the pillows, and straightened all the couch cushions.

"Stressing isn't going to help anything," he said. "I'm sure they're going to be just fine. It's probably taking longer than they thought to track down Avalon Tammy, or whatever her name was."

"I know," Charlotte said with a sigh. "I wish I was as capable of handling myself as they are of handling themselves. Mothers get trained in how to deliver their children, how to care for and nurture them, how to develop their motor skills and self-esteem—but no one trains you in how to *stop worrying about them*! They say childbirth is the worst part, but it's just the beginning of the pain!"

Charlotte sat on the couch in defeat. Bob sat next to her and put his arm around her.

"I hate to say it, but this is the price you pay for raising two wonderful, intelligent, and responsible young adults," he said.

"I almost wish they weren't so independent," she confessed. "It'd be nice if they needed *their mother* once in a while. Maybe I'd get to see them more often."

The binder suddenly popped open on its own and the beam of light shot straight out of it. A moment later, Conner poked his head out of the beam and had a look around the living room. The sight of Conner's floating head made the eavesdropping Book Huggers flail around the flower bed. They covered one another's mouths so their screams weren't heard.

"Hey guys!" Conner happily greeted his mom and step-dad. "Good news! We found the pirates."

"That's terrific!" Charlotte said. "I was so worried. What took you so long? Was everything all right?"

"Everything went *great*," Conner said with a laugh. "Actually, it couldn't have gone *smoother*. It just took a little longer to track down Auburn Sally than we thought."

"Oh, *Auburn Sally*—that's her name," Bob said. "See, Charlotte, I told you everything was going to be fine."

"Can we bring the pirates into the house now?" Conner asked.

"Just a second," Charlotte said. She retrieved the welcome mat from the porch and set it beside the binder. "Have them wipe their feet on the mat on their way in. I just vacuumed."

Conner nodded and popped back into the world of Starboardia to have a quick word with the *Dolly Llama* crew.

"Remember what I told you guys to say if my mom asks about Starboardia?" he asked.

The pirates and sailors repeated what they had rehearsed. *"It was a piece of cake. Nothing remotely dangerous happened at all,"* they said in unison.

"Perfect," Conner said. "Now, everyone step through

the beam and wipe your feet on the mat—my mom just vacuumed."

The pirates and sailors were puzzled—what was *vacuumed*?

One by one, the *Dolly Llama* crew followed Conner through the beam of light and stepped into the house. Not knowing what to expect, the pirates charged inside with their weapons raised—which nearly gave Charlotte and Bob heart attacks.

"Everybody calm down!" Conner ordered. "You're all safe here!"

The living room filled up very quickly with the characters from "Starboardia." They looked around at all the furniture, decorations, and lighting fixtures in awe. It was the most extraordinary place they had ever been to. The spying Book Huggers had their camera and tape recorders ready, but they were so stunned to see the pirates appear, they dropped their devices and just watched in shock.

"It's like we've stepped into the nineteenth century!" Admiral Jacobson said.

"It's the twenty-first century, actually," Bob said.

"This chamber is so elegant," Winking Wendy said. "Does a royal family live here?"

"No—but thank you," Charlotte said. "It's amazing what a couple of throw pillows and an accent chair will do to a room."

Siren Sue was mesmerized by all the framed photographs on the mantel.

"Commander Bailey, these small portraits of you and your sister are so detailed," she said. "Your face was so round when you were younger."

"That's called a *school picture*," Conner said. "And it was right before a growth spurt."

Peg-Leg Peggy stared up at the ceiling in terror. "What sort of torture device is *that*?" she asked, and pointed her rifle at it.

"That's just a ceiling fan," Conner said. "Relax, it's not going to hurt you."

The pirates and sailors split up to explore the house. They bounced on the mattresses in the bedrooms, turned all the lights on and off, used the toilets to splash water on their faces, and opened and closed the appliances in the kitchen.

"I've found a cupboard that's as cold as winter!" Too-Much-Rum Ronda announced. "And it's full of fruit, vegetables, and colorful liquid!"

"That's the refrigerator, Ronda—stay out of there!" Conner said. "No one touch anything without asking!"

Charlotte and Bob watched nervously as the crew invaded and inspected every corner of their home. They weren't sure which pirate or sailor to follow, because everyone clearly needed supervision.

"Conner, we only have one guest bedroom," Charlotte said. "Where are all your friends supposed to sleep?"

"Don't worry, none of the pirates or sailors are sleeping inside," Conner said.

He said it like it should have been a relief, but it only

concerned his mother more. Charlotte was going to ask him for more details, but she was distracted when Alex suddenly leaned out from the beam of light.

"Hi, Mom—hi, Bob!" she said, then looked to her brother. "Conner, we're ready!"

Alex leaned back and disappeared. Conner went to the window and had a good look at the large pool in their backyard.

"Hey, Bob, how deep is the pool?" he asked.

Bob shrugged. "Ten, maybe twelve feet," he said. "Why do you ask?"

Before Conner could answer, he scooped up the binder and ran into the backyard. The Book Huggers quickly got to their feet and ran to the other side of the property. They peeked between boards and through holes in the fence to see into the backyard. Conner stood at the edge of the pool and aimed the binder's beam of light directly at the water.

"Go for it, Captain!" he said.

Bob and Charlotte joined Conner outside just in time to see the *Dolly Llama* emerge from the binder and land in the pool. Charlotte and Bob screamed and grabbed on to each other. The splash knocked half the water out of the pool and drenched Conner and his parents.

It was too much for the Book Huggers to take. All four girls fainted at once and collapsed in a pile behind the fence.

"*Charlotte,*" Bob said quietly, in shock. "*There's a pirate ship in our pool....*"

"Sorry," Conner said. "The captain was adamant about bringing her ship along. But the good news is that the pirates live in it, so you don't have to worry about them sleeping in the house."

"*Right,*" Charlotte said with large eyes. "*Nothing to worry about.*"

Had the *Dolly Llama* been just a tiny bit bigger, it wouldn't have fit in the pool. Auburn Sally and Alex were standing on the upper deck behind the wheel and had a great view of the neighborhood. The Rosary Chicken was perched on the ship's railing beside them.

"So this is the land of Sycamore Drive?" Auburn Sally asked.

"It's just one of many neighborhood streets in the town," Alex said.

"I like it," the captain said. "The cottages in this village are very charming."

Auburn Sally kicked down a gangplank and she, Alex, and the Rosary Chicken climbed down from the *Dolly Llama*. The Rosary Chicken happily waddled onto the grassy yard and pecked at bugs. The twins introduced Auburn Sally to Bob and Charlotte, and the captain gave them each a very firm handshake.

"It's an honor to meet you," Auburn Sally told them. "You have very crafty children."

"Tell me about it," Charlotte said.

"It's never a dull moment," Bob said. "Wait, is that chicken wearing a rosary?"

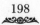

Now that the twins had successfully escorted the *Dolly Llama* crew into the Otherworld, they immediately began planning their next venture. Conner opened his binder to the second tab, retrieved the Portal Potion from his backpack, and poured three drops on the pages of his next story. Another beam of light appeared and shined into the sky like a spotlight.

"Time for our second stop," Conner said.

"What's your next story about?" Alex asked.

"'Galaxy Queen' is an intergalactic space odyssey," he explained. "It takes place in the year 3000 and follows the queen of a Cyborg civilization as she travels through the universe."

Alex took a deep breath. "It doesn't get easier after 'Starboardia,' does it?"

"Not really," Conner said. "But at least we *learned* a lot from 'Starboardia.'"

"Is there anything I can help with beforehand?" Alex asked. "Think about it."

"There is, actually—we're going to need space suits," he said.

Alex snapped her fingers and their clothes transformed into chic, shiny, and futuristic space suits. Their suits were silver and had round helmets, and there were oxygen tanks attached to their backs.

"These are perfect!" Conner said excitedly.

Charlotte put a hand over her heart. "You both look *so cute!*" she said. "Stay right there—I need a photo of this!"

"Mom, we really don't have time to take a—"

Charlotte gave her son a dirty look that said a thousand words, but most specifically: *There are fifty pirates in my house and a ship in my backyard pool. You WILL take a photo for me whether you like it or not.* Conner didn't say another word, and his mother ran into the house and returned with her camera.

"Stand on the grass so I can get the pirate ship in the background," Charlotte instructed. "That's nice! Now put your arms around each other—smile! This is going on the Christmas card!"

"Mom, this is top secret! You can't put this on a Christmas card!" Conner said.

"Calm down, no one is going to know what you're doing," Charlotte said. "Everyone will just think we took a vacation to a theme park—you know, like *normal families* do. Okay, now just a couple more with my phone!"

Begrudgingly, the twins smiled and posed as their mother took a dozen pictures. Once she was finished, they were permitted to continue their plans. The twins tightened their helmets, turned their oxygen tanks on, and toed up to the binder of short stories.

"Next stop, 'Galaxy Queen'!" Conner said.

CHAPTER THIRTEEN

GALAXY QUEEN

The twins stepped into the beam of light and re-entered the world of Conner's handwriting. The words *the universe* stretched around them, and before they knew it, they were floating through an endless galaxy. They were surrounded by thousands and thousands of stars—it was a breathtaking sight, and the twins had never felt so small in their lives.

All gravity disappeared, and the weightlessness gave the twins a falling sensation in the pit of their stomachs that didn't go away. They moved their arms and legs and tried swimming through the emptiness, but there was absolutely nothing to swim against.

Conner barely caught the corner of his binder before it floated out of reach, and tucked it safely into his backpack with the flask of Portal Potion.

In the distance, Alex and Conner could see a large white planet with multi-colored clouds, but they were still thousands of miles away from its atmosphere. The planet looked delicious—like a large piece of candy floating in space.

"What's that?" Alex asked.

"That's Jawbreakeropolous," Conner said. "I had a sweet tooth when I wrote this story."

It was difficult to make out at first, but the twins saw a small light traveling toward the planet. It orbited around Jawbreakeropolous and after the eighth or ninth rotation it shot out a green laser that engulfed the planet. In a matter of seconds, Jawbreakeropolous shrunk and vanished from the universe.

"What just happened?" Alex asked. "Why did the planet disappear?"

"It didn't disappear, it was *uploaded*," Conner explained. "That thing circling Jawbreakeropolous is the *BASK-8*, the Cyborg Queen's spaceship. She travels the galaxy looking for habitable planets in other star systems' Goldilocks zone. When she finds a planet she likes, her spaceship uploads it into its hard drive, and then she takes it back to her home solar system."

"What's a Goldilocks zone?" Alex asked.

"It's the area of every solar system that's *not too hot* and *not too cold* to host life," Conner said. "That's actually what scientists call it—I swear I'm not making it up!"

"Why does the Cyborg Queen need so many planets?"

"The Cyborgs have outgrown their home planet and need more room," he said. "The queen travels with an army aboard her ship in case she runs into any trouble. We need to get aboard the *BASK-8* and convince her to let us borrow her soldiers."

Conner opened the binder and aimed the beam of light in all directions around him, like a busted lighthouse, to get the *BASK-8*'s attention. It must have done the trick, because the spaceship zoomed toward the twins and within a few seconds was hovering just a hundred yards away from them. The *BASK-8* was the shape and size of a cruise ship. It was made from red steel and had wings like a plane. A cluster of satellites and antennas near the top made the spaceship look like it was wearing a crown.

"Whatever happens, just follow my lead," Conner told his sister. "I'm not going to tell them I'm their creator—I learned that lesson in 'Starboardia'—but I think I've got something up my sleeve that will work."

"You're the boss," Alex said.

Large speakers stuck out on both sides of the *BASK-8* and someone aboard spoke to the twins. The voice was very proper and sounded awfully familiar, but Alex couldn't tell who it reminded her of.

"Attention, unidentified life-forms," the voice said. "Please state your name, species, and home star system."

"I'm Conner Bailey and this is Alex," he announced. "We're human beings from the planet Sycamore Drivious of the Willow Crestian system."

"What are you doing in the middle of space?" the voice asked.

"Our spaceship was hijacked by Orphianotics," Conner said. "Would you mind giving us a lift back to our planet?"

Conner was confident the tall tale would grant them admission to the *BASK-8*, and he gave Alex a thumbs-up. She hoped whatever plan he had cooking was going to work. There was silence from the speaker as whoever was on the other end considered the request.

"Any enemy of the Orphianotics is a friend of ours," the voice said. "Please, come aboard."

A large compartment door opened and two steel claws reached out of the *BASK-8* and plucked the twins from space like stuffed animals in an arcade prize machine. They were pulled into a large hangar where several smaller spaceships were kept. The *BASK-8* had artificial gravity, so the twins hit the floor as soon as they entered.

Once the compartment door was shut behind them, a pair of automatic doors on the other side of the hangar opened. A lizard the size of a man walked in with two Cyborgs on either side of him.

The lizard had big yellow eyes and red slimy skin and wore a gray jumpsuit with several buttons. The Cyborgs were half human, half robotic in a variety of combinations. Some were human with robotic arms and legs; others were split evenly down the middle. They all wore red goggles and held guns with barrels that pulsated bright blue light. They also wore vests that monitored their heartbeat and/or remaining battery percentage.

Alex and Conner quickly got to their feet and the Cyborgs raised their weapons toward them. The lizard man cautiously looked the twins up and down.

"Neither Sycamore Drivious nor the Willow Crestian system are registered in the intergalactic database," the lizard man said with the same voice they had heard outside.

"Oh..." Conner said. "That's because we hate solicitors."

The lizard man stepped toward the twins to inspect them further.

"You're awfully young to be traveling through the universe by yourselves," the lizard man said. "Were there more in your crew?"

"We had an android chaperone, but the Orphianotics stole him, too," Conner explained. "Darn those filthy creatures!"

The lizard man nodded to the Cyborgs and they lowered their weapons.

"I'm Commander Newters," the lizard man said. "Welcome to the *BASK-8*. You may remove your helmets—this ship is equipped with oxygen."

The twins unscrewed their helmets and shook Commander Newters's hand.

"Thank you so much for rescuing us," Conner said. "We would have been goners if it weren't for you."

"I'm sorry to hear about your unfortunate encounter with the Orphianotics," Newters said. "The Cyborg Queen has made many exhausting requests to the United Universe Council to ban them from our quadrant of the galaxy, but they won't listen to her."

"What are the Orphianotics?" Alex asked, forgetting to go along with the story her brother was describing. "They stole our ship so quickly, I didn't get a good look at them."

"They're a terrible species," Newters explained. "They destroyed their home planet, and now they travel through the galaxy stealing resources from other star systems."

"But isn't that sort of what the Cyborg Queen does, too?" Alex asked.

"That's *exactly* what the United Universe Council said," Newters said. "Never mind that, we would be happy to escort you to your home planet. The queen loves traveling to new star systems—I'm sure she'd be delighted to see Sycamore Drivious in Willow Crestian."

A loud alarm suddenly went off, startling the twins. The hangar was filled with flashing red lights. Commander Newters and the Cyborgs looked around in panic.

"Oh no!" Newters said. "This is terrible!"

"What's happening—are we under attack?" Alex asked.

"Worse," Newters said. "That alarm means the queen has awoken early from her charging slumber! She's always

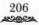

in a terrible mood if she doesn't get a full twenty hours. I must get to the Command Bridge before she arrives!"

Newters and the Cyborgs bolted through the automatic doors and the twins ran after them. They ran through the spaceship, passing several hallways full of frantic half-human, half-robotic men and women. The alarm was even louder outside the hangar and was accompanied by a voice that repeated, *"The queen is awake, the queen is awake, the queen is awake."*

They finally reached the Command Bridge in the center of the ship. It was a wide room with a gigantic set of windows that had a view of the galaxy ahead. The walls were covered in screens with information about different parts of the space-ship, the queen's location, and the universe around them. There were dozens of control stations scattered around the Command Bridge like desks in a classroom. Each station was covered in hundreds of blinking buttons, dials, and levers.

In preparation for the Cyborg Queen's arrival, the Cyborg crew throughout the Command Bridge lubricated their joints, tightened their screws, and polished the steel covering their bodies.

"How close is she?" Newters asked the nearest Cyborg.

"She's descending from her chambers now, Com-mander," the Cyborg said. "The levels of her emotion chip are off the charts—she must be upset about something!"

The Cyborg pointed to the queen's private elevator in the back of the Command Bridge. All the Cyborgs stood at their control stations just as the elevator doors opened. There was a collective hiss as their mechanical bodies compressed into bows. Alex and Conner followed their example and bowed, too.

The Cyborg Queen was more robotic than anyone else aboard the *BASK-8*. She was only humanoid from the chest up, and even that was questionable. Her nose, her chin, and most of her forehead were covered in metal plates. Her left eye was a camera lens, and instead of hair, her head was covered in wires that wove through a beehive of gears like the film in a projector. On the top of her head, above the wires and gears, was a steel crown. The word *QUEEN* blinked on it like the numbers on a digital alarm clock.

The queen had thin metal arms, and her steel body was shaped to look like she was wearing a gown. She had wheels instead of legs and rolled out of the elevator and into the Command Bridge. The twins could tell she was mad because her lens was twitching and a few of her wires snapped and stuck straight up.

"Your Majesty," Commander Newters said with a deep bow. "We weren't expecting you to wake early. Did you have a restful charge?"

"*Someone* left the gravity on in my chambers while I was charging," the Cyborg Queen said sharply. "Not only did it prevent me from a restful charge, but when I awoke, the human side of my face was *puffy!*"

With this, Alex realized why the "Galaxy Queen" was so familiar—she was embarrassed it had taken this long to click. Without a doubt, the Cyborg Queen was based on Red Riding Hood, Commander Newters was based on Froggy, the Orphianotics were based on the orphans Red despised, the *BASK-8* was a clever play on *basket*, and the Cyborg Queen's passion for collecting planets was based on Red's passion for real estate.

"You *didn't*," Alex whispered to her brother.

Conner knew exactly what she was referring to by her smile.

"Yeah, I *did*," he whispered back.

The Cyborg Queen rolled through the Command Bridge and glared at her Cyborg crew, waiting for one of them to step forward.

"Well?" she said. "Someone better claim responsibility or I'll take away battery privileges for the entire ship!"

The smallest Cyborg in the Command Bridge became so nervous, he began short-circuiting. Sparks flew out of his mechanical neck and his head started spinning. He fell to his metal knees and pleaded for forgiveness.

"I'm so sorry, Your Majesty!" the small Cyborg said. *"I was inspecting the artificial gravity generator and forgot to adjust the pressure in your chambers!"*

The Cyborg Queen rolled her human eye and her lens pointed upward.

"Commander Newters, please have this Cyborg re-started before he catches on fire," she ordered. "And have him re-programmed to remember the priorities of his assignments."

"Yes, ma'am," Newters said, and nodded to the Cyborg soldiers. "Take him to the Upgrade Center."

Against the small Cyborg's will, the soldiers escorted him out of the Command Bridge. The Cyborg Queen rolled to the center of the room and the bottom half of her body transformed into a throne. The Cyborg crew took it as a cue to be seated at their control stations.

"Was Jawbreakeropolous uploaded successfully?" the Cyborg Queen asked.

"Yes, Your Majesty," Newters said. "It's been safely added to the hard drive and will be a wonderful addition to your home system.

"Then why are we still in *this* solar system?" the queen asked. "Shouldn't we be at Gumdropida by now?"

"We were en route to the next planet when we answered a distress call," Newters informed her.

"A distress call?" the Cyborg Queen asked. "From whom?"

Newters cleared his throat and gestured for the twins to come stand beside him. Alex and Conner cautiously approached Newters and the Cyborg Queen. Her lens popped several inches out of her head to examine them.

"Who are you?" she asked.

"Hello, Your Electronicness," Conner said. "My name is Conner and this is my sister, Alex. We're human beings from the planet Sycamore Drivious of the Willow Crestian system."

The Cyborg Queen squinted her human eye at them.

"I've never heard of such places," she said. "What are you doing in this part of the galaxy?"

"We were stranded and left for dead after our ship was stolen by Orphianotics," Alex said. "Your commander kindly saved our lives and brought us aboard."

The mention of the Orphianotics' name infuriated the Cyborg Queen. Two exhaust pipes shot out of her shoulders and steam erupted from them.

"I HATE Orphianotics!" she yelled. "I'll admit there are few alien species I can stomach, but the Orphianotics are *extra-terrible extraterrestrials*! I've begged the United Universe Council to do something about it, but they refuse! They had the audacity to tell me collecting planets is no different from the destruction those scoundrels cause! But I don't *steal resources* from other planets, I just move them into a better neighborhood!"

Conner waited for the Cyborg Queen to let off all her steam before he said another word.

"You know, the Orphianotics aren't allowed in our solar system," he said. "They were kicked out eons ago. If you wouldn't mind giving us a ride back to Sycamore Drivious, we'd love to give you a tour of the Willow Crestian system."

"No Orphianotics, you say?" the Cyborg Queen asked. "Perhaps I should move my planets to your system. What type of star does Willow Crestian revolve around? White dwarf? Blue dwarf? Yellow dwarf? Red giant? I like knowing I have at least two hundred billion years left in a new system before making such a big commitment."

Conner wasn't sure how to answer. "It's a *seventh* dwarf," he said. "Yup, seven white dwarves from the Milky Snow White Galaxy combined into one and *boom*—the Willow Crestian system was formed."

The Cyborg Queen nodded as she gave it some thought. She had never heard of stars combining in such a manner, and the impossibility intrigued her.

"I'd like to see this Willow Crestian," she said. "We'd be delighted to give you a lift to your home planet. Unfortunately, there are a few stops we need to make along the way. There are a handful of planets I need to inspect and collect before the Orphianotics get to them. I hope you don't mind waiting."

"No worries," Conner said. "We'd be happy to accompany you!"

"Marvelous," the Cyborg Queen said. "Commander Newters, take us to Gumdropida, please."

"Full speed to Gumdropida!" Newters ordered the crew.

The Cyborgs went to work pressing buttons at their control stations. The *BASK-8* shot through the galaxy at light speed. The powerful jerk almost knocked Alex over and she screamed. The Cyborg Queen gave her a funny look—surely this wasn't her first time experiencing light speed.

"She doesn't get out much," Conner said.

The *BASK-8* whizzed through the stars and then slowed down as it approached the new planet. Gumdropida was bright orange and covered with snowy mountain ranges. The spaceship orbited the planet, and information about Gumdropida loaded on all the screens in the Command Bridge. A detailed hologram of the planet appeared in front of the Cyborg Queen's throne.

"Gumdropida," Newters read from a screen. "It has a diameter of three thousand four hundred seventy-eight miles. Surface temperatures range from negative ninety degrees to positive thirty degrees Fahrenheit. Atmosphere is made of helium. Currently there is no life on the planet, but forty percent of it is habitable for a Cyborg population."

"It would be perfect for that ski resort I've been itching to build," the Cyborg Queen said. "Upload the planet!"

The green laser shot out of *BASK-8* and surrounded Gumdropida. Just like Jawbreakeropolous had, the orange planet shrank and disappeared from the universe. The words *Upload Complete* appeared on all the screens in the Command Bridge.

"The upload was successful, Your Majesty," Newters said.

"Splendid. Please proceed to the next planet," the Cyborg Queen ordered.

The *BASK-8* raced through the galaxy in a different direction and arrived at the next planet. It was green and had white clouds spiraling through its atmosphere. Whatever sweet tooth Conner had when he wrote this story was contagious, and suddenly Alex had a strong craving for candy.

"Mintune," Newters read from the screen. "It has a diameter of fifty-four thousand six hundred thirty-two miles. Surface temperatures range from five degrees to two hundred and three degrees Fahrenheit. Atmosphere is made up of sulfuric gases. The planet is home to an alien species known as Gas Whales, but only five percent is habitable for a Cyborg population."

"*Pass,*" the Cyborg Queen said. "Five percent isn't worth an upload—and I loathe neighbors. Proceed to the next planet."

The queen was served hot oil in a teacup as the *BASK-8* traveled through space to the next planet. However, when the spaceship arrived, they found nothing but a field of crunchy-looking asteroids.

"Oh dear," Newters said. "It appears Granolia was hit by a comet and this is all that remains. Shall we continue ahead, Your Majesty?"

At first the Cyborg Queen slouched with disappointment, but her attitude quickly changed when an exciting idea popped into her head. The twins knew she had had an idea because a flashing lightbulb stuck out of her crown.

"You know, our solar system could use a *belt*," the queen said. "Upload the asteroids and we'll place them between Blousery and Skirturn when we get home."

The Cyborg crew did as they were told and then proceeded to the next stop. The back-to-back light speed was making Alex a little nauseated. The subsequent planet was a russet color and had a rocky surface.

"Nutfugdus," Newters read from the screen. "It has a diameter of two thousand seven hundred seventy-nine miles. Surface temperatures range from fifty degrees to three hundred degrees Fahrenheit. Atmosphere is very thin and made of carbon monoxide. Fifty-six percent of the planet is habitable for Cyborg life. Nutfugdus once hosted an alien species known as the Desert Ferrets, but they're extinct."

"Wonderful!" the Cyborg Queen said. "I love a good dry heat. Upload!"

Once again, the *BASK-8* crew followed their queen's instructions. When the upload was finished, the spaceship zipped across the galaxy to the location of the following planet. Alex pulled her brother aside as it traveled.

"How much longer until we ask the Cyborg Queen to borrow her army?" Alex asked.

"Soon," Conner said. "There's only one more Goldilocks zone left with a planet the queen is going to go nuts over. We're going to help her upload it in exchange for the use of her Cyborg soldiers."

"Did you *intentionally* base a story about a queen who steals things from Goldilocks zones on Red Riding Hood?" Alex asked. "I can't decide if it's brilliant or brutal."

"Oh, I never thought about that," Conner said. "Red is going to kill me if she ever finds out."

The *BASK-8* arrived at the next planet. It was purple with turquoise rings and by far the most beautiful of all the planets they had visited so far. The Cyborg Queen was enchanted by it. Her throne transformed back into a gown and she rolled over to the hologram to take a closer look at the majestic world.

"What's the name of *this* beauty?" she asked.

"Lollipopigust, Your Majesty," Newters read from the monitor. "It has a diameter of three thousand ninety-nine miles. Surface temperatures range from twenty-five degrees to ninety degrees Fahrenheit. Atmosphere is made of pure oxygen, and ninety percent of the planet is habitable for Cyborg life."

"*I LOVE it—it's meant to be!*" the Cyborg Queen said, and clasped her metal hands together. "Upload it immediately! I'll share Jawbreakeropolous, Gumdropida, and Nutfugdus with the Cyborgs at home, but I want Lollipopigust for myself!"

The green laser engulfed the purple planet. But as Commander Newters read more information about Lollipopigust, a grave expression came over his red face. The commander bolted to a control station and pulled a red lever to abort the mission.

"*What are you doing?*" the queen demanded.

"Forgive me, Your Majesty, but I just read some troubling information," Newters said. "One thousand years ago, scientists from another planet sent a vial of insects to Lollipopigust to see if it would sustain life. The high oxygen levels in the atmosphere made the insects grow to enormous sizes and now they dominate the planet. If we upload Lollipopigust, it would be like uploading thousands of tiny viruses into our hard drive! The entire ship would crash."

The flashing lightbulb reappeared above the Cyborg Queen's crown. "Can't we send the army to Lollipopigust to terminate the insects?" she asked desperately.

Commander Newters shook his head. "The *BASK-8* has been traveling for so long, it doesn't have enough power to charge the soldiers' battle batteries," he said.

The queen's lightbulb went off again. "Can't they use their solar panels to charge their battle batteries?" she asked.

Commander Newters gulped. "That would only work while the soldiers were on the surface—but most of the insects live in colonies under the ground," he explained.

All the Cyborgs knew their queen wouldn't take the news well, so they dived under their control stations. The Cyborg Queen was so mad, the lightbulb above her crown burst and fiery blasts erupted from her exhaust pipes. Four robot legs wearing boots emerged from her steel gown and stomped the floor. Tears rolled down from her human eye and oil dripped from her lens.

"All I want is every habitable planet within a trillion-mile radius—it's not like I'm asking for *the world*!" the Cyborg Queen lamented. "Everyone put your brains and A.I. chips together! There's got to be something we can do!"

Once the fiery blasts had finished, Conner stepped toward the Cyborg Queen and tapped her on the exhaust pipes. Alex had no clue what her brother was up to.

"Excuse me, Your Mechanicalness, but I might have a solution," he said. "You see, my sister and I just happen to be the children of the best exterminator in the galaxy!"

"We are?" Alex said.

"Yes, *we are*!" Conner said, and sent her a dirty look. *"Meteor Magazine* gave our father four and a half nebulas out of five in their review, and the *Alien Voice* gave him three appendages up! Those are the most popular publications in the Willow Crestian system!"

The Cyborg Queen's eye and lens darted between Alex and Conner. Her eyebrows turned into tiny windshield wipers and cleaned the tears off her face.

"So the two of you could exterminate all the insects on the planet for me?" the queen asked hopefully.

"We *could*..." Conner said, lowering his head dramatically. "You've already been so kind to us by offering transportation back to our planet. I hate to ask you for *another* favor in exchange for exterminating the insects, but there is something *else* my sister and I could use your help with."

The Cyborg Queen wanted Lollipopigust so badly, she was willing to strike whatever bargain it took. "That's quite all right, just tell me what you have in mind."

"It's not for us, it's for our friends," Conner explained. "They live on a small planet called Fairytaletopia in the Storybookian Galaxy. Their planet has recently been invaded by a savage race known as the Literarious Villainomous."

"Bless you," Alex said.

Conner ignored his sister. "The Literarious Villainomous are twice as bad as the Orphianotics and ten times more powerful! The worst part is, Fairytaletopia has no way of defending itself."

"That sounds terrible!" the Cyborg Queen said.

"It is," Conner said. "But it's nothing your Cyborg army couldn't help with. If my sister and I exterminate the insects on Lollipopigust, would you lend us your soldiers to help our friends fight the Literarious Villainomous?"

It wasn't every day the Cyborg Queen was asked to lend out her army—however, it wasn't every day she came upon the planet of her dreams, either. She turned to the hologram of Lollipopigust and stroked it with her metal hand.

"Fine," the Cyborg Queen said. "Wipe that planet clean of insects, and I will let you use my Cyborg army to save Fairytaletopia."

Conner shook her metal hand appreciatively. "Thank you so much, Your Engineeredness," he said. "We couldn't be more grateful! Right, Alex?"

"Sure . . . *grateful*," she said unenthusiastically.

"Sure, sure," the Cyborg Queen said. "Commander Newters, please see that the humans from Sycamore Drivious have everything they need for their extermination plan. I'm going to my chambers now to finish my charge. Please see that the gravity is turned *off*, and wake me when the extermination is over."

"Yes, Your Majesty," Newters said with another deep bow.

The Cyborg Queen rolled into her private elevator and ascended through the ship. Alex yanked her brother aside.

"*Bugs?*" she asked. "*That's* your plan? We're going to kill bugs in exchange for soldiers?"

"Oh, come on," Conner said. "We'll get to travel to another planet and shoot at some overgrown pests! It'll be fun—like we're in a video game!"

Alex shook her head—she couldn't believe she had gone into this situation willingly. There were many times when Alex was convinced she and her brother were from different planets, and this just about proved it.

"Commander Newters," Conner said happily, "lead the way!"

CHAPTER FOURTEEN

UNIVERSAL PESTS

We're going to need two short-range blasters, one Omega GDD, and one Bio-Mat Compass," Conner said. "Oh, and the *2999 Moon Jumper Express* to get us there."

Commander Newters gave him a peculiar look. "You're very well informed as to our armory for someone who's never been aboard this ship before."

As if the *BASK-8*'s arsenal were a vending machine, Newters punched the codes of the devices Conner had requested into a touchscreen and they were brought out on a conveyor belt. The short-range blasters were long and silver with a bright blue light pulsating from the barrels, just like the Cyborg soldiers' guns. The Omega GDD was short and round like a propane tank and had a small keypad at the top. The Bio-Mat Compass looked like a thick silver watch with a holographic arrow.

The commander handed a blaster to each of the twins, and Conner fastened the compass around his wrist. The Omega GDD was heavy, so Alex and Conner carried it together.

"What do the Omega GDD and the Bio-Mat Compass do?" Alex asked.

"The Omega GDD stands for gamma detonation device—it's a very powerful bomb that uses gamma rays to vaporize its targets," Newters explained. "The Bio-Mat Compass detects biological material within a three-hundred-yard radius."

Alex gulped. "I'm sorry I asked," she said.

"To detonate the Omega GDD, type in the code *LRRH215*, wait for confirmation, and then run," Newters said. "The *2999 Moon Jumper Express* is in the spacecraft hangar. I'll show you to it."

The twins followed the commander through the spaceship. The short-range blasters and Omega GDD made Alex uneasy, and she held them away from her body. She was terrified the tiniest bump or tap would set them off and injure someone. Conner, on the other hand, couldn't have been more excited to be holding the weapons from his story.

When he was a kid, he used to spend hours pretending he was fighting evil aliens on a distant planet with the devices now in his hands. He was eager to get to Lollipopigust and live his childhood fantasy.

Conner twirled and pointed the blaster around the halls as they walked through the *BASK-8*. He re-enacted scenes from his favorite action movies and even made the sound effects to go along with it.

"Conner, knock it off!" Alex said. "You're gonna hurt someone with that!"

"Relax, I have the safety on," he said. "Oops—okay, *now* I have the safety on."

The commander and the twins walked through a set of automatic doors and arrived in the hangar. He showed them to a small spacecraft with the words *2999 Moon Jumper Express* engraved along the side of it. The spacecraft was the size of an SUV and looked like a mini version of the *BASK-8*. It was made of red steel and had two wings and a small crown of satellites and antennas. Newters pressed a button on the side of it and the door of the spacecraft slid open. There were two seats inside and compartments to store their weapons, but no sign of steering controls.

"How are we supposed to fly this thing?" Alex asked.

"The *2999 Moon Jumper Express* is controlled from the *BASK-8*," Newters said. "It prevents our spacecraft from being hijacked by Orphianotics—no offense."

Alex was relieved. If her brother had been planning to pilot the *2999 Moon Jumper Express* himself, she wasn't sure they would have made it to Lollipopigust. The twins stored their weapons in the compartments, tightened their helmets, and then strapped themselves into the seats. Newters hesitated before closing the spacecraft door behind them.

"Are you sure you know what you're doing?" he asked like a concerned father.

"One hundred percent," Conner said. "Once you've exterminated one alien insect species, you've exterminated them all. By the way, would you mind holding on to this until I get back?"

Conner handed the commander his backpack.

"It'll be safe with me," Newters said. "Good luck, exterminators. May the cosmos smile upon you."

The commander moved three fingers in a circle through the air and then pointed to his heart. Conner copied the motion exactly and Alex did her best to mimic him, but it was bizarre to her. Newters shut the door of the *2999 Moon Jumper Express* and headed out of the hangar.

"*'May the cosmos smile upon you'?*" Alex laughed. "Is that, like, a 'Galaxy Queen' catchphrase?"

"Do you know how hard it is coming up with an original science-fiction saying?" Conner asked. "Nearly impossible."

Once the commander was safely out of the hangar, the large compartment door opened to space. The gravity disappeared and the twins would have floated out of their seats if they weren't strapped in so securely. The engines of the

2999 Moon Jumper Express roared to life, and the space-craft flew out of the *BASK-8* hangar and headed toward the planet of Lollipopigust below.

The ride was smooth and serene. The purple planet and its turquoise rings glowed exquisitely. Even though she wasn't thrilled they were en route to exterminate bugs, Alex couldn't deny how amazing it was to be glid-ing between a massive spaceship and the atmosphere of an alien planet.

"I have to admit, this is pretty cool," she said.

Conner didn't respond. Alex turned to check on him and saw tears glistening in his eyes. He had seen so many things from his imagination come to life, but seeing *an actual planet* was surprisingly emotional.

"Are you okay?" she asked.

"I'm fine," Conner said. "Just allergies."

"In *space*?" She laughed.

"Yeah, I think there might have been a cat in here before us."

Alex just smiled and didn't press it further. "Well, what-ever you're reacting to, thanks for sharing it with me. This is an experience I would never have had without you."

The tender moment was interrupted by a loud beeping sound. The twins looked around the spacecraft nervously, afraid something was broken. The beeping was followed by an automated voice.

"Five . . . four . . . three . . ." it said.

"Conner, what are they counting *DOOOOWN*—"

The *2999 Moon Jumper Express* blasted toward Lolli-popigust with the power of a thousand rockets. The twins were slammed back into their seats by so much force, it felt like invisible elephants were sitting on them. Their teeth rattled and their cheeks rippled. They were moving so fast, they couldn't breathe, let alone speak or scream.

The spacecraft zoomed under the turquoise rings, shot through Lollipopigust's atmosphere, and headed straight for the purple surface. They were moving thousands of miles per second and showed no sign of slowing down. Right when the twins were convinced the spacecraft was going to crash, it suddenly jerked upright and pointed its engines to the ground. The *2999 Moon Jumper Express* made a surprisingly gentle landing on the Lollipopigustian surface.

The spacecraft door opened automatically. "You've arrived at your destination," said the same automated voice. "Enjoy your visit to *Lo-lee-pop-ee-gust*."

Alex's and Conner's hearts were racing so fast, they felt frozen in one perpetual beat. When their bodies finally caught up with their minds, they both let out a long, terri-fied, and overdue scream.

"Alex, I think I peed a little...." Conner said.

"Me too," she said.

The twins climbed out of their seats and stumbled off the spacecraft. They had a look around the planet's surface as their hearts returned to normal and feeling came back to their arms and legs.

Lollipopigust was covered in rolling purple hills and had a bright pink sky. The planet's turquoise rings arched above them and cast a shadow over the ground. The gravity wasn't as high on the planet as it had been on the *BASK-8*, and the twins felt stronger and lighter in their space suits.

They retrieved the weapons out of the spacecraft's compartments and ventured onto the planet. Conner glanced between the compass and the land around them, but there wasn't a sign of life anywhere.

"What kind of bugs are we looking for?" Alex asked. "Ants? Beetles? Flies?"

"The ones we have to find are called *polycrabs*," Conner told her. "They're a spider, scorpion, and wasp combination."

Just the description of the insects made Alex gasp and choke on the air.

"What the heck is wrong with you, Conner?" she asked. *"How could you even think of something so terrible?"*

"Sorry, it was in one of my nightmares," he said. "I thought it'd make a great alien monster, so I put it in the story. It's not like I *planned* to meet any of the villains in my stories."

"If that's what's crawling around your subconscious, you need *deep* psychological help," Alex said. "What's the plan to exterminate them?"

"It'll be simple," Conner said. "All we have to do is find the entrance to their colony, drop the Omega GDD inside, and then take off!"

Alex shook her head. "You and I both know it's never that easy," she said. "Who would have killed these bugs if we weren't here?"

"The Cyborg Queen would have been so desperate, she would have teamed up with the Orphianotics," Conner explained. "They would have exterminated the polycrabs but would have had to share Lollipopigust afterward."

"Then we make a nice plot twist for her," Alex said. "By the way, I've been meaning to ask, what is Commander Newters's deal? How did he end up working for the Cyborg Queen?"

"She saved his planet from being sucked into a black hole," Conner said. "Newters was so thankful, he devoted his life to working for her. Also, it's helpful to have *someone* aboard the *BASK-8* who's not connected to a battery, in case of a power outage."

The Bio-Mat Compass suddenly lit up and an arrow appeared on its screen.

"Looks like we've got our first catch of the day," Conner said.

The compass guided the twins through the purple hills to the edge of a deep, wide hole the size of an empty swimming pool. The compass pointed to something with biological material at the bottom of it. Alex and Conner held their short-range blasters tightly with their fingers against the triggers and cautiously peered into the hole.

Instead of a polycrab, they found a teal worm the size of

a small dog. It was chubby and had several rolls like a cater-pillar, but was shaped more like a jelly bean than a noodle. It had big black button eyes, no nose, and a wide mouth that was naturally shaped into a smile. The worm merrily rolled around the hole without a care in the world. It laughed and talked to itself like a happy baby.

"That is the cutest thing I've ever seen," Alex said. "What is it?"

"A Blissworm," Conner said. "They're a species of worm that's always happy, regardless of the situation they're in. The Blissworms are one of the few remaining species left on this planet. The polycrabs have hunted all the other bugs."

"What's it doing at the bottom of the hole?" she asked. "Does it live there?"

"No, the polycrabs dig holes to trap prey," Conner said. "The poor little guy must have fallen inside."

The Blissworm certainly didn't look like it had fallen into a trap. It giggled as it somersaulted across the hole. It looked up at the twins and waved with one of its four tiny hands.

"Oh, let's rescue it," Alex said. "It's too adorable to be eaten."

The twins lowered their weapons and slid down the side of the hole. The Blissworm was so excited to have company, it curled around their feet and purred like a kitten. Alex pet-ted the friendly bug. Its body felt like a gummy bear.

"I think it likes us," she said. "Would it survive on earth?"

"You want to take it *home*?" Conner asked.

Alex leaned down and the Blissworm crawled into her arms. It pressed its mouth against the glass of her helmet and gave her a big, slobbery kiss. Alex was filled with a warm fuzzy feeling, and she hugged the Blissworm like it was a long-lost pet.

"You know, maybe we should re-think this extermination thing," she said. "Maybe instead of *killing* all the polycrabs, we could just set traps and release them on another planet. The polycrabs are really no different from this Blissworm—they never asked to come to Lollipopigust. Let's be humane about it."

The Blissworm crawled to the ground and curiously circled the Omega GDD. It stretched its mouth over the top of it and swallowed the bomb whole. Since the detonation device was bigger than the Blissworm, its body stretched around it like a sock over a soda can.

"That worm better cough up our bomb or it's about to have some really bad heartburn," Conner said.

"It must be hungry," Alex said. "What does it usually eat?"

"Space weeds and stuff," Conner said. "Which is really strange, because polycrabs don't eat herbivores—they prey on other predators."

Suddenly, the twins and the Blissworm were eclipsed by a large shadow. Alex and Conner turned around and saw an enormous creature climbing into the hole behind them. It had big red eyes, fangs, two claws, eight legs, and three tails like a scorpion. At the tip of each tail was a long, sharp stinger. The creature's fangs dripped with saliva and it snapped its claws as it approached them.

It was easily the most terrifying thing the twins had ever seen and they both froze. The Blissworm waved at the monster and blew it a kiss.

"And *that's* a polycrab," Conner said.

"It has ten limbs and three tails," Alex noted. "That's thirteen appendages—why would you name it a polycrab? *Poly* means seven."

"Oh," Conner said. "That explains why I failed that geometry quiz."

Alex thought making sense of the creature would somehow make it less scary, but it did the opposite. The more she realized how little her brother knew about the alien insect he had created, the more frightening it became.

"Now I get why the worm was in the hole. It wasn't prey—the polycrab was using it as *bait*!" Conner said.

Alex was afraid to even ask. "Bait for what?"

"Us."

The polycrab vaulted toward the twins with its claws and stingers raised. Alex dived behind her brother and used him as a shield.

"Forget what I said about being humane!" Alex yelled. *"Kill it! Kill it! Kill it NOW!"*

Conner pointed his short-range blaster and shot at the

creature seconds before it tackled them. A bright blue blast hit the polycrab and it exploded into slime and guts. The innards rained down on the twins, and they almost became sick at the sight of it. Alex tried wiping the guts off her helmet, but they only smeared over the glass.

"Next time, I'm going to need a full itinerary *before* we travel into one of your short stories," she said.

"You got it," Conner said.

The Bio-Mat Compass started flickering more than ever before. The arrow spun out of control as something made of biological material approached the hole aboveground.

"We've got to get out of here!" Conner said.

The twins didn't have time to pry the Omega GDD out of the Blissworm, so they each grabbed one of the worm's hands and carried the Blissworm and weapon out of the hole as one. The Blissworm happily swung between them like it was on a trapeze.

Alex and Conner's problems only became worse aboveground. A dozen polycrabs surrounded them and there were even more running in from all directions. The twins set the Blissworm-covered Omega GDD on the ground and stood back to back. They raised their blasters and pointed them at the approaching polycrabs.

"Ready?" Conner said.

"Ready," Alex said.

"It's exterminating time!"

Alex and Conner opened fire on the polycrabs. The purple hillside was consumed in bright blue blasts and pieces of exploding alien insects. The Blissworm swayed and grooved to the sound of battle like it was a song with an electronic beat.

A polycrab in the twins' blind spots knocked them apart with one stroke of its claw. Alex and Conner tumbled onto the ground in different directions. The polycrabs were even harder to shoot at from the ground. The twins had to quickly roll back and forth to avoid being stepped on or stabbed by a polycrab's stinger.

No matter how many they killed, the monstrous insects kept coming. The polycrabs sprayed webs out of their center stingers, and the twins and the Blissworm became entwined in it. Alex and Conner struggled to break free from the sticky restraints, but their arms and blasters were confined against their torsos. The Blissworm rolled onto its back and tried to make snow angels in the web.

The polycrabs scooped up the twins and the Blissworm. But instead of eating them, the polycrabs carried them off into the distance, scurrying over the purple hills like a school of crabs across the sand.

"Now what?" Alex asked. "Where are they taking us?"

"To their colony to feed us to their queen," Conner said.

The Blissworm clapped giddily, as if they were being taken to an amusement park.

"The worm is right—this is actually a good thing," Conner said. "The deeper we get into the colony, the more effective the Omega GDD will be."

The herd of polycrabs arrived at a huge mound that

looked like an anthill the size of a mountain. They crawled into the entrance at the top and then down a long tunnel that snaked deep into the ground. It reminded Alex of the time she and Conner were kidnapped by trolls and goblins and taken to their underground territory.

They entered the largest cavern of the colony. Every inch of it was covered with polycrabs. The insects crawled across the dirt floor and the walls and hung by their tails from the ceiling. The polycrabs snapped their claws, rattled their tails, and hissed in celebration as the twins and the Blissworm were brought inside. The Blissworm waved and pointed at the creatures like it was the front-runner in a polycrab election.

The twins spotted the polycrab queen in the back of the cavern. She was a giant compared to her offspring and shared all their features. The queen also had tall horns protruding out of her head and a pair of wings she wore like a high collar. Under her tails was a thick, long abdomen that curved into a corner of the cavern where she laid eggs. A massive spiderweb hung behind her like a national flag.

Alex noticed the queen bore a slight resemblance to Trollbella. She had a sneaking suspicion the Troll and Goblin Territory was the inspiration behind the polycrab colony.

"Conner, is that supposed to be Trollbella?" Alex asked.

"Of course it is," he said without shame. "She's the biggest pest I know!"

The polycrabs carrying the twins and the Blissworm joined a line of other polycrabs headed for the queen. The creatures each presented the queen with a Lollipopigustian insect they had captured that day. The queen looked each victim over and spit green or yellow mucus on it.

"That's disgusting," Alex muttered to her brother. "What's the purpose of that?"

"The queen is separating the prey," Conner said. "Green mucus means she wants to eat the prey herself, yellow mucus means she wants it to be fed to the larvae, and no mucus..."

The twins watched as the queen inspected an alien that resembled a mantis. When no mucus was produced, the alien was dragged to the center of the cavern and the entire colony attacked it. They savagely tore the insect limb from limb as they feasted upon it. It was hard to watch, and the twins looked away.

Conner was the first prey the polycrabs in their party presented to the queen. As she examined him, her large red eyes grew even bigger and saliva dripped from her fangs. It was similar to how Trollbella looked at Conner—she wanted him all to herself. The polycrab queen covered him in green mucus, picked him up with her claw, and tossed him into the web behind her.

Just like a fly caught in a spiderweb, the more Conner struggled to free himself, the more entangled he became.

Alex was presented to the queen next. It was no surprise that the queen wasn't nearly as impressed with her as she was with Conner. She spit yellow mucus all over her and Alex was dragged to the corner of eggs.

The Blissworm was the last in their group to be presented to the queen. The worm was delighted to see her and eagerly reached up like it wanted to hug the gigantic insect. The queen didn't even bother inspecting the worm. With no mucus, the polycrabs dragged the Blissworm to the center of the cavern to eat it themselves.

"Shoot! They'll set off the bomb if they eat it!" Conner said. "Alex, do something!"

Both twins were still wrapped in web from their surface encounter with the polycrabs, but Alex managed to free one of her hands and she snapped her fingers. Suddenly, the polycrab queen tilted her head back and let out a massive sneeze, and the Blissworm was showered in green mucus. When the queen looked down and saw the worm, she didn't realize the green mucus was accidental. She picked it up and tossed it into the web behind her, too.

The Blissworm stuck to the web just a few feet away from Conner. The worm waved at him like they were two friends running into each other at the supermarket. The queen continued separating the other prey her children had brought into the colony.

"Conner, I'm going to cast a spell on our space suits to make them web resistant," Alex said. "Hang on."

She snapped her fingers again and the web covering their bodies melted away, freeing their arms and the short-range blasters that had been compressed against their torsos. Conner hung on to the queen's web like it was a wide rope ladder.

Alex heard snapping and crunching sounds coming from nearby—the polycrab eggs had started hatching. The small larvae poked their heads out of the eggs and looked around for their first meal. As soon as one larva noticed Alex, they all turned their heads to her as if they were connected on the same wavelength.

Alex pointed her gun at the newborns and Conner waved to stop her.

"Don't shoot them!" Conner yelled. "We need to activate the Omega GDD before you cause a scene!"

"Then get to it!" Alex said.

Conner climbed across the web to where the Blissworm hung. He pulled the worm off the web with a *snap* and carried it down to the ground. The Blissworm was very heavy with the bomb inside its body. At first he tried pulling the Omega GDD out through the Blissworm's mouth, but the jolly worm made a game of it and kept its mouth tightly shut.

"You stupid little parasite!" Conner said. *"Just spit it out!"*

He tried squeezing the Omega GDD out of the Blissworm, but it only tickled the worm. The Blissworm kept its mouth shut but Conner felt the laughter building up inside of it.

"So you like being tickled, huh?" Conner said. "I'm gonna *goochie-goochie-goo* that bomb right out of you!"

Conner tickled the Blissworm with both hands. The worm had never been so amused in its whole life, and so much laughter built up inside its body that the Omega GDD looked like it was covered in a teal balloon. Finally, the Blissworm couldn't take the tickling anymore and opened its mouth to laugh. The Omega GDD shot out like a cannonball. Luckily Conner grabbed its handle before it got away.

Meanwhile, in the corner, the larvae started crawling out of their eggs. Once they figured out how to walk, they crawled toward Alex. She kicked them away with her boots, but they were relentless. Each egg hosted several larvae, so the number of newborns coming toward her doubled by the second.

"Hurry up!" she yelled at her brother. *"I'm about to become alien baby food!"*

Conner punched *LRRH215* into the Omega GDD keypad and a red light started to flash.

"The Omega GDD will detonate in thirty seconds," said a calm voice from the device.

"It's set!" Conner announced, and dashed toward his sister.

"Don't forget the Blissworm!" Alex said. *"We can't leave it here!"*

Conner grunted and then dashed back. The Blissworm was waiting with its hands up like a toddler wanting to be lifted, and Conner scooped it up.

The larvae started leaping on Alex—she had no choice but to shoot them. The blasts echoed through the cavern, and all the polycrabs snapped their heads toward her. Conner quickly thought of a distraction to save his sister. He fired his blaster at the corners of the web behind the queen, and it fell on top of her like a net. The polycrab queen hissed and all her children forgot about their newborn siblings and hurried to help her.

Alex and Conner met in the middle of the cavern and ran for the tunnel in the back. The Blissworm waved good-bye to the polycrabs as they passed them. Alex and Conner entered the tunnel and shot at the ceiling behind them as they ran, causing large chunks of dirt to fall and block the passageway so the polycrabs couldn't follow them.

The twins ran as fast as their legs could carry them. The Blissworm held on to Conner's helmet like a jockey clutching the reins of a racehorse. It even slapped Conner's bottom as if that would make him run faster.

"Cut it out!" he said. *"That hurts!"*

They only had a few seconds left before the Omega GDD detonated. They saw light ahead and knew they were almost out of the colony. They heard a thunderous explosion erupt behind them and the whole tunnel vibrated. Alex, Conner, and the Blissworm re-surfaced just in time and rolled down the mound. A powerful gamma ray exploded out of the colony's entrance, vaporizing everything it touched. The purple hills shook and cracked for miles like they had been hit by a powerful earthquake. When the gamma ray dissipated, there was nothing left of the colony but a massive hole in the ground.

With the polycrabs successfully exterminated, Lollipopigust was safe for the *BASK-8* to upload. The twins stayed on the ground as they caught their breath.

"From now on, I'm only writing about bunnies," Conner said, panting.

A spacecraft a teeny bit bigger than the *2999 Moon Jumper Express* descended from the sky and landed near the twins. It was black and its shape was similar to the body of a wolf. *CLAW-DS* was engraved along the side of the spacecraft. Alex and Conner got to their feet as the Cyborg Queen charged out of the *CLAW-DS* followed by Commander Newters and a handful of Cyborg soldiers.

"Well done, exterminators!" the Cyborg Queen said. "We had a bet going on the *BASK-8* that you wouldn't survive—now I owe my crew a week of double battery privileges!"

The twins could tell she was fully charged because she seemed to be in a much better mood than before. The commander shook the twins' hands and gave Conner his backpack.

"Excellent work," Newters said. "I haven't seen the Cyborg Queen so pleased since the time a constellation was named after her!"

The Cyborg Queen clapped her metal hands and a team of short gray aliens with large heads and eyes ran out of the spacecraft. They carried holographic blueprints, laser measuring tapes, and toolboxes that hovered beside them.

"Who are those guys?" Conner asked.

"Once she was certain you would succeed, Her Majesty had the best architects in the galaxy flown out to immediately start construction on the planet," Newters said.

The Cyborg Queen rotated and pointed the gray aliens to different parts of the Lollipopigustian surface.

"I think I'll build the palace right *there* in the eclipse of the rings so it doesn't get hot in the summer," she thought out loud. "And since there's already a gigantic hole in the ground over there—wish someone had warned me that might happen, but oh well—that's where I'll put the gasoline pool."

The Cyborg Queen rolled over to join the commander and the twins.

"Your Magneticness," Conner said, "now that we've exterminated the polycrabs, may my sister and I borrow your Cyborg army to save our friends?"

"A deal is a deal," she said. "You may take us to Fairytaletopia whenever you're ready."

"Wait, *you're* coming with us?" Alex asked.

"Indeed," the Cyborg Queen said. "They're going to start building my new residence as soon as we take the planet to my home system—I'm going to need something to do while it's being constructed. How long is the journey? I must warn you, anything longer than seventy-four seconds makes me irritable."

"We're actually going to make a stop in Sycamore Drivious first, but it won't take long at all," he said. "In fact, I just remembered I have a transportation device right here."

Conner reached into his backpack and pulled out his binder of short stories.

"Lovely," the Cyborg Queen said. She rolled away from the twins and covered her nose. "Friendly word of advice: You might want to change before seeing your friends. You both smell horribly of *bug guts*."

CHAPTER FIFTEEN

THE APPLE MEETS THE TREE

Emmerich wasn't getting much sleep. The witches at Dead Man's Creek stayed up all night like nocturnal animals. They cackled and brewed foul-smelling potions until the sun came up and then rested during the day. Their loud snoring, growling, and mumbling was impossible for Emmerich to sleep through. Like a neglected pet, he wasn't being fed much, either. So he became weaker the longer he stayed there as the witches' prisoner.

He thought his exhaustion was starting to play tricks on

his mind, because one day at sunrise, after all the witches went to bed, he saw a strange man tiptoeing through the camp toward him. He had pale blue eyes and several scratches along the side of his face. He walked with a limp and his left arm was in a sling.

Emmerich had never seen the man before and had no idea what he was doing there. He circled the tree Emmerich was restrained to and quietly untied the chains.

"Who are you?" Emmerich asked.

The man motioned for him to be silent. *"I'm here to rescue you,"* the man whispered.

Once he unwrapped the chains around Emmerich's body, the man offered his good hand and helped the boy to his feet. It was difficult for both of them since the man was injured and Emmerich hadn't been on his feet for a long time.

The man gestured for Emmerich to follow him, and they snuck into the forest, far away from Dead Man's Creek.

"Are you hurt?" the man asked, and inspected the boy front to back.

"No," Emmerich said. "Tired, hungry, and scared—but they didn't harm me."

The man reached into his sling and handed Emmerich an apple. The boy was so hungry, he forgot all politeness and immediately started eating it.

"Make sure you chew your food," the man said with a smile. "Remember what happened to Snow White?"

The Masked Man played the part of a Good Samaritan

very well. With just a few kind gestures, he had the little boy convinced he was a hero.

"Thank you for rescuing me," Emmerich said. "Who are you?"

"You don't know who I am?" the man asked.

Emmerich shook his head. The two had never been face-to-face before, but the Masked Man needed to be certain his reputation hadn't found his son first.

"I'm from the Otherworld," the Masked Man lied. "I've come to rescue you and take you back home."

The little boy was so happy about the prospect of going home, tears came to his eyes and he gave the Masked Man a giant hug. It hurt his broken rib, and the Masked Man pushed Emmerich away.

"I'm sorry," Emmerich said. "I've been away from home for a very long time. My mother must be worried sick about me!"

"Right..." the Masked Man said. "Your *mother*."

He paused for a moment to observe his son. The resemblance he shared with Bo Peep was even more striking up close.

"How did you find me?" Emmerich asked.

"Oh," the Masked Man said, thinking on his feet. "Your friends in the Otherworld sent me."

"You mean Conner and Alex?" the boy asked.

The Masked Man was shocked that Emmerich knew the names of his niece and nephew. If he didn't know his own father, how could he possibly know about his cousins?

"Why . . . *yes*," the Masked Man said.

"Are they here?" Emmerich asked.

The little boy looked around the forest excitedly, as if the twins were about to jump out from behind a tree.

"They're in the Otherworld waiting for us," the Masked Man said.

"How do you know the twins?" Emmerich asked.

The Masked Man needed to be careful with the information he shared—especially if Emmerich was friends with the twins. If his plan was going to work, he needed his son's absolute trust.

"Have they ever mentioned their uncle Lloyd?" he asked.

"No," Emmerich said. "I didn't even know they had an uncle."

"Good," the Masked Man said. "I mean—*good for me*. Now I get to introduce myself to you. I'm Lloyd Bailey, Alex and Conner's *favorite* uncle."

Emmerich shook the Masked Man's hand as enthusiastically as if he were meeting a member of his own family.

"It's wonderful to meet you," Emmerich said.

"And you as well," the Masked Man said. "Now, we must hurry out of the woods before the witches realize you're gone. I've just returned from following the witch Morina— she led me to a portal in the Eastern Kingdom that will take us to the Otherworld. We must move very quietly, though; it's a dangerous time to be traveling through this world."

The Masked Man led the way and Emmerich followed.

Even with an injured leg, the Masked Man moved with so much determination that Emmerich had difficulty keeping up with him. Although his head was filled with a hundred more questions, Emmerich followed the man's instructions to stay quiet.

They traveled through the forest for miles without making a sound. Suddenly, a loud crunch came from under the Masked Man's foot. He looked down at the ground and saw he had stepped on a small statue of a bird made from a pale stone. It was an odd thing to find in the middle of the woods.

"Look, there are more!" Emmerich said.

The boy pointed to the treetops above them. The statue under the man's foot was one of many. The branches were covered with hundreds of stone birds—enough to make an entire flock. Each bird looked terrified, as if it had been frozen while fleeing from a predator.

"What strange decorations," Emmerich said.

"These aren't decorations," the Masked Man said. "They've been turned to stone by a terrible monster creeping through the forest. We need to get far away from here as quickly as possible before we're next!"

Emmerich didn't need any further explanation. He and the Masked Man hurried through the woods faster than before. But even with a monster loose in the woods, Emmerich was glad to be away from Dead Man's Creek. Little did the boy know, he would have been better off with the witches than in the Masked Man's care.

CHAPTER SIXTEEN

FULL HOUSE AND
FULL HEARTS

The perseverance of the *Dolly Llama* crew had been put to the test when they entered the Other-world, but after only one day in the house on Sycamore Drive, the pirates and sailors of "Starboardia" had grown very accustomed to life in the twenty-first century. In fact, they had become a little *too comfortable* for Charlotte's taste. The twins' mother had spent the entire day following pirates and sailors from one room to the next as if she were babysitting fifty toddlers.

Auburn Sally, Admiral Jacobson, Siren Sue, and the navy sailors were spread out in the living room watching television. They shared bowls of popcorn and candy as they watched a program Charlotte didn't recognize.

"What are you watching?" Charlotte asked.

As if it had cast a spell on them, the men and women never looked away from the screen.

"A very wealthy family with very frivolous problems," Auburn Sally said. "It's hard to tell who the parents are, because they *all* act like spoiled children."

"And for whatever reason, we can't stop watching it," Admiral Jacobson said.

Suddenly, they all jumped at the sound of a blender. Charlotte ran into the kitchen to see what the others had gotten into. She found Too-Much-Rum Ronda pouring a red slushy liquid into mugs for herself, Not-So-Jolly Joan, Catfish Kate, and High-Tide Tabitha.

"Can I help you with something, ladies?" Charlotte asked.

"We couldn't be better," Too-Much-Rum Ronda said. "I've recently discovered how to create a marvelous con- coction called a strawberry daiquiri! It's a delicious and cold drink that's so sweet, you can't even taste the rum! It's the nectar of the gods, I tell you! Would you like one?"

"No, thank you," Charlotte said.

Not-So-Jolly Joan, Catfish Kate, and High-Tide Tabitha quickly slurped down their frozen drinks and then held their heads in pain.

"You've poisoned us!" Not-So-Jolly Joan yelled.

"My head is going to explode!" Catfish Kate shouted.

"Quick—put us out of our misery!" High-Tide Tabitha said. She tried to hand Charlotte her rifle.

"Ladies, relax," Charlotte said. "You're having a *brain freeze*—it's what happens when you drink cold beverages too fast. Pace yourselves and it'll go away."

A clump of red slush fell and splattered across the counter. Charlotte looked up and saw the kitchen ceiling was covered with strawberry daiquiri.

"What's all that?" she asked.

"Sorry, that was my first round," Too-Much-Rum Ronda said. "It took me a couple tries before I mastered the pitcher of spinning blades."

Before Charlotte had a chance to clean up the mess, she was distracted by a giant splash that came from the second story. She ran up the stairs and dashed into her and Bob's bathroom.

Winking Wendy and Fish-Lips Lucy were taking a bubble bath in Charlotte's tub fully clothed. Stinky-Feet Phoebe was sitting on the tank of the toilet with her feet in the bowl. She flushed the toilet and sighed with relief as the rushing water gave her a foot massage. All three pirates had clearly gone through Charlotte's things, because they wore green beauty masks and were reading romance novels.

"Hello, Charlotte!" Stinky-Feet Phoebe said. "You blokes certainly know how to live! This is by far my favorite invention of the future."

She patted the side of the toilet happily and flushed it again. Charlotte took a deep breath and slowly let it out. A headache was forming right between her eyes.

"That's not what the toilet is for, Phoebe," Charlotte said.

Stinky-Feet Phoebe was shocked. "Then what *is* its purpose?"

"Human waste," Charlotte said.

The pirate immediately removed her feet from the toilet bowl and wiped them with a hand towel.

"Then what's that bucket in the corner with the pedal that opens the lid?" Fish-Lips Lucy asked.

"That's a trash can," Charlotte said.

Winking Wendy's and Fish-Lips Lucy's faces filled with guilt.

"I wouldn't look inside it if I were you," Winking Wendy said.

Before Charlotte could reprimand the women in her bathroom, she caught sight of something out of the corner of her eye. She stepped into her bedroom and saw that the comforter on her bed had been replaced with a large black flag with the skull of a llama on it. Charlotte rushed to the bedroom window and looked at the pirate ship in the backyard. Big-Booty Bertha was hoisting the lavender bedspread above the *Dolly Llama* like a new flag. The twins' mother hurried downstairs and ran out into the backyard.

"Bertha, that's my comforter!" Charlotte shouted.

"Do you like it?" Big-Booty Bertha asked. "I thought

the ship could use a little color. Don't get me wrong, I like our old flag, but this flag says, *'Yes, we're pirates, but we're also totally in touch with our femininity!'*"

Clink-clink! As soon as Charlotte took her first step to climb aboard the ship, she heard a strange sound coming from the side yard. *Clink-clink!* She inspected the noise and found Pancake-Face Patty playing darts with her nicest silverware.

"Stop that!" Charlotte said, and quickly gathered the utensils. *"This is my great-grandmother's silver! It's a family heirloom!"*

"And fine taste she had," Pancake-Face Patty said. "They're very easy to throw. Your great-grandmother must have been quite a bandit!"

Charlotte could feel her blood pressure rising. She went inside and locked herself in the laundry room before she lost her temper. The racket throughout the house was blocked by the sound of the dryer. It was the first peaceful moment Charlotte had had all day. She was so happy to be helpful to her children, but she hadn't expected that watching the pirates and sailors would be such a chaotic task.

There was a knock on the laundry room door and Charlotte cringed.

"What now?" she asked.

"Charlotte, it's Bob," her husband said. "I just got home. Are you all right?"

Charlotte quickly let him in and shut the door before a pirate followed him inside.

"To be honest, I'm losing my mind a little bit," she confessed. "And these are only the characters from the *first* story! What am I going to do when Alex and Conner get back from 'Galaxy Queen'? The house is too small for all these people!"

"I think we've bitten off more than we can chew," Bob said. "The sailors made a rope net out of my ties, and the Rosary Chicken turned my hamper into a nest. She also laid eggs in all my shoes—I wish I had been warned before I got dressed for work this morning."

"And we *both* have to work tomorrow," Charlotte said. "We can't leave them in the house alone. They'll burn it down by the time we get back."

"It's not like we can call a sitter," he said. "And we certainly can't take them with us to the hospital."

Bob had unintentionally given Charlotte an idea, and her eyes lit up.

"That's it!" she said. "What if we take them to the new wing of the children's hospital? They just finished construction and the inspections don't start until next week. It's empty and spacious—exactly what we need!"

Before Bob could argue with her, the dryer door popped open and Somersault Sydney rolled out of it. The pirate was very warm and dizzy. When her eyes stopped spinning, she looked up at Bob and Charlotte.

"What time is it?" Somersault Sydney asked.

"Almost half past five," Bob said.

"Dang it," Somersault Sydney said. "I was hoping that was a time machine."

A loud *crash* came from the living room. Charlotte and Bob sprinted through the house and found their television on the floor with its screen shattered. Auburn Sally and Admiral Jacobson were helping Siren Sue to her feet beside it.

"What happened?" Charlotte asked.

"The privileged family disappeared and were replaced by a series of merchants," Auburn Sally explained. "First a woman was bewitching us into purchasing a mop of miracles, then a man swallowed a tiny pebble that soothed his aching bones, and then an old woman fell onto the floor and couldn't get up!"

Siren Sue looked down at the floor. "I tried to save her," she said.

Bob and Charlotte looked around their house at all the pirates and sailors and shared a long sigh.

"You're right," Bob said. "We can't let them stay here. We'll take them to the hospital with us. At least we'll be able to check on them while we're working."

"But they're still going to need supervision," Charlotte said.

Conner's binder of short stories was kept safely in the corner of the living room. The cover flipped open and a beam of light illuminated the house. Alex and Conner stepped out of the beam in their newly cleaned space suits with huge smiles on their faces. The Blissworm sat on Alex's shoulder and *oohed* and *aahed* as it saw their house.

"Hey, guys!" Conner said. "Good news—we've recruited the Cyborg army to help us!"

The pirates and sailors cheered, then stopped, sharing the same puzzled expression.

"What's a Cyborg?" Admiral Jacobson asked.

"You'll see," Conner said. "They'll be in the house shortly. The Cyborg Queen was just waiting on a New Planet Construction Permit from the United Universe Council—it's a long story."

The broken television and the messy kitchen caught the twins' attention.

"What happened in here?" Alex asked. "Was there an earthquake?"

"We need to talk," Charlotte said.

Bob and Charlotte pulled the twins into the dining room for a private word.

"The house is getting smaller by the minute," their mother said. "Bob and I were talking, and we think it might be best if we take your characters to the new wing of the children's hospital. There's lots of room there and no one will see them."

"That's a great idea," Conner said. "I was wondering where we'd put a thousand Cyborg soldiers. Good thinking."

"Which brings us to our next concern," Bob said. "We need help taking care of all these characters—your mother and I can only do so much. Is there anyone you know who can help us supervise?"

The Blissworm raised its hand, confident it was the worm for the job. The twins looked to each other and thought of possible candidates.

"We should probably check in with the others in the fairy-tale world," Alex said. "What if we bring Jack and Goldilocks back to help Mom and Bob?"

"Yeah, they're probably worried about us," he said. "We can let everyone else know we've recruited half an army—they might need some good news."

Even though the Blissworm had no idea what the twins were talking about, it nodded along approvingly. It was the first time Bob and Charlotte had noticed the worm on Alex's shoulder, and they both took a step back from it.

"How should we get to the fairy-tale world?" Conner asked. "Grandma's old storybook?"

"Yes, but instead of activating the magic within the storybook, we should use the Portal Potion on it," Alex suggested. "We'll have an easier way of getting back here."

Bob and Charlotte listened to Alex and Conner like they were speaking another language, but if the twins were satisfied with this plan, so were they.

"Where is Grandma's old storybook, anyway?" Conner asked.

"It's on the bookshelf in Alex's room upstairs," Charlotte said.

"Great!" Conner said. "Thanks for being so organized, Mom!"

Alex snapped her fingers and their space suits turned into normal clothes again. She handed Charlotte the Blissworm and the twins ran up the stairs to Alex's room.

Despite its energetic attempt for a hug, Charlotte held the Blissworm away from her body like it was poisonous.

"Charlotte," Bob said in shock, "there's an alien worm in our house."

In her bedroom upstairs, Alex scanned her bookshelf until she found the spine of her grandma's emerald storybook. She pulled it out and read the golden title aloud.

"*The Land of Stories,*" Alex said.

"More like *The Land of Troubles*." Conner laughed.

Naturally, the book was nostalgic for the twins, but they didn't have time to walk down memory lane. Conner placed the storybook on the floor, removed the flask from his backpack, and poured three drops of the Portal Potion onto the pages. They lit up as another bright beam of light shined out of the book.

While Conner got the storybook ready, the title of another book on the shelf caught Alex's eye: *King Arthur*. It made her heart sink and her face fall.

"Is something wrong?" Conner asked her.

"Not at all," Alex said. "Go ahead, I'll be right behind you."

Conner stepped into the beam of light and disappeared from the bedroom. Alex pulled her copy of *King Arthur* off the shelf and stared at it. The image on the cover was of an old, weary king seated at the head of a round table. He had bags under his eyes, a long, graying beard, and a mind full of troubles. It made her laugh because the Arthur she knew couldn't have been more different.

Alex wondered what Arthur was doing at that very moment. She wondered if he thought about her as much as she thought about him, if he missed her as much as she missed him, and if he longed to be with her as much as she longed to be with him. Even though it was entirely her choice to leave him in his own world, not a single day went by that she didn't think of him and wonder if she had made the right decision.

Oddly, just holding the book made Alex feel closer to Arthur, as if he were on the other end of an open telephone line. She stuffed the book into her backpack, stepped into the beam of light, and followed her brother into the Land of Stories.

In the world of King Arthur, the once and future king was battling an enchanted scarecrow in the middle of a large open field. The duel would have been a spectacle to any passing observer, but to Arthur it was just another lesson in his training to become the king of England. Merlin and Mother Goose sat in plastic lawn chairs to the side and drank iced tea as they cheered him on.

"That's it, young Arthur!" Merlin said. "Always remember, enemies will come in different shapes, sizes, and materials!"

"Ar-ty! Ar-ty! Ar-ty!" Mother Goose chanted like she was at a football game. "Show that scarecrow who's boss! Kick the hay outta him!"

Arthur was the least enthusiastic of all of them. In fact, he resembled the King Arthur on the cover of Alex's book more than the adventurous young man she remembered. Defeating the scarecrow was an easy challenge, but his heart wasn't in it. Only one thing had been on Arthur's mind for weeks, and he couldn't let it go.

The scarecrow tackled Arthur to the ground. It punched and kicked him with its soft hay hands, but Arthur didn't even try to shield himself. He just lay on the ground and let the enchanted object beat him.

Merlin and Mother Goose did everything they could to encourage him. They magically set off fireworks, they did the wave like a crowd in a stadium, they even danced with pom-poms, but nothing motivated him.

"He's been depressed since Alex left," Merlin said. "Unless we do something to inspire him soon, England will have a very bleak future."

"Let me talk to him," Mother Goose said. "If there's one thing I'm good at, it's convincing young men to do things against their will. Trust me, I had two dates to every school dance, and it wasn't because of my looks."

Merlin shrugged. He was out of ideas himself and willing to try anything. He snapped his fingers and the scarecrow was disenchanted.

"Let's take a break," Merlin told Arthur. "I need to return to the cottage and stir my wormtail ragu so it won't be lumpy for dinner."

The wizard kissed Mother Goose on the cheek and then

headed into the forest to give her and Arthur a moment alone.

"Hey, Arty! Come have a seat next to me," Mother Goose called.

Arthur pushed the scarecrow off his body and sluggishly took Merlin's seat next to her. He kept his eyes on the empty field and let out a deep sigh.

"Why the long face, Arthur?" Mother Goose asked. "You look like I did when the Beatles broke up."

"I'm having a difficult time concentrating on Merlin's lessons," he said. "I don't feel like myself these days."

"Because you miss Alex," she said matter-of-factly.

Arthur's knee-jerk reaction was to deny the accusation, but when he opened his mouth, he couldn't find the words to argue. Instead, he just nodded and sank into his seat. Mother Goose put a comforting hand on his shoulder and smiled sweetly.

"Young love," she said. "It doesn't matter how old you get, you always remember it. You spend five minutes with someone and suddenly you never want to spend a moment apart. They become your sole focus and make you happier, more excited, and more inspired than anything before. They become your armor and give you strength and bravery and make you feel unstoppable. Life doesn't seem so bad now that you have someone to share it with."

Arthur gulped—he couldn't have described it better himself.

"That is, until it *stops*," Mother Goose said. "Then

everything comes to an earth-shattering, heartbreaking, and rude-awakening halt. You feel foolish for ever having been so happy, and embarrassed for letting it show, and the world has never seemed so terrible."

"Sounds familiar," Arthur said.

Mother Goose leaned a little closer to him, and seriousness grew in her eyes.

"Love is wonderful, magical, and beautiful, but it can also be maddening, damaging, and dangerous," she said. "It blinds us more than anything. It makes us selfish, it makes us feel like nothing else matters, and it tricks us into thinking the rest of the world doesn't exist—but it *does* exist. Whether you're on the high or low side of love, the world always moves on."

"So you're saying love is a weakness?" Arthur asked.

"That depends on you," Mother Goose said. "There's a reason we've got hearts *and* brains—we're supposed to listen to them both. A good man follows his heart, but a wise man follows his heart without ignoring his brain. Finding the right balance is one of the hardest parts of life."

"It appears Alex and I are on opposite ends of that scale," Arthur said. "She believes being together would alter my destiny, and I can't imagine a destiny without her."

"Destiny is an awfully big gamble for one relationship," Mother Goose said. "It doesn't matter how strongly you feel about something—even the most stubborn people can change. What if you and Alex grew apart a couple of years down the road? Could you imagine the guilt you'd both feel if you let down the people of England for nothing?"

"But like you said, life is about finding a *balance*," Arthur said. "Surely there's an outcome where we can fulfill our destinies *and* be together? Why does it have to be so black-and-white?"

"Young people from the Otherworld are overly dramatic these days," Mother Goose said. "Every relationship has to be *all-or-nothing*, there's no example of *give-and-take*—I blame television and vampire novels. Alex doesn't want to keep King Arthur from England—so she's keeping King Arthur away from her."

Arthur went quiet and looked at the sky. He thought over and over again about what Mother Goose had just said. An enticing idea came to him and he smiled from ear to ear.

"Then to prove her wrong, I have to prove she won't be depriving England of anything," he said. "If I accomplish everything in the legend she holds me to, Alex will have nothing to put between us!"

Mother Goose was confused. She was trying to convince Arthur to get over Alex and move on with his life, not to get over his life and move on with Alex. She had no idea how her advice could have backfired so easily.

"I suppose you're right," she said. "Heck, Arty, if you founded Camelot, assembled the Knights of the Round Table, located the Holy Grail, and *still* had feelings for Alex after you were done—I'd take you to her myself."

Arthur looked at Mother Goose with deep desperation in his eyes. "You would?" he asked.

"Um . . . *sure*," Mother Goose said. "But I think you're missing my—"

"Then I'd better get back to work!" he said.

Arthur excitedly ran back into the field. She wasn't entirely sure how it had happened, but Mother Goose was pleased to see his spirits change. She snapped her fingers and the scarecrow got to its feet. Arthur fought it with more vigor and purpose than he had ever fought anything before.

Merlin returned to the field and couldn't believe his eyes. He sat beside Mother Goose with an astonished look on his face.

"It's a miracle!" Merlin said. "How did you manage it?"

Mother Goose shrugged. "I have such a way with words, even I'm not sure what I said."

CHAPTER SEVENTEEN

REGROUPING

Alex and Conner stepped through the beam of light and found themselves somewhere near the base of the Northern Mountains in the Northern Kingdom. If it weren't for the range of snowy peaks stretching across the horizon, they wouldn't have recognized the Land of Stories. The smoky sky and the prominent burned smell in the air made them feel like they had stepped into a war zone, not the world of classic fairy tales. But unfortunately, these days they were one and the same.

"This place looks awful," Conner said. "What has Uncle Lloyd done to it?"

"We're not far from the Northern Palace," Alex said. "Let's sneak over and take a look—it might give us some information."

The twins picked up the emerald storybook from the ground next to them and traveled through the woods of the Northern Kingdom, carefully avoiding roads and paths to stay out of sight. Soon the green domes of the Northern Palace came into view above the trees, and the twins crept closer to get a glimpse of it.

If the Northern Palace was any indication, the fairy-tale world was in the worst shape it had ever been in. Snow White's former home was so battered, it was a miracle parts of it were even standing. Captain Hook's flying ship, the *Jolly Roger*, hovered above the palace like a docked hot-air balloon. The grounds were covered with groups of patrolling Winkies and card soldiers.

On the front lawns of the palace, the twins saw villagers constructing three enormous statues: the Wicked Witch of the West, Captain Hook, and the Queen of Hearts. They were watched over by a flock of flying monkeys that pushed and kicked the villagers as they carried supplies past them.

"What have they done to Swan Lake?" Conner exclaimed. "All the villagers from all the kingdoms must be in there!"

"Look up there," Alex said.

She pointed to the palace balcony, where Captain Hook, the Queen of Hearts, and the Wicked Witch of the West watched the villagers build their monuments. The villains were seated on large cushioned chairs and were being served drinks and sweets by Mr. Smee.

"Where's Uncle Lloyd?" Alex asked. "Why isn't he sitting with them or having his own statue constructed?"

"It's weird, isn't it?" Conner said. "Let's get to the cave—the others will know."

Alex held her brother tightly, and with a bright flash she magically transported them to the cave in the mountains. They were expecting to find their friends the Merry Men, the Lost Boys, and soldiers from the Northern and Charming Kingdoms inside, but there wasn't a trace of them anywhere. The cave was completely empty.

"Where did everybody go?" Alex asked. "You don't think they were found and captured, do you?"

Conner looked around the vacant cave, fearing the same thing.

"No, they would have put up a fight," he said. "There's no sign of a struggle anywhere. They must have moved to a different location."

"Maybe they left a clue behind so we'd know where to find them," Alex said.

She and Conner searched the cave, but they didn't even find a footprint that could lead them in the right direction. They stepped out of the cave and looked around at the forest and the mountains surrounding them. Something large emerged from the trees and caught Conner's eye.

"I don't think they left *something* behind—I think they left *someone*," he said.

Conner gestured to the woods ahead, where a chubby unicorn with a broken horn stood.

"*Cornelius!*" Alex said excitedly.

The twins ran to the unicorn and gave him a huge hug. He was so happy to see them, he neighed eagerly and did an animated dance with his front hooves.

"Cornelius, we're looking for Jack and Goldilocks," Alex said. "Do you know where they and the others went?"

The unicorn nodded his large head up and down.

"Could you take us there?" Conner asked.

The unicorn knelt to the ground and the twins climbed onto his back. His horn glowed like a lantern, and he raced through the forest faster than any normal horse could. Although they zipped past trees at a high speed, the twins could tell how empty the woods were. They didn't see a single living thing in the forest besides each other.

Cornelius took Alex and Conner deep into the Dwarf Forests, to the West Hills. Neither had been to these parts of the woods before, so they didn't know what to expect or what to look for. The unicorn stopped at a large boulder sticking into the hillside.

"Are you sure this is it?" Alex asked.

Cornelius nodded, but even the unicorn was baffled. Jack and Goldilocks had left him near the cave in case the twins returned, knowing his magic horn would guide them to their new location, but they didn't give him any instructions for what to do once they got there.

"It must be some kind of secret entrance," Conner said.

The twins climbed down off Cornelius and inspected the boulder. They knocked on it as if it were a door, but nothing happened. Alex tried using magic to move it aside, but the boulder didn't move.

"There must be a spell keeping it in place," Alex said. "Hagetta must have charmed it to keep intruders out. It must need some sort of password."

"It doesn't need a password, it needs a whistle," said a voice behind the twins.

Alex and Conner turned and saw Rook Robins standing on a hill nearby. Given their history, the twins weren't overjoyed to see him, but it was nice to see a familiar face nonetheless.

"Rook, it's good to see you!" Alex said. "Do you know where we are?"

"We're in the West Hills of the Dwarf Forests," Rook said. "Jack, Goldilocks, and all the others are hiding in an abandoned mine on the other side of that boulder."

"Do you know how to get inside?" Conner asked.

"Only a special birdcall will open it," Rook said. "But I know another way in. There's a tunnel on the other side of the hills—it's how I got out. Follow me!"

Alex and Conner still had reservations about trusting Rook, but they didn't have another choice. The twins and the unicorn followed him over the hills to a small tunnel whose entrance was camouflaged in the hillside. Rook held back cobwebs like a curtain and escorted Alex, Conner, and Cornelius inside.

Rook had to give the unicorn a big push to squeeze him through the narrow entrance. The tunnel was very long and dark, but thanks to Cornelius's glowing horn, they could see where they were going.

"Do you know why they changed locations?" Alex asked Rook.

"The cave became really crowded after Jack and Goldilocks started rescuing refugees," Rook explained. "My village was among the first they saved from the Literary Army. They've been retrieving people when and where they can, but it's been more difficult since the Masked Man rounded up all the citizens and put them in the lake. The royal families were the last to arrive—Jack and Goldilocks barely saved them from being executed."

Knowing the royals were safe felt like a giant weight was being lifted off the twins' shoulders. They sighed with relief and walked a little taller.

"Where is the Masked Man?" Alex asked. "We didn't see him with the villains at the Northern Palace."

"You haven't heard?" Rook asked.

"We haven't been around in a while," Conner said. "What happened?"

"The Masked Man is dead," he said. "The villains took over and had him killed."

The news made Alex and Conner stop in their tracks.

"Well, that's . . . *something*," Conner said, and shared a look with his sister.

A person they hated and felt so much anger toward was gone, but on the other hand, a family member was dead. The strangest part was not feeling any grief whatsoever for him.

After thinking about it, they realized the loss didn't really change a thing. The face and name they were fighting against may have changed, but their mission was still the same. Hopefully the battle ahead would be easier without him. Perhaps this meant the Literary Army would implode like a circus without a ringleader.

"Everyone is going to be thrilled to see you," Rook said. "How have you been?"

He unintentionally directed the question at Alex, and her brother suddenly felt like a third wheel. As uncomfortable as it made Conner, it was nothing compared to how Alex felt.

"We've been busy," Alex said. "My brother and I are recruiting an army to help us fight the villains."

"I know I'm still earning your trust back, but let me know if I can help," Rook said.

Alex kept trying to incorporate her brother into the conversation to make it less awkward, but Conner wanted nothing to do with it.

"Thank you, but I think we've got it under control," Alex said. "And for the record, we do trust you."

Rook smiled at her, but there was sadness in his eyes. Obviously, he was hoping to regain a lot more than trust. When Alex didn't smile back, the rest of Rook's face matched his eyes. They continued on through the tunnel, walking in a silence that said a thousand words.

The worst part about life in the abandoned mine was the constant waiting. It might have been easier if the refugees had an indication of what they were waiting *for*, but with each passing day, there was no good or bad news to share. They were becoming so restless that *any* information would have been better than none at all.

To pass the time, the refugees formed a little academy within the mine and taught one another different skills. Jack and the Tin Woodman taught the villagers how to sculpt using their axes. Soon, there wasn't a stalagmite in the mine that hadn't been carved into a squirrel, a beanstalk, a tower, or a mermaid.

Robin Hood and the Merry Men gave the queens archery and sword-throwing lessons. The Sherwood natives became a little invasive of the queens' personal space while showing them how to improve their form and received dirty looks from the kings.

Red's granny and the Old Woman from the Shoe Inn kept the kings and soldiers busy with sewing lessons. After a few days, the men had produced their first quilt and proudly hung it on display for the rest of the mine to see it.

"Remember, any man can shape a nation with a crown, but it takes a real man to start a quilt from a thread," Granny said.

Trollbella tried to teach Peter Pan and the Lost Boys to dance, but they weren't enthusiastic students. It didn't matter how many times she went over the steps of her routine, the boys only goofed off and teased one another.

"I don't know how to be more clear with you," Trollbella said. "It's step-touch, step-touch, kick-ball-change, reach to the right, reach to the left, kick-ball-change, shimmy to the front, shimmy to the back, pirouette, and pose! There's no nose-picking, pants-dropping, eye-poking, or tongue-showing in any of my choreography!"

Peter made a funny face at the troll queen behind her back. All the Lost Boys laughed, and she turned around just in time to see it. When Trollbella had first laid eyes on the Boy Who Never Grew Up, she was completely smitten, but the more his true colors showed, the more she disliked him; he was all sparkle and no substance.

The troll queen figured it was time to break the news to him. She looked Peter Pan directly in the eye and caressed his face.

"I had such high hopes for us, but I'm afraid it's not going to work out," Trollbella said.

She covered Peter's mouth to silence his protest, even though he didn't try to argue.

"We simply have different needs," Trollbella explained. "I'm looking for *romantic strolls*—you need a *stroller*. I'm looking for *love* and *lust*—you need a *leash*. I'm looking for a *Butterboy*—you're just a *Buttertoy*. Let's part as friends."

Trollbella sauntered away from Peter Pan and the Lost Boys. The boys exchanged puzzled looks, not sure if that was part of the dance lesson or not.

Goldilocks lay in the corner of the mine using Lester as a pillow and Clawdius as a footstool. The expectant mother was overdue and very eager to deliver the baby. Her backaches and irritability increased every day. Jack had to take all sharp objects away from her so she wouldn't have anything to throw during a mood swing.

Hagetta boiled some herbs in her cauldron and gave the concoction to Goldilocks for the pain. The Traveling Tradesman dangled a triangular stone on a string over her pregnant belly and studied the movement very closely. Red watched the Tradesman like he was a lunatic.

"What are you doing?" Red asked.

"I'm predicting the child's gender," the Traveling Tradesman said. "If the stone swings in a circle, it's a girl. If it moves back and forth, it's a boy."

"And what if it gets ripped out of your hand and thrown across the mine?" Red asked.

"It's all right. I already know it's going to be a boy," Goldilocks said.

"How could you possibly know that?" Red asked.

"Mother's intuition," Goldilocks said. "It's the one perk that comes with the bloating, the back pain, and the unstable emotions."

"A *niece* would be better for me," Red said. "I could dress her up in little dresses, apply blush to her tiny cheeks, and put dainty bows in her hair! I suppose I could do that with a nephew, too, but he might resent me for it later."

Goldilocks rolled her eyes. "Your request has been submitted," she said.

Red grabbed the string of the Tradesman's triangular stone and forced it to swing in a circle above Goldilocks's stomach, as if that would do the trick.

"Have you chosen a name yet?" Hagetta asked.

"Not yet," Goldilocks said. "I want his name to be special, I want it to mean something and inspire him for his whole life."

"You know, *Red* works for both a boy and a girl," Red said. "And *I* happen to be a very special, meaningful, and inspiring person."

Goldilocks cringed at the thought of bringing another Red into the world.

"Absolutely not," she said. "I want it to be original and freeing, like River or Robin or—*Alex and Conner*!"

Red scrunched her nose and crossed her arms. "How are *Alex* or *Conner* original and freeing?"

"*No—Alex and Conner are here!*" Goldilocks yelled. "*Look over there!*"

Goldilocks sat up and pointed to the back of the mine. Everyone went dead silent and turned toward where she was pointing. When they saw Alex and Conner entering with

Rook and Cornelius, the refugees burst into cheers and the mine vibrated with joy. Although it hadn't been too long since they'd seen most of them, the twins felt like they were walking into a reunion. Their friends surrounded them and stood in lines to embrace them. There were so many familiar faces they weren't expecting to see, they didn't know who to say hello to first. Everyone looked more tired, thinner, and paler than before. Living in the mine had worn them down.

"It's so wonderful to see you!" Alex said.

"Goldilocks, you look like you're about to explode!" Conner said.

"From your mouth to God's ears," Goldilocks said.

"Are you guys doing okay?" Alex asked. "Is everyone healthy and unharmed?"

"We're taking it one day at a time," Jack said. "How are you two? Where have you been?"

Alex and Conner shared a smile, knowing their news would excite them.

"We've been in the Otherworld recruiting an army to fight the literary villains," Conner announced.

"That's terrific!" the Tin Woodman said. "What kind of army?"

"An army of *my* characters," Conner said. "We've used the Portal Potion on my short stories from school. So far we've enlisted pirates, sailors, and Cyborgs—I'll explain what those are later."

All the refugees turned to the Traveling Tradesman.

The old geezer crossed his arms, leaned on a stalagmite, and glared at the others with a look that said *I told you so!*

"That's the best news we've heard in ages," Sir Lampton said. "How soon until it's ready for battle?"

"It won't be long," Alex said. "We just have two more stops and the army will be complete."

"DID YOU HEAR THAT, MEN?" Robin Hood asked the Merry Men. "SOON WE SHALL BE OUT OF THE SHADOWS OF SOLITUDE AND UNDER THE SUNLIGHT OF WAR! HOW MARVELOUS!"

Red pushed past the villagers, animals, and other royals to get closer to the twins. "Excuse me, pardon me, a *real friend* coming through," she said. "Alex and Conner, it's so lovely to see you're all right!" She suddenly grabbed them both by the shirt and looked frantically into their eyes. "You've got to get me out of here! There are peasants, animals, and men who talk to marbles! And Charlie isn't here to calm me down!"

The twins gently removed her hands from their clothes and took a step away.

"That's actually why we're here," Conner said. "Our mom and stepdad are watching my characters for us while we recruit others, but they need a hand. We were hoping a few of you could come back with us to help them supervise. There are more characters than they can handle."

"How many people do you need?" Jack asked.

Alex and Conner looked around the mine. Red wasn't the only one who looked desperate for a break. The twins would have a hard time refusing anyone's help.

"The more the merrier," Conner said. "But let's hurry. The people in this world need us."

Alex set the storybook on the ground and opened the cover. The beam of light was the brightest thing many of the refugees had seen in days and they shielded their eyes from it.

Before Conner could even explain where they were going, Red ran into the beam of light and disappeared from the mine. She was followed by Clawdius, Jack and Goldilocks, Robin Hood and the Merry Men, Lester and the Tin Woodman, and Peter Pan and the Lost Boys. Conner had lost count of how many people were traveling into the Otherworld when he felt a tap on his shoulder.

"You've come back for me, Butterboy," Trollbella said. "I don't know why I worried so. You've never let me down before. I know the pain of being away from each other can be overwhelming, so please don't waste your energy with a personal request for me to accompany you—*I'd be delighted to visit the Otherworld*!"

Before Conner could stop her, Trollbella ran into the beam of light with the others.

"Okay, we've definitely got enough help," Conner said. "We should get back and finish recruiting the army. If any of you need us, we'll just be on the other side of this beam."

"We'll stay behind and look after the others," Sir Lampton said.

"Thank you," Alex said. "We'll be back soon with help. Everyone stay safe!"

The twins stepped through the beam of light and returned to the Otherworld. Sir Lampton, Sir Grant, Hagetta, the Traveling Tradesman, Rook, Cornelius, Red's granny, the Old Woman from the Shoe Inn, the royal families, the villagers, and all the animals lowered their heads in a moment of silence. They all collectively said a prayer for the twins' success to continue and for them to be able to form an army to save the fairy-tale world.

Unfortunately for the occupants that remained, their quiet moment was interrupted by another unexpected visitor. Unbeknownst to Alex and Conner, they had been followed through the Dwarf Forests and into the secret tunnel.

The refugees saw something moving in the back of the mine. They heard hissing and rattling coming from a large silhouette.

"What was that?" Sir Grant asked.

The soldiers drew their swords and walked toward the sounds as a pair of bright red eyes glowed from the shadows. All the refugees froze where they stood, but they were frozen by much more than fear....

CHAPTER EIGHTEEN

SAINT ANDREW'S CHILDREN'S HOSPITAL

It took five trips in each of Charlotte's and Bob's cars to transport the characters from "Starboardia" to Saint Andrew's Children's Hospital. They covered each pirate and sailor in scrubs and medical masks and quickly escorted them through the hospital to the empty commissary in the brand-new wing.

It would have been simpler if the *Dolly Llama* crew weren't such a curious bunch. They pocketed medical supplies as they passed unoccupied countertops, snuck charts off hospital-room doors, and stole pens out of the lapels of unobservant physicians. By the time they reached the commissary, the pirates' pockets were full of scissors, Band-Aids, and medical tape, and a few of them wore bed-pans as hats.

The commissary was a wide and colorful room. It had dozens of tables, hundreds of chairs, adjoining bathrooms, and a large, never-been-used kitchen. It was the perfect place for temporarily hosting Conner's characters.

Ironically, the commissary had been decorated with a classic storybook theme. The walls were covered with murals of Alex and Conner's friends, and the support beams had been painted to look like book spines.

Anticipating her children's return from the fairy-tale world, Charlotte had cleared a space in the corner of the commissary and placed the *Land of Stories* book and Conner's binder of short stories on the floor. Once all the characters from "Starboardia" had been successfully escorted inside, the emerald storybook flipped open and the beam of light appeared.

Red ran out of the beam like a bull released from a pen and looked around the commissary. She sighed with relief and stretched her arms out.

"Thank God," she said. "I'm indoors!"

"Hi, Red!" Charlotte said. "Long time no see!"

Without even making eye contact with the twins' mother or the *Dolly Llama* crew, Red ran to the window and yanked the blinds open. Rays of sunlight shined inside and Red blissfully spun in them.

"*Daylight*—I've missed you so much!" Red said, and turned to the others. "No one look at me for at least twenty minutes. I haven't seen the sun in weeks! I'm paler than Snow White with a stomach flu!"

"Good to see you, too, Red," Bob said under his breath.

It wasn't long before the others from the fairy-tale world joined her. Clawdius ran out from the beam behind Red. Unlike his mother, the wolf was very social. He did an excited lap around the commissary and visited with every human he saw.

Jack and Goldilocks stepped out of the beam next and Jack helped his pregnant wife to the closest seat. They were joined shortly afterward by Robin Hood, the Merry Men, Lester, the Tin Woodman, Peter Pan, the Lost Boys, and Trollbella. Just like the characters from "Starboardia" did when they arrived on Sycamore Drive, the characters from the fairy-tale world and classic literature stared in awe at the wondrous new world around them.

"Welcome to Saint Andrew's Children's Hospital!" Charlotte said.

"So this is the Otherworld?" Jack said, and whistled at the sight.

"It's *colorful*," Goldilocks said. She side-eyed the decorations. "They certainly make reading a lifestyle here."

Before Bob and Charlotte began the complicated task of

introducing the new characters to the old characters, Alex and Conner popped out of the beam of light beside them.

"Oh cool, we're already at the hospital!" Conner said, and cleared his throat. "Ladies, gentlemen, chicken, and Blissworm from my stories, allow me to introduce you to the ladies, gentlemen, goose, and wolf from classic literature and fairy tales."

The introduction didn't go as well as the twins had hoped. The characters circled one another like animals meeting in the wild.

"*Pirates!*" Peter shouted at the *Dolly Llama* crew.

"Guys, knock it off!" Alex said. "We're all on the same side here. These people are going to help us defeat the Literary Army."

"Sorry," Peter said. "For whatever reason, I'm always inclined to shout '*Pirates*' whenever I see them—bad habit."

The Rosary Chicken fearfully laid an egg as soon as she saw Clawdius, and he chased after her. The Blissworm didn't want to miss out on the fun, so it jumped aboard the wolf and rode him like a cowboy. Lester thought the Blissworm was the most delicious-looking worm he had ever seen, so he chased after the others, forming a bizarre parade of fictional creatures.

"Rule number one," Conner said. "No one is allowed to eat anyone else!"

The Rosary Chicken clucked with relief. Clawdius and Lester stopped in their tracks and slumped. The Blissworm tugged on Clawdius's collar—Conner didn't say *the fun* had to stop.

It took the fairy-tale characters a few moments to realize that pictures of many of them were painted on the walls throughout the commissary. They walked to their respective murals and stared at the artwork worryingly.

"Look, boys, we're on the wall!" Peter said, and pointed to a mural of them. "Wait a moment. Is this place a church? Are we *gods* in this world?"

"Don't flatter yourself," Conner said. "People just like your story here."

The Tin Woodman found himself in a mural of *The Wonderful Wizard of Oz* but didn't recognize the three others he was traveling with down the yellow brick road.

"Who are the people I'm linking arms with?" the Tin Woodman asked.

"That's Dorothy, the Scarecrow, and the Cowardly Lion," Alex explained. "You would have met them in Oz if we hadn't found you first."

"Did *they* drop a barn on me as well?" the Tin Woodman asked.

"Um . . . I don't remember," Alex lied.

Robin Hood and the Merry Men gathered around the mural of *Robin Hood.* The resemblance between the real Merry Men and the painted Merry Men was striking; however, Robin Hood was depicted very effeminately in the painting. He wore bright green tights and had a short curly bob and no facial hair.

"I DON'T UNDERSTAND," Robin Hood said. "WHAT IS MY MOTHER DOING IN THIS PAINTING?"

Trollbella stared up in awe at a beautiful mural of Cinderella in a ball gown. She smiled from ear to ear and clutched her hands over her heart.

"Oh my Troblin heavens, it looks *just* like me!" she said. "There are some very talented painters in the Otherworld."

Red let out an earsplitting scream when she saw the mural of *Little Red Riding Hood*. The twins looked between the real Red and the painted Red, but they couldn't figure out what was so offensive. All they saw was an adorable girl in a red cape running from the Big Bad Wolf.

"Red, what's the problem?" Alex asked.

"They made me a *brunette*!" Red yelled.

The twins rolled their eyes. Red turned her back to the room and pouted as she continued soaking up the sun.

"That reminds me," Conner said. "I need to go back to 'Galaxy Queen' and get the Cyborgs."

He went to his binder of short stories, flipped it open to "Galaxy Queen," and vanished into the beam of light. As he went, Alex noticed that Goldilocks and Jack were whispering to each other and suspiciously glaring across the room.

"Is everything okay?" Alex asked.

"Alex, are my hormones driving me mad, or do that man and woman look exactly like Jack and me?" Goldilocks asked.

Alex looked at Auburn Sally and Admiral Jacobson on

the other side of the room. They were also whispering to each other and shooting peculiar glances at Jack and Goldilocks. Clearly they were having the exact same conversation.

"A lot of Conner's characters are based on people he knows," Alex said. "But trust me, it could be a lot worse than the captain and the admiral."

As soon as she said this, the Cyborg Queen charged out of the "Galaxy Queen" beam of light. She ignored everyone in the commissary and rolled directly to the windows where Red stood. Two large solar panels came out of her metal shoulders and she pointed them toward the sun.

"*Daylight*, thank goodness," the Cyborg Queen said. "I haven't had a solar charge in weeks!"

The Cyborg Queen stretched her solar panels so far, she took up the whole window.

"Excuse me," Red said. "You're blocking my light."

"Who says it's *your* light to begin with?" the Cyborg Queen said.

Red was appalled by her rudeness, so she left the window and took a seat by Jack and Goldilocks.

"I don't know who or what that woman is, but she's *terrible*," Red said.

Goldilocks fought a smile and leaned close to Alex. "I see what you mean," she said.

Conner and Commander Newters hurried out from the "Galaxy Queen" beam and cleared a large area of the commissary, stacking chairs and tables on top of one another until there was a large open space.

"Conner, what's that for?" Charlotte asked.

"The Cyborgs," he said.

Newters removed a small remote from his belt and pointed it at the beam. Twenty mechanized wagons carrying fifty Cyborg soldiers each rolled out of the beam of light. The Cyborgs were deactivated and were stacked on top of one another like folding chairs. Newters steered the wagons into the cleared area and parked them.

"Is that . . . *humane*?" Bob said with wide eyes.

"Probably not," Newters admitted. "But if we keep them deactivated until battle, we'll save a fortune on our electric bill."

The characters settled into groups throughout the commissary like high school cliques. The people of each dimension had their own sets of tables and cautiously eyed one another from afar.

"Will they be okay?" Charlotte asked.

"They'll warm up to each other," Conner said, and then whistled to get the room's attention. "Everybody listen up! Alex and I have to head into my next story to recruit more characters. Everyone please be nice to one another while we're gone. My mom and Bob are in charge unless they're at work—then Jack and Goldilocks are in charge."

The characters from "Starboardia," "Galaxy Queen," the *Land of Stories*, Sherwood Forest, Neverland, and Oz all nodded respectfully, then quickly returned to watching one another apprehensively. Alex and Conner hugged

Charlotte and Bob and went to the binder of short stories. Conner flipped it open to his next story and poured three drops of the Portal Potion on the pages.

Conner stepped toward the beam of light that appeared, but Alex stopped him before he entered it.

"Hold on a second," she said. "You're supposed to tell me what to expect at the next stop—and don't spare the details this time. If there are bug guts, I want to be prepared."

"The next story is called 'The Ziblings,'" Conner explained. "It's about four kids with superhuman powers. They all lost their parents at an early age and went to live at the same orphanage. One night, an asteroid carrying cosmic radiation hit their orphanage and affected their DNA, giving them phenomenal abilities. They were adopted by a billionaire astrophysicist named Professor Wallet and taken to his laboratory, where he raised them and trained them to become superheroes."

"Professor *Wallet*?" Alex asked.

"Yeah, I lost my wallet the day I wrote it and thought it was a good name," Conner said. "Moving on, we're going to travel to their city and meet them at the scene of a bank robbery. While they're saving the bank, we'll sneak inside the Zibling Mobile, follow them back to their secret laboratory, and ask them to join us."

"Will they cooperate?" she asked.

"The Ziblings are very competitive siblings," Conner

said. "They never pass up a challenge, especially if there's an opportunity to outshine each other."

"Okay," Alex said with a nod. *"Zounds zuper."*

"Leave the jokes to me," Conner said.

The twins stepped into the beam of light and disappeared from Saint Andrew's Children's Hospital.

CHAPTER NINETEEN

THE ZIBLINGS

C onner's handwriting wiggled and zoomed through the air as the world of "The Ziblings" was created around him and his sister. The word *highway* stretched beneath their feet, and Alex and Conner were suddenly standing in the middle of a wide country road. Cars and large trucks honked and swerved to avoid them, and they dashed to the side of the highway to avoid getting hit.

Alex and Conner looked up and saw a large city-limits sign above them. The sign read:

BIG CITY, USA
POPULATION 7,654,321

Once the handwritten words finished constructing the new dimension, the twins saw that the highway led to an enormous city a couple of miles in the distance. It had the tallest and leanest skyscrapers Alex had ever seen; the skyline looked more like a bundle of pencils and pens than a row of buildings.

"Big City, USA?" Alex asked. "You couldn't come up with anything more original than that?"

"It was supposed to be a placeholder until I came up with a better name, but Big City, USA, grew on me," Conner said. "Now let's go to the bank before it gets robbed without us."

Alex laughed. "Now, *that's* something I've never heard before," she said.

The twins walked down the road and entered the busy city. The world of the Ziblings was like a highly exaggerated version of the Otherworld. The buildings were more colorful, the streets were cleaner, and the cars were shinier. Even the people were more extravagant. The men were taller and had broader shoulders and wider jaws. The women had impeccable hair, makeup, and clothes. Even the children were cuter and better behaved. It was like the twins had entered a 1950s cartoon.

Alex and Conner zigzagged through the city streets. They walked down Main Street, made a right on Center

Road, and then a left on First Avenue. Alex wasn't sure which city Conner was emulating for "The Ziblings" setting because Big City, USA, had characteristics of every American city she could think of. There were subway stations like in New York City, bridges like in San Francisco, surrounding Great Lakes like in Chicago, and BIG CITY, USA, was written across a hillside like the Hollywood sign.

They eventually found Big City Bank, in the middle of First Avenue. It was a large white building with thick pillars and a massive dome. It reminded Alex of the Capitol Building in Washington, DC. The twins walked up the front steps and went inside.

The bank had marble floors, golden pillars, and wooden counters. There were high ceilings, tall windows, and lots of elaborate lighting structures. A long line of Big City citizens waited patiently to be helped by one of a dozen bank tellers. There were also desks scattered throughout the bank where bankers helped other citizens open new accounts and apply for loans. No one appeared to have been rejected, because all the applicants had big smiles on their faces as they happily shook the bankers' hands.

Conner took his sister to the far end of the bank, near a back door. He got down on the floor, lay facedown, and put his hands over his head.

"Are you doing yoga?" Alex asked.

"No, I'm getting ready," he said. "We're just in time."

"For what?"

"The *robbery*," he said, as if it were obvious. "It should be starting in five...four...three...two..."

Five armed robbers stormed into the bank. They wore all black and had mouse ears and whiskers attached to their masks. The robbers fired their guns into the air to get everyone's attention. It was startling even to Alex, and she'd known it was coming.

"Everyone on the ground now!" the largest robber shouted. "Facedown with your hands on your heads! No talking! Don't make me tell you twice!"

The citizens screamed and did what they were told. Alex joined her brother on the floor and copied his pose. The robbers threw big duffel bags on the wooden counters and pointed their guns at the tellers.

"Empty the safe!" the largest robber shouted. "And don't you dare try any funny business or I'll blow you all to the sky!"

The trembling tellers did what the robbers demanded. They opened the gigantic safe in the back of the bank and began filling the duffel bags with stacks of cash and bars of gold.

"What's up with the ears and whiskers on their masks?" Alex whispered to her brother.

"It's part of their gimmick," he said. "These guys are called *the Rat Pack*—they're the most infamous bank robbers in Big City, USA. The tallest one's name is Frank, he's the leader, and then there are his henchmen: Sammy, Dean, Joey, and Peter."

"Just like the Rat Pack from the sixties!" Alex said.

Conner scrunched his forehead. "Dang it!" he said. "I thought I made it up—I must have heard about them from someone."

"*You two! I said no talking!*" Frank yelled, pointing his gun at the twins.

Alex and Conner went silent. The Rat Pack walked around the bank and patrolled their hostages. They nudged the terrified citizens with their feet and laughed wildly as the hostages cowered and squirmed. After a few minutes of lying uncomfortably on the floor and watching the robbers torment the men and women, Alex was very eager to see the Ziblings come to the rescue. It was taking all her self-control not to transform the Rat Pack into actual rodents.

Conner tapped his sister and gestured to one of the windows. Alex looked up and saw the silhouette of a man wearing a cape. He stood heroically with his hands on his hips. Alex was so excited to see a real superhero that her stomach filled with butterflies, but the feeling quickly subsided. It took a moment for the superhero to enter the bank, not because he was conducting a plan, but because he couldn't open the window.

Finally, with a strong tug, the hero managed to pry it open. He crawled through the small opening, but then he stepped on his cape and slipped off the windowsill. He crashed onto the floor behind a desk with a very loud *thump*. Everyone in the bank heard the crash and jerked their head toward it. The Rat Pack clutched their guns tighter and slowly approached the desk. The hostages waited on pins and needles, hoping it was someone who had come to their rescue.

The superhero jumped out from behind the desk and struck the same heroic pose he had held in the window. After a closer look, Alex was surprised to see he was actually an adorable boy no more than twelve years old. He wore a sky-blue suit and a dark blue mask, with matching gloves, boots, and cape. He had messy dark hair, plump cheeks, and green eyes.

Upon seeing him, the robbers snickered and the hostages lost all hope. Apparently no one had much faith in the hero's capability.

"Don't worry, boys, it's just Bolt." Frank laughed. "The Ziblings have sent the *runt* of the litter!"

Bolt shifted uncomfortably at the blatant disrespect.

"Hello, Rat Pack," the boy said in a tone obviously deeper than his real voice. "I see you've escaped prison and gone right back to your old tricks. I guess you can take the rats out of the garbage, but you can't take the garbage out of the rats!"

"*'But you can't take the garbage out of the rats,'*" Frank mocked him. "You really need to work on your playful jargon if you want to be taken seriously."

"And *you* need to work on following the law," Bolt said. "Good thing there are people like me to put you back in your place!"

Frank turned to his henchmen. *"Get him,"* he said. "But don't waste your bullets—he isn't worth it."

The boy's face turned bright red. "Oh, yes I am!" he argued. "I'm worth all the bullets you got!"

Bolt became angry and his superpowers were activated. His body was covered in static electricity, his messy hair rose above his head, and tiny electric waves buzzed around his fingertips. Bolt somersaulted toward Frank, and with the lightest touch of his index finger, he zapped the robber on the leg.

"Ouch," Frank said. "That *almost* hurt a little."

The boy cartwheeled to Sammy and Dean and shocked them on the arms. He dived to the other side of the bank and zapped Joey on the nose and Peter on the ear. Bolt was very proud of himself, but his efforts did little to wound the Rat Pack. They just looked more irritated than before.

"I changed my mind. *Shoot him,*" Frank instructed.

Bolt flew through the air to avoid the bullet, not with the grace of an eagle or a hawk, but with the clumsiness of a baby bird. His erratic flight pattern made it very difficult for the Rat Pack to aim their guns at him, so they flipped their weapons over and swung them like baseball bats. Frank knocked Bolt out of the air and the not-so-super-hero hit the floor.

"Tie him up," Frank ordered, and eyed the hostages. "And for the rest of you—show's over, *back to work*!"

The Rat Pack tied Bolt to a chair and the tellers continued emptying the vault. Eventually the vault was cleared out entirely and the duffel bags were bulging with cash and gold. The tellers handed the bags back to the Rat Pack and the robbers headed for the door. Bolt tried to free himself from the restraints, but they were too strong.

"This transaction has been a *pleasure*," Frank announced to the bank. "See you next time!"

Suddenly, a thunderous *crash* came from above. Three more superheroes dropped in from the domed ceiling—*the rest of the Ziblings had arrived*!

The oldest Zibling was about sixteen and very athletic. He wore a bright yellow tank top, baggy yellow pants, big sneakers, and a headband. His muscly arms were bare and caught fire as soon as he touched the ground.

The second-oldest Zibling was a fifteen-year-old girl. She wore a pink suit with a built-in miniskirt. She had sandy-blond hair that was braided into two long pigtails. She had complete control over her hair and twirled her braids like the blades of a helicopter until she came to a safe landing.

The third-oldest Zibling wore a dark green suit and a leather jacket. Instead of a mask, he wore very dark sunglasses. His arms transformed into large feathered wings as he glided to the floor, then transformed back once he landed.

All the citizens, tellers, and bankers sighed with relief at the older Ziblings' arrival. The Rat Pack robbers simultaneously gulped and eyed one another nervously. Bolt rolled his eyes at his siblings' splashy entrance—he had been hoping to handle the Rat Pack without them.

"Hello, Frank, Sammy, Dean, Joey, and Peter," the oldest said, acting as the Ziblings' leader. "Have you come out of the sewer for fresh air?"

"Hello, Blaze, Whipney, and Morph," Frank said. "Have you come to save your little brother?"

"I don't need to be saved!" Bolt said. *"Being tied to this chair is part of my plan, which you guys are kind of ruining!"*

The Ziblings ignored their little brother as if he weren't even in the room. They locked eyes with the Rat Pack and never looked away.

"We've come to take you and your boys back to prison, Frank," Blaze said. "You belong in a cage just like all the other rodents."

The Ziblings charged toward the Rat Pack and the robbers ran for the door.

Morph jumped in front of them and transformed into a brick wall. His sunglasses were his only remaining physical trait. He was now blocking the robbers' exit, so they ran for the back door. Whipney whipped her head back and forth and her braids wrapped around Sammy's and Dean's ankles. She raised them into the air and knocked them into each other, and they fell unconscious to the ground.

Joey and Peter aimed their guns at Blaze. He pointed at them and two fiery geysers blasted out of his fingertips. The robbers were set on fire and they dropped to the floor and rolled around to extinguish the flames. Morph transformed into a huge cage and Whipney scooped up Dean, Sammy, Joey, and Peter with her hair and threw the robbers inside it. They had caught all the rats in the pack except for one.

Frank jumped over the wooden counter and ran to the back of the bank. He jumped inside the vault and locked the enormous metal door behind him. Blaze followed him and pressed his palms against the vault door. He heated the vault so much, the door turned bright orange and melted away. Whipney reached into the vault with her hair, pulled Frank out, and tossed him into the cage with the others.

The bank hostages leaped to their feet in celebration. They cheered and applauded their rescuers. Everyone was thrilled the Ziblings had saved another day in Big City, USA—everyone but Bolt.

"You're in so much trouble," Blaze told his little brother.

"Why?" Bolt said. "I had everything under control before you showed up."

"You know the rules," Whipney said. "No crime fighting until your homework is done, and Dad doesn't want you doing it without us!"

"I can take care of myself," Bolt said. "I can do anything you guys can, you just never give me the chance! You never let me prove myself!"

"*Prove yourself?*" said the cage Morph had turned into. "You can't get out of that chair!"

"How are you supposed to help people if you can't even help yourself?" Whipney said.

Tears came to Bolt's eyes and he looked away from his siblings. It was an expression layered with embarrassment, frustration, self-doubt, and heartache all in one. Alex knew that look. She could have sworn she'd seen it somewhere before.

Suddenly, memories surfaced like a movie playing in her mind. Alex flashed back to when she and Conner were in elementary school.

"Let's go around the room and say what we all want to be when we grow up," their second-grade teacher told the class.

"A doctor!" said a boy.

"A senator!" said a girl.

"A teacher!" Alex remembered saying.

Her brother sat up at his desk, excited to share his answer.

"A fireman!" he said. "I want to help people!"

Even then, Conner wasn't as good a student as Alex was. He had trouble learning to read, how to spell, and how to do math. He was always asking Alex for help with his homework and she became mad that he couldn't keep up with her. So when Conner gave his answer about his plans for the future, Alex was inclined to respond.

"A fireman?" she asked. "How are you supposed to help people if you can't help yourself?"

Everyone in the class laughed. Alex didn't mean any harm by it; she was so young, it just slipped out of her mouth. Even though it had happened almost ten years before, the expression on Conner's face had been engraved in her memory forever. It was exactly how Bolt looked at his siblings now.

Soon, the front steps of the bank were filled with police and reporters. Morph transformed back into his human form and he, Whipney, and Blaze pushed the Rat Pack robbers outside and into the hands of the police. The Ziblings spoke with the reporters about what had happened. They took all the credit and soaked up the attention, leaving Bolt tied to the chair inside.

"Now's a good time to sneak into the Zibling Mobile," Conner whispered to Alex.

The twins exited the Big City Bank through the back door and Alex followed Conner into the alley behind it. The Zibling Mobile was a bright red convertible with rocket engines and a bright yellow *Z* painted on the side. The car was parked out of sight between two dumpsters, but Conner knew exactly where to find it.

He felt around the back tire and pulled a spare key out of a hidden compartment. He opened the trunk and crawled inside it.

"Come on," Conner said, and offered his sister a hand.

Alex hesitated before joining him. Something heavy was weighing on her heart.

"Quick question," she said. "Is this story based on anything that happened in real life? Anything that might have happened between us?"

Conner thought about it, but shook his head.

"Nope, this one is completely made up," he said. "I just loved superheroes when I was a kid. 'The Ziblings' was one of the first stories I ever wrote."

Alex didn't press the issue further; she just nodded and climbed into the trunk with him.

Conner may have forgotten what happened in the second grade, but Alex couldn't shake it. It wasn't just the mean exchange in elementary school that bothered her, though. Alex was worried "The Ziblings" was much closer to home than Conner realized, and that *she* might be the story's villain.

CHAPTER TWENTY

PROFESSOR WALLET'S SECRET LABORATORY

The Zibling Mobile zoomed through the streets of Big City, USA, tossing Alex and Conner around the trunk like clothes in a washing machine. Every turn was sharper than the one before, every acceleration was more forceful, and the vehicle never slowed down or came to a stop. It had only two speeds: *fast* and *faster*.

"Who the heck is driving this thing?" Alex asked.

"Blaze just got his license," Conner said. "He's a little zealous about it."

The Zibling Mobile ran over speed bumps, causing the twins to slam into the top of the trunk.

"I bet his driving puts more people in danger than all the robbers and criminal masterminds combined!" Alex said.

It was pitch-black in the trunk, so the twins had no clue which street or neighborhood the vehicle was cruising through. Conner was able to track their whereabouts to a certain point, but Blaze's reckless diving was so discombobulating, he didn't even know if they were still headed for Professor Wallet's laboratory.

"How much longer are we going to be in this thing?" Alex asked. "I feel like a scrambled egg."

"The laboratory is deep underground just a few miles outside of the city," Conner said. "At the speed Blaze is driving, it shouldn't take much longer."

"And how exactly do we *get* to the laboratory?" Alex asked. "I'm assuming there's more involved than just surface streets."

"They have to go into the Big City Lake, through the sewer, and down an abandoned subway tunnel," Conner said.

"Can their car go underwater?" Alex asked.

"Of course their car doesn't go underwater," Conner said. "It turns into a submarine first."

The twins heard a bunch of mechanisms moving throughout the vehicle as it converted into a submarine. Then they heard a big *splash* outside, and a moment later the trunk began filling with water.

"We must be in the lake," Conner said.

"I thought you said the vehicle turns into a submarine!" Alex said.

"Apparently everything but the trunk," he said. "Gosh, I never thought I'd have to be *that* specific!"

Alex snapped her fingers and the water stopped. The Zibling Mobile moved into the sewer, and the twins gagged and covered their noses with their shirts. There wasn't enough magic in the world to keep out the smell.

The Zibling Mobile converted back into a car, and its tires touched solid ground again. The vehicle rattled and shook as it drove over the tracks of the abandoned subway passage. It was so bumpy, the twins became nauseated. Right before they were about to vomit, the car came to an abrupt stop.

They heard the vehicle's doors open and close as the Ziblings got out.

Conner popped the trunk just a crack, and he and Alex peered out.

"We're here," he whispered. "This is Professor Wallet's secret laboratory."

The underground laboratory was built on a former subway platform. The Zibling Mobile was parked on the subway tracks below it and was only one of many methods of transportation. There was a Zibling Jet, a Zibling Speedboat, Zibling Motorcycles, Zibling Segways, and even a Zibling Carriage with robotic horses.

The laboratory had everything a secret superhero base

could need. There was a wall of televisions with live news feeds from every major city in the world. There were giant computers, microscopes, test tubes, data servers, and generators. In the center of the laboratory was a big red lightbulb that went off whenever a crisis occurred. All the appliances were neatly labeled in case there was any confusion over what the object was.

Not only was Professor Wallet a devoted astrophysicist, he was also a proud father. The laboratory was decorated with photos of his adopted children and tokens of their accomplishments. The Ziblings' very first superhero suits were framed and hung on the walls. There was a lit candle with a plaque that read "Blaze's First Flame." A lock of hair and a pair of mangled scissors were on display and tagged "Whipney's First Haircut." There was a photo of a trash can wearing sunglasses marked "Morph's First Transformation." Another photo, of a toddler sucking on a glowing lightbulb like a binky, was labeled "Bolt's First Spark."

There was also a wall covered with a giant map of Big City, USA. The map was bordered with mug shots of all the criminals the Ziblings had brought to justice. Pieces of yarn stretched from the mug shots to the places on the map where the criminals had been caught.

Each Zibling had a corner of the laboratory filled with personal belongings. Blaze had a collection of hot sauces, matches, and fire extinguishers. Whipney had a vanity full of hair products and industrial-strength brushes and combs. Morph had framed butterflies, moths, beetles, wasps, and shelves of photography books—all inspiration for metamorphosis. Bolt had a desk where he made figurines out of old batteries.

Whipney printed out five mug shots of the Rat Pack and placed them on the wall with the others. Blaze went to the computer and dialed a number on the keypad.

"What are you doing?" Bolt asked.

"I'm calling Dad," Blaze said. "He needs to know you left the laboratory without permission—*again*."

"*Tattletale!*" Bolt said.

A few moments later, Professor Wallet appeared on the computer screen. He was an older man with a gray beard and thick glasses that magnified his blue eyes. He wore a turquoise turtleneck and a white lab coat. The professor held his communication device way too close to his face and the camera was aimed up his nostrils.

"Hello, children," the professor said. "Is this an emergency? I'm just about to step into a meeting with the German chancellor about her new anti-matter research program."

"It's not an emergency, but *someone* snuck out of the laboratory to fight crime on his own again," Blaze said, and nodded at Bolt.

The professor rubbed his eyes under his glasses. "Oh, Bolt," he said disappointedly. "What am I going to do with you?"

"It's not fair!" Bolt said. "Blaze, Whipney, and Morph

306

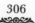

were allowed to fight crime on their own when they were my age!"

"Young man, we've been over this a hundred times," Professor Wallet said. "Your abilities haven't reached their full potential yet. The radiation from the asteroid reacted differently with each of your DNA, meaning your powers will peak at a different time than your siblings'. Remember, not all flowers bloom in the spring."

"What if I'm more like a Venus flytrap than a flower?" Bolt argued. "Maybe my powers are just waiting for an opportunity to show up!"

"Science doesn't work that way," the professor said. "I don't make the rules to upset you—I make them to protect you. You're grounded until I get back home."

Bolt grunted and stomped his feet. He sulked over to his corner of the laboratory, zapping Blaze on the ear as he went, and then pouted at his desk.

"I'm being summoned into the chancellor's office," the professor said. "I'll call you tonight when I get to my hotel room."

"Tell the chancellor we said hello," Morph said.

"And tell her I love the new highlights!" Whipney said.

The professor looked confused. "Of the anti-matter program?" he asked.

Whipney sighed. "No, Dad, in her *hair*," she said.

"Oh, of course," the professor said. "I will pass along the message. Good-bye, children."

The professor hung up and disappeared from the computer screen. The Ziblings went to their respective corners to decompress. Blaze drank a bottle of hot sauce like it was water and did push-ups. Whipney's hair unbraided and brushed itself while she flipped through a magazine. Morph looked at a photography book and practiced transforming into the objects he saw. Bolt played with his battery figurines and tied a tissue around one to give it a cape.

Conner quietly closed the trunk of the car to have a private word with his sister.

"Here's my plan," Conner said. "We're going to get out and tell them we're reporters from the *Otherworld Times*, a syndicated school newspaper that runs in twenty-five states. We'll say we're looking to do a personal-interest piece on the bravest, strongest, and smartest superhero in the country. And to prove which one of them deserves the title, we'll take them to the fairy-tale world, where whoever defeats the most soldiers in the Literary Army will be the winner. What do you think?"

Alex definitely saw some flaws in her brother's plan, but she kept them to herself. She was still consumed by guilt from her realization at the bank. She never wanted to discourage her brother again.

"Brilliant!" she said. "That's a great idea—no, it's an *amazing* idea! Gosh, all your ideas are so wonderful. I don't know how you do it."

Even though the trunk was dark, Conner gave his sister a funny look. Something was up. Alex was never *that* supportive. He worried she might have hit her head in the car ride over.

"Alex, are you feeling okay?" he asked.

Before she could answer, the red lightbulb in the center of the laboratory started flashing and a loud siren went off. The Ziblings jumped to their feet like protective canines and ran to the wall of televisions. They scanned the screens and saw a frantic reporter on the French news. Blaze turned up the volume and pressed a button so the reporter's words were translated into English.

"Paris is under attack," the reporter said from the newsroom. *"The mad scientist and criminal mastermind known as the Snake Lord, notorious for his interactions with the Ziblings in Big City, USA, has taken over the Eiffel Tower!"*

The news program played footage of the Snake Lord from earlier that day. He was a tall, muscular middle-aged man with a villainous scowl. His eyes were yellow with narrow pupils like a reptile. He wore a large helmet shaped like the head of a king cobra and a long purple cape. The Snake Lord licked his lips and exposed a forked tongue.

"That slithering son of a gun!" Blaze said.

The Snake Lord was accompanied by two sidekicks, a man and a woman—but neither appeared to be entirely human. They had scaly green skin, large nostrils, and reptilian eyes. The man had an orange Mohawk and a collar like a frilled lizard. The woman had red horns and long nails like the claws of a raptor.

"*Collared Joe* and *Lizzy Liza* are with him!" Whipney said, and raised a lock of hair at the screen.

"He's got more friends than that," Morph said. "Look!" The three criminals were followed by a long procession of thousands and thousands of serpents. There were boa constrictors, pythons, anacondas, and even tiny garden snakes. The serpents were colorful and moved behind the Snake Lord like a slithering rainbow.

The news showed footage of the Snake Lord and his scaly accomplices storming the base of the Eiffel Tower. They knocked down security guards in their way, and hundreds of tourists ran for their lives. The snakes formed a circle around the Eiffel Tower and didn't let any of the Parisian police pass.

The camera zoomed in on a device the Snake Lord was carrying that looked like a mini-satellite.

"The Snake Lord has the *Reptilalizer*!" Bolt said in horror.

"*At this time, the Snake Lord hasn't made any demands and isn't holding any civilians hostage,*" the reporter said. "*It is a complete mystery as to why he has come to Paris and what he wants with the Eiffel Tower.*"

The Ziblings shared fearful looks with one another.

"It isn't a mystery to us!" Blaze said. "We've got to get to Paris and stop him! *Ziblings to the jet!*"

The four superheroes ran straight to the Zibling Jet parked on the subway track.

Conner was more upset by the news than any of the superheroes were. "This is *terrible*," Conner said.

"Hold the phone," Alex said. "The Snake Lord? The Reptilalizer? You never mentioned any of that before we left."

"That's because I forgot how short this story is. It moves much faster than the other ones," he said. "The Snake Lord is the Ziblings' arch-nemesis. He was a scientist who used to work with Professor Wallet. A failed experiment turned him and his research assistants into partial reptiles. When Professor Wallet couldn't reverse the effects, the Snake Lord became evil. He invented a helmet that gave him control over all reptiles. The Reptilalizer is his newest invention, and it turns mammals into reptiles. It has to be activated from the tallest point in a city—that's why he's at the Eiffel Tower!"

"So once he activates it, he'll turn everyone in Paris into a reptile and be able to control them!" Alex said as she figured it out. "That's intense!"

The Ziblings climbed aboard the jet and strapped themselves into the seats, but Blaze blocked Bolt from entering.

"What do you think you're doing?" Blaze asked.

"I'm going to Paris to fight the Snake Lord with you guys," Bolt said.

"No you're not," Blaze said. "You heard Dad—you're grounded."

"Oh, come on," Bolt argued. "The Snake Lord is the

toughest bad guy we've ever fought! You're going to need help!"

"Exactly. Which is why you need to stay in the laboratory," Blaze said. "We'll have our hands full saving the people of Paris—we won't be able to watch you. If you come with us, you'll just be a burden."

Bolt's posture sank almost an entire foot. He had never been called a *burden* before.

"But...but...but I'm a *superhero*," Bolt said with a quivering lip.

Blaze sighed. "No you're not," he said. "You're just a kid with tricks."

Blaze closed the jet's door right in front of Bolt's face and joined Whipney and Morph in the cockpit. The engines roared and the Zibling Jet rocketed down the abandoned subway, heading for Paris.

Bolt waited until his brothers and sister were gone and then burst into tears. He went to his corner of the laboratory and cried at his desk. Once it was out of his system, he tried to make himself feel better by playing with his homemade figurines. He picked up the one with the tissue cape and moved it through the air like it was flying.

"Here he comes now to save the day!" Bolt said, pretending he was a news reporter. "It's the world's favorite Zibling—it's *Bolt*!"

Fantasizing about being a real superhero only made him feel worse. Bolt crumpled up the figurine until it was nothing but a pile of used batteries. He rested his head on his desk and continued crying.

"We need a new plan to recruit the Ziblings," Conner whispered to Alex. "Any ideas? Alex?"

He turned to his sister and saw that the sad little super-hero had brought Alex to tears. In fact, she looked sadder than Bolt did.

"Alex, are you okay?" he asked.

"Conner, I'm so sorry." She sniffled.

"Sorry for what?" Conner asked.

"Sorry if I ever made you feel like *that*," Alex cried. "I know you don't remember, but there was a time I treated you exactly like the Ziblings are treating Bolt—and just like them, I had no idea how much I was hurting you. This story is much more personal than you think. It's about *us*."

"Alex, I think you're over-reacting," he said.

"You just don't see it," Alex said. "Since we were kids, people have always compared us to each other. Everyone always shamed you for not getting good grades like me, for not being as mature as me, or for not being as organized as me. But no one ever made *me* feel bad for not being more like *you*—I had no idea what it was like. But now that I'm watching Bolt, I see how painful it must have been."

At first Conner thought his sister was crazy. There was no way a silly story he wrote could have been *that* meaning-ful. But the more she explained, the more sense it made. Alex had always been capable of so many things, she was like a superhero in his mind, a superhero he could never live up to.

"I apologize if I ever made you feel bad about yourself or made you feel left behind," Alex said. "You've always been so supportive of me, and I should have returned the favor more often. You're so gifted and deserve a lot more champions than just Mrs. Peters. I'm sorry it took a trip into your stories for me to see that."

Conner had no idea what to say. He looked around at the world of the Ziblings as if he were seeing his own story for the first time.

CHAPTER TWENTY-ONE

CITY OF LIGHTNING

*T*he Ziblings have arrived in Paris! I repeat, the Ziblings have arrived in Paris!" the French reporter announced. "Parisians can take a deep breath! It looks like help is here!"

The twins were still sitting in the trunk of the Zibling Mobile. Conner was trying to come up with a new plan to recruit the superheroes, but all he could think about was his sister's analysis of his story. Was there really more to the Ziblings than he realized?

"So what happens next?" Alex asked.

"The Snake Lord captures the Ziblings at the Eiffel Tower," Conner said. "When Professor Wallet returns to the laboratory, he gives Bolt a pep talk that boosts his confidence. Bolt goes to Paris to save his brothers and sister, and when he faces the Snake Lord, the rest of his powers kick in and he saves the day."

"Oh, Professor Wallet must be based on Mrs. Peters!" Alex said. "She's the person who gave you the confidence to write—and it activated the rest of *your* abilities!"

"Stop analyzing and focus," Conner said. "Professor Wallet doesn't get back to the laboratory for a week. *We* need to boost Bolt's confidence or we'll be stuck here for a couple days."

"Can't you and I just go to Paris and save the Ziblings ourselves?" Alex asked.

"No. The Ziblings are too divided right now," Conner explained. "We need them working as a team if we want them to help us fight the Literary Army. When Bolt saves them, he restores their bond as a family."

"Got it," Alex said. "So how do we make him confident enough to go?"

Conner scratched his head as he thought about it. He peeked out of the trunk and saw that Bolt was still pouting at his desk.

"He wants nothing more than to be a superhero," Conner said. "So let's make him *feel* like a superhero. We'll still pretend we're student reporters from the *Otherworld Times*, but we'll say we're doing a story all about him."

Alex nodded. "Let's look the part," she said.

She snapped her fingers and a notepad and pen appeared in Conner's hands. Alex snapped again and a camera appeared hanging around her neck. The twins quietly crawled out of the Zibling Mobile, tiptoed across the subway tracks, and climbed onto the platform. Conner knocked on the wall of mug shots like it was a door.

"Excuse me?" he called into the laboratory. "Is this Professor Wallet's secret underground laboratory?"

The voice startled Bolt and he jumped up from his desk. He had never seen strangers in the laboratory before. He eyed the twins suspiciously and made fists with his hands.

"What are you doing in here?" he asked.

"Oh my goodness!" Conner said. "It's the incredible Bolt himself! We must be in the right place!"

"Oh my gosh, I can't believe we're seeing him in person!" Alex said.

The twins acted starstruck. They giddily jumped up and down like they were meeting their idol. Their enthusiasm made Bolt stand a little taller.

"Who are you?" he asked. "How did you find the laboratory?"

"I'm Conner and this is my photographer, Alex," Conner said. "We're from the *Otherworld Times*. Professor Wallet didn't tell you we were coming?"

"No," Bolt said. "What's the *Otherworld Times*?"

"It's a syndicated school newspaper that's printed in over twenty-five states nationwide," Conner explained.

"We're here to do a human-interest piece on you. We asked our readers who their favorite Zibling was, and over seventy percent of those polled said it was you. Congratulations!"

Bolt couldn't believe it. His eyes grew wide and his mouth dropped open. He had never been anyone's favorite *anything* before.

"Me?" he said in shock. "But...but...but *why*?"

Conner hadn't thought this part of his plan through yet. He looked to Alex for help.

"Because you're the Zibling our readers identify with," she said. "They think it's very brave of you to fight criminals much bigger and older than you. You inspire young kids around the country to go after their own dreams—despite their size or age!"

Bolt held a hand over the lightning bolt on his chest. He had never been so honored in his life.

"I never thought I was so *inspirational*," he said.

"Would you mind if we interviewed you and took some pictures?" Conner asked.

"Would I *mind*?" Bolt asked. "Please—I insist!"

The superhero checked his reflection in the computer screen and straightened his hair. He pulled up two chairs for him and Conner to sit in while they chatted. Conner scanned his blank notepad as if it were full of questions. Alex walked around them and took photos while they spoke.

"Now, tell us, what's it like being a superhero?" Conner asked.

Bolt hesitated to answer. Truthfully, he had never felt more *unlike* a superhero than today. But he didn't want to disappoint the readers of the *Otherworld Times*, so he gave the answers he thought they'd want to hear.

"It's the best job in the whole world!" Bolt said. "The asteroid hitting our orphanage was the best thing that ever happened to me."

Conner scribbled down notes so quickly, he wasn't even writing real words.

"What's your favorite part about being a hero?" Conner asked.

"Oh, that's easy," Bolt said. "Helping people! I love seeing the relief in their eyes after they're rescued from a burning building, or a runaway train, or a sinking ship. Actually, I've never saved anyone myself, but I've been with my brothers and sister when they have."

The thought made Bolt a little sad and he sank in his chair. Conner quickly changed the subject to keep his spirits up.

"Our readers love watching you fly," he said. "Do you have any special techniques that get you off the ground?"

"Actually, I'm still working on the whole *flying thing*," Bolt said, like it was a secret. "Hopefully I'll get better at it one day. Never go so high you're afraid to look down: That's my motto."

"Words to live by," Conner said. "And what about all that electricity you produce? Where does it come from?"

"According to my dad, my body generates a lot of

friction, which pulls the electricity out of the environment around me," Bolt said. "Right now I can light up a fourteen-watt battery all by myself, but I'm hoping to get to a sixty-watt by the end of the year."

"That's *very* impressive!" Conner said. "It makes perfect sense why our readers said they'd prefer having *your* powers over any of your siblings'."

"Really?" Bolt asked. "That's crazy because most of the time I wish I could switch! I think it would be so cool to create fire like Blaze, or turn into stuff like Morph, or use my hair for chores like Whipney."

The more Conner buttered him up, the happier he became. With every picture Alex took, Bolt had a bigger and bigger smile. So far, their plan seemed to be working.

"Nice. This is all such great stuff," Conner said. "What would you say to someone who wanted to be a superhero as amazing as you?"

It took Bolt a few moments to respond. He had never thought anyone would want to be a superhero like *him*. He wanted to give his followers an answer from his heart.

"I suppose it would be to never give up," he said. "Courage is what makes a superhero super!"

Suddenly, the red lightbulb in the center of the laboratory lit up and the crisis alarm sounded again. The twins and Bolt turned to the television and saw that the situation in Paris had become much worse.

"Breaking news," the panicked reporter said. *"The Snake Lord has captured the Ziblings! I repeat, the Snake*

Lord has captured the Ziblings! Something has gone wrong in their attempt to save the city. There is still no information at this time of what the Snake Lord is doing at the Eiffel Tower or what he is now planning to do with the Ziblings."

The news played live footage from a helicopter circling the Eiffel Tower. Blaze, Whipney, and Morph were wrapped around the base of the tower's antenna by a large anaconda. They were so close together, Blaze couldn't use his powers without burning his brother and sister. It was so tight between them that Morph couldn't transform into anything. A rattlesnake was covering Whipney's head like a turban, constricting her hair.

The Snake Lord was standing on a small platform at the very top of the Eiffel Tower's antenna. Screw by screw, he attached the Reptilalizer to the antenna and connected it to the tower's power. He operated unwaveringly and never looked up from the device.

Bolt was horrified to see that his family had been captured. Even though they'd known it was coming, Alex and Conner pretended to be just as surprised as him.

"This is awful!" he said. "The Snake Lord is going to turn everyone in Paris into a reptile!"

"Good thing there's still *one* Zibling left who can save them," Alex said.

The boy shook his head and paced back and forth. He couldn't fathom facing such a threat without the help of his brothers and sister.

"I can't defeat the Snake Lord on my own!" Bolt said.

"My powers haven't reached their full potential yet! I'm no match for him."

"Sure you are," Conner said. "You're the *Otherworld Times*' favorite superhero!"

"No I'm not!" Bolt exclaimed. "Your readers got it wrong. I'm not even a real superhero. My own family said it! I'm just a boy with tricks! The Snake Lord is going to win, and there's nothing I can do about it!"

Bolt went to his corner of the laboratory and sat at his desk. Alex and Conner exchanged worried glances. They had built up his ego only to watch it collapse like a building under demolition.

"I don't think we can convince him," Conner said to his sister. "To be honest, I'm not sure I would go to Paris if I were in his shoes."

"But you *were* in his shoes once," Alex said. "Bolt is you. He represents the little boy inside you who used to doubt himself. You have to be *his* Mrs. Peters—tell him exactly what you would have wanted to hear."

It was unsettling how Alex understood Conner's characters better than he did, but that's how he knew she was right. He let out a deep sigh and walked over to Bolt.

"For what it's worth, I know how you feel," Conner told him. "I used to doubt myself a lot. When people told me I wasn't good enough, I believed them. It's hard not to when you're young."

"Tell me about it," Bolt said. "Does it get better when you're older?"

"It did for me," Conner said.

"How?" Bolt asked.

"Someone else believed in me," Conner said. "All it took was one person's approval and suddenly I believed in myself, too. It gave me a shield to block out all the doubt and negativity. It made me realize I was just as capable and deserving as the people I compared myself to. But you know what? I was wrong."

"You were?" Bolt asked.

"Totally," Conner said. "I didn't *need* someone else. I had confidence in myself, deep down inside, the whole time. Approval is just a shortcut to self-worth, but sometimes we have to find things out on our own. Sometimes if we want something bad enough, we have to inspire ourselves to get it. Sometimes we have to be our own superhero."

Out of everything Conner said, he could tell this reso- nated with the boy the most. If he wanted to help people, maybe he had to start with himself.

"But what if I fail?" Bolt asked. "What if the Snake Lord wins and I don't save anyone? Then I'll *never* be a superhero."

"A very wise man once told me that 'courage is what makes a superhero super,'" Conner said. "He never said anything about succeeding."

Bolt looked down at the pile of used batteries on his desk. If the batteries had feelings, he imagined they'd feel the same way he did: useless, crumpled, and empty. But if he could glue junk together and turn it into a hero, he knew he could make a hero out of himself, too. Bolt stood up from his desk and looked Conner in the eye.

"Let's go to Paris," he said. "I've got a family and a city to save."

"Attaboy!" Conner said. He patted Bolt on the back. The contact shocked Conner's hand and he yelped. "Sorry, I forgot who I was talking to."

"How am I supposed to get to Paris in time?" Bolt asked. "My brothers and sister took the jet."

"Luckily for you, Alex and I happen to have a teleportation device," Conner said. "It'll get us there in a matter of seconds."

Alex did a double take. "We *do*?" she asked.

"Yes—*you do*," Conner mouthed at his sister. *"We'll use your magic."*

"Oh, right." Alex played along. "I completely forgot about the *teleportation device*. I have it right here in my hand—it's small and invisible. Boy, it sure is easy to misplace."

Bolt was impressed. "My dad doesn't even have one of those," he said. "How did two school journalists get one?"

"Our school has a great science department," Conner said. "More on that later. Do you want to get to Paris or not?"

Alex put her arms around Bolt and Conner and they formed a group hug. She had never magically transported between locations in one of her brother's stories before. She hoped it would work like it did in the fairy-tale world. Alex

324

closed her eyes and visualized the Ziblings tied to the Eiffel Tower's antenna by the anaconda and also remembered how desperately she and Conner needed the superheroes to defeat the Literary Army.

"Activating the teleportation device," she said. "Here goes nothing."

With a bright flash, the twins and Bolt disappeared from Professor Wallet's secret laboratory. The first thing they felt was a cool night breeze. They looked around and saw lush rectangular lawns, fountains, and a winding river. There were gorgeous buildings for miles around with tall windows, domes, columns, steeples, and French flags. Every building was lit up like the entire city was in the middle of a photo shoot.

"We're definitely in Paris," Alex said. "But I don't see the Eiffel Tower anywhere."

"That's because we're *in* the Eiffel Tower," Conner said. "Check it out!"

After further inspection, she realized they were hundreds of feet in the air. Alex had transported them directly onto the roof of the lower observation deck. The rest of the structure towered above them like the skeleton of a steel giant. It was so tall, the twins got vertigo just looking at it. Despite the circumstances, the Eiffel Tower was a breathtakingly beautiful sight.

On the ground below, they saw the Snake Lord's circle of serpents keeping the Parisian police at bay. Beyond the police were thousands of French citizens observing the scene. A dozen news helicopters flew in the air around the Eiffel Tower and they shined their spotlights on Bolt and the twins as soon as they arrived.

It was a blessing they did, because the spotlights illuminated Collared Joe and Lizzy Liza sneaking up behind them.

"Bolt, look out!" Conner yelled.

Collared Joe leaped toward Bolt and knocked him to the floor. Lizzy Liza stood on her hands and kicked the twins. Alex and Conner rolled across the roof and over the edge. Conner grabbed on to the ledge with one hand and his sister with the other. They swung from the roof like rock climbers without a harness. The observers below gasped and screamed.

As they climbed back over the ledge, Collared Joe and Lizzy Liza started circling Bolt as he got to his feet. Collared Joe puffed his frilled neck out like an umbrella around his head. Lizzy Liza scraped her claws across the roof and hissed at the boy. They were like predators surrounding their prey.

"What a treat," Collared Joe said. "All four Ziblings in one day! The Snake Lord will be thrilled!"

"I say we keep the little one between us," Lizzy Liza said. "I could use a *Znack,* if you know what I mean."

The overgrown reptiles cocked their heads and laughed. At that moment Alex noticed something on the roof behind Bolt that had the potential to help him, and she hoped he'd get the same idea when he saw it.

"Bolt—behind you!" Alex yelled.

Bolt turned around and saw the bucket of water she was referring to. He ran to it and kicked it over. The water spilled across the roof as Collared Joe and Lizzy Liza charged after him. Bolt put both hands down and sent electric waves through the spill. The evil sidekicks' feet and legs were electrocuted. They hopped around the roof like it was covered in broken glass. They tripped on each other and then fell over the edge of the observation deck and never returned.

The twins crawled back onto the roof and Bolt helped them to their feet.

"Smart thinking, guys," Conner said.

"My dad always says, 'Science is a superpower in itself,'" Bolt said.

With Collared Joe and Lizzy Liza gone, the Snake Lord was the only person preventing them from saving the city. The twins and the youngest Zibling went to the edge of the roof and looked up at the Eiffel Tower's highest observation deck.

"We've got to get up there," Alex said.

"No, it's too dangerous," Bolt said. "You both need to stay here. This is between me and the Snake Lord."

Alex opened her mouth to argue, but Conner gave her a look to keep quiet. As he had explained before, for the Ziblings to reunite, Bolt had to face the Snake Lord alone.

"Good luck, Bolt," Alex said.

"We believe in you," Conner said.

Bolt gave them a nervous salute. He flew into the air and

ascended the Eiffel Tower, gliding from steel beam to steel beam like a flying squirrel jumping from branch to branch. Eventually, he made it all the way to the roof of the highest observation deck, where he saw the other Ziblings at the base of the antenna. Blaze, Whipney, and Morph were shocked and upset to see their little brother.

"Bolt, what the heck are you doing here?" Blaze asked.

"I'm here to save you and the city," Bolt said.

"No, get out of here while you still can!" Whipney said. "You can't face the Snake Lord alone!"

"You need to get Dad!" Morph said. "You can't help us—you aren't strong enough!"

"It doesn't take *strength* to be a superhero," Bolt said. "It just takes *courage*."

Just like Conner, Bolt pretended he had a shield protecting him from all the doubt and belittlement his siblings were sending him. He flew over them to the antenna's ladder and climbed up to the platform where the Snake Lord stood.

The Snake Lord had reached the final step of the Reptilalizer's installation, and a pleased grin stretched across his face. It would only be a matter of time before everyone in Paris was transformed into a reptile, and he would have total control over the world's most cosmopolitan city.

The Snake Lord was distracted by movement coming from beneath his feet. He looked down just as the youngest Zibling was pulling himself onto the platform. The Snake Lord kicked Bolt hard in the chest and he slipped down the ladder.

It knocked the wind out of Bolt, but as soon as he caught his breath, he climbed back up. When he reached the platform, the Snake Lord kicked him down again. But no matter how many times the Snake Lord kicked Bolt down the ladder, the boy was never going to give up. Even if he was kicked down a hundred more times, Bolt was going to do whatever it took to keep the Snake Lord from activating the Reptilalizer.

On the boy's fifth trip up the ladder, the Snake Lord stared down at him pityingly. Bolt's determination amused him. Instead of kicking him down again, the Snake Lord grabbed Bolt by the lightning logo on his suit and looked the boy closely in the eye.

"You're a brave little hero, I'll give you that," the Snake Lord said. "But there's a thin line between *bravery* and *stupidity*—and I'm afraid you just crossed it."

"And there's a thin line between *bad breath* and *halitosis*," Bolt said. "I'm afraid you crossed *that* a while ago."

The remark angered the Snake Lord to no end, so rather than putting Bolt with his siblings, he threw the boy off the antenna. The youngest Zibling plummeted toward the ground, falling so fast he couldn't fly.

"Bolt!" the Ziblings yelled as they watched helplessly.

He fell past Alex and Conner on the lower observation deck and landed somewhere among the trees below the Eiffel Tower. It was over before the twins even knew what was happening. They looked at each other in total shock.

"This is all my fault," Conner cried. "I pushed him too

far. I made him face the Snake Lord when he wasn't ready! *I killed him!* Now the Ziblings will never be united!"

Conner was so ashamed of himself, he buried his face in Alex's shoulder. She felt just as responsible and couldn't find the words to comfort him.

"You murderer!" Blaze yelled at the Snake Lord.

"How could you do that to a child?" Whipney screamed.

"He was just a boy!" Morph shouted.

The Ziblings struggled against the anaconda binding them, but the large snake only tightened its squeeze. The Snake Lord finished the final phase of the Reptilalizer's installation and laughed uproariously to himself.

"The Reptilalizer is complete!" he announced. "Not only have you lost a brother, but once I activate my invention, you'll be the first people in Paris to turn into reptiles! And with no Ziblings left, no one will ever stop me! Soon the whole world will be in my control!"

The Snake Lord flipped the switch on the Reptilalizer and the machine came to life. A thick green gas spewed from the antenna and traveled down the Eiffel Tower like a looming fog. But just before it reached the Ziblings below, the Eiffel Tower's power unexpectedly went out. The Reptilalizer shut off and the green gas dissipated in the night breeze.

"What in the name of Kaa?" the Snake Lord said, and desperately tried to re-start his machine.

As the twins mourned the loss of Bolt, a strange phenomenon occurred in the city around them. Not only did the Eiffel Tower lose its power, but all the buildings in a ten-block radius blacked out, too. It was like the Reptilalizer had blown Paris's fuse.

"Wait a second," Alex said. "Didn't Bolt say his power comes from absorbing the electricity around him?"

"Yeah, when he was alive," Conner said. "But he's dead—isn't he?"

Suddenly, the twins' hair rose above their heads and their bodies were tickled by a strong wave of friction. They looked down to the trees where Bolt had landed. The trees were buzzing and emitted a glowing bright white light.

Bolt launched from the trees like a missile: He was alive and more powerful than ever. Strong electric waves charged out of his body like he was a human plasma ball. His body was producing so much friction that the air hummed around him. His hair stood straight up above his head and his eyes glowed with energy. Bolt had never looked so confident or capable in his life.

"It worked!" Conner said. *"Bolt's reached his full potential!"*

"Go, Bolt!" Alex yelled.

Conner couldn't have been more proud of the little superhero. Watching Bolt flourish made him feel like a part of him had succeeded and beaten the odds, too. The twins hugged in celebration.

Bolt soared back to the antenna of the Eiffel Tower. He pointed a finger at the anaconda and rattlesnake restraining his siblings and zapped the reptiles with electricity. The snakes curled into balls and fell to the ground. The Ziblings couldn't believe their eyes. It took them a moment to realize that their rescuer was their brother.

"Bolt?" Blaze said.

"You're alive!" Whipney said.

"And POWERFUL!" Morph said.

The youngest Zibling could have gloated, he could have made his brothers and sister feel as lousy as they had made him feel, but none of that was as important as saving the city.

"I have two friends on the roof of the lower observation deck," Bolt said. "Get them to safety and I'll take care of the Snake Lord."

The Ziblings didn't argue with their brother. Blaze jumped off the tower, and fiery blasts erupted from his feet like he was standing on a jetpack. Whipney swung down the Eiffel Tower beam by beam, as if her hair were the long arms of an orangutan. Morph turned into a huge paper airplane with sunglasses and glided down to the lower observation deck to retrieve the twins.

"Hop on!" Morph told them.

Alex and Conner climbed aboard the paper airplane, and the Ziblings escorted them to the rectangular lawns below. Once they were safely on the ground, the twins and Ziblings all looked up at the Eiffel Tower and anxiously watched as Bolt went head-to-head with the Snake Lord.

At the top of the antenna, the Snake Lord was fidgeting

with the wires and gears of the Reptilalizer, but nothing he adjusted made the device regenerate. Bolt landed on the platform behind him with so much force, the entire structure rattled. He raised both hands toward the Reptilalizer and fired it with electricity until it exploded.

If looks could kill, the Snake Lord would have murdered Bolt with his hateful glare.

"You think *you're* powerful?" he asked. "You have no idea what power is!"

The eyes on the Snake Lord's helmet started to glow. As if they were connected by a wireless frequency, he sent instructions to the serpents guarding the base of the Eiffel Tower. The snakes joined their bodies together and formed one monstrous beast. Thousands of snakes made up of hundreds of species were now slithering in perfect synchronicity. The gigantic reptile coiled up the Eiffel Tower toward the antenna to join its master and attack Bolt.

The observing twins, the Ziblings, the police, and the Parisian citizens all screamed. They had never seen such a gargantuan creature take form. Bolt only laughed at the approaching giant. In the Snake Lord's ruthless quest for power, the mad scientist had forgotten one basic scientific fact.

"Science 101," Bolt said. "Nothing helps electricity move faster than metal, and you just sent your entire entourage into a steel structure."

The Snake Lord's yellow reptilian eyes widened and his pupils shrank into narrow slits. He had made a grave mistake. Bolt looked toward the sky above the antenna and sent a wave of friction into the clouds, causing a mighty bolt of lightning to descend and strike the Eiffel Tower.

The lightning illuminated the tower and it shone more brightly than it ever had in history. Every lightbulb on the tower burst, covering it in tiny explosions. The electricity coursing through the structure electrocuted the Snake Lord and his scaly accomplices until there was nothing left of them but burned dust.

When the lightning had finished, a thunderous roar erupted throughout Paris. The Ziblings, the twins, the police, and all the witnessing Parisians cheered and applauded the little superhero. Bolt flew down to the rectangular lawn and joined the twins.

"Way to go!" Conner said. "I'd hug you, but I'm definitely not touching you after all that!"

"We knew you could do it!" Alex said.

Blaze, Whipney, and Morph sheepishly stepped toward Bolt. They hung their heads shamefully, feeling so guilty they couldn't even look their brother in the eye.

"Bolt, we're so sorry," Blaze said.

"Thank you for saving our lives," Whipney said.

"We should have believed in you," Morph said.

Bolt stared blankly at his brothers and sister, not knowing what to say to them. A sly grin appeared on his face. It felt so good to finally *prove himself* that he didn't care about *proving them wrong*.

"It's okay," he said. "All that matters is that I believed in myself. And I'll definitely find ways for you to make it up to me."

The Ziblings went to speak with the French police and press. Blaze, Whipney, and Morph gave all the credit for saving the city to their little brother. The reporters crowded around him and praised him for his efforts. The Parisians chanted Bolt's name, and Blaze and Morph lifted their brother onto their shoulders so the people could get a better look at him.

Bolt had never smiled so big in his whole life—he was finally a *real* superhero.

"That's so sweet," Alex said. "This is such a great story, Conner."

"Thank you," he said. "You know, I've been thinking a lot about what you said in the trunk of the Zibling Mobile. You were right. 'The Ziblings' is definitely about us."

Alex took a deep breath. "I told you," she said. "And just to reiterate, I want to apologize for anything I might have—"

"But you were wrong about one thing," Conner interrupted. "Blaze, Whipney, and Morph aren't based on you. Alex, you might not realize it, but *you* were the first person to encourage me to write. *You're* my Professor Wallet, not Mrs. Peters."

"Me?" Alex said. "But...but...*Mrs. Peters*—"

"Mrs. Peters also tried getting me to finish my homework and study for tests, but that never happened," Conner said. "I don't remember the second grade, but I do remember the seventh. Just before we went into the fairy-tale world to fight the Enchantress, I showed you my stories for the first time. You liked them, you said they were special, and *you* gave me the confidence to keep writing. It was *your* approval that inspired me—*you* were my champion."

Alex was more relieved than words could describe. Thinking she had somehow harmed him in the past was the worst feeling in the world. She hugged her brother, squeezing him so tight that he could barely breathe.

Professor Wallet appeared in the crowd of Parisians and pushed his way through the people toward his children. He was so out of breath and sweaty, he looked like he had run all the way from Germany.

"Dad!" Bolt said when he saw him.

"I'm sorry I didn't get here sooner," the professor said. "The chancellor let me borrow her plane. I've been watching the whole thing unfold on the news!"

"I'm sorry I broke the rules again," Bolt said. "I know I was grounded and shouldn't have left the laboratory, but the others were in danger, and I didn't want the Snake Lord to win, so I—"

Professor Wallet silenced his son with a hug. The embrace was slightly electrifying, but the professor didn't care.

"We can talk about the logistics at a different time," Professor Wallet said. "But right now, I couldn't be more proud to be your father. It took a lot of bravery for you to save all these people—bravery you must have found on your own.

Paris is known as the City of Light, but after tonight, I believe it'll be remembered as the City of *Lightning*."

It was a touching display, and many of the observers teared up. The reporters tried sticking their microphones closer to the father and son, but the Ziblings pushed them back to give Bolt and the professor some privacy.

"It wasn't all thanks to me," Bolt said. "If it weren't for my new friends, I would never have had the confidence to come here. They taught me how to believe in myself. I couldn't have done it without them."

Bolt led the professor to the rectangular lawn in front of the Eiffel Tower and introduced him to the twins.

"Conner and Alex, meet my dad, Professor Wallet," he said.

"It's a pleasure," the professor said, and shook their hands. "Thank you for giving my son the inspiration he needed to save his brothers and sister. If there is anything we can do to return the favor, please don't hesitate to ask."

Alex and Conner exchanged quick smiles.

"As a matter of fact," Conner said. "We *could* use your help with something. . . ."

CHAPTER TWENTY-TWO

A CASTLE OF QUESTIONS

After a long and exhausting journey across the fairy-tale world, Emmerich and the Masked Man arrived in the woods of the Eastern Kingdom. They had only stopped to rest once since leaving the Dwarf Forests, and Emmerich was so tired that he was falling asleep as they walked.

"We're almost there," the Masked Man said. "Keep up, boy."

The closer they got to the portal, the more cross the Masked Man became. Emmerich was starting to realize he wasn't as nice a person as he had first thought. The longer Emmerich accompanied the twins' uncle, the louder a voice in the back of his mind urged him not to trust the man.

They entered an area of the forest that Emmerich recognized. It was the part of the woods he had entered with Conner and Bree on his first trip to the fairy-tale world. He would never forget seeing the Grande Armée soldiers raining down on the trees after they arrived.

"This is it," the Masked Man said. "This is where I saw Morina activate the portal. Now all I need is the magic panpipe. Let me think, which tree did the witch stash it in?"

The twins' uncle searched all the trees in the area. He stuck his hand in every hole, crack, and bird nest in every tree trunk. Finally, he found the instrument in the back of a squirrel's nest.

"Aha!" the Masked Man said with delight. "I found it. Now I just need to play the right tune and the portal will open."

The Masked Man played a series of melodies on the panpipe. He waited a few moments after each one, but none of the notes did the trick. Even when he was certain he had remembered the correct tune, a portal to the Otherworld did not appear.

"Blast that damn witch!" the Masked Man said. "Why isn't it working?"

"Is it the right panpipe?" Emmerich asked.

"Of course it is," he said. "Morina stole it from the

fairies. I watched her open the portal just a few days ago. For whatever reason, it won't cooperate with me."

Emmerich thought back to when Conner played the panpipe and opened the portal in Neuschwanstein Castle. He remembered there was something very specific the instrument needed in order to work.

"It needs to be played by a person of magic blood," Emmerich said. "That must be why it isn't working. My friend Bree thinks she and I might have magic in our blood. Would you like me to give it a try?"

The magic in the Masked Man's blood had been taken away a long time ago, so it made sense that the portal wasn't opening for him. However, if his son was able to do the trick, not only would it grant them entrance to the Other-world, it would also prove the Masked Man's plan would work. He glanced down at his son, trying to conceal the eagerness in his eyes.

"Be my guest," he said, and handed his son the panpipe.

Emmerich licked his lips, held the instrument to his mouth, and blew the eight notes he remembered Conner playing at the castle. Almost instantaneously, a bright light appeared out of thin air among the trees. The light grew bigger and bigger, and it started to spin, sucking all the leaves on the forest floor inside it like a wormhole.

Emmerich smiled. He had activated the portal all by himself! This confirmed Bree's theory that there was magic in his blood. More than ever, Emmerich couldn't wait to get home so he could tell her.

Unbeknownst to him, the Masked Man had other plans for the boy. He stared at the portal as it grew, mesmerized by its spinning light. He placed his hand on the back of Emmerich's neck and pushed his son toward it.

"Good boy," he said softly. "*Very* good boy..."

Bree and the Sisters Grimm had spent the entire week in Germany searching for clues to Emmerich's disappearance. Just as they expected, nothing in the Bavarian countryside revealed where the boy was or who had taken him. There was only one place that might give them more insight, and unfortunately, it wasn't an easy location to get to.

After days of trading voice mail, Cornelia finally got through to the groundskeeper of Neuschwanstein Castle. She told the man she and her family were private investigators from the United States and needed access to the castle. The groundskeeper wouldn't hear a word of it until Cornelia mentioned it was regarding Emmerich Himmelsbach. By now all of Bavaria had heard of the missing boy, and the groundskeeper was inclined to help her.

Late one night, once all the tour guides and tourists had left and the janitors had finished their shifts, the groundskeeper snuck Cornelia, Wanda, Frenda, and Bree inside the castle.

"You have one hour," the groundskeeper said. "I can't give you any more time than that or I might lose my job."

"We really appreciate this," Cornelia said.

"Would you mind showing us around to the lower levels of the castle?" Wanda asked.

The groundskeeper escorted Wanda and Frenda to the stories below, giving Cornelia and Bree a chance to thoroughly inspect the Singers' Hall without supervision. Bree looked around at all the instruments, the pillars, the chandeliers, and the mural of the enchanted forest: She couldn't believe it had been more than a year since she and the boys were there.

"That's where the portal is," Bree said, and nodded to the mural.

Cornelia removed a cross-dimensional emission-tracking device from her purse and waved it around the painting. The device beeped with gusto.

"If I didn't know that before, I would now," Cornelia said. "The detection rates are off the charts. This portal was activated recently—*very* recently."

"I knew it. Emmerich isn't in this world," Bree said. "Whoever kidnapped him took him back to the fairy-tale world."

Bree sat on the floor and sighed. Cornelia kneeled next to her and put the tracking device aside.

"Sadly, I think we've done all we can do," she said. "We should think about heading back to the States tomorrow morning."

Bree would have stayed in Germany for months if she

could. She felt like she was abandoning Emmerich by leaving, but Cornelia was right. There was no point in staying if there was nothing they could do.

"Have you contacted the Bailey twins and told them about Emmerich yet?" Cornelia asked.

"I tried calling Conner as soon as I found out Emmerich was taken," Bree said. "At the time, his mom didn't even know where he and his sister were. I bet they're still somewhere in the fairy-tale world."

"Then perhaps Conner will find Emmerich," Cornelia said. "The three of you were brought together by chance— we need to have faith it'll happen again."

Bree nodded. "Let's go," she said. "I don't want to waste any more of anyone's time."

Just as she got to her feet, the tracking device began a beeping frenzy: Something otherworldly was headed their way. A bright light appeared in front of the mural and became brighter and brighter. It grew bigger and bigger, swirling like a vortex.

"My word!" Cornelia gasped. "What's happening?"

"It's the portal!" Bree said. "Someone must have activated it from the fairy-tale world!"

Instead of pulling them in like it had before, the portal blew powerful gusts of air into the room, knocking all the furniture and instruments to the floor. Bree and Cornelia held on to each other so they weren't knocked off their feet. Leaves from the fairy-tale world blew inside the hall, and

Bree could make out the silhouettes of two people stepping through the portal. It was so bright she couldn't tell who they were.

Finally, the portal closed and the swirling vortex disappeared.

"Bree?" said a familiar voice with a German accent.

As soon as her eyes adjusted, Bree saw Emmerich running toward her. She couldn't believe it—all her prayers had been answered! She embraced her friend and twirled him around in a circle.

"Emmerich!" Bree cried thankfully. "We've been looking all over for you!"

"I was kidnapped by witches!" Emmerich said. "They held me prisoner at their camp in the woods until this man rescued me!"

Emmerich gestured to the Masked Man behind him. Even though Bree was overjoyed to see her friend, there was something very peculiar about the man with Emmerich. He seemed familiar, but Bree couldn't think of who he reminded her of.

"Thank you for saving my friend," Bree said. "Who are you?"

"He's Alex and Conner's uncle Lloyd!" Emmerich exclaimed. "They sent him to find me and bring me home!"

"You know my niece and nephew, too?" the Masked Man asked. "Well, it's certainly a *small world.*"

From the sarcastic tone in his voice, he was anything but thrilled by the connection.

"We go to the same school," Bree said. "I didn't even know they had an uncle."

"We aren't close," the Masked Man said.

Emmerich was so happy to be back home in Germany, he hugged Cornelia before being introduced.

"I'm Emmerich," he said. "Who are you?"

"My name is Cornelia Grimm," she said. "It's so wonderful to see you're alive and well!"

"Cornelia is my cousin," Bree said. "When I heard you were missing, she brought me here in her very own plane and helped me look for you. She's part of a secret group of women called *the Sisters Grimm*—they're descendants of the Brothers Grimm and they know all about the fairy-tale world."

Emmerich's eyes grew wide and he jumped up and down.

"Bree, that reminds me of something I have to tell you!" he said. "I activated the portal from the fairy-tale world all by myself! You were right—there's magic in our blood! That must mean that you, Cornelia, and I are all related!"

"Actually, Emmerich," Bree said, "we found out some information while we were visiting with your mom. It turns out you're not related to the Brothers Grimm like I thought, you're from the—"

Her train of thought was interrupted when Cornelia suddenly screamed. Bree and Emmerich looked up and saw that the Masked Man was pointing a revolver at them.

"What are you doing, Lloyd?" Emmerich asked.

The Masked Man ignored him. He stepped toward Cornelia and aimed the gun at her. The old woman raised her hands in the air.

"Did the girl say you have a *plane*?" he asked.

"Well...yes," Cornelia said. "I do."

The Masked Man jerked his head and gun toward Bree next.

"And you go to school with my niece and nephew," he said. "Do you know where they live and how to get there?"

Bree was scared speechless. *"I...I...I..."* she mumbled.

"JUST ANSWER THE QUESTION!" the Masked Man yelled.

"Yes!" Bree said.

Emmerich was petrified. He regretted not trusting his instincts in the woods. Clearly, the man wasn't who he said he was.

"You're not Alex and Conner's uncle, are you?" he asked.

"Yes, I most certainly *am*," the Masked Man said. "Actually, I'm a lot more than what you realize, but we'll have plenty of time for that later. The four of us are going on a little trip to the twins' house—*right now!*"

"But Alex and Conner aren't there," Bree peeped. "They're in the fairy-tale world!"

The Masked Man chuckled. "Stupid girl," he said. "I never said I was looking for *the twins*."

CHAPTER TWENTY-THREE

FAMILIAR STRANGERS

I n the commissary, the Blissworm was standing on a table entertaining all the pirates and sailors from "Starboardia." The space worm theatrically re-enacted the twins' encounter with the polycrabs on Lollipopigust. It used sound effects, large gestures, and impersonations to tell the exciting tale. Although it never articulated any words, the *Dolly Llama* crew seemed to understand everything the worm was saying. They *oohed* and *aahed* at the descriptive story; some even covered their eyes like they were watching a scary movie.

"You're telling us that Alex and Conner found you in a hole the polycrabs dug to capture prey?" Winking Wendy asked.

"Then you were all captured and taken to the polycrabs' colony deep underground?" Siren Sue asked.

"And after Conner rescued you from the queen polycrab's web, he detonated a massive bomb that vaporized the whole species?" Stinky-Feet Phoebe asked.

The Blissworm nodded happily. They were a very attentive audience. All the pirates and sailors were astonished by the story. The *Dolly Llama* crew had never heard such an adventurous tale, and *they* were *pirates*.

The commissary was still segregated. The characters from the fairy-tale world glared at the characters from Conner's short stories from their table across the room. They were also astonished, not by the events in the story, but that the *Dolly Llama* crew understood what the worm was saying.

"How do they know what it's talking about?" Jack whispered to Goldilocks.

"They're all from Conner's imagination," Goldilocks said. "They must share some kind of language."

Red casually slid into the seat across the table from Jack and Goldilocks. Her eyebrows were raised and she pursed her lips tightly to keep from smiling: She obviously had a secret she was dying to share. Red leaned over the table so only Jack and Goldilocks could hear her.

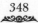

"Have you noticed how *familiar* all these strangers are?" Red whispered.

Jack and Goldilocks stared at her blankly. Was she just now realizing that?

"Can't say I have," Jack said. "Have you, Goldie?"

"Familiar?" Goldilocks said. "Whatever do you mean?"

Red was so eager to talk about it, she didn't realize they were being sarcastic. Her eyes enlarged like her theory was scandalous.

"All the characters on *that* side of this odd ballroom are from Conner's short stories, right?" Red said. "But I'm not convinced they're entirely from his imagination. I think many of the people in this room are *based* on people he knows—people like *us*."

Red swiped the table like she was laying out a winning hand of cards. Jack and Goldilocks both sighed. Sometimes Red was so naïve, it was impressive.

"I think you're onto something, Red," Jack said.

"Nothing gets by you," Goldilocks said.

Red was so pleased with herself, she shimmied her shoulders. Captain Auburn Sally walked by their table and Red waved her down.

"Excuse me, lady with the big hat!" Red called. "Come sit with us!"

Red patted the seat next to her. The captain looked around the room to make sure Red wasn't speaking to someone else, and then sat down next to the queen, with no clue of her intentions.

"It's rather silly for us to share such close quarters and not get to know each other," Red said. "Allow me to introduce myself. I'm Queen Red Riding Hood. These are my subjects Jack and Goldilocks."

Jack and Goldilocks glanced at each other. *Subjects?*

"It's nice to meet you," Auburn Sally said. "I'm Captain Auburn Sally of the *Dolly Llama*."

"Tell me everything," Red said. "Where are you from, what do you do for a living, what are your hobbies, et cetera, et cetera?"

"Well, like I said, I'm the captain of a ship," Auburn Sally said. "We're the only all-female vessel in the Caribbean, but one of the most feared in the sea. We spend our days sailing across the ocean, looking for buried treasure. Occasionally we'll meet other women like ourselves, on the run from their pasts, and we invite them to join our crew."

Red was so charmed by the captain, she gently placed her hands over Auburn Sally's. The queen smiled like they were long-lost sisters who had finally been reunited.

"You must be *me*," Red said.

Auburn Sally was confused. She understood what Red was insinuating, but the queen didn't seem to notice that *Goldilocks* could have been the captain's identical twin.

"Are you sure?" the captain asked. "No offense, but I would have guessed someone *else* was inspired by you."

The captain gestured to the Cyborg Queen in the corner

of the commissary. She was sitting in throne mode as Commander Newters tightened the wires around the gears on top of her head.

"Don't be so humble," Red said. "I'm certain you're me. The similarities are uncanny! Both of our names start with colors, we're both very powerful and accomplished women, and we're both very flamboyant dressers. My style is more *privileged and pampered* but the *dirty-and-daring* look works well on you."

Auburn Sally looked to Jack and Goldilocks for help.

"Just play along or it'll never stop," Goldilocks whispered to the captain. "I think you're right, Red. Auburn Sally is definitely based on you."

"You're practically the same person," Jack said, and nodded over-dramatically.

Red happily turned to the crew of the *Dolly Llama*. She now saw the pirates from a completely different perspective.

"Pardon me for a moment," she said. "I'm going to introduce myself to *our* crew—oh, what fun this has turned into!"

The queen skipped to the table of pirates and sailors and introduced herself. Auburn Sally stared at Red like the queen had just escaped from an asylum.

"She's not sailing with a full set of sails, is she?" the captain asked.

Across the commissary, the twins' mother was happy to see the characters finally warming up to one another. Charlotte took the intermingling as a sign that she was succeeding as a glorified babysitter. Things had gotten significantly easier now that they were in the hospital. There was plenty of room for all the characters, no one was breaking Charlotte's possessions, and everyone was getting along for the most part. There was only one thing missing to make it an enjoyable experience: Alex and Conner. Spending several hours a day with her son's characters made Charlotte miss Conner more than ever. He had never shared his stories with his mom, so it was nice for her to see them come to life piece by piece.

Charlotte heard a familiar jingle and turned toward the door of the commissary. It swung open and her heart sank into the pit of her stomach—*they had company*!

Dr. Sharon Jackson, a clinical psychologist at Saint Andrew's Children's Hospital, stepped into the commissary with an elderly couple. Sharon was an African American woman with curly black hair who wore several bracelets around each of her wrists that jangled as she walked.

"And *this* is the new storybook commissary," Dr. Jackson told the couple as she escorted them inside.

The psychologist was floored to see that it was filled with so many strange people. The elderly couple cleaned the lenses of their glasses to make sure their eyes weren't deceiving them. All the characters in the room froze and went dead silent—*they had been caught*!

"Hi, Sharon," Charlotte said. "What brings you to the new commissary?"

"Charlotte, meet Mr. and Mrs. Carmichael," Dr. Jackson

said. "They're two of the donors who paid for the construction of the new wing. I was just giving them a tour of the facility. *Who are all these people?*"

Charlotte's options were limited. Telling her co-worker the truth was out of the question, and there were very few lies that could explain why so many costumed adults were gathered there. Coming up with something that wouldn't get her and Bob into trouble with the hospital was nearly impossible.

"They're *performers*," Charlotte said. "Bob and I wanted to surprise the patients and the staff with a little entertainment."

The characters were impressed by how convincing Charlotte's lie was, especially one that had been thought of on the spot. Dr. Jackson and the Carmichaels were touched by Charlotte and Bob's generosity.

"Oh, how wonderful!" Mrs. Carmichael said. "They remind me of the circus! When is the performance? We'd love to see it."

"Tomorrow night," Charlotte fibbed again. "In the multi-purpose room, at eight o'clock."

"It'll be a late night for us, but we'll be there!" Mr. Carmichael said.

"That is so kind of you, Charlotte," Dr. Jackson said. "What show are they performing? Is it something I know?"

Charlotte eyed the characters for assistance, but none of them were helpful. They watched the twins' mother like she was a show herself.

"They're still figuring it out," she said. "That's why everyone is dressed so differently. They're going to rehearse all the shows in their repertoire for me so I can select one that will be best for the children."

"We'll be looking forward to it!" Dr. Jackson said. "May I spread the word, or are you still keeping it under wraps?"

Charlotte laughed. "I guess the cat is out of the bag now," she said. "Feel free to let everyone know."

"Sounds terrific!" Dr. Jackson said. "The kids are going to love it! We'll let you get back to rehearsals."

Dr. Jackson escorted the Carmichaels out of the commissary. Charlotte faced the characters in a panic. Her face turned bright red, and she was thinking only in swear words.

"Looks like we're putting on a show," she said. "Anyone have an idea of what we should do?"

"William Shakyfruit has a collection of hysterical plays, but I don't think we can pull one of them off by tomorrow night," Red said.

"Anyone *else* have a suggestion?" Charlotte asked.

Trollbella was the only character to step forward. She went to the center of the room, looked up at the fluorescent lighting, and spread her arms out like she was having a religious experience.

"My time has come," she said in a trance. "Finally, life has presented me with an opportunity to show my purpose. At last, I have an outlet to combine all my talents for something that matters."

"You mean, besides being a queen?" Goldilocks asked.

"Governing is just a side gig," Trollbella said. "My true calling has always been the performing arts. I have the perfect performance for our predicament. It's the greatest story ever told."

"'Little Red Riding Hood'?" Red asked.

"'THE PRINCE OF THIEVES'?" Robin Hood asked.

"'Peter Pan'?" Peter asked.

Trollbella raised a finger to silence them. "No," she said. "'The Life and Times of Queen Trollbella'!"

The troll queen flicked her hands through the air and mimed falling confetti. The other characters slumped— each thought *their* story was a much better choice.

"We need to start at once!" Trollbella said. "I'll write, direct, and narrate the performance myself, as nobody knows Trollbella like Trollbella. I'll need the pirates to build the sets and the Cyborgs to adjust the overhanging fireless torches."

"Those are called *lights*," the Cyborg Queen said.

"Now for casting," Trollbella said. "The Merry Men will be my goblins, the Lost Boys will be my trolls, handsome Jack will be my Butterboy, beautiful Red will play the title character, and fat Goldilocks will be the creature that keeps us apart."

"I'm pregnant," Goldilocks said.

Trollbella winked at her. *"Of course you are."*

"Can I have a bigger role?" Peter Pan asked.

"I have the perfect part for you," Trollbella said. "No one can portray the highs and lows of life like a boy who can fly! You will symbolize my heart and personify the joy, the conflict, and the agony I've experienced in my very short life."

"Wicked!" Peter Pan said.

Trollbella took charge of the room like a mad conductor, and her eyes widened with power.

"This will be the best surprise performance in the history of Saint Andrew's Children's Hospital!" Trollbella declared. "The audience is going to be so invigorated, so inspired, so dumbfounded—it's a good thing medical professionals will be standing by!"

The characters throughout the commissary were a little frightened by the troll queen. None of them had given her the authority to direct the performance, but none of them were going to take it away from her, either.

"Don't just sit there like porcelain porcupines—*let's get to work!*" Trollbella ordered.

Right away, the characters split into the groups she had assigned. Trollbella walked around the commissary and met with each cluster privately to discuss her vision in greater detail.

As they deliberated over the performance, the binder of short stories flipped open and the twins stepped out of the beam of light with Professor Wallet, Blaze, Whipney, Morph, and Bolt. The Zibling characters looked around the commissary in wonder. The other characters were so

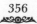

busy planning the performance, they didn't even look up at the superheroes.

"Welcome to the Otherworld," Alex told the Ziblings.

"Wow!" Bolt said. "A whole other dimension! This is so cool!"

"There's no science to prove this is possible, but I've always said there is too much world for just one planet," Professor Wallet said.

Conner whistled to get the room's attention. "Hey, everybody," he said. "These are our friends the Ziblings—they're superheroes and have agreed to help us fight the Literary Army."

"Can one of you sew?" Trollbella asked.

"I can transform into a sewing machine," Morph said.

"That'll do," Trollbella said. "You'll be in charge of costumes."

The troll queen grabbed Morph's hand and pulled him into her group of set designers.

"Costumes for what?" Alex asked.

"We were caught by one of my co-workers," Charlotte told the twins. "I didn't know what to say, so I told her the characters were performers. The good news is she believed it. The bad news is we have to put together a show for tomorrow night."

"Oh, *Butter-in-law*," Trollbella sang to Charlotte. "Is there a place we can get materials, or can we use the table-cloths and the wood from the walls?"

"Yikes," Alex said. "I'd better get them some supplies before Trollbella tears this place apart."

"I could probably travel into the next story alone if you want to stay here and help," Conner said.

"Are you sure you won't need a hand?" Alex asked.

"Positive," Conner said.

Alex didn't want to desert her brother, but she knew he'd be fine on his own. Charlotte was glad Alex was sitting the next one out because it presented a wonderful opportunity—one she had been hoping for.

"Conner, I have today and tomorrow off," Charlotte said. "Maybe I could join you in the next one? I would love to travel into one of your stories and see everything you've created."

Having his mom tag along seemed like the worst idea in the world. It was like she wanted to walk him to his classroom when dropping him off at school. He forced himself to smile so he didn't hurt her feelings.

"Oh . . . *great*," he said through his teeth.

Charlotte could tell her son wasn't thrilled by the idea. "Only if I won't be a burden," she said sadly. "I would hate to interfere. I'm just as happy to stay here and continue watching the characters."

He couldn't tell if she was *intentionally* making him feel guilty or not, but the effect was strong. Obviously it was something Charlotte really wanted to do, and Conner didn't have the heart to tell her no.

"It'll be totally fine," he said. "I'd *love* to have you there."

Charlotte clapped cheerfully. "What's the next story about?" she asked.

"It's called 'The Adventures of Blimp Boy,'" Conner explained. "It's about a young archaeologist in the 1930s who travels across the world on a giant blimp. He searches through ruins and finds precious artifacts before they're stolen by tomb raiders, and then donates them to museums."

"How exciting!" Charlotte said. "Is there anything special we need to do while we're there?"

"We have to find a magical talisman in an ancient pyramid," Conner said. "Whoever possesses the talisman is granted control over a legion of mummified soldiers. Once we bring the mummies here, we'll finally be finished recruiting the army we need to face the literary villains."

"I can't wait!" his mom said. "Let me just find my purse. Alex, if you see Bob, tell him I briefly stepped into another dimension with your brother."

Charlotte searched the commissary for her bag. Alex gazed at Conner with her deepest sympathies.

"Good luck," she said.

Conner sighed and shook his head. "What could be better than an afternoon of *mummies and Mom*?"

CHAPTER TWENTY-FOUR

THE ADVENTURES
OF BLIMP BOY

Conner poured the Portal Potion on his next story, and he and his mom stepped through the beam of light. Charlotte marveled at the world of handwritten words waiting on the other side. She laughed and gasped as her son's handwriting whirled around them.

"Conner, this is incredible!" she said. "Where are all the characters?"

"Mom, we're not in the story yet," he said. "This is just

the area that creates the story around us—it's like the Portal Potion's lobby. 'The Adventures of Blimp Boy' starts in India. You'll know we're there when you see a jungle."

"How fun!" Charlotte said. "I've never been to a jungle before."

She watched in wonder as the words *jungle trees*, *temple ruins*, and *screeching monkeys* stretched and filled the empty space around them. Word by word, a tropical Indian wilderness was created before their eyes. There were thousands of thick trees with large, drooping leaves and vines. It was very warm and so humid that their clothes stuck to their bodies. Playful monkeys growled and shrieked as they climbed through the tree branches above. Over the treetops, Conner and Charlotte could see the spiraling towers of an ancient temple in the distance.

"This is it," Conner told his mom.

Charlotte dug through her purse and pulled out a bottle of lotion. She rubbed it on her face and arms and then handed it to her son.

"What's that?" Conner asked.

"It's insect repellent with SPF," Charlotte said. "I don't want us getting sunburned or bitten while we're in the jungle."

Conner could already tell this was going to be a long trip. He rubbed the repellent on his skin and handed it back to his mom. Charlotte walked around the jungle like she was inspecting a house for sale.

"Well, it's *nice*," she said. "There are lots of plants and interesting animals to watch, but that heat really gets to you, doesn't it?'"

"Don't worry, we won't be here very long," Conner said. "The lead character should be running by any minute now."

They heard a rustling in the jungle as someone ran toward them from the temple. A few moments later, a fourteen-year-old boy appeared. He came to a halt when he saw Conner and Charlotte. They were the last things he had expected to see in the jungle.

The boy wore an aviator hat with goggles and flaps over his ears, a fitted brown leather jacket, khaki pants, and tall boots. His face was bright red and he panted from running. He held a golden relic shaped like a human hand tightly under his arm. The boy looked like he could have been Conner's little brother.

"Who are you?" he asked them.

Charlotte shook his hand excitedly. "Hi there," she said. "I'm Conner's mom, Charlotte. It's very nice to meet you!"

The boy stared at her strangely: Was he supposed to know her son? Conner sighed and slapped his palm against his forehead.

"Mom, he doesn't know who we are yet," he whispered to her. *"We have to act like this is the first time we're meeting him."*

"My apologies," Charlotte whispered back. *"I'll let you do all the talking."*

Conner turned toward the boy and tried to smooth things over.

"Forgive my mom," Conner said. "She's a little delirious. We got separated from our tour guide and have been lost in the jungle for days! It's so good to see another human being. What's your name?"

"I'm Beau Rogers," the boy said.

A series of thunderous growls came from the jungle behind him. Beau glanced back and gulped nervously. Although they couldn't see what was coming, they could hear a group of animals rushing through the trees toward them.

"We're all about to become *lunch* if we don't get out of here," Beau said. "Follow me if you value your life!"

Beau sprinted into the trees and gestured for Conner and Charlotte to come with him. Conner ran after him, but when he turned around he saw his mom hadn't moved. She was standing in the same spot, stretching her feet and legs.

"Mom! We've got to go!" Conner yelled.

"I know, I heard him," she said. "But I'll really regret it if I don't stretch before running. You'll know what I'm talking about when you get to be my age. Okay, now I'm ready."

Another roar sounded through the jungle. Conner and Charlotte could see that the commotion was coming from a pack of tigers running straight toward them. Charlotte screamed and ran after Beau faster than Conner had ever seen her move before. He followed but could barely keep up with her.

"I never knew you ran so fast!" Conner said.

"I ran track in college," Charlotte said. "Those are *real tigers* chasing us! What are *real tigers* doing in your story?"

"What were you expecting? Puppets?" Conner asked.

"I guess I was expecting everything to be more innocent, like a school project!" she yelled. "I didn't think I'd be running for my life!"

Conner and Charlotte caught up with Beau, but as they gained distance, the tigers did, too. They got closer by the second, and it wasn't long before they were close enough to swipe at them. Whenever a tiger got too close, Charlotte smacked it in the nose with her purse.

To add to their troubles, Beau was leading Conner and Charlotte right to the edge of a cliff. The tigers started slowing down, assuming their prey had nowhere to go. Beau didn't seem discouraged at all by the cliff, though; in fact, it made him run even faster.

"We're almost there!" Beau said.

"Almost *where*?" Charlotte said. "We're trapped between *death* and *death*!"

"Mom, Beau knows what he's doing!" Conner said. "When we get to the cliff we have to jump!"

"*WHAT?*" Charlotte yelled.

"You have to trust me or you'll be cat food!" Conner said.

Charlotte ignored every instinct to slow down and continued running with the boys.

Right when they reached the cliff, a massive blimp rose above the edge like a sunrise. The blimp was bright white like an oval cloud, and a long silver gondola with several round windows stretched under its belly. An old woman aboard the blimp slid its wide door open just in the nick of time, and Beau, Conner, and Charlotte jumped over the cliff and landed inside. They collapsed on the blimp's floor and stayed in a dog pile until they caught their breath.

The tigers on the ground dropped their jaws in unison. They had never seen their lunch float away in a giant balloon before.

"Time to diet, you overgrown felines!" the old woman yelled at the tigers below, and she slammed the door shut with gusto.

The old woman wore pearls, high heels, and a fur coat, with goggles and an aviator hat just like Beau's. She had a familiar raspy voice and saucy attitude. It only took Charlotte a couple of seconds to realize the old woman was based on Mother Goose.

"That was closer than the run-in I had with Bonnie and Clyde," the old woman said. "I see you picked up some friends, Beau."

"I wasn't expecting the temple to be filled with tigers!" Beau said. "Why are ancient ruins always filled with giant predators? Just once I'd like to walk into a tomb and find a flock of sheep."

"I wasn't talking about the cats," the old woman said.

"Oh, obviously," Beau said. "Aunt Emgee, this is Conner and his mother, Charlotte. I found them in the jungle right after I left the temple. Apparently they got separated from their tour guide and have been lost in the jungle for a couple of days."

Emgee eyed Conner and Charlotte over her goggles. "You look awfully cleaned-up for being lost in the jungle," she said.

"My mom's really into personal hygiene," Conner said.

"I'm a nurse," Charlotte said with a shrug.

Emgee was pleased to hear it. "I always love meeting a fellow working woman," she said. "Welcome aboard the *Charlie Chaplin*!"

The old woman helped Beau, Conner, and Charlotte to their feet and shook their hands.

"Did you name the blimp after the actor?" Charlotte asked.

"Actually, he named himself after the blimp," Beau said. "He's Emgee's ex-boyfriend."

Emgee twirled her pearls and blushed. "Oh, no, he was just a *fling*," she said. "Poor kid fell madly in love with me, but I was too old for him and had already vowed not to date any more actors. Speaking of ancient history, did you get the relic, Beau?"

Her grand-nephew held up the golden hand. "Presenting the fourth and final Golden Hand of Shiva!" he said happily.

"Way to go, kiddo!" Emgee said. "You've collected them all! The Delhi Museum will be ecstatic!"

Beau placed the golden hand on a shelf with three

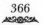

identical relics. Conner and Charlotte looked around the blimp with wide eyes. There were shelves and cases filled with artifacts, statues, tools, coins, and jewelry from ancient ruins around the world. All the walls in the *Charlie Chaplin* were covered in maps of various places with pins indicating where Beau and Emgee had traveled.

Conner knew where each and every artifact came from and the different adventures Beau had had collecting them. The only one he didn't recognize was a small doll made of rope. Beau slapped his hand as he reached for it.

"Don't touch that—*it's cursed*," Beau warned him.

Conner nodded. He remembered it now. Charlotte looked around the blimp at all of Beau and Emgee's belongings. She couldn't believe her son had created a world with such unique details and original characters.

"You've collected all of these?" Charlotte asked.

"Not *us*—it's all *him*," Emgee said, and patted her grand-nephew on the back. "Beau is the youngest archaeologist in the world. He earned his doctorate when he was just twelve years old!"

"It was actually my second," Beau clarified. "I got my first doctorate in political science when I was ten, but that was before I realized archaeology was my passion."

"That's extraordinary," Charlotte said. "I'm sure your parents are very proud!"

Beau lowered his head sadly. "Actually, my parents died when I was five," he said. "My mom was a flapper and my dad was a musician. They were performing at an under-ground nightclub when the building above it collapsed from all the barrels of gin the owner was hiding in the attic."

"*Prohibition.*" Emgee groaned. "It took away so much joy from so many people. I've been caring for the little rascal ever since. I've supported him through every step of his archaeology ambitions. A lot of my friends thought I was crazy when I sold my brownstone and bought a blimp to travel the world, but if you ask me, it was a great invest-ment. Everyone's crazy about *planes* these days, but I think blimps will be the transportation of the future."

"We've had some good times aboard the *Charlie Chap-lin,*" Beau said. "We've gone on so many adventures, seen so many astonishing places, and met so many interesting people. Speaking of which, where are you guys headed? Is there a place we could drop you off at?"

With just a look, Conner reminded his mom to let him do all the talking.

"The rest of our group headed to Egypt," he said. "You wouldn't by chance be headed in that direction, would you?"

Emgee was so tickled by the coincidence, she slapped her knee.

"You're in luck!" Emgee said. "We're headed to the Ancient Pyramid of Anesthesia right now! Beau's got his heart set on a mythical talisman."

Charlotte was confused. *"Anesthesia?"* she whispered to her son.

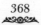

"I heard you and Bob talking about it once and thought it sounded like an ancient pyramid," Conner whispered back. "Tell us more about this talisman. It sounds super-neat!"

Beau was more than excited to talk about it. He retrieved a rolled-up map from a stack in the corner and spread it over the table in the center of the gondola. The map was of southeast Egypt and showed a giant pyramid located near the Nile a few miles south of Cairo. Beau yanked an illustration of a talisman off the wall and placed it on top of the map. The talisman was a gold medal with several Egyptian hieroglyphics carved into it.

"The Lost Talisman of Pharaoh Eczema," Beau said theatrically. "According to legend, the pharaoh was so beloved by his people, they presented him with a golden talisman. Unfortunately, the token of appreciation made the gods jealous. When the pharaoh grew old and became ill, he was afraid the gods would punish him unfairly in the Underworld. So at the time of Eczema's death, one thousand of his most devoted soldiers were killed, mummified, and buried with him in the pyramid so he wouldn't enter the Underworld alone. The gods were furious and denied the soldiers entrance to the Underworld, forcing them to roam the pyramid as the undead. Since they can't protect the pharaoh in the Underworld, the soldiers devotedly protect his remains in the pyramid."

"Wow," Charlotte said, and glanced at Conner. "That's unsettling."

"But wait, there's more!" Beau said. "The legend also states that Pharaoh Eczema's soul bestowed mythical powers on the talisman. Whoever wears it has complete control over the mummified soldiers in his pyramid. The pharaoh was buried with the talisman in a golden chamber deep in the Pyramid of Anesthesia. The chamber is surrounded by a maze, and the pharaoh's casket is patrolled by his most treasured and loyal guardian."

"Conner, that sounds *just* like the talisman you wanted to collect," Charlotte said. "Is it the same or is there more than one?"

The horrified gaze Conner sent his mother was the exact expression Beau sent him. Once again, Conner slapped his palm against his forehead, and Charlotte knew she had made a mistake by sharing their plan.

"*You're* after the talisman, too?" Beau asked.

"Um...kind of," Conner said. "I happen to dabble in archaeology as well. My mom and I are planning to find the talisman and donate it to...um...the Not-So-Natural History Museum in Cairo."

"Well, you can forget about it!" Beau yelled. "The talisman is mine! It's one of the reasons I went into archaeology! Emgee, open the door—let's kick these tomb raiders off the *Charlie Chaplin*! I should never have saved you in the jungle!"

"Easy, Beau," Emgee said. "Technically the talisman doesn't belong to either of you. It belongs to Pharaoh Itchy, or whatever his name is. Seems only fair to get you both to the pyramid and let you duke it out the old-fashioned way."

Beau nodded. "You're right, Aunt Emgee," he said. "We'll fight to the death!"

Emgee sighed. "No, Beau," she said. "I meant you'll have to *race* for it."

"That seems reasonable," Charlotte said. "We can even set a starting mark so it's completely fair."

Conner quickly pulled his mother aside. "Mom, stop agreeing! You know I need the talisman to recruit the mummies into our army!"

"If my son is going to become a warlord, he's going to come by it honestly! Besides, I am not letting you go inside that pyramid alone now that I know it's filled with zombie mummies!" Charlotte snapped. "How much longer until we reach the Pyramid of Anesthesia?"

"It'll take all night, but we'll get there by morning," Emgee said.

"Then it's settled," Charlotte said. "Tomorrow you can both go into the pyramid together, and whoever finds the talisman first can keep it."

Neither of the boys was happy about having to race for the talisman. Conner never pictured a scenario where the hero of his story would turn into his competition. He had created the Pyramid of Anesthesia, so hopefully it wouldn't be too hard to navigate it, but he had also written Beau to be the best archaeologist in the world. It wasn't going to be an easy race.

Emgee shifted the gears of the *Charlie Chaplin*, and the blimp sailed into the western sky.

"Anesthesia or bust!" the old woman said.

After a long evening of reminiscing, Emgee convinced Charlotte and Conner she had single-handedly put the *roaring* in the Roaring Twenties. While she sipped from a jug of homemade potato gin, she told them all about her five failed marriages, her many connections to organized crime, and her early days of performing on a burlesque circuit.

Even though Beau had found a reason to resent their guests, Emgee loved having an audience besides her grand-nephew.

Beau spent the whole evening looking over his map of the pyramid and the illustration of the talisman. He only glanced up to glare spitefully at his new opponent. Conner became so tired of the hateful looks, he moved his seat so his back faced the archaeologist.

At night, Emgee pulled out some guest cots and set them up for Charlotte and Conner to sleep on. She tied down the gears of the *Charlie Chaplin* so it would continue floating west while they slept, and then she and Beau retired to their rooms in the back of the gondola.

Spending the night on a blimp was anything but restful. The sudden bursts of elevation and unexpected turbulence made it very difficult for Conner and his mom to stay asleep. However, Charlotte was kept awake by much more than the bumpy ride. Something had been eating at her since she learned about Beau's parents, something she was desperate to get out.

"Conner, are you awake?" she asked.

"I haven't been able to sleep since that sudden dip over Persia," he said.

"Well, I just wanted to tell you how proud I am of you, honey," Charlotte said. "I'm really amazed by everything you've created, not just in 'The Adventures of Blimp Boy' but in all of your stories. Why have you never shared them with me before now?"

"I guess I just never wanted to bother you," he said. "I first started writing shortly after Dad died. You were always so busy with work and taking care of us, I never wanted to put one more thing on your plate."

Unknowingly, Conner had just answered a difficult question she had been meaning to ask him.

"I suppose that's why there aren't any mothers in your stories," Charlotte said. "Your writing represents so many facets of your life, and I spent so much time away from you, I can't expect any representation of me in your writing. You know, I think one of the reasons I'm so afraid you and your sister are missing out on your lives is because *I've* missed out on so much of your lives. I'm sorry there have been so many times you felt like you didn't have a mom. It's never the kind of mom I wanted to be—life just had other plans."

This was as heartbreaking for him to hear as it was for Charlotte to confess. "The Ziblings" was the first story that made Conner realize just how meaningful each character in his writing could be; he never thought the *lack* of a character could be so symbolic, too. But even though there were no mothers in his stories, it didn't mean Charlotte was missing from them. She didn't see the stories like Conner did.

"Mom, you've got it all wrong," Conner said. "You're in my stories a bunch, you just don't realize it. Auburn Sally is based on more people than just Goldilocks. There's a reason I made her hair the same color as yours. After Dad died, you sailed through all the hard times so bravely; it reminded me of a pirate sailing through a storm. You were the real inspiration behind 'Starboardia.' Jack and Goldilocks just helped me add some layers to it."

"Really?" Charlotte asked. "You're not just saying that?"

"You'd know if I was lying to you—you always do," Conner said. "That's not all, though! Every day when you went to work and took back-to-back shifts just so we could get by, I always thought you must have had superpowers to get through it. That's why I made Bolt's superhero suit the same color as your nursing scrubs. You might have been gone a lot, but you were still a superhero to me and Alex."

Charlotte was moved to tears. She leaned over Conner's cot and kissed him on the cheek.

"I love you so much, sweetheart," she said. "And from now on, I want to be the very first person you share your stories with."

"The next one'll go straight off the presses and into your hands," he said. "I promise."

Charlotte's heart gave a sigh of relief. Knowing she wasn't missing from her son's imagination felt like a weight had been lifted off her chest. And Conner rarely got to reassure his mom about anything, so he was happy he could put her mind at ease. They both finally drifted off to sleep as the blimp drifted over Arabia.

The following morning, Conner and Charlotte awoke as the sun rose and shined through the *Charlie Chaplin*'s round windows. It felt even hotter than it had in the jungle in India. When Conner looked out the window, he saw they were floating above an endless sandy desert. He could barely see the tip of a triangle peeking out on the horizon.

"The Pyramid of Anesthesia!" Conner shouted. "We're almost there!"

His excited declarations woke up Emgee and Beau. They hurried out of their rooms dressed in pajamas and joined Conner at the window. Emgee couldn't see until she strapped on her goggles and used them like prescription glasses.

"That's the pyramid, all right!" she said. "Personally, I would have built my own pyramid closer to a beach, but to each their own."

Less than an hour later, Emgee was piloting the *Charlie Chaplin* toward the sandy earth beside the pyramid. The landing alone was enough evidence for why blimps never became the transportation of the future as Emgee had predicted. The bottom of the gondola bumped across the sand over a dozen times before the blimp came to a stop. Each contact made the whole gondola rattle, and things toppled overboard.

Once they landed, the boys got ready for the race to the talisman. Beau fastened the straps of his aviator hat, laced his boots, and zipped up his leather jacket. Conner tied his sneakers, applied sunblock, and put his backpack over his shoulders. Conner tried offering Beau a friendly handshake before they started, but Beau wouldn't even look at him.

Outside the blimp, Emgee drew a line in the sand and made Conner and Beau stand behind it. The old woman raised a revolver in the air, careful not to aim it at the *Charlie Chaplin*.

"I want a good, clean race," Emgee said. "No cheating, no sabotage, and no swearing! May the best archaeologist win!"

"Good luck, honey!" Charlotte said. "Please watch where you're going—pyramids are dark and dusty."

Emgee fired the revolver and Beau and Conner charged toward the Pyramid of Anesthesia. The thick sand was almost impossible to run in. But even wearing tall boots and a leather jacket in the desert heat, Beau was much faster than Conner. Once Beau was in front of Conner, he purposely kicked the sand backward, aiming for Conner's eyes.

"Hey!" Conner said. "That's cheating!"

"Eat my dust!" Beau said.

The boys reached the base of the Pyramid of Anesthesia. Beau immediately ran up the north side like the pyramid was a wide stone staircase. Conner knew the entrance was on the south side of the pyramid, so he ran around it. Beau noticed Conner going in a different direction, so he followed him from higher ground. They arrived at the entrance on the south side of the pyramid at the same time.

"How did you know where the entrance was?" Beau asked him.

"Because I made it," Conner said truthfully in a sarcastic tone, so Beau was none the wiser.

The young archaeologist kicked the entrance open and a gust of sandy air almost knocked the boys down the pyramid. The entrance led to a long, dark, and dusty hall. The walls were hung with a row of unlit torches and were engraved with hieroglyphics from floor to ceiling. Cobwebs draped across the hall like torn curtains. Clearly there hadn't been another person in the pyramid for thousands of years.

Beau took a torch off the wall and pulled a matchbox out of his pocket. He struck a match using the zipper of his jacket and lit the torch. Conner removed the flashlight from his backpack and hit it against the wall until the batteries worked. The boys ran down the hall, venturing farther into the pyramid.

The hall was just the beginning of a multi-dimensional maze that zigzagged through the pyramid. As soon as the maze split into different directions, Beau purposefully chose the path opposite from Conner, hoping it would get him to the pharaoh's chamber faster. Conner just rolled his eyes and took the route he knew would get him there quickly.

After a mile of winding narrow passages, steep staircases, and sharp turns, Conner stepped into an enormous room at the very bottom of the pyramid. The walls were covered with layers and layers of tombs like novels stacked on a giant's bookshelf. The crypts contained the mummified corpses of the pharaoh's soldiers. The room marked the halfway point of the pyramid's maze, which continued on the other side.

Beau entered the room several moments after Conner. He was red-faced and winded. Obviously the archaeologist was having a rougher time navigating the maze than Conner was. Beau looked around in astonishment. He had never seen so many tombs in one place.

"What is *this*?" Beau asked.

"This is the pharaoh's army," Conner said.

Beau saw where the maze continued on the other side and dashed toward it, hoping to get a head start on Conner.

"No, Beau! Wait!" Conner yelled after him.

"Nice try, but I'm not falling for—"

Beau suddenly tripped on a rope that was so thin he couldn't see it. The rope snapped, and two enormous metal gongs fell from the ceiling and crashed to the floor on either side of him. The noise was deafening and the boys covered their ears before it damaged their eardrums.

"That's loud enough to wake the dead!" Beau said.

"That's the whole point!" Conner said.

All the crypts began shaking at once. One by one, the lids were pushed off and the pharaoh's mummified soldiers slowly crawled out of their tombs. They moaned and groaned in agony and crept toward Conner and Beau.

"Mummies!" Beau yelled. *"So the legend is true! It's all true!"*

Beau and Conner continued into the second half of the maze and the mummies chased after them. Once again, Beau took an alternative route from Conner on purpose.

Conner knew the second part of the maze even better than he knew the first. He had no hesitation whatsoever as he snaked through hall after hall, climbing higher and higher into the pyramid. Each level he reached became smaller and smaller the closer he got to the top of the pyramid. Soon he came to a pair of golden double doors with the hieroglyph of a phoenix carved into them.

"I did it!" Conner said proudly. "I made it to the pharaoh's chamber!"

His victory was cut short by a blood-chilling scream coming from the maze behind him. It was followed by a clamor of monstrous wails and growls. It sounded like the mummies had caught up with Beau.

"Help!" Beau screamed. *"Help me!"*

Conner was conflicted about what to do next. He was only a few short steps away from retrieving the talisman, the only thing he needed to complete his army and save his friends in the fairy-tale world. For a split second, Conner thought Beau deserved to be attacked by mummies for the way he had acted. However, Conner knew his mom would be upset if only one of them came back alive. So to avoid a potential guilt trip (and because it was the right thing to do), Conner turned around and went to save the archaeologist.

"Stupid conscience," Conner mumbled to himself. "It never knows when to quit."

He followed the screams through the maze as he carefully took note of the route to get back to the pharaoh's chamber. Conner found Beau in a corner of the maze surrounded by eight mummies. He was on the floor, and the mummies were viciously hitting and kicking him.

"Hey!" Conner said. "Toilet-paper heads! Over here!"

The mummies turned to Conner and crept toward him. He shined his flashlight directly in their eyes, temporarily blinding them. The mummies scattered like roaches, and Conner helped Beau to his feet.

"You saved my life!" Beau said in shock.

"I *gave* you life," Conner said under his breath.

"I wasn't expecting you to come back for me, especially after how I treated you," Beau said. "Thank you!"

"You can thank me later," Conner said. "I found the pharaoh's chambers. Follow me! There are a lot more mummies where these guys came from!"

Conner quickly retraced his steps through the maze to the highest point in the pyramid where the pharaoh's chamber was located. Beau was amazed by how effortlessly he was moving through the pyramid. Finally, the boys arrived at the golden doors with the phoenix, and Conner grabbed the handles to push them open.

"Wait," Beau said. "Remember, the pharaoh's chamber is patrolled by his most treasured and loyal guardian. It might take both of us to defeat it."

Conner let out a light laugh. "Yeah..." he said. "I wouldn't worry about that if I were you."

He pushed open the doors and the boys stepped into Pharaoh Eczema's chamber. Unlike the rest of the pyramid, the chamber was spotless. The walls were made of pure gold and the pharaoh's colorful casket rested on a platform in the center of the room. They knew they were at the top of the pyramid because the high ceiling rose to a peak above them. There was a small opening in the ceiling that allowed a ray of sunlight to shine directly on the casket.

Beau eyed the chamber nervously: Something was missing. "Where's the pharaoh's most treasured and loyal guardian?" he asked.

The boys heard high-pitched barking. Peeking around the casket on the floor was a small mummified dog.

Although it barked at Conner and Beau, it was clearly more frightened of them than they were of it.

"It's a *dog*?" Beau asked.

"I don't know anything more treasured and loyal than someone's dog," Conner said.

Conner held out his hand, and the dog slowly approached it and sniffed around it. There was something familiar about Conner, and the mummified dog became excited when he sensed it. He happily ran around Conner's feet and rolled on his back, allowing him to rub the wraps covering his belly.

"Good boy, Bones," Conner called. "Who's a nice three-thousand-year-old pup, huh?"

"You know the dog's name?" Beau asked him suspiciously.

"Um...yeah," Conner said. "I must have read it somewhere."

They heard stomping echo through the maze outside the chamber. Conner and Beau turned and saw hundreds and hundreds of mummies creeping toward them.

"We've got to get to the talisman!" Conner said. "Those mummies are about to take out millenniums' worth of pent-up aggression on us!"

The boys hustled to the casket and tried sliding the lid off. It was incredibly heavy and they had to use all their strength. Just as the mummies entered the chamber, Conner and Beau knocked the lid over and saw the golden talisman around the neck of the mummified pharaoh. It grossed him out to touch a dead body, but Conner pulled the talisman off the corpse and put it over his own neck.

"*Knock it off!*" Conner yelled at the approaching mummies.

Now that Conner had complete control over them, all the mummified soldiers froze and attentively put their hands at their sides. Beau looked at the talisman around Conner's neck and became very depressed. The young archaeologist had spent most of his life dreaming about the day he'd find it, only to see it in someone else's possession. He looked so pathetic, Conner couldn't help feeling sorry for him.

"Look, I only need the talisman for a little while," he said. "I'm going to use the mummies to help out some friends. When I'm done, you can have it."

Beau was overjoyed to hear this. "Really?" he asked.

"Totally," Conner said. "Besides, it won't be worth much where I'm from."

The archaeologist squinted at Conner. He had been trying to figure out how Conner knew so much about the pyramid and had finally come to the only probable conclusion he could think of.

"You're Pharaoh Eczema reincarnated, aren't you?" Beau asked. "That's how you knew where the entrance was, how you moved so quickly through the maze, and how you knew the name of his dog."

"It's way more complicated than that," Conner said. "I'm not sure you'd even believe me."

"Try me," Beau said. "I'm an archaeologist—I *live* for complication."

Conner sighed. After their race through the pyramid, he was too tired to come up with any more lies.

"Okay, fine," Conner said with a shrug. "But before I explain, let me ask you this: How familiar are you with classic fairy tales?"

Chapter Twenty-Five

"THE LIFE AND TIMES OF QUEEN TROLLBELLA"

Written and Directed by Trollbella

D r. Sharon Jackson had been the resident clinical psychologist at Saint Andrew's Children's Hospital for over two decades, and today she was facing the most difficult patients of her career. Four stubborn teenage girls sat across from her with their arms folded. They each wore the same hospital gown and the same defiant expression. Unbeknownst to the girls, their worried parents were watching them through the mirror on the wall.

"Hello, ladies," Dr. Jackson said. "My name is Dr. Sharon Jackson and I'm a psychologist here at Saint Andrew's. I've been asked to have a word with you. How are you all feeling today?"

"Don't answer any of her questions," Mindy told her fellow Book Huggers. "The less we say, the less they can use against us."

"I promise you, we are only trying to take care of you," Dr. Jackson said. "Do you remember why you were brought to the hospital?"

Cindy tilted her head in suspicion. "Were we *brought* to the hospital or were we *sent* to the hospital?" she asked.

"Well, you were *brought* to the hospital by an ambulance," Dr. Jackson said. "And it was *sent* here because all four of you were found unconscious on a sidewalk. Does that answer your question?"

The Book Huggers shared a look—their newest suspicion had been all but confirmed.

"Do *you* work for *them*?" Lindy asked.

"For who?" Dr. Jackson asked.

"The people who don't want us knowing what we know," Mindy said.

"*What* do you know?" Dr. Jackson asked. "And *who* doesn't want you knowing it?"

The Book Huggers could tell that the psychologist was

genuinely confused. Perhaps she wasn't as informed as they thought.

"Maybe it's best if we don't tell you," Lindy said. "They might lock you up next!"

"We've been here for three days—but they can't keep us in here forever!" Cindy said.

"We know our rights!" Mindy said.

Wendy leaped out of her seat and went to the door. She yanked on the handle with all her might, but the door didn't budge.

"Ms. Takahashi, if you'd like to leave, just *push* the door open," Dr. Jackson said. "No one is keeping you here against your will."

Wendy turned the door handle and pushed it open easily. She blushed and took her seat.

"Prisoners or not, we know that someone very high up doesn't want us spreading *the facts*," Cindy said. "That's the real reason we're here!"

"I'm glad you brought that up," Dr. Jackson said. "I think it would do us all some good if we go over the facts together and take a break from suspicions."

Dr. Jackson went down a list on her notepad, hoping it would comfort the girls if she put things into perspective.

"You were found unconscious—that's a fact," the psychologist listed. "Just like any young person found in your condition, you were brought to this hospital to be examined—that's also a fact. When you regained consciousness, you told the doctors that you had seen 'pirates appear out of thin air,' and that you had overheard a discussion about 'recruiting armies of fictional characters' and a 'threatened fairy-tale world.'"

"Yeah," Mindy said. "Because we *did!*"

"Why do you think we fainted in the first place?" Cindy asked.

"That aside, usually when patients awake from a trauma and describe such eccentric events, I'm asked to have a word with them to make sure there isn't any psychological damage," Dr. Jackson explained. "This is all standard procedure, and I assure you that no one *high up* has any control over you."

The Book Huggers slumped in their chairs. Given the circumstances, perhaps the psychologist had been brought in for legitimate reasons. Maybe it wasn't part of a big conspiracy against them like they thought.

"We're just so tired of being told we're wrong when we know we're right," Mindy said.

"It's very unlikely four different people would have the exact same hallucination at once," Cindy said.

"But no one will listen to us," Lindy said. "Every time we try to tell someone what we've uncovered, they either hang up, point to the door, or threaten restraining orders."

The Book Huggers were getting worked up. Dr. Jackson raised her hands to calm them down.

"Ladies, it's *my job* to listen," Dr. Jackson said. "Tell me what you saw, what you heard, and what you're worried about. I'll be honest about what I believe is real or exaggerated, but I'll also be open-minded."

The Book Huggers eyed one another apprehensively. Dr. Jackson was the first person to have shown interest willingly. She took vigorous notes as the teenagers explained the cause of their paranoia.

"It started in junior high," Mindy said. "Alex and Conner Bailey disappeared without a trace, and no one could give us a good reason why. We wanted to know the truth, but the more answers we looked for, the more questions we found."

"It seemed like there was something our school, our city, and possibly the government were keeping from us," Cindy said. "Finally, after a year of searching, we saw the twins in a restaurant called the Storybook Grill four days ago!"

"We heard them talking about 'recruiting armies of fictional characters' to save a 'fairy-tale world,' " Lindy said. "It confirmed all our suspicions that something much deeper was going on! That's when we snuck to their house, peered through the window, and saw the pirates and their ship appear out of thin air!"

To their surprise, Dr. Jackson was *relieved* to hear this. She set her notes aside and a big smile came to her face. She even gave a thumbs-up to the mirror, which the Book Huggers thought was very odd.

"Ladies, I have good news for you," the psychologist said. "I believe every word you just said."

The Book Huggers were shocked. They had never

heard those words come out of someone's mouth before. For a second, they thought Dr. Jackson—not the pirates at the twins' house—might be a hallucination.

"You believe us?" Cindy asked.

"Absolutely," Dr. Jackson said. "You aren't experiencing delusions or hallucinations—you're suffering from a simple *misunderstanding*. You see, the twins' mother and stepfather work at this hospital. As a surprise, they hired a group of entertainers to perform for the patients in a show. The pirates you saw at their house are just performers and the ship was probably a set piece."

"A set piece?" Lindy asked. *"But it appeared out of thin air!"*

"Haven't you ever seen a magician or a Broadway show?" Dr. Jackson said. "That's what good set pieces do—it's all part of an illusion."

The Book Huggers shook their heads and covered their ears. They didn't want to believe what the psychologist was telling them—it was all too simple!

"No!" Mindy said. "That can't be it! There has to be more to the story than that!"

"I understand your confusion," Dr. Jackson said. "I met the performers yesterday. Their costumes were so colorful and elaborate, had Mrs. Gordon not explained to me who they were, I might have been just as puzzled as you."

"But that doesn't explain the conversation we heard over dinner!" Cindy said. "Why would they say things like 'recruiting armies' to save 'a threatened fairy-tale

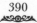

world'? Those aren't words normal people use to describe a show!"

"I imagine they were using code words to keep the performance a secret," Dr. Jackson proposed. "I'm sure it took them a very long time to put it together, and they were being extra-cautious. This is a small town—people talk, and clearly people listen."

The Book Huggers had put so much time and effort into tracking down and exposing the Baileys—it couldn't have all been for a *performance*! They were intelligent girls; they should have spotted a misunderstanding from a mile away.

The teenagers rocked in their seats, trying to think of where they went wrong. Dr. Jackson glanced up at the clock.

"Actually, the performance is tonight," she said. "But if it's *that* unsettling to you, I would recommend sitting it out. Now that we know you aren't suffering any psychological damage, I recommend you all go home and get a good night's rest. Doctor's orders."

Once the psychologist prescribed the troubled Book Huggers some sleep, she escorted the girls back to their parents and headed to the hospital's multi-purpose room.

Thanks to the characters' hard work, Trollbella's thorough direction, and a little touch of Alex's magic, they had put together a performance for Saint Andrew's Children's Hospital in just under a day. The quality of it was questionable, but it was a performance nonetheless. The tedious and frantic task had created a much-needed union among the characters and taught them to work together— which was necessary if they planned on joining forces to defeat the Literary Army.

The pirates of the *Dolly Llama* and the Tin Woodman constructed a large stage with red velvet curtains at the far end of the multi-purpose room. The sailors set up the chairs and made sure every patient, their families, and all the hospital employees had a seat.

Cyborg soldiers were hung from the ceiling and their illuminated body parts were pointed toward the stage like lights. The Cyborg Queen herself converted into a large spotlight and was operated by Commander Newters. Instead of using the hospital's electricity, all the Cyborgs were hooked up to Bolt, who functioned like a human generator.

The other Ziblings were working behind the scenes. After Morph had assisted with costumes by turning into a sewing machine, the shape-shifter transformed into the set. Since Whipney had the most dexterity, she was put in charge of props. Blaze was assigned special effects, but it was the easiest job in the entire show since there was only one, at the very end.

Trollbella insisted the performance have programs so the audience would have something tangible to take away. Bob helped her design the exact flyer she had in mind, and one was laid on every seat. The programs read:

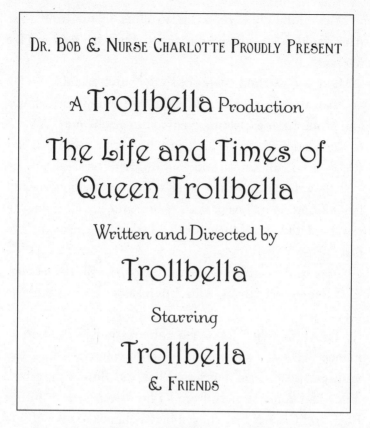

DR. BOB & NURSE CHARLOTTE PROUDLY PRESENT

A Trollbella Production

The Life and Times of
Queen Trollbella

Written and Directed by

Trollbella

Starring

Trollbella
& FRIENDS

At around fifteen minutes to eight o'clock, the multi-purpose room began filling up with an eager audience. Doctors, nurses, and other hospital staff escorted the patients and their families to their seats. Some children were rolled in on wheelchairs or transported in their hospital beds. Although the children weren't feeling their best, they looked around the room keenly, curious about what was waiting for them on the other side of the curtain.

Alex and Bob were sitting together in the front row. Alex couldn't sit still and nervously shook her legs and bit her nails.

"Are you worried about the show?" Bob asked.

"Not the show," she said. "I'm worried about Conner and Mom. I was expecting them to be back by now."

Bob laughed. "You look just like your mother when she's worried about you and your brother," he said.

"Now that I know how it feels, I'm never going to keep her waiting again," Alex said. "I hope they're all right. It's not that I don't trust them, or that I think they need *me*, it's just...just..."

Alex couldn't think of the words to describe the feeling.

"You just *love* them, Alex," Bob said. "It's as simple as that."

To Alex's relief, just a few minutes before the performance started, Conner and Charlotte hurried into the multi-purpose room and found her and Bob at the front. They had come straight from "The Adventures of Blimp Boy" and Conner hadn't even had a chance to take off his backpack.

"Well?" Alex asked. "How did it go? Did you find the talisman?"

Conner and Charlotte exchanged a smile. Conner pulled the talisman out from under his shirt and showed his sister.

"Let's just say there's a blimp parked in the field next

to the hospital and there's a thousand mummified soldiers and one mummified dog in the commissary," Conner said.

"So it's done!" Alex said. "We've recruited all the soldiers we need to take on the Literary Army!"

The twins were so thankful the recruitment was finally over. They couldn't have done it without the help of their mom and stepdad, so they pulled Bob and Charlotte into a tight family hug. It may not have been the family vacation their mom was looking for, but the twins and their parents had accomplished something extraordinary together.

Bob noticed a foul scent lingering around Conner and Charlotte.

"What's that smell?" he asked.

"Mummies," Charlotte said. "I sprayed each of them with perfume and disinfectant, but *decay* isn't an easy odor to take off."

"Should we tell the others before or after the performance?" Conner asked.

"Let's wait," Alex said. "If they pull off the performance, we'll have two miracles to celebrate."

"Is it any good?" Conner asked.

Alex hesitated to answer. "Let's just say it probably won't be your *favorite* show," she said. "Trollbella took some *liberties*."

The lights dimmed and all the audience members sat in their seats. The Cyborgs illuminated the stage, and Commander Newters aimed the Cyborg Queen's spotlight at the center of the curtain. Trollbella stepped through the curtain and waved to the crowd. All the children gasped—they had never seen such a lifelike troll before. The troll queen went to the microphone stand and greeted the audience.

"Good evening, big room of small people," Trollbella said. "Welcome to tonight's performance. As you probably know, I am Queen Trollbella of the Troblin Kingdom. If you don't know, please ask the person beside you to slap you. I am known for many things in my kingdom: beauty, intelligence, charisma, elegance, *passion*—but I'm best known for bringing my nation together. Thanks to my brilliant leadership, what was once a territory of greedy trolls and obnoxious goblins is now a kingdom of respectable and sophisticated Troblins. Tonight you will see that transformation before your symmetrical human eyes in 'The Life and Times of Queen Trollbella'!"

Conner was already annoyed and it was just the introduction. The audience sat on the edge of their seats—they were loving it. Trollbella dragged the microphone stand to the side of the stage and snapped at Commander Newters to keep the spotlight on her.

The curtains opened to reveal a dismal set depicting the Troll and Goblin Territory. The Merry Men and the Lost Boys ran onstage in ridiculous costumes. The men were dressed in green and wore goblin ears over their own. The boys wore brown and headbands with horns. All of them looked very uncomfortable.

"We are the goblins!" the Merry Men announced.

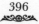

"We are the trolls!" the Lost Boys said.

"The kingdoms of man have forced us to live with the trolls," the Merry Men said.

"The kingdom of fairies has forced us to live underground with the goblins," the Lost Boys said.

"None of us are pleased," they said together.

"OH THE AGONY!" Robin Hood said. *"SORRY, THAT WASN'T IN THE SCRIPT. I JUST THOUGHT THE SCENE COULD USE A LITTLE PIZZAZZ."*

The Merry Men and the Lost Boys were terrible performers. Many of them stood motionless with dead eyes and said their lines like robots. Others put way too much effort into their characters and pranced around the stage. Some of them were terrified to be in front of an audience; others enjoyed it too much. Despite their problematic stage presence, they were entertaining to watch. The children in the audience laughed at everything they said.

"WHY DON'T WE PUT ASIDE OUR DIFFERENCES AND FORM OUR OWN NATION?" Robin Hood said.

"Robin, you're skipping lines!" Tootles said.

"APOLOGIES!" Robin Hood said. "I AM THE GOBLIN KING AND I HATE TROLLS!"

"And I am the Troll King and I hate goblins," Tootles said. "How can we live together underground? *Now say it!*"

"WHY DON'T WE PUT ASIDE OUR DIFFERENCES AND FORM OUR OWN NATION?" Robin Hood asked.

"That is a good idea!" Tootles said. "We will form the Troll and Goblin Territory, start our own society, and prove we are not savage creatures!"

"Hooray," the men and boys said with very little enthusiasm.

Trollbella cleared her throat to get the audience's attention. "The trolls and goblins lived harmoniously in the underground territory for many years, until tragedy struck!" she narrated.

All the performers froze on the stage. They waited for something to happen, but nothing did.

"I said *until tragedy struck!*" Trollbella repeated. *"Braid girl, that's your cue!"*

"Sorry, I was texting!" Whipney called from backstage.

Using her hair, Whipney lowered onto the stage two pillows painted to look like rocks. The "rocks" gently touched both Robin Hood and Tootles on the head. The actors fell to the floor and acted out dramatic death scenes. Tootles's performance was much simpler than Robin Hood's, who convulsed around the stage for almost five minutes before he lay still.

"GOOD-BYE, CRUEL WORLD!" Robin Hood shouted. *"THAT WASN'T IN THE SCRIPT, EITHER! I BELIEVE IT'S CALLED AN ABBY LID!"*

Trollbella shot him a dirty look and then turned to the audience.

"Sometimes rocks fall and you die—that's just life," Trollbella said into the microphone. "With the Troll King and the Goblin King both gone, the territory needed a new ruler!"

Red suddenly rose from a trapdoor in the center of the stage. She was dressed similar to Trollbella, with horns and a brown dress. All the performers sang like an angelic chorus as she entered, but none of them could find the right note or harmonize.

"I am the Troll King's only daughter, Trollbella," Red said. "I will be your new queen and guide you to prosperity! And...and...*what's the rest of my line?*"

"My heart is so full!" Trollbella whispered.

"Yes, that's it," Red said. "And my heart is so full, I can't imagine needing anything else but the affection and gratitude of my people!"

Peter Pan suddenly flew across the stage wearing a large cardboard heart. It was completely unexpected, by both the audience and the other performers. The children pointed him out to one another, wondering how the boy was able to fly.

"Not yet, Peter!" Trollbella snipped, and continued the narration. "Although she thought her heart was full, the young queen soon realized something was missing. There was a void in her life that the trolls and goblins couldn't fill."

Jack stepped onstage dressed in jeans, sneakers, and a T-shirt.

"I'm the handsome Butterboy," Jack announced. "I'm the queen's soul mate. I just don't know it yet because I'm emotionally immature. *Sorry, Conner.*"

Conner was so embarrassed, he sank into his seat and covered his face with his backpack. Trollbella was sporting a wide grin—this was her favorite part of the show. Red struck a theatrical pose with her hands over her heart.

"Be still my heart, for I am in love!" Red announced.

"Now, Peter!" Trollbella whispered.

Peter soared out from backstage and flew in circles over the audience. The children laughed and clapped—they reached up and tried to touch him. Conner was irritated by how much they were enjoying the show.

"Hello, Butterboy!" Red said to Jack. "Would you like to be my king and rule the trolls and goblins with me? Oh, how happy we will be together!"

"Oh boy, that sounds wonderful!" Jack said. "How lucky I am to be loved by such a beautiful and brilliant troll queen. I will never find someone like her ever again—nope, not once, no how, no way, not going to happen! I want to be with Trollbella for all eternity!"

"I never said that!" Conner shouted from his seat. "She's making this up!"

Trollbella glared down at him from the stage. *"If you get to tell stories, so do I!"*

Jack and Red ran toward each other in slow motion across the stage. Suddenly, the lights began flickering melodramatically. Goldilocks stomped onto the stage dressed as a large yellow toad with big warts and a purple beanie. Of all the performers, she looked the least excited to be there.

"I am the terrible Bree Monster," Goldilocks announced. "My mission in life is to rid others of happiness. I must keep Butterboy away from Queen Trollbella so their powerful love does not inspire others. I will bewitch Butterboy with a curse so he thinks he has feelings for me, when in reality, I'm so hideous I can't be loved by anyone."

"Oh, come on!" Conner said. "This is just ludicrous!"

The audience booed as Goldilocks dragged Jack off the stage. Red lowered her head and pretended to cry.

"After Butterboy was taken from her, Trollbella became very sad," Trollbella narrated. "But luckily, the troll queen was so commonsensical, she bounced back quickly. She used her misfortune to create something positive!"

"If I can't have my Butterboy, I'll put all my energy into being queen!" Red said with a big smile. "I'll help the trolls and goblins improve their image by combining them into *the Troblins*! We'll turn our territory into a brand-new kingdom so the world will see how much we've changed!"

"The troll queen made the world a much better place for the trolls and goblins," Trollbella said. "Although it broke her heart to be away from Butterboy, the distance taught the queen a valuable lesson and a secret to success: When you can't have what you want, make the most out of what you have!"

A big sign hanging above the stage suddenly caught on fire. It burned THE END and the curtains closed.

Conner was thankful the show was over. "Well, that was probably the worst piece of theater in the history of—"

He was interrupted by thunderous applause coming from behind him. Conner turned around and saw every patient in the hospital clapping ecstatically and smiling from ear to ear. Trollbella's show might have been stupid and silly, but it was exactly what the audience needed. It gave the patients of Saint Andrew's Children's Hospital a night off from their troubles and an evening of mindless fun.

When the curtains opened again, Trollbella and her company reappeared and took a bow. The audience cheered loudly and the patients who could stand gave them a standing ovation. The performers could feel the patients' gratitude in the applause and they bowed again and again until the clapping stopped.

After the show, the characters came down off the stage and mingled with the audience. They took pictures, signed autographs, and did everything they could to make the patients feel special. The doctors and nurses appreciated how the performers "stayed in character" while visiting with the children, never suspecting the actors were actually who they claimed to be.

Dr. Jackson and Mr. and Mrs. Carmichael found Bob and Charlotte in the crowd and shook their hands.

"Thank you for such a *unique* performance," Mrs. Carmichael said.

"It wasn't Shakespeare," said Mr. Carmichael. "But on the bright side, *it wasn't Shakespeare*."

"I've never seen so many smiling faces in this hospital,"

Dr. Jackson said. "It was so kind of you to treat the children to a night of fun."

"It was our pleasure," Charlotte said. "It's amazing what a story can do."

It was getting late, and the doctors and nurses escorted the patients out of the multi-purpose room and back to their own rooms. Tootles was a little confused about where to go and wandered off with the other children. Luckily the twins spotted him before he went too far.

"I'll get him," Alex told Conner. "Actually, it's probably best if I do a lap around the hospital to make sure he isn't the only one who's wandered off. You should share your good news with the others!"

Alex followed Tootles out of the multi-purpose room. Conner waited until everyone had left but his parents, the characters from "Starboardia," "Galaxy Queen," and "The Ziblings," and his friends from the fairy-tale world. He stood on a chair and whistled to get the group's attention.

"Congratulations on a good show, everyone," Conner said. "Trollbella put together a really *creative* and *totally fictional* show. You should all be very proud of yourselves!"

"Fiction is a matter of opinion, Butterboy," Trollbella said, and winked at him.

Conner ignored her. "Now, I have some great news to share!" he said. "My mom and I went into my last story and recruited one thousand mummified soldiers into our army! We finally have enough people to face the literary villains and take back the fairy-tale world!"

The characters erupted into cheers and applause of their own. Their spirits were already high from the performance, but the news sent their spirits soaring. Jack, Goldilocks, and Red shared a celebratory hug.

"That's fantastic!" Red said. "I was getting so tired of that commissary!"

"Good job, my friend," Jack said, and patted Conner on the back.

"Well done, Conner," Goldilocks said. "We couldn't have done it without YOOOOOUU!"

Her words turned into a scream, and the room went silent. The color drained from her face and her mouth dropped open. Goldilocks looked to Jack and grabbed his hand.

"Goldie?" Jack asked. "What is it?"

"Jack, my water just broke," Goldilocks said. *I'm going into labor!*"

All the characters glanced at one another in panic. This was such an anticipated moment, but no one was prepared for it. They were characters from children's stories—none of *them* knew how to deliver a baby!

"Quick! We need scissors, boiling water, and recycled paper!" Red shouted. "Or is that for papier-mâché?"

Trollbella covered her eyes. *"Keep it inside while I'm in the room!"* she said. *"I don't want to see a baby come out of you!"*

"CALL THE MIDWIFE AND WET NURSE!"

Robin Hood yelled. "BUT DON'T TELL THEM I SENT YOU!"

"Everyone calm down," Charlotte said. "I'm a nurse—I know what to do. Bob, make some calls and see if there's an ob-gyn close by. I'll take her to the operating room in the new wing of the hospital and get her prepped."

"Got it," Bob said.

"Isn't Bob a doctor?" Red asked. "Can't he help?"

"He's not that kind of doctor," Conner said.

"There are different *kinds* of doctors in the Otherworld?" Red asked. "That just seems unnecessarily complicated to me."

Bob immediately got on his phone and Charlotte quickly retrieved a wheelchair. They were in a room filled with cutthroat pirates, advanced Cyborgs, and daring superheroes—but Charlotte was the one taking the situation by the horns. It was fun for Conner to watch his characters gawking at his mom. Just like he told her on the blimp, she was the true hero.

Charlotte gently sat Goldilocks in the wheelchair and pushed her down the hall. Jack held Goldilocks's hand as they traveled and Red followed them.

"You guys stay here!" Conner told his characters. "When Alex gets back, tell her where we are!"

"Good luck!" all the characters said together.

Conner ran down the hall and caught up with the others.

"Goldilocks, how's the pain?" Charlotte asked.

"Not terrible, actually," Goldilocks said. "The contractions aren't nearly as bad as I was expecting— NEVER MIND, THEY'RE BAD! THEY'RE REALLY, REALLY BAD!"

"Ouch, my hand!" Jack cried.

"Thank goodness you're in a children's hospital, Goldie!" Red said. "I can't imagine a better place in the world to have a baby! Good timing!"

"Red, babies aren't born in children's hospitals," Conner said. "They're usually delivered at standard hospitals."

"That makes absolutely no sense!" Red said. "This world is so backward!"

They traveled through Saint Andrew's to the operating room in the new wing of the hospital. Conner ran ahead and held the doors for the others to enter. When they went into the operating room, there were three people waiting inside—two of whom were the last people Conner was expecting to see.

"Bree? Emmerich?" he said in shock. "What are you doing here?"

His friends were standing with an old woman no one recognized. Conner could instantly tell that Bree and Emmerich weren't their normal selves. They both looked pale, exhausted, and frightened.

"Conner!" Bree said frantically. "I didn't know you would be here, too!"

"Bree, what are you guys doing here?" Conner asked. "Is something wrong?"

Bree burst into tears. "I'm so sorry," she cried. "I didn't want to bring him, but I had no choice."

The doors slammed shut and locked behind them. Conner, Charlotte, Jack, Goldilocks, and Red turned around and saw the Masked Man behind them. He had a crazed look in his eye and he raised a revolver toward them.

Tonight's surprises were just getting started.

CHAPTER TWENTY-SIX

ALEX ALONE

Alex found Tootles before he wandered into the Saint Andrew's ICU and escorted him back to the multi-purpose room. Alex completed a quick round of the hospital, and the Lost Boy appeared to be the only character who had strayed from the group.

Right before Alex rejoined the others in the multi-purpose room, she saw something out of the corner of her eye: A woman with horns was entering the women's rest-room down the hall. Alex could have sworn Trollbella was with the others when she left, but she decided to inspect the bathroom just to be sure. Who else would have horns in a hospital?

Alex searched the women's restroom, but didn't find the troll queen anywhere.

"Trollbella?" Alex asked. "Was that you?"

Morina suddenly lunged out of a bathroom stall and blew a handful of magic dust directly into Alex's face. Alex was so startled she gasped, breathing the dust deeply into her lungs. She coughed like she was choking on poisonous gas, and her eyes watered like she had been hit with pepper spray.

"What . . . what have you done to me?" she cried.

"I've enhanced you," Morina said with a wicked smile.

Alex collapsed on the floor and tried to recuperate, but she couldn't catch her breath or stop crying. The witch stared down at Alex, like a vulture waiting for its prey to die.

"That's it," Morina said. "Let it sink in, let it course through your veins, let it *consume* you. . . ."

The coughing and tears eventually subsided, but the irritation was replaced by even harsher symptoms. Alex was filled with more anger than she had ever felt in her entire life. She tried to fight the magic manipulating her emotions, but the struggle only infuriated her even more. Why was her life a constant battle? Why did she have to fight so hard? Why did *she* always have to save so many others?

To comfort herself, Alex thought of the people she

loved, but the dust wouldn't let Alex *feel* love. As visions of her friends and family flashed before her eyes, the spell convinced her that they all secretly hated her and wished she would disappear. She thought her brother resented her, that her mother was ashamed of her, that her grandmother had died disappointed in her, and that her father had died just as an excuse to abandon her.

Alex grabbed the sink and pulled herself to her feet. She looked into the mirror but didn't see her own reflection. Alex only saw the face of a complete failure. The dust altered not only her perception of the world, but also how she viewed herself. She saw a girl who didn't deserve affection, who was unworthy of success, and who was incapable of anything but making mistakes.

She wasn't going to save her friends, she wasn't going to defeat the Literary Army, and she wasn't going to save the fairy-tale world. It would fall apart like everything else in her life, and Alex had only herself to blame.

"Do you feel the anger boiling inside of you?" Morina asked. "Let it grow, let it shape you, let it blind you.... Let it *become* you."

The bathroom walls and floor started to shake and the lights flickered. Alex's eyes began to glow, and her hair rose above her head like flames in slow motion. She disappeared from her body and the magic dust transformed her into someone else entirely....

CHAPTER TWENTY-SEVEN

CEMETERY OF THE UNDEAD

Conner was so stunned to see the Masked Man in the hospital, he lost his train of thought. He didn't stop to wonder what Bree and Emmerich were doing with the Masked Man, how they'd got there, or who the older woman with them was. All he could think about was getting his friends and his mom away from such a dangerous man.

"They said you were dead," Conner said.

"I've lived to seize another day," the Masked Man said. "Sorry to disappoint you."

Charlotte looked at the Masked Man like she was seeing a ghost. Despite his injuries and tattered clothes, he was the spitting image of her late husband. Alex and Conner had tried so carefully to keep his existence a secret from their mother, but the disturbing reality was right in front of her face.

"Mom, this man isn't Dad," Conner said. "It's his younger brother, Lloyd. He's a criminal from the fairy-tale world, don't believe a word he—"

"I know who he is, Conner," Charlotte said. "Your father told me all about him before you were born. I'm sorry you know about him. Your father never wanted you to find out you were related to such a horrible person."

"You're not the only person he's related to, Conner," Bree said. "Emmerich is the Masked Man's son—he's the child the Masked Man had with Bo Peep!"

The information was so unexpected, Conner felt like he had been slapped. He remembered the story Hagetta had told him and his sister about hiding Bo Peep's child from his father, but that was long before they discovered who the Masked Man really was. Conner had forgotten all about the child until this moment.

"I guess that makes us cousins," Emmerich said.

"This has turned into quite the family affair," the Masked Man said. "But I'm afraid it won't be remembered as a *pleasant* reunion."

"What do you want from us?" Conner said.

The Masked Man grunted. "*Teenagers*," he sneered.

"You always think both worlds revolve around you. To be frank, dear nephew, you're quite useless to me."

"Then what do you want with Alex?" Conner asked.

"He's not here for your sister, either," Bree said. "He's come to the hospital to take your mom!"

"Me?" Charlotte said. "What could you possibly want with me?"

"I'm in need of an Otherworld nurse," the Masked Man said. "You see, the medical knowledge of the fairy-tale world isn't as advanced as it is here, and I'm in the market for a complicated procedure."

Goldilocks moaned as another contraction began.

"This woman is about to have a baby," Charlotte said. "Please, we need to get her to a doctor immediately."

"What a coincidence—I'm going to need a lift out of the hospital," the Masked Man said. "I thought I'd have to give the old woman here a bullet wound to do it, but the mother-to-be is even more convenient."

"You won't lay a finger on her!" Jack yelled.

Jack charged toward him, but the Masked Man fired his gun into the air and Jack froze.

"That was my only warning," the Masked Man said. "I will not *waste* another bullet—that goes for all of you."

Their captor was growing visibly impatient. His most recent scheme was so close to fruition, he could almost taste it. He paced around the room and gave his hostages more insight into what he had in store.

"This is what's going to happen," the Masked Man said.

"Charlotte is going to collect from this room whatever she needs to perform a *blood transfusion*. Then she, Emmerich, and myself are going to escort Goldilocks downstairs to the emergency room. We're going to tell the paramedics Goldilocks needs to be transferred to another medical facility, and as they load her into the ambulance, we're going to steal it. Then we're going to drive far away, where Charlotte will transfer my son's blood into my own veins, until there isn't a drop left in the boy."

His plan was so barbaric, it took Conner a moment to understand the reasoning behind it.

"If Emmerich is your son, that means there's magic in his blood," Conner thought aloud. "You want his blood to regain your powers. You're so obsessed with power, you're willing to kill your own son!"

"I'm willing to kill more if I have to," the Masked Man warned.

"I'm not draining your son's blood!" Charlotte said.

The Masked Man pointed his gun at Conner. "I'll find ways of convincing you," he said.

The tense silence was broken by another painful cry as Goldilocks's contractions increased.

"It's okay, Charlotte," Emmerich said. "I'm not scared—I'd rather he hurts me than anyone else. I'm sure it'll just feel like I'm falling asleep."

Charlotte would have sacrificed herself before harming a child, but Emmerich had given the nurse an idea. The Masked Man nudged her toward the supply cabinet and she collected syringes, gauze, bags, surgical tape, and other equipment. Charlotte put everything she needed for a blood transfusion into a large bag—and pocketed a little something extra.

"Now everyone else lie on the floor," the Masked Man ordered. "Emmerich, take those ACE bandages out of the cupboard and tie their hands and feet together. Make sure the knots are tight—I'll be checking before we leave."

With no alternative options in sight, Conner, Jack, Cornelia, Red, and Bree did as the Masked Man demanded. Emmerich tied their hands tightly behind their backs and their feet together. The Masked Man inspected his son's knots to make sure they'd last. Once he was satisfied, he tucked the revolver under his sling—making a point to show his hostages it was hidden but easily accessible if he needed it.

"Now let's go," he said.

Charlotte wheeled Goldilocks out of the room with the bag of supplies, and they headed for the emergency room. The Masked Man pushed Emmerich out the door, and they followed the women. The others left in the operating room struggled against the bandages with all their might, but they wouldn't budge.

"We have to do something!" Jack said desperately. "Goldilocks is about to give birth! Who knows what that madman might do to her!"

"Help us!" Cornelia yelled. *"Help us!"*

"Let me try," Red said. "No offense, but I'm an attractive young blonde—someone's more likely to answer me! HELP US! HELP US!"

"Guys, we're the only people in an empty hospital wing!" Conner said. "No one can hear us!"

"We have to stop him!" Bree said. "He's going to kill Emmerich if we don't!"

"You see, this is why I'm not close to my own relatives!" Red said. "Families are nuts! They give you life, then you're lucky if you survive them!"

Red's rant inadvertently reminded Conner of something in his bag—something they could use!

"Survival!" Conner said happily. "That's it!"

Charlotte had packed Swiss Army knives in the twins' backpacks before they left for "Starboardia." Thankfully, the Masked Man hadn't instructed Conner to take his backpack off before he was tied up. If he could just reach the knife inside it, he might be able to cut himself free.

Conner rolled onto his back and with his tied hands painfully reached up to the backpack's front pouch. Just when it felt like he was about to break his arms, he pried the zipper open with his fingertips.

"Bree, see if you can find the Swiss Army knife in my bag," Conner said.

They shuffled around the floor until they were back to back and Bree was able to remove the small knife from his backpack.

"I got it," Bree said, and unfolded it. "Stay still—I'm going to cut the bandages around your wrists."

She sawed the small blade against Conner's bandages until she cut through them. Once Conner's hands were free he removed the bandages around his feet and sliced them off the others. They helped one another to their feet and ran out of the operating room, but Cornelia stayed behind.

"Cornelia, are you coming?" Bree asked.

"I can't keep up," Cornelia said. "Go! Get to them before it's too late! I'll call Wanda and Frenda and let them know where we are!"

"Cornelia, go to the multi-purpose room," Conner said. "Find my sister and tell her what's happened—her name is Alex and she looks like me."

"I will," the old woman said. "Now hurry!"

Conner, Bree, Jack, and Red ran through the hospital as fast as they could. They followed the signs to the emergency room, pushed past the people waiting in the lobby, and ran out to the driveway where the ambulances were parked.

They arrived just in time to see two paramedics loading Goldilocks into the back of an ambulance. As soon as they shut the doors behind her, the ambulance screeched down the driveway, and the paramedics watched helplessly as the vehicle was stolen in plain sight. They ran inside the hospital to call the police. As the ambulance passed Conner and the others, they saw the Masked Man at the wheel and Charlotte and Emmerich sitting in the front beside him.

The driveway curved around the hospital like a horseshoe. If Conner ran straight ahead, he might be able to stop the ambulance—but with *what*? What did he have that could stop a speeding vehicle? As soon as he thought of the question, the answer hit him like a bolt of lightning hitting the Eiffel Tower.

"They're getting away!" Bree yelled.

"Oh no they're not!" Conner said. He ran across the driveway and retrieved the binder of short stories from his backpack. He flipped it open to the very last page and dived in front of the ambulance. Just before the vehicle ran him over, the beam of light hit the ambulance and it disappeared into his short story.

Jack and Red sighed with relief—they couldn't believe Conner had pulled it off. Bree had no clue what had just happened, but she was amazed by what she saw.

"Come on!" Conner said. "Follow me!"

With no time to lose, Conner jumped into the beam of light and his friends followed him inside.

Since he had opened the binder to the very last page, Conner was certain he had sent the ambulance into "The Adventures of Blimp Boy." He expected to see an Egyptian desert and the Pyramid of Anesthesia, but Conner didn't recognize the world around him at all. In fact, he had never seen the strange environment they had landed in, not even in his imagination.

They were standing on a tall knoll surrounded by rolling hills of dark soil. A full moon peeked through dark clouds above them, and a misty fog hung in the air. In the distance they saw a tall wrought-iron fence along the perimeter of an enormous and eerie cemetery. The fence guarded a sea of gothic tombstones, and through the fog beyond the graves, they could make out a forest of stone mausoleums.

The tombstones were so old they were cracked and covered in mildew and their engravings were virtually illegible. They were decorated in crucifixes and macabre statues of angels and the grim reaper. Even though the fog distorted the view, the cemetery seemed as endless as the deserts of Egypt. There wasn't a sign of life anywhere; there were no trees, grass, or flowers, only tombs for miles and miles around.

"Conner, were you in a bad mood when you wrote this story?" Red said.

"This isn't my story," Conner said. "I never wrote about anything like this."

Suddenly, they saw something moving across the graveyard. A red fox was prancing among the tombstones. The animal batted its eyes and twirled its tail flirtatiously, almost as if it were trying to lure them into the cemetery. Bree recognized the fox and rubbed her eyes to make sure she wasn't seeing things.

"Conner, where was that beam of light supposed to take us?" Bree asked.

"It should have transported us into one of my short stories," he explained. "We've been using a potion to travel into my writing, but I have no clue where it's taken us."

Bree gulped nervously. "I do," she said. "This is *my* short story—we're in 'Cemetery of the Undead'! I wrote it in the eighth grade!"

Conner tried to make sense of the situation. How could they be in one of Bree's stories?

"I got my stories from Mrs. Peters," Conner said. "She must have mixed your writing with mine when she gave them to me! It's been in the back of my binder the whole time! I didn't have a divider between them, so the Portal Potion must have seeped through my writing and into yours."

Traveling into his own stories had been a jarring experience for Conner, but at least he knew where he was going. He couldn't imagine how Bree felt after accidentally stumbling into a world from her imagination with no prior warning.

"Look over there!" Jack said, and pointed.

They saw tire tracks and followed them into the cemetery. The ambulance had crashed into the fence just beside a wide-open gate. They checked the vehicle, but it was empty. A moan came from somewhere in the graveyard and they ran toward it.

"Goldie!" Jack shouted. *"We're coming!"*

They found Goldilocks on the ground a few hundred feet inside the graveyard. She was leaning against a tombstone, with beads of sweat covering her forehead, and she was breathing deeply. Jack knelt beside her and held her hand.

"The Masked Man..." She panted. "I couldn't keep up, so they left me here....He took Emmerich and Charlotte somewhere over there....I didn't see which one they went inside...."

Goldilocks pointed to the mausoleums, but there were hundreds of them. Finding Emmerich and Charlotte among them would be like finding a needle in a haystack.

"Let's get you back to the hospital," Jack said. He tried to get Goldilocks to stand, but she wouldn't move.

"My contractions are too close together," Goldilocks said. "I can't stand! This baby is being born right here!"

Jack and the others exchanged fearful looks— Goldilocks needed help.

"You guys stay with Goldie," Conner told them. "I'm going to find Emmerich and my mom. As soon as I get them away from the Masked Man, I'll send my mom here to help."

"I'm coming with you," Bree said.

"You can't, it's too dangerous," Conner said.

"Conner, I know you're used to being the hero of your own stories, but this is mine," Bree said. "I know this cemetery like the back of my hand. Besides, we only have twenty minutes until midnight—we have to get everyone out of here before then!"

"What happens at midnight?" Red asked.

Bree looked frightened. "The characters come out," she said.

"What's wrong with you writers?" Red yelled. "If you wrote instruction manuals, we wouldn't have this problem!"

Goldilocks moaned again and squeezed Jack's hand. They didn't have much time before the baby arrived. Conner and Bree ran into the cemetery and searched through the mausoleums one by one.

The Masked Man had taken Emmerich and Charlotte deep into the cemetery and forced them inside a mausoleum with stained glass windows and a statue of a fallen angel on the roof. He and his son sat on the casket inside as Charlotte prepared the equipment for the blood transfusion. The Masked Man kept a watchful eye on the nurse and a steady grip on his revolver as she worked.

To keep up appearances, Charlotte drew blood from Emmerich and let it fill a small bag. Emmerich watched the blood drain from his body as if it were sand pouring out of his personal hourglass.

"If you see my mom, please tell her I love her." The little boy sniffled.

"You can tell her yourself—I promise," Charlotte whispered, and winked at the young boy.

Next, the nurse prepared the Masked Man's IV. She made it as unpleasant for him as possible. She forcefully straightened his broken arm and stuck him with the dullest needle she had.

"Easy!" he barked.

Charlotte pulled a small vial out of her pocket and filled a syringe with its clear liquid. She started injecting the solution into the Masked Man's IV but he became suspicious and stopped her.

"What is that?" the Masked Man snarled.

"It's just saline," Charlotte said. "It's to prevent infection."

"I don't want you putting anything inside my veins except the child's blood."

"I can't put his blood into your system until the area is sterilized," Charlotte said. "If you don't want me to do my job correctly, then there was no point in leaving the fairy-tale world."

The Masked Man glared at her, held his revolver a little tighter, and allowed her to proceed. Charlotte injected the solution into his arm and watched him closely. The Masked Man suddenly felt very tired. His eyelids became heavy and the small mausoleum started spinning around him—*he had been tricked*! Charlotte hadn't injected him with *saline* but with a *sedative*!

"YOU WENCH!" the Masked Man yelled, and raised his revolver.

Charlotte twisted his broken arm and the Masked Man shrieked in agony. He dropped the gun and scrambled to the floor to retrieve it. Charlotte threw the IV pole at the stained glass window and it shattered. She and Emmerich quickly crawled through it just as the Masked Man got his gun. He shot at them, but the sedative made him a lousy shot and he missed. The bullet ricocheted off the mausoleum's stone wall and hit the side of his right leg. He screamed in pain.

Conner and Bree were searching the mausoleums nearby when they heard the sounds of broken glass, gunfire, and screaming.

"Mom!" Conner gasped.

"Emmerich!" Bree said.

They ran toward the sounds, praying nothing had happened to either of them. A dark and foggy graveyard was scary by itself, but knowing a dangerous man was lurking nearby with a gun made Conner and Bree feel like they were in a real-life horror movie. They jumped at every statue they saw, afraid it was the Masked Man looming through the fog. Luckily, they ran into Charlotte first.

"Mom!" Conner said. "Thank God you're okay! Where's Emmerich?"

Charlotte's eyes darted around the cemetery. "He was right beside me a moment ago," she said. "We escaped from your uncle but got separated in the fog."

Another scream echoed through the cemetery, but this time it was coming from Goldilocks.

"Mom, you have to go and help her," Conner said. "Bree and I will find Emmerich."

From the look in her eyes, Conner knew leaving him and Bree alone was the last thing his mother wanted to do.

"We'll be fine," Conner said. "Right now, Goldilocks needs you!"

Charlotte was torn between her obligations as a mother and her duties as a nurse. But she had to remind herself she wasn't the mother of a normal child—she knew Conner was more than capable of taking care of himself. He had proven it time and time again.

"I love you, sweetheart," Charlotte said. "Be safe."

She hugged her son and kissed him on the cheek. Then Charlotte followed Goldilocks's moans to the front of the graveyard and prepared to deliver the child.

Conner and Bree hurried in the opposite direction, looking for their friend.

"Emmerich!" Bree whispered. *"Where are you?"*

They found Emmerich crouching behind a tombstone. He was trembling and looking around with large, frightened eyes. The fog was the thickest in this part of the cemetery, and he hadn't been able to tell who Bree and Conner were until they were just a few feet away from him.

"There you are!" Bree said.

"Conner! Bree!" Emmerich cried with relief. "Where's Charlotte?"

"She went back to help Goldilocks," Conner said. "Come on, let's get you out of here."

"NOT SO FAST!" shouted a voice behind them.

Conner and Bree slowly turned around and saw the Masked Man creeping toward them. He was in the worst shape of his life: His limp was much worse now that he had a sprained ankle *and* a bullet wound on the same leg. His clothes were covered in blood, and the sedative had made the bags under his eyes droopier than usual. He was fighting the medication off with all his remaining strength.

"The boy is coming with me!" the Masked Man yelled.

Conner stood between his uncle and Emmerich.

"No one is going anywhere with you!" he said.

"Stupid boy!" the Masked Man said. "Get out of my way or I'll shoot!"

"Go ahead!" Conner said. "You'll never be satisfied no matter how many people you kill and no matter how powerful you become! And if I can't stop you, my sister will! Good luck facing her once she finds out you killed me!"

The Masked Man ignored Conner and pointed his gun at his nephew's head. *"Give my regards to your father."*

Just as he was about to press his finger against the trigger, they were all startled by a loud scraping sound. The lids of three stone caskets nearby were pushed open, and the corpses inside suddenly stood up from their graves.

"What's going on?" Conner whispered to Bree.

She glanced down at her watch. "It's midnight," she said. "All the bodies in the cemetery come back to life for a few minutes every night to stretch their legs and visit with each other. It's supposed to be a morbid representation of what break time is like in a public high school!"

All three corpses were women, and although in Bree's story they were less decomposed than they would have been in real life, each had obviously been dead for a long while. Their skin was so pale, it was a shade of blue, there were dark circles under their eyes, and parts of their bones stuck out from their skin.

The women wore very specific clothing from different eras in history. The first woman wore early-fifteenth-century armor, and her skin was partially burned. The second woman wore a dress with wide sleeves, a necklace with the letter *B*, and a headband with a long veil. The third woman wore an enormous ball gown and lots of jewelry and had a towering white wig. The two women in dresses also had stitches around their necks, as if their heads had been detached from their bodies and then sewn back on.

"Who are they?" Conner asked. "Why do they look so familiar?"

"This area of the cemetery is called 'Wronged Women Row,'" Bree said. "These are the women I thought had unfair deaths in history. That's Joan of Arc, Anne Boleyn, and Marie-Antoinette."

The historical figures stretched and yawned as they came back to life. It was like they were waking from a long nap rather than coming back from the dead.

"I just adore our nightly stretches," Joan of Arc said. "Don't you, Anne?"

"It certainly gives us something to *live* for." Anne Boleyn giggled.

"You know what I always say," Marie-Antoinette said. "Death is what you make of it. Just like everything else, it's all in the *execution*!"

The corpses laughed wildly among themselves. Apparently nothing tickled them more than jokes about their mortality. The women turned to a fourth casket in their row whose occupant hadn't risen yet.

"It looks like Bo is sleeping in again," Joan of Arc said.

"She'd better wake up and stretch, otherwise she'll be very stiff tomorrow," Anne Boleyn said.

"Oh, Bo, darling?" Marie-Antoinette called to the casket. "It's midnight, dear! Come out and join us!"

The lid on the casket slid open and a fourth corpse stood up in her grave. She wore a dainty dress and a bonnet and held a staff. She must have been the most recently departed, because she was far less decomposed than the other corpses were.

"Sorry, girls, I was counting sheep," the woman said. "It helps me pass the time between stretches."

"What's your count up to now?" Joan of Arc asked.

"Twenty-eight million, nine hundred and seventy-four thousand, eight hundred and sixty-three," the woman said.

Conner recognized the woman immediately. It caught him completely off guard because he thought he'd never see her again—even in a fictional story.

"That's Bo Peep!" Conner whispered to Bree. "You put *her* in 'Cemetery of the Undead'?"

"This must be my second draft," Bree said. "I was upset by how Bo Peep died, so I added her to the story."

As strange as it was to see their deceased acquaintance, it was nothing compared to how Emmerich felt at the sight of his birth mother. He had hundreds of questions he wanted to ask, but he was too afraid to speak.

Seeing her corpse come to life made the Masked Man feel like he had stepped into a nightmare. He couldn't tell if she was really there or if she was just a hallucination brought on by the sedative.

"Bo Peep?" he asked in shock.

All the undead women turned to the sound of his voice. It was the first time they realized their row had visitors.

Bo Peep was enraged to see him. *"Lloyd!"* she yelled.

The other corpses gasped.

"Is this the man you were telling us about, Bo?" Joan of Arc asked.

"Yes, he is," Bo Peep said. "He's the one who *used* me, who *tricked* me, and who *broke my heart*! He's the whole reason I'm in this cemetery! I'd still be alive if it weren't for him!"

"And look—he's not alone," Anne Boleyn pointed out. "There are three young people with him."

"I know them, too," Bo Peep said. "What are the three of you doing with a man like *him*?"

"I promise, it's not by choice!" Conner said. "He's holding us hostage!"

Hearing this angered Bo Peep to no end. She stepped out of her casket and charged toward the Masked Man. He had never been so terrified in his entire life. He aimed his revolver at her, but it didn't stop her from approaching him.

"Don't come any closer or I'll shoot!" he warned her.

"You can't hurt me anymore," Bo Peep said.

She reached toward him with her cold dead hands, and the Masked Man shot at her—using the third and final bullet in the revolver. Bo Peep looked down at the bullet hole in her torso, but it only infuriated her even more.

"Kill me once, shame on you. Kill me twice, shame on *me*!" she said.

"Get away!" the Masked Man said. "I'm warning you!"

"Your threats are as empty as your soul!" Bo Peep said.

The Masked Man hobbled away from her as quickly as his injured leg would allow. He wasn't paying attention to where he was going, though, and fell right into an empty grave with an unmarked tombstone. He tried to climb out of it, but dozens of decaying hands suddenly stuck up from the dirt below and grabbed hold of him. They pulled on his legs, his arms, and his clothes and pulled him into the ground with them.

"UNHAND ME AT ONCE, YOU DEMONS!" the Masked Man yelled.

He screamed and tried to free himself, but there were too many for him to fight. The more he struggled, the more hands appeared. Even after he was completely underground, his screaming could still be heard aboveground, but the sound of his voice became fainter and fainter as he was pulled deeper and deeper into the earth.

When the noise had finally disappeared completely, an engraving appeared on the tombstone: HERE LIES LLOYD BAILEY—BELOVED BY NONE.

As much as Conner hated the Masked Man, it was still a terrifying thing to witness. He wondered if his uncle was really gone for good, but when he turned to Bree, he saw she looked just as frazzled as he did. Bree's story of the undead had taken on a life of its own.

"Well, that's all the excitement I can handle for one night," Joan of Arc said.

"Time to go back to sleep," Anne Boleyn said with a yawn.

"See you tomorrow night, girls," Marie-Antoinette said. "Same time, same place—for all eternity."

The women lay back down in their graves. They pulled the lids over their caskets, tucking themselves in for a good night's rest. Bo Peep wandered back to her casket, but Bree stopped her before she stepped inside it.

"Bo?" Bree said. "I'm not sure this is the right thing to do, but if I were you I would want to know. It's so difficult to say—I guess I'll just spit it out: Emmerich is your son."

Bo Peep stared at the young boy in bewilderment. If she still had a pulse, it would have been racing. If she still needed to breathe, she would have been breathless.

"You're my *son*?" she asked.

"Yes," Emmerich said.

"Hagetta said she would find you a good home. Did she?"

"She did," he said. "I have a mother—an adoptive mother, who loves me very much."

"That's good to hear," Bo Peep said. "Knowing that, I might finally be able to rest instead of counting sheep."

Emmerich eyed Lloyd's grave. "Is my father ever coming back?" he said.

"Not from where he's going," Bo Peep said. "He'll never harm you or anyone else ever again."

Bo Peep removed a small necklace from around her neck and placed it in her son's hand. Bree and Emmerich remembered her showing it to them while they traveled down the secret path with the royals the year before. It had a thin chain and a small stone heart with a crack across it.

"Here, something to remember me by," Bo Peep said. "You seem like a kind child. I'm sorry I didn't raise you myself, but you were better off with your adoptive mother. I was too young and foolish to be a mother. You didn't deserve to inherit my mistakes."

"I understand," he said.

"Good night, Emmerich," she said. "I hope we see each other in our dreams."

Bo Peep lay back in her casket and pulled the lid over her body. Bree put her arm around Emmerich as he watched her go. Once she was gone, he looked down at the necklace and held it tightly in his hand.

"Speaking of mothers," Conner said, "we should probably find my mom and the others."

Conner, Bree, and Emmerich hurried to the front of the cemetery to regroup with their friends. The closer they got, the louder and clearer the others' voices became.

"Push, Goldilocks!" they heard Charlotte shout. *"Push! Push! Push!"*

"ERRRRRRRR!" Goldilocks grunted.

"You can do it, Goldie!" Jack encouraged his wife. *"You're almost there!"*

"I can see the head!" Charlotte declared. *"Just one more push!"*

"OH MY GOD, WHAT IS THAT?" Red screamed loudest of all. "I AM NEVER HAVING CHILDREN!"

Soon the sounds of a crying infant echoed through the cemetery. By the time Conner, Bree, and Emmerich found the others, Goldilocks and Jack were the proud parents of a healthy and beautiful baby boy. There wasn't a dry eye in the bunch.

Charlotte cleaned the baby off and wrapped him in towels she found in the ambulance. He had his mother's golden curls, his father's strong chin, and his aunt Red's doe-eyed expression.

"Jack, we're parents," Goldilocks said tearfully. "We have a son!"

"We're an official family," Jack said affectionately.

"We did it!" Red said, and burst into happy tears. *"I only wish Charlie was here to see it!"*

Although she had had nothing to do with creating the child, she hugged Jack and Goldilocks as if she were a new parent, too.

"What are you going to name him?" Conner asked.

"Hero," Goldilocks said confidently. "That way, it won't matter where he's from, what he becomes, or who his parents are—he'll always be the hero of his own story."

CHAPTER TWENTY-EIGHT

A SITUATION

As soon as they stepped through the beam of light and returned to the Otherworld, Charlotte and Jack took Goldilocks and Hero to the Saint Andrew's emergency room to be examined by a doctor. Conner, Bree, Emmerich, and Red went straight to the multi-purpose room to tell the others what had happened in the "Cemetery of the Undead" and to share the good news of Jack and Goldilocks's son.

Conner figured Cornelia must have spread the word about the Masked Man, because everyone in the multi-purpose room had a long, somber face and seemed worried sick. Even the Blissworm's smile wasn't as pronounced as it usually was. Bree and Emmerich were a little overwhelmed by all the people they didn't know but could have sworn they recognized.

"Conner!" Bob shouted. "Are you all right? Where's your mother?"

"Everything is fine, we're all safe," Conner said. "Mom is in the emergency room with Jack and Goldilocks. They have a son and they named him Hero! They're just getting checked out to make sure everything is okay."

"And what about that horrible man?" Cornelia asked.

"The Masked Man is gone," Conner said. "And this time, he's not coming back."

The news wasn't as comforting as Conner thought it would be. In fact, the expressions of the characters around the room didn't change. They didn't even seem excited about the new baby.

"Guys, what's wrong?" he asked. "You all look like someone died."

The characters parted and Conner realized they were gathered around the Tin Woodman. He sat in a chair beside Blubo, the small flying monkey. The monkey was distraught and his eyes were puffy from crying.

"Blubo?" Conner asked. "What are you doing here? Why aren't you in the fairy-tale world with the others?"

"We wanted to share the good news about completing our army with the others back in the mine," the Tin

Woodman said. "We traveled through the emerald storybook but when we arrived, they were all gone. *Everyone in the mine had been turned into stone!* Blubo was the only one who wasn't affected."

Conner shook his head as if he were trying to clear out the words he didn't want to hear.

"What?" he said. "You mean the royal families, the animals, the citizens, Hagetta, the Tradesman—"

"THEY WERE ALL STATUES!" Robin Hood said. "STILL AS ROCK AND PALE AS BONE."

"Oh no. *Granny*." Red gasped. "What happened to them?"

"Right after you left the mine, we were attacked by a horrible monster." Blubo sniffled. "I was so afraid, I hid and covered my eyes. I never even got a good look at it."

Conner had an idea of what had happened. "The creature that turned the Fairy Council into stone must have found a way into the mine," he said.

He walked in a circle around the room, wondering what to do next. Apparently he had left one crisis only to stumble into another. He looked for his sister but didn't see her.

"Has anyone seen Alex?" Conner asked.

"She hasn't been here since I arrived," Cornelia said.

"I'll check to see if she's in the bathroom," Red said.

Red left the room and sprinted down the hall. As soon as she opened the door of the women's restroom she let out a bloodcurdling scream.

"Conner!" Red yelled. *"Come quick! You need to see this right away!"*

He was already headed toward her before she finished the sentence. As Conner dashed down the hall, all the characters followed him. Whatever Red had found was so bad, she hadn't even needed to step inside the bathroom to see it. The queen just held the door open and stared inside in total shock.

Conner arrived at her side and peered into the bathroom—but there wasn't a bathroom to see. He saw the night sky and other buildings outside. He looked up and saw into an empty office above; he looked down and saw into a deserted basement below. There was drywall, sparking electrical wires, and broken water faucets—it looked like an explosion had gone off.

Even though there was no evidence that Alex had caused it or that she had even been present for it, Conner knew in the pit of his stomach that it had something to do with his sister.

"Alex…" Conner said. *"What's happened to you?"*

⬅✏

President of the United States Katherine Walker was sitting in the Oval Office of the West Wing with two foreign ambassadors.

"Gentlemen," President Walker said, "I understand it's difficult for the prime minister and the sultan to agree on a location, but I'm not going to sit here day after day while innocent people are suffering because of their negligence. If we can't find a way to resolve this matter in the next forty-eight hours, I will put troops on the ground."

The meeting had been a major priority on the president's schedule and was booked weeks in advance. As far as she was concerned, no other matter was more important, and her entire afternoon had been cleared for the discussion. So it was surprising when the door of the Oval Office swung open and her Chief of Staff interrupted.

"Madam President," the Chief of Staff said. "I'm sorry for the interruption, but you're needed in the Situation Room immediately."

"What's wrong?" President Walker asked.

"It's best if you see it for yourself," the Chief of Staff said. "There's a *situation* in New York City."

"Terrorism?"

"No, ma'am," he said with difficulty. "Our most educated analysis, with all means of science and technology in mind, is that it's *magic....*"

ACKNOWLEDGMENTS

I'd like to thank Rob Weisbach, Alla Plotkin, Rachel Karten, Derek Kroeger, Heather Manzutto, Marcus Colen, Jerry Maybrook, and the amazing Brandon Dorman. Also, I couldn't have written this book without the support of Alvina Ling, Bethany Strout, Melanie Chang, Nikki Garcia, Megan Tingley, Andrew Smith, Kristin Dulaney, Svetlana Keselman, and everyone at Little, Brown. And, of course, all my friends and family! Thanks for being mine!

TURN THE PAGE FOR A SNEAK PEEK
OF THE BOOK THAT STARTED IT ALL!

THE LAND OF STORIES

A TREASURY OF
CLASSIC FAIRY TALES

AVAILABLE OCTOBER 2016

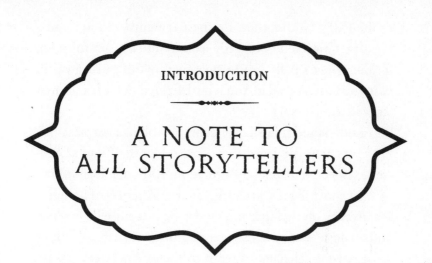

A NOTE TO ALL STORYTELLERS

I magine a world with *magic*. Now imagine this place is home to everything and everyone you were told wasn't "real." Imagine it has fairies and witches, mermaids and unicorns, giants and dragons, and trolls and goblins. Imagine they live in places like enchanted forests, gingerbread houses, underwater kingdoms, or castles in the sky.

Personally, I know such a place exists because it's where I'm from. This magical world is not as distant as you think. In fact, you've been there many times before. You travel there whenever you hear the words "Once upon a time." It's another realm, where all your favorite fairy-tale and nursery-rhyme characters live. In your world, we call it *the Land of Stories*.

For those of you familiar with fairy tales, I'm known

as the Fairy Godmother. I'm best remembered for transforming Cinderella's raggedy clothes into a beautiful gown for the prince's ball—but I won't give anything else away in case you haven't read it. You'll be delighted to see it's the first story in this treasury.

I understand this all may come as a bit of a surprise. It's not every day you learn that a place like the Land of Stories exists outside one's imagination. Although it shouldn't be *that* shocking if you think about it: After all, if fiction is inspired by mythology, and myths are just embellished legends, and legends are exaggerated history, then *all* stories must have an element of truth to them. And I can assure you that the fairy-tale world is as real as the book you're holding in your hands.

You're probably wondering *how* the stories of the fairy-tale world became so prevalent in your world. Allow me to explain, for I am entirely to blame.

Many centuries ago, I discovered your world by accident. After a long and wonderful career of helping people (like Cinderella) achieve their dreams, I was only eager to do more. So one day I closed my eyes, waved my magic wand, and said, "I wish to go someplace where people need me the most." When I opened my eyes, I was no longer in the Land of Stories.

When I first arrived, your world was enduring a time known as *the Dark Ages*, and there couldn't be a better description. It was a period consumed with poverty, plague, and war. People were suffering and starving, and they were very doubtful that conditions would get any better.

I did what I could to help the people I met: I treated the sick, I fed the hungry, and I even tried to stop the violence throughout the land. Unfortunately, nothing I did prevented the disease and destitution from spreading.

However, it wasn't *interaction* your world needed; it was *inspiration*. In a world dominated by ruthless kings and warlords, the ideas of *self-worth* and *self-empowerment* were unheard of. So I started telling stories about my world to entertain and raise spirits, especially the poor children's. Little did I know it would become the greatest contribution of my lifetime.

I told stories about cowards who became heroes, peasants who became powerful, and the lonely who became beloved. The stories taught many lessons, but most important, they taught the world how to dream. The ability to dream was a much-needed introduction to *hope*, and it spread like a powerful epidemic. Families passed the stories from generation to generation, and over the years I watched their compassion and courage change the world.

I recruited other fairies to help me spread the tales from the Land of Stories around the world, and the stories became known as *fairy tales*. Over time, we asked writers like the Brothers Grimm, Hans Christian Andersen, and Charles Perrault to publish the stories so they would live on forever.

During that time, I realized how important *storytelling*

is. While philosophy and science help enhance our mind and body, storytelling stimulates our spirit. It broadens our imagination, teaches us valuable lessons, shows us that things are not always as they seem, and encourages us to reach our greatest potential.

With that said, I have a favor to ask of anyone reading this: *Become a storyteller!* Read to others the fairy tales in this book. Read them stories from another book. If you can, create your own stories to share. When you pass along the art of storytelling to your family and friends, you make the world a better place.

By inspiring someone, you stimulate that person's creativity; and when someone is gifted with creativity, he or she inherently holds the source of *progress* and *prosperity*. Creativity is the simple but powerful ability to make something from nothing, and it just so happens that *making something from nothing* is also the definition of *magic*.

Become a storyteller and help us keep fairy tales alive. Even if people don't believe in magic, never let the world forget what it represents. Wherever there is a storyteller, there will always be hope.

Thank you, and may you all have a *happily-ever-after*!

With love,
The Fairy Godmother

FOR BARNES & NOBLE READERS ONLY:
TURN THE PAGE FOR AN EXCLUSIVE LOOK AT
MOTHER GOOSE'S FAIRY-TALE SURVIVAL GUIDE FROM

A TREASURY OF
CLASSIC FAIRY TALES

Have you noticed anything funny about your *Treasury*? Have the pages started glowing at random times and become brighter every day? Is this glowing followed by a strange but inviting humming noise? Did you lean too far into the book and wind up falling into a different dimension? Then you're in luck, because this survival guide is for you!

When you purchased this book from the store, or checked it out from the library, or "borrowed" it from a friend, you probably weren't expecting it to transport you into a world where fairy tales are real. Life is full of surprises; sometimes it rains when it's supposed to be sunny, and sometimes children's books turn out to be portals into different dimensions. Relax; these things happen.

So if you find yourself in a fairy tale, there's no reason to panic. The fairy-tale world can be a very dangerous place, but if you follow my instructions carefully, you'll be back in your own world before you can say "and they all lived happily ever after." (Trust me, if there's one thing I'm good at, it's *surviving*. You're in good hands.)

Rule #1: Don't panic. Let it out.

Everyone's first trip is always a little jarring. Don't let your shock, terror, and confusion build up inside of you; that will only lead to panicking. Treat yourself to a good scream, a nice cry, or a release of bodily fluids. However, make it short. You don't want to attract any unwanted attention from the shifty creatures in the forest.

Rule #2: Don't blame yourself.

Remember, none of this is your fault. It doesn't matter how careful or responsible you are—CDT happens to the best of us. (Oh, that stands for *Cross-Dimensional Travel*—I coined it myself.) Yes, you could have called the police when the book *first* started glowing. No, you didn't *have* to lean so far into the book that you lost your balance and fell inside it. But hey, no one ever got anywhere by playing it safe; just ask the Wright brothers.

Rule #3: Assess what kind of fairy tale you're in.

Take a look around: What do you see? Are you in a colorful garden with pixies and unicorns? Do you see handsome knights riding off into the sunset with beautiful maidens? Great! You're in a harmless bedtime story. Feel free to look around and take a few pictures.

Are you surrounded by a thick and creepy forest? Are you standing in a large, smoky cave? THEN RUN—*you're in a cautionary tale!* Something is about to make a meal or an example out of you! Don't stop until your surroundings match the description above.

Rule #4: If it's got claws, it don't follow laws.

The food chain applies to every animal, even if it talks. Just because something can communicate, that doesn't make you any less delicious. Never tell a wolf where you're headed, don't trespass into the home of bears, and don't take directions from a fox! You'd think this would be common sense, but after you read the *Treasury* (especially the rhymes about the idiots I know), you'll realize common sense isn't common in the fairy-tale world.

Rule #5: Never trust old people.

The fairy-tale world is full of seniors looking for a way to get even with youngsters (present company excluded, of course). Never make a trade with an old geezer; you'll only end up with a giant beanstalk growing in your backyard.

Never accept a gift from an old hag; you'll get stuck raising a daughter the size of a shot glass.

However, you must never *deny* them anything! If an old woman knocks on your door in the middle of the night looking for shelter, *give her a room with a view!* If an old beggar man stops you on the road and asks you for food, *cook him a gourmet meal!* Whatever you do, DO NOT tick off the elderly, or you may end up cursed as a beast or living as a frog!

Rule #6: Avoid strangely built structures.

I don't care how interesting it looks from afar—if you see something oddly placed or constructed, don't approach it! It will only lead to trouble.

For example, if you find a tower standing alone in the woods, *get out of there*—it belongs to a witch! Suppose you come across a bridge over a small stream—*better to get your shoes wet* than become lunch to the hungry troll living underneath it!

Rule #7: If something seems too good to be true, it is!

In the fairy-tale world, coincidences usually come with consequences. If you find yourself in an unfortunate situation and miraculously stumble upon a solution that perfectly suits all your needs, you're most likely being tricked into an even worse situation!

For example, if you're lost in a vicious storm and the only shelter in sight is a magnificent castle with large, spacious rooms, chances are there's a beast waiting for you inside. If you're starving and wandering aimlessly through the forest, that gingerbread house down the path was probably built to lure poor saps like you. Remember, in the fairy-tale world, traps come in all shapes, sizes, and flavors.

Rule #8: Don't be a jerk.
Here's a good tip! As difficult as it may seem, try to keep a positive attitude during your visit. The fairy-tale world tends to reward the generous and punish the selfish. Be kind and treat everything with respect, and you'll be amazed at what a difference it makes. Also, lots of fairies and witches like to dress up in disguises, so be careful about whom you upset.

Rule #9: When in doubt, find a fairy.
If you're not looking to stay and see the sights, the fastest way to get back home is to find a fairy. Tell it about your treasury, how it glowed, hummed, and transported you into the fairy-tale world, and the fairy should be able to help you out. Most fairies are familiar with CDT and can get you back home.

However, don't tell them I sent you. I'm not very popular among fairies these days. In fact, it's better not to mention my name at all. Otherwise, when they send you home, you might end up on a desert island in the Bermuda Triangle—it's a long story!

Well, I hope this guide has been helpful! A lot of people

thought it was silly to write it, but if this book were in my hands, I'd want to be prepared. If you do find yourself in the fairy-tale world, don't forget to stop by and say hello. I'll be at a pub in the Charming Kingdom called *The Stepmother* with an overgrown gander named Lester. Just follow the feathers...

Cheers!
Mother Goose

Acknowledgments

I'd like to thank my mom, my stepdad, Goldie, Jack, Red, Froggy, M.G., and especially Mrs. Peters. Also, a big thank you to my sister, Alex. I wouldn't have survived these stories without you!

Rosary Chicken

Bolt

The Dolly Llama

Bones

Isle of Skulls